THE HOUSE OF DEATH

THE HOUSE OF DEATH

A Mystery of Alexander the Great

PAUL C. DOHERTY

CARROLL & GRAF PUBLISHERS, INC.
NEW YORK

Carroll & Graf Publishers, Inc.
19 West 21st Street
New York
NY 10010–6805

First published in the UK by Constable,
an imprint of Constable & Robinson Ltd 2001

First Carroll & Graf edition 2001

ISBN 0–7867–0853–0

Printed and bound in the EU

To Captain Frank and Phyllis McKenzie
of Arlington, Virginia
Lovers of Greece

"Πράξεις δὲ μεγίστας κατεγρασόμενος οὐ μόνον τῶν πρὸ αὐτου βασιλευσάντων, ἀλλά καὶ τῶν οὐστερον ἐσομένον μέχει του καθ᾽ ἡμάς βίου."

"He achieved greater deeds than any, not only of the kings who had lived before him but also of those who came later down to our own time."

Diodorus Siculus, *Library of History*,
Book 17, Chapter 117

THE GREEK WORLD, 334 BC

BLACK SEA

ILLYRIA

MACEDONIA

THRACE

•Pella

THASOS

SAMOTHRACE

SEA OF MARMARA

Sestos Lampascus

Elaeus

Zeleia Granicus Dascylium

Troy Abydos

HELLESPONTINE
PHRYGIA

THESSALY

AEGEAN SEA

TROAD

ASIA MINOR

Chaeronea

EUBOEA

LESBOS

Delphi

Thebes

CHIOS

•Sardis

Olympia

Corinth

Athens

SAMOS

•Ephesus

Argos

Sparta

MEDITERRANEAN

RHODES

CRETE

SEA

N

Historical Personages Mentioned in the Text

The House of Macedon

PHILIP   King of Macedon until his assassination in 336 BC. Father of Alexander
OLYMPIAS OF MOLOSSUS (Born Myrtale). Philip's queen, Alexander's mother. Co-regent of Macedon during Alexander's conquest of Persia
ALEXANDER   Son of Philip and Olympias
EURYDICE   Philip's wife after he divorced Olympias. She was niece of Philip's favourite general, Attalus. Eurydice, her baby son and Attalus were all executed after Philip's death.
ARRIDHAEUS   Philip's son by one of his concubines, poisoned by Olympias. He survived but remained brain damaged for the rest of his life.

The Court of Macedon

BLACK CLEITUS   Brother to Alexander's nurse. Alexander's personal bodyguard
HEPHAESTION   Alexander's boon companion
ARISTANDER   Court necromancer, adviser to Alexander
ARISTOTLE   Alexander's tutor in the Groves of Mieza; Greek Philosopher
SOCRATES   Athenian Philosopher. Found guilty of "impiety", forced to drink poison.
PAUSANIAS PHILIP OF MACEDON'S ASSASSIN

Alexander's Generals

PARMENIO, PTOLEMY, SELEUCUS, AMYNTAS, ANTIPATER (left as co-Regent in Macedon), NEARCHUS

The Court of Persia

DARIUS III   King of Kings
ARSITES   Satrap of Phrygia. Persian commander-in-chief at the Granicus
MITHRIDATES AND NIPHRATES   Persian commanders
MEMNON OF RHODES   A Greek mercenary in the pay of Persia, one of the few generals to defeat Macedonian troops.
CYRUS AND XERXES   Former great emperors of Persia

The Writers

Aeschylus, Aristophanes, Euripides, Sophocles Greek playwrights

HOMER   Reputed author of the two great poems the *Iliad* and the *Odyssey*

DEMOSTHENES   Athenian demagogue, ardent opponent of Alexander

HIPPOCRATES OF COS   Greek physician and writer, regarded as the father of medicine.

The Mythology of Greece

ZEUS   Father god

HERA   His wife

APOLLO   God of light

ARTEMIS   Goddess of the hunt

ATHENA   Goddess of war

HERCULES   Greek man-god. One of Alexander's reputed ancestors

AESCULAPIUS   Man-God; a great healer

OEDIPUS   Tragic hero king of Thebes

DIONYSIUS   God of wine

EYNALIUS   Ancient Macedonian god of war

The Trojan War

PRIAM   King of Troy

HECTOR   Priam's son and Troy's great general

PARIS   Hector's brother whose abduction of the fair-faced Helen led to the Trojan War.

AGAMEMNON   Leader of the Greeks in the Trojan War

ACHILLES   Greek hero and warrior in the Trojan War, the slayer of Hector. He was eventually killed by an arrow fired by Paris. Alexander regarded him as a direct ancestor.

PATROCLUS   Achilles' lover, his death in the Trojan War led to Achilles' homicidal rage.

ULYSSES   King of Ithaca: he fought against Troy and his journey home became the subject of Homer's poem.

AJAX   Greek commander in the Trojan War: his violation of the priestess and prophetess, Cassandra, led to his own death.

Preface

I n 336 BC, Philip of Macedon died swiftly at his moment of supreme glory, assassinated by a former lover as he was about to receive the plaudits of his client states. All of Greece and Persia quietly rejoiced – the growing supremacy of Macedon was to be curbed. The finger of suspicion for Philip's murder was pointed directly at his scheming wife – the "Witch Queen", Olympias – and their only son, the young Alexander whom Demosthenes of Athens dismissed as a "booby". Macedon's enemies quietly relished the prospect of a civil war which would destroy Alexander and his mother and end any threat to the Greek states as well as the sprawling Persian Empire of Darius III. Alexander soon proved them wrong. A consummate actor, a sly politician, a ruthless fighter and a brilliant general, in two years Alexander crushed all opposition at home, won over the wild tribes to the north and had himself proclaimed Captain-General of Greece. He was to be the leader of a fresh crusade against Persia – fitting punishment for the attacks on Greece by Cyrus the Great and his successors a century earlier.

Alexander proved, by the total destruction of the great city of Thebes, the home of Oedipus, that he would brook no opposition. He then turned east. He proclaimed himself a Greek ready to avenge Greek wrongs. Secretly, Alexander wished to satisfy his lust for conquest, to march to the edge of the world, to prove he was a better man than Philip, to win the vindication of the gods as well as confirm the whisperings of his mother – that his conception was due to divine intervention.

In the spring of 334 BC, Alexander gathered his army at Sestos while, across the Hellespont, Darius III, his sinister spymaster the

Lord Mithra and his generals plotted the utter·destruction of this Macedonian upstart. Alexander, however, was committed to total war, to leading his troops across the Hellespont, to conquering Persia and marching to the rim of the world . . .

Prologue I

"Darius became King before the death of Philip . . . but when Philip died, Darius was relieved of his anxiety and despised the youth of Alexander."

Diodorus Siculus, *Library of History*,
Book 17, Chapter 7

O nce it was a lonely plain, shrouded in silence, fringed by mountains and covered in leafy fields and mist-ringed fir trees. A place where the dust devils blew in summer, the lair of the wildcat and savage wolf. Cyrus the Great had changed all this. It had become the sanctuary of the Holy Fire, the Treasury of Heaven, the Shrine and Glory of Ahura-Mazda, the god of light, the Lord of the Hidden Flame, of the Sun Disc, the Ever-Seeing Eye, borne aloft on the wings of eagles. Persepolis, the house of god's representative on earth, Darius III; King of Kings, Lord of Lords, the owner of men's necks. A city which lay like the hub of a great wheel, the centre of empire, Persepolis stood on artificial, well-watered terraces between the Mountain of Mercy and the River Araxes. The mud-caked walls of its palaces rose over twenty yards high and were glazed with gold. Its porches and entrances boasted columns of marble and precious wood to support roofs of Lebanon cedar.

At the heart of the royal palace, surrounded by three huge walls and defended by bronze-plated gates flanked by flagstaffs, lay the Apanda, the House of Adoration in the Hall of Columns. This holy of holies was guarded by the immortals, the personal bodyguard of the King of Kings, garbed in bronze-studded cuirasses over kilts of red cloth and striped leggings: on their heads, soft caps with thick cheek guards; these could be pulled round and wrapped across the mouth and nose to protect the wearer when he marched and ate the dust of his Lord of Lords. The immortals stood in silent array in porticoes, along colonnaded walks, in courtyards and paradises. Immobile as statues, in their hands were rounded shields and long spears, counterweighted by golden apples from which they earned their nickname, the "Imperial Apple Bearers".

Dusk had fallen. The Persian court, its officers and chamberlains, the Imperial Fan Bearer and Fly Swatter, the Medes and Magi, all knew that, tonight, their Lord of Lords would show his face: he had agreed to grant an audience to his favourite, the renegade Greek, General Memnon of Rhodes. They had whispered about it all day. They'd gathered in chambers to savour the news. Others, more wary of their master's legion of spies, met in the sweet-smelling groves of the fertile paradises, those elegant gardens where every flower and shrub of the empire, flourished in black fertile soil especially imported from Canaan. These whisperers all agreed on one thing: the King of Kings was troubled. A dark shadow had emerged on the edge of his empire. The news was on everyone's lips: Alexander of Macedon was coming! Alexander, son of Philip the Tyrant and Olympias the Witch Queen. Alexander, whom Demosthenes of Athens had dismissed as a "stripling", "a mere booby". Alexander seemed to have all the power of the under-world supporting him. He had clawed his way to the top, crushed conspirators, crucified rebels, and extended his sway over those wild tribes Darius had bribed so heavily to ravage Macedon's borders. Now these same barbarians had bent their heads, taken the bread and salt and swore great oaths of loyalty to Alexander of Macedon. Everyone thought he'd perished in the sombre, icy forests of Thessaly but he had loped back like some ravenous wolf and torn apart his enemies. Athens was crushed. Its leading citizens, whom the King of Kings had supported with golden darics, hid out in desert places or skulked like beaten dogs in whatever village would house them. Even Thebes, the city of Oedipus, was nothing more than a devastated ruin, a place of blood where the scavengers hunted and swarms of black flies buzzed around unburied corpses.

Now Alexander of Macedon had turned his eyes east. Captain-

General of Greece, he had sworn holy oaths to wage eternal war, with fire and sword, by land and sea, against the King of Kings. Already the spies had come galloping in. Alexander had left Pella. Alexander was marching east. Alexander was at the Hellespont, staring hungrily across its blue, fast-running waters to the glories of Persepolis. Some said that he marched at the head of a great army. More sensible people said this was only 30,000 or 40,000 men and, surely, the great King of Kings could defeat such a rabble. Darius' harmony was certainly disturbed. He had tried to keep Macedon at bay with gold but now the wolf was sniffing outside his door. Darius had sent for Memnon of Rhodes, saying it takes a wolf to fight a wolf. Memnon had spent time as a hostage in the Macedonian court; he had studied the souls of Philip and his son; he had watched the Macedonian phalanx, with their short shields and long spears, shatter one Greek army after another. Memnon had eventually escaped from Macedon and now had the ear of the King of Kings. Memnon knew all about such wolves. He had fought courageously against Parmenio, the veteran Macedonian general sent across the Hellespont to establish a bridgehead.

On that particular night, however, waiting in the antechamber at the foot of the stairs leading to the Apanda, Memnon didn't feel highly favoured. He stood with his mute servant Diocles and his Master of Horse, Lysias, and tapped his sandalled foot imperiously at the delay. The chamber was stiflingly hot, guarded by the "Apple Bearers" and thronged with courtiers and chamberlains – Medes, not Persians, in their brightly decorated robes and trousers, faces heavily coated with cosmetics, rings flashing at earlobes. They, too, caught this barbarian's unease and moved restlessly about, their high-heeled boots tapping on the floor. Now and again they would stop and glance sly-eyed at Memnon. They did not like Greeks, whoever they were. In particular, Memnon, his bald head glistening with oil, that craggy face, weatherbeaten and suntanned, his squat nose slightly broken and twisted, bloodless lips and darting, cruel eyes.

"Never trust a Greek" ran the Persian proverb. There were no exceptions!

"How long?" Memnon spoke in Greek, a hard, jarring sound. It disturbed the songbirds in their golden cages which hung on silver cords from the cedarwood beams.

"Be patient, my lord."

Memnon's companion, the Persian Prince Arsites, satrap of western Phrygia, smiled tactfully and bowed, raising his hand to cover his mouth as if scratching his well-oiled moustache and beard. If Arsites had his way, Memnon, that stupid-looking Diocles and the shifty-eyed Lysias, would be hurled into the crocodile pool; however, Memnon was highly favoured. He had been shown great honour when he had arrived the previous evening. Escorted through the shadowy, perfume-filled chamber of Darius' harem, Memnon was proclaimed as "Friend of the King of Kings" and solemnly greeted by Darius' women in their silks and precious cloths, bright as fireflies, necks, ankles and wrists shimmering with precious jewels. They had dipped plates into their sacks of gold and filled the chest a eunuch had carried beside Memnon. The Greek was to take this away, a token of the emperor's friendship and pleasure. Memnon had also been shown the imperial treasury, the Red House, its walls and ceilings of blood-like stone, where tens and tens of thousands of talents of gold lay stowed away in chests, coffers and baskets.

Arsites turned his sallow face away and dabbed elegantly at the drop of sweat above the stiff-rimmed collar of his gown. Darius had been too gracious. The satrap played with the gold chain round his neck. He walked towards the wall as if interested in the carving of a Mede courtier sniffing at a lotus flower. Arsites recalled Darius' words: "Show Memnon my favour. Show Memnon my power and, above all, show Memnon my terror." Arsites lowered his head. He had done all three. He had taken Memnon out into the paradises, with their fountains and shadowy grottoes, to savour the cool shade of the tamarind, sycamore and terebinth trees, and enjoy the fragrance of the pomegranate, apple and cherry orchards. Suddenly, without warning, they had turned into the garden which lay just beneath the Apanda – a long lawn, though one not bordered by flowers or herbs, but by a row of crosses on which Darius crucified those who had incurred his displeasure. On this occasion, a unit of cavalry men, guilty of cowardice and treachery;

each had been stripped, castrated and then crucified against the soaring wooden beams. A few had died immediately; others would linger for days. Oh yes, Memnon had been shown terror.

Arsites moved to the window. Lanterns and lamps had been lit in the gardens below. He relished the perfume of the flowers on the evening breeze, but he was at heart a soldier. He stood, all senses straining; he caught it: the iron tang of blood and the low moans of those who still survived.

"Will the Great King listen to my plan?"

Arsites sighed, glanced quickly at one of the chamberlains and shook his head slightly, secretly warning him not to reproach Memnon. After all, the Rhodian was a barbarian. He did not know the protocol and etiquette of the Divine One's court: that silence was to be observed so one could prepare the heart and soul for the great favour soon to be shown.

"I do not know what is in my lord's mind," Arsites replied, walking back. "But, when he opens his heart to us, you shall see his wisdom." Arsites' gaze moved to Lysias. "And his justice!"

Memnon felt a prickle of unease. He had been out campaigning, collecting troops, hiring mercenaries. He had done well: thousands of hoplites under arms. Veterans of many a war, a well-trained war horde, yet there was something wrong. If only he could act on his own. Yet, everywhere he went, the King of Kings' spies followed him. Memnon had listened to rumour and gossip. His Persian officers maintained traitors skulked in the Greek camp. Memnon refused to believe this. Now, however, waiting in this shadow-filled chamber, surrounded by silent guards and sly-eyed courtiers, was something wrong? Memnon knew he was disliked. He held favour with Darius for two reasons. First, he had proved his loyalty. Second, he had beaten the Macedonians. Yet Darius himself was a demon! Volatile and at times cruel in the extreme, he had fought his way to the imperial throne, slaying rivals before rounding on those who had helped him: slitting noses, gouging eyes, removing hands and feet. Darius hadn't killed all of them. He'd allowed some of his victims to wander like doleful ghosts around the palace: a warning to all who might threaten the golden throne. Darius could be gentle and kind, even generous to a fault but, to keep this great

5

empire in check, he would indulge in sudden flashes of terror, like lightning across a summer sky. May the gods help those whom Darius had marked down for destruction!

"He awaits!"

A chamberlain's voice echoed through the room. Memnon breathed in deeply and wiped his sweaty hands on his white robe – obligatory dress for such an occasion. Arsites walked before him, the chamberlains behind. The immortals turned, a silent file on either side as they climbed the steep steps to the Hall of Audience. Memnon felt as if he was scaling Olympus, the sacred mountain, going up into the court of the gods. Hundreds of torches, fastened in the walls, spluttered and danced in the draught, bringing to life the dramatic friezes on the walls. The paintings depicted Darius and his ancestors in victorious battle against foreign enemies – even demons of the underworld, particularly the lion-headed griffin and savage sphinx. Memnon missed his footing and quietly cursed. He smelt the lotus blossom which strewed the sacred steps. He glanced to his left. Diocles' face shimmered with sweat and the mute glanced quickly at his master with the furtive look of a hunted gazelle. Memnon forced a smile. He had two great loves: his wife Barsine and this body-servant who would give his life for him. Memnon stretched out his hand and lightly touched Diocles' wrist, a gesture to remain calm. Lysias, on his right, kept his head down betraying no emotion except, now and again, by scratching at the well-cropped white beard or, more surreptitiously, removing a trickle of sweat from his brow.

"Great glory awaits us," Memnon whispered. "Do not show your fear!"

They reached the top of the staircase. The bronze-plated doors were flung open and Memnon entered the Hall of Audience all ablaze with light. He remembered protocol. On the marble floor, just within the doorway, stretched a broad, blood-red carpet leading up to the hearth where the sacred flame leapt up from its log-based platform. This was the sacred fire of Ahura-Mazda, the god of the Persians. It was tended by priests and burnt continuously through the king's life: it would only die when he did. The carpet was sacred, to be trodden only by Darius himself. Memnon and his

6

group knelt by the side. Further down, beyond the sacred fire, under a silver and scarlet banner bearing the eagle's wing and sun disc, sat Darius on his golden throne. He drank specially boiled water, ate barley cakes and sipped wine from a golden, egg-shaped cup, watched by officials and members of his family. The royal enclosure was now screened off by a thick white veil; in front of this stood three lines of immortals in gorgeous battle armour. Memnon waited. The air was sweetened by hundreds of flower baskets placed along the walls. From one of the adjoining passageways echoed the soft melodies of court musicians.

"Bow your heads!" a chamberlain's voice thundered. "Look now! Darius, King of Kings, Lord of Lords, beloved of Ahura-Mazda the possessor of men's necks!"

Memnon glanced up. The immortals had now disappeared. The white gauze veil had been pulled aside. Darius sat on his golden throne, in one hand a white wand of office, in the other a jewel-encrusted fly whisk. He was dressed in robes of silver and purple under a heavy cloak of gold embroidery; his ankles and throat shimmered with jewels which reflected the glare from the sacred flame. On the king's head was a brimless top hat of purple and his feet, resting on a silver footstool, were sheathed in padded sandals of purple satin.

"Adore!" the chamberlain behind Memnon ordered.

Memnon bowed his head. Time passed slowly. The music stopped and Memnon heard the soft pad of slippers. From the paradise below came a cry of agony like that of an animal trapped in a thicket.

"You may approach!"

Memnon sighed and got to his feet. Darius had now dispensed with ceremony, given up the white wand and the fly whisk. The gold embroidered cloak had been removed. He now sat on a divan of cushions just beyond the sacred flame. Led by Arsites, Memnon and his two companions walked up, made their obeisance and sat on the cushions provided. A small table separated them from the king. On this stood three goblets of wine, bowls of fruit and strips of roast goose. Memnon's throat was parched but, according to court etiquette, he would not eat until Darius gave the sign. The hall seemed empty; the immortals stayed in the shadows, in the window enclosures and the long passageways, ready to act at the slightest sign of danger to their master.

"My friend," Darius' voice was deep and throaty. "You may look upon my face."

Memnon did so. Darius seemed at peace: his black, ringleted hair, moustache and beard were drenched in the most exquisite perfume; his olive-skinned face shimmered with oil. Memnon sighed in relief. At times Darius' eyes could be slits of black obsidian – now they crinkled in welcome.

"My hawk, my falcon, my lion of Rhodes!" Darius smiled. "My courtiers may not like you, Memnon, but I love you as a brother." Darius' smile widened. This was the Greek who would defend his empire, drive back the Macedonian barbarian.

"My lord, why am I here?" Memnon asked in the tongue of his master.

"To gaze on my face. To see life. To receive honour." Darius paused. "And my justice."

Memnon caught his breath. Darius raised his hand.

"So he comes." His gaze held Memnon's. "Alexander of Macedon will cross the Hellespont. How many men will he bring?"

"Some people say as few as thirty thousand; others forty."

Darius glanced at Arsites.

"You could swat him like a fly."

"My lord," Memnon interrupted. "I have seen the Macedonian phalanx. Think of a moving wall, a block or a wedge. Shields locked, the long sarissas coming down."

"We have cavalry," Arsites said.

"They will split themselves on the Macedonian spears," Memnon retorted.

"Why?" Darius took a grape and held it between his forefinger and thumb. "Why can't we squeeze and eat such a puny force?"

Memnon closed his eyes. He thought of the Macedonians: tough, hard, a moving wall of death, aiming for the centre while their cavalry poured into the enemy flanks like fire from heaven.

He opened his eyes. "My lord, you have to see it to believe it.

They have a power and a cunning, a savage ferocity. Numbers mean little to them. Cunning and speed, power and strength do. Alexander is committed to total war. You have heard the rumours, my lord?"

Darius shook his head.

"Alexander is short of money. He has given away all his lands. One of his generals asked what did he have left? Alexander replied, 'My dreams.'" Memnon couldn't resist a smile at the courage of his young, would-be opponent.

"And?" Darius asked softly.

"'What about the future?' This same general asked. Alexander replied, 'My hopes.'"

"How old is he?"

Memnon spread his hands. "Twenty, twenty-one summers."

"And what does he look like, this Macedonian gnat who wants to sting my empire?"

Memnon recalled his own memories as well as news from his spies. "A small man who seems tall," he replied slowly. "Alexander is thick-set with the body of an athlete. He walks with a slight limp."

"His hair?"

Memnon tapped his own bald head and grinned. "Some say blond, the colour of wheat, curled and cropped round the nape of the neck and brow. Flatterers say he has golden skin. He is of ruddy complexion, pleasant and well proportioned. He does not have the snub nose of his father, though he has Philip's laughing mouth."

"And the eyes?"

Memnon gazed at Darius. "They always remark on his eyes, my lord, of different colour, one blue the other brown. Alexander possesses all the skill of an actor: a liquid glance, girlish they say, smiling, mocking but, when required, as hard as iron, as unyielding as the coldest marble. He tends to keep," Memnon mimicked the gesture, "his head down, chin almost touching his chest. Sometimes he turns his head slightly sideways. When he talks to you, Alexander treats you as if you were the only person who mattered."

"Remarkable," Darius murmured. "And what other qualities does this so-called stripling have?"

9

"He is generous, brave, a superb horseman. He has an interest in all things, whether it be plants . . ."

"Or the writings of Aristotle?"

"Aristotle was his tutor," Memnon agreed. "Alexander and his companions were educated by the Athenian fop in the groves of Mieza."

"Ah!" Darius rocked backwards and forwards on his cushions, a far-away look in his eyes. "And how is the Lady Barsine?"

"As lovely as the night, my lord."

Memnon felt a frisson of fear. Darius had still not invited him to eat or drink. Arsites seemed tense, head down, constantly stroking his oil-drenched beard as if he was either listening intently or distracted by something else.

"And as a general?" Darius' voice was harsh. "This Alexander?"

"He has mercenaries, Thessalian light horse, but they are only chaff in the wind compared to his own troops."

Memnon himself was distracted. In his mind's eye he could see the massed ranks of the Macedonian phalanx: the long sarissas coming down, the tramp of sandalled feet, the battle paean, the thunder of cavalry.

"If they are the chaff," Darius smirked, "what is the plant?"

"More like a harvest," Memnon whispered. "A moving corn-field, my lord, but its stems are wood and cruel steel. Can you imagine?" Memnon held up his hand. "They hit their opponents in the flank or even head-on. The sarissa is some six yards long. It can pierce and penetrate before their enemy even engages."

"You could use archers," Arsites interrupted.

"The phalanx moves too fast, they could form a shield wall."

"We could counter them," Arsites declared.

From the paradise below a nightingale sang, clear lucid notes, an incongruous sound in this chilling hall, with its silent, brooding menace.

"The pikemen of Macedon are born and raised as warriors," Memnon declared. "It's not just the power of their arm but their speed, strength and confidence."

"Show me their tactics." Darius gestured, pointing to small sticks of incense on the banqueting table.

Memnon laid them along the table. "This is the enemy, my lord." He smiled apologetically. "Or should I say our Macedonian opponents? Infantry in the centre, cavalry on the wings, yes? The danger posed by Macedon is threefold. First, the cavalry led by Alexander. He will base himself on the right wing. Second, in the centre, the foot brigades, divided into two: the shield-bearers and light infantry, very fast but deadly . . ."

"And, third, the pikemen?" Darius intervened.

"Alexander's tactics are speed and movability," Memnon continued. "He will concentrate his attack on the enemy's wing which extends itself to meet him. The brigades come up, the enemy line is divided, it's simply a matter of surrounding and killing."

"Ah!" Darius breathed. "So, he breaks and divides; he surrounds and kills?"

Memnon nodded. "It requires strength of will," he agreed. "Determination and tight control. Time and again it's proved effective."

"So, what do you advise?" Darius asked.

Memnon breathed in deeply. "Never meet him in battle."

"What?"

Arsites' exclamation was echoed by Darius. Out of the corner of his eye Memnon saw the shadows move but Darius raised his hand, gesturing slightly.

"Let him come on," Memnon urged. "Burn your lands, your crops, your towns. Lure him deeper and deeper into the maze. Wait till he's hungry and thirsty, his men demoralized."

"So, you would have us burn our crops?" Arsites exclaimed.

"No, no, listen." Darius held his hand up. "This Macedonian booby, as Demosthenes calls him . . ."

"Demosthenes may be a great orator, my lord, but, every time he has met the Macedonian in battle, he has run away."

"I know." Darius picked up a grape, popped it into his mouth and chewed slowly. "You talk of Alexander's strengths. What are his weaknesses?"

"He will have to leave Macedon and Greece," Memnon remarked, "under the co-regency of his mother Olympias . . ."

"Ah, that wild-eyed bitch!" Darius exclaimed.

11

". . . and the old General Antipater."

"But they hate each other!" Arsites exclaimed.

"Precisely!" Memnon snapped.

Darius held his hand to his face and chuckled. "The more I hear of this Alexander the more I like him. So, Antipater and Olympias will watch each other." His face became serious. "But what other weaknesses?"

"He'll have to leave some of his troops at home," Memnon continued in a rush. "When he crosses the Hellespont, Alexander will be cut off from home. His treasury is empty and Greece seethes with resentment. In name, Alexander is Captain-General, but Athens resents him. No one has forgotten the destruction of Thebes. Greece has two eyes. One, Athens, is dimmed. The other, Thebes, has been extinguished forever."

Darius sucked on his teeth, listening intently.

"So, Alexander will have to live off the land?" Arsites asked.

Memnon felt more confident at the calculating look in Darius' eyes: he was explaining a strategy the King of Kings understood.

"What other weaknesses does this man have?" Darius asked.

"The reputation of a bloody tyrant: thirty thousand Thebans were sold into slavery . . ."

"No!" Darius snapped. "Weaknesses as a *man*."

Memnon glanced away. He could mention treachery. Yet, that was as common in Macedon as it was in Athens or Persepolis.

"He has two weaknesses," Memnon replied slowly. "First, his parents. They hated each other. Alexander himself has remarked that his mother charges a constant high rent for the nine months he spent in her womb. Olympias considers herself a mystic. She regularly taunted Philip at how Alexander had been conceived by a god. They say Philip himself spied on her during certain mysterious rites."

"And that's how he lost his eye." Darius smirked. "I've heard the story."

"Philip and Olympias came to hate each other," Memnon continued. "In fact, he divorced her and married the niece of one of his generals. At the wedding banquet this general, Attalus, proclaimed a toast, 'At last Macedon will have a legitimate heir, a

12

true Macedonian.' Alexander, defending Olympias, cursed him roundly. Philip, drunk as usual, tried to attack his son. He drew his dagger, leapt from the couch but collapsed on the floor. 'Look,' Alexander jibed, 'here is a man who wants a pass from Europe to Asia but hasn't got the strength and skill to cross from one couch to another.' "

"And then?" Darius asked.

"Alexander went into exile but later returned. Philip's new wife gave birth to a son."

"And Philip was murdered?"

"Yes, he was hosting a great festival, a meeting of all the Greek states when a former lover, Pausanias, who had been sodomized by some of Philip's friends, ran forward and drove a Celtic winged dagger up into his heart."

"And this Pausanias was killed?"

"He tried to run away but tripped over a vine. Philip's body-guards killed him. The corpse was crucified."

"And the real assassin?" Arsites asked.

"Rumours abound that Olympias was the power behind Pausanias. Whispers circulate that Alexander himself knew of the plot."

"But he protested his innocence?" Darius asked.

"Of course, my lord. Olympias, however, placed a wreath on the gibbetted Pausanias' head, burnt his corpse and sprinkled his ashes over Philip's grave."

"And Philip was not warned of the plot?"

"He received an enigmatic warning from the Oracle at Delphi." Memnon moved restlessly.

"The bull is wreathed for sacrifice!" Darius exclaimed. "All is ready. The slayer awaits!"

"Yes, my lord. Philip thought the bull was you."

Darius laughed deep in his throat. "Continue, Memnon."

"Alexander is confused. He loves Olympias. He claims one of her tears is worth more than a thousand letters, yet he is repelled by her. She threw Philip's new baby son onto a bed of charcoal and made the mother watch until the young woman, driven out of her wits, hanged herself. Olympias has filled Alexander's mind with doubts about his own paternity as well as vague dreams that he is

13

the son of a god. She constantly reminds Alexander that Achilles is one of his ancestors."

"Ah yes, I've heard this," Arsites intervened. "Alexander keeps a copy of Homer's *Iliad* next to the dagger beneath his pillow."

"His favourite line," Memnon agreed, quoting the *Iliad*, "is 'Achilles born of an immortal mother'. He sees himself as the reincarnation of Greece's greatest hero."

"You mentioned a second weakness?" Darius urged.

"Given his parentage," Memnon couldn't resist the taunt, "Alexander is riven between deep superstition and an almost insatiable desire to confront the gods, to demonstrate he's their equal."

"Does he like gold?"

"He gives it away as if it was sand on the seashore."

"And women?"

"He respects them."

"My spies," Darius interjected, "claim he has a male lover, Hephaestion."

Memnon was about to agree when he recalled the old adage: "Know your enemy truly". Memnon prided himself on one thing – the truth.

"His enemies whisper that," he confessed. "Others say Hephaestion is a father figure, Alexander's close counsellor."

"So?" Darius leaned back on the cushions. "Why does he come? For glory?"

Memnon shrugged. "For conquest. To fulfil his mother's dream that he is Achilles come again. To wage holy war against the Persian Empire of Xerxes and Cyrus, to prove he's a god . . ."

"Or," Darius added drily, "to prove he's a better man than his father. So we know," he nodded, speaking as if to himself, "that he will come, but how?"

"His fleet is meagre," Memnon replied. "When he crosses the Hellespont, you . . ."

"No, no." Darius shook his head. "I want him to come with his puny force so I can embrace him to my bosom and strangle the very life out of him. I want to show all of Greece what happens. When I have defeated Alexander, I will visit the Parthenon in Athens to demonstrate who is their true master."

"There is poison, the assassin," Lysias suddenly spoke up.

Darius ignored the interruption, running a finger round his wine-coated lips, the other hand playing with the tassels on a cushion. "I have traitors at the Macedonian court." Darius snapped his fingers. "I could take Alexander's life as I could snuff out the wick of an oil lamp. But, if I do, they might still come. No, no, I will trap and catch this Alexander. I will parade him in chains through Persepolis and then," he pointed to his feet, "my 'cowled ones' will take him to rot in a Tower of Silence. I will slit his corpse from neck to crotch and fill it with gold dust from my treasury and use it as a footstool."

The King of Kings bowed his head. Memnon, despite the perfumed warmth, felt a chill of fear. Darius had schemed and plotted.

"You mentioned a spy!" Memnon exclaimed. "What is his name?"

"Naihpat." Darius raised a finger to his lips as a sign for silence. "Alexander," the King of Kings mused, "will cross the Hellespont. He will make his devotions in the ancient city of Troy. He will have guides and advance down the western coastline of my empire. He will blunder about like a man in a fog. Then we shall kill him."

"How?" Memnon asked.

Darius remained silent. Memnon stared longingly at his wine and cup. He abruptly realized what had troubled him. To eat and drink in the presence of the great king was a great honour. There were four of them, but only three goblets – silver-fluted and jewel-encrusted – not a fourth. He glanced up. Darius was watching him curiously. The Persian king then stared at a point behind Memnon. The Greek kept his harsh face impassive. He heard a light footfall and knew that Darius' "cowled ones", the black-garbed assassins of the Persian court, were not far away.

"Is all ready?" Darius asked.

Memnon didn't hear any reply. Darius abruptly clambered to his feet. He grasped his jewel-encrusted fly whisk, tapping this against his thigh.

15

"My lord," Arsites exclaimed, getting to his feet. "What is wrong?"

Darius was already walking away, gesturing with his fly whisk for them to follow. Near a window overlooking the paradises, Darius paused and turned.

"Memnon, my friend. You know what a tower of silence is?"

Memnon stared back.

"Go on," the Persian king urged, "tell your companions!"

"It is a tradition of your people, sire. They take their dead into such a tower and suspend the corpse by ropes from beams."

"And?" Darius insisted. "What happens then, Memnon?"

"The corpse is allowed to corrupt, the flesh falls away; it rots and cannot pollute any living thing."

"So the living remain clean?" Darius murmured.

Memnon glanced quickly at the window, drawn by faint sounds and the glare of torchlight.

"We must all remain clean." Darius walked slowly back. "I mentioned spies. Did you know, General Memnon, that I have a spy close to Alexander?"

"The person you called Naihpat?"

"The person called Naihpat," Darius agreed. "Naihpat is owned by Mithra, the master of my secrets."

Memnon didn't react. Some of this he knew from rumour and gossip. He had never met this Mithra. Yet, Darius trusted him so much, people called this elusive keeper of secrets "the king's shadow".

"And did you know, Memnon, my friend, that Alexander has a spy close to you? Perhaps two, even three?"

Memnon's mouth went dry. He felt his legs tense. "My lord, that is not . . ."

Memnon bit his tongue; to call any Persian a liar was the greatest insult.

"I have eyes and ears," Darius replied. "I am the great king. Come!"

They walked to the window. Memnon stared out. Down below a great wooden gibbet had been erected. A man, naked except for the gag in his mouth, had been crucified against it, his body a mass of bruises from brow to toe. Memnon's stomach clenched as he realized the condemned man had also been castrated, a seeping, bloody mess where his genitals had been. He heard a low moan and turned quickly. Lysias stood pallid as a ghost, beads of sweat lacing his forehead.

"Do you recognize that man, General Memnon? Or perhaps you wouldn't. Your good friend Lysias does."

Memnon stared down at the crucified man, his hair shorn like that of any convict. "It's Cleander!" Memnon stared in horror at Lysias. "He's one of your commanders! A Theban, yes?"

"He's also Lysias' messenger," Darius declared.

Lysias stood, his back against the wall, trembling as in a fever. "I can explain all!" he stuttered.

Memnon confronted him, his face only a few inches away. "Lysias, what is this?"

"I sent Cleander with a message to Alexander: I would meet him in Troy. I offered to betray you."

"You!" Memnon stepped back, raising his hand.

Lysias shook his head. "Not treason. You know that."

"Then why?"

"I am Theban." Lysias found it hard to speak. "My wife, my family, all perished in Thebes. I have a blood feud with the Macedonian. I would not have betrayed you, my lord. I meant to meet Alexander and kill him."

"That is not," Arsites spoke up, "what Cleander told us."

Lysias turned, his face twisted into a snarl. "Well, of course he wouldn't, if tortured! My lord king." He got down on one knee. "Is this Arsites' doing?" Lysias gazed beseechingly at Memnon. "You know how much they hate us! They hate you: when we take the field, they'll have their way and impede you at every twist and turn. The only way to stop Alexander is to kill Alexander. I was doing it for you. For me." He stared round. "For all of us!"

"In which case," Arsites interrupted smoothly, "why did Alexander agree? My lord, I apologize." Arsites turned, a smirk on his face. "But our scouts captured Cleander on his return from across the Hellespont."

"Did you know he had gone?" Darius asked.

Memnon shook his head.

"But why didn't Lysias tell you about his plot?"

"I would have done," Lysias stammered, "but I had to be sure. I thought Cleander had been delayed."

Memnon stared down at his Master of Horse. On the one hand Memnon believed him, but on the other? To send an envoy to the enemy's camp yet not seek his permission?

"Did you know that Alexander was visiting Troy?" Darius' voice was just above a whisper.

Memnon shook his head.

"Nor did I," the King of Kings continued. "Not until Cleander fell into the clutches of Arsites." Darius touched Memnon gently on the wrist. "Even if it were true," he murmured, "who is Lysias to decide strategy? I do not want Alexander murdered, to become a hero, a martyr, for all of Greece. It would simply delay the inevitable for a few months, even years. Let Alexander cross. Let him meet the fate I have prepared for him."

Lysias tried to clutch Memnon's white robe but the general stepped away. He glanced over his shoulder at Diocles; his servant gazed back, stricken.

"There's nothing you can do, my lord," Darius declared, gesturing with his fingers.

Black-garbed figures swept out of the darkness. They surrounded Lysias, seizing him by his arms, dragging him to his feet.

"You were in my pay," Darius accused. "You are mine, body and soul. I am the King of Kings, the possessor of your neck. You are a mere pebble beneath my sandals. Take him to the Tower of Silence!" he ordered. "Lash him to a cage. Let him be suspended between heaven and earth!"

Lysias screamed and struggled. The cowled guards dragged him away.

"As you lie there," Darius shouted, "and wait for death, a long time coming, reflect on the just fate of a traitor!"

Prologue II

"Pausanias' body was immediately hung on a gibbet: but, in the morning, it appeared crowned with a golden diadem, Olympias' gift, to show her implacable hatred of Philip."

Quintus Curtius Rufus, History,
Book 1, Chapter 9

"**W**elcome back, Telamon, son of Margolis!"

"My lady, why am I here?"

"Because you have the gift of life." Olympias lifted her head. "While I have the gift of death."

"My lady, both lie in the hands of the gods."

"You don't believe in the gods, Telamon!"

"My lady, I believe in the same as you!"

Red-haired Olympias, widow of Philip, mother of Alexander, laughed loudly, a girlish sound which ill-suited both her mood and appearance. She sat garbed in a dress of sea-green clasped at the shoulder with a gold brooch displaying the head of Medusa. Her hair and long, olive-skinned face were shrouded in the sky-blue hood of her mantle; her feet, incongruously, were shod in soldier's marching sandals. The small acacia-wood table beside her bore a goblet and next to it all the jewellery she had taken off – her rings, necklaces and bracelets – as if their very touch was unpleasant. She tapped her feet and stared up at the ceiling, distracted by the picture of Bacchus riding a panther.

You haven't changed, Telamon considered. Of all the women he had ever met, indeed of all the people he had ever met, Olympias, of the tribe of Molossus, truly frightened him. He studied her face: wrinkle-free, the sharp nose above full red lips, but it was the eyes which drew him, like those of a wildcat, gleaming, restless; they would stare at you as if trying to draw the very life from your soul. Telamon swallowed hard and listened to his breathing. He knew the rules of the game: never show fear to Olympias. She thrived on that. She was now playing the role she had decided upon: teasing, flirtatious but, underneath, an air of brooding menace. Telamon felt as if he was acting in one of Sophocles' plays. Taking him abruptly from his mother's house, the captain of Olympias' guard was courteous but firm: he was to be the guest of the co-regent of Macedon.

"Why?" Telamon had asked.

The officer removed his helmet, wiped the sweat from his brow and stared across at the fountain in the small courtyard.

"Because that's the way she wants it."

Telamon had washed his face and hands, changed his tunic, put on a mantle, kissed his mother goodbye and, escorted by the Foot Companions, made his way up to the royal residence. He had first been taken to the Corpse house and, as instructed, studied the cadaver sprawled on a wooden table. Afterwards he had been given wine, some cheese and bread and brought here to the heart of the palace, the centre of Olympias' web.

Telamon moved restlessly on the chair. Olympias was still staring at the ceiling, lounging slightly on the wooden silver-gilt throne. On either side of the dais stood officers of the Foot Companions in full dress uniform: blue helmets with scarlet plumes on either side, the gold rims shading their eyes; the purple, flared neck guards stretching down to just above their shoulders. They stood like statues in their elaborate corselets, kilts and silver red-rimmed greaves; spears grasped in one hand, rounded shields in the other, displaying a wild-eyed, savage-faced maenad, Olympias' personal symbol.

Telamon coughed. Olympias still stared at the ceiling so the physician distracted himself by staring around this gloomy chamber, warmed only by a crackling brazier and bronze dishes full of spitting charcoal. Had something been sprinkled on the top, Telamon wondered. A strange perfume? The leaves of laurel or myrtle? Certainly not incense; perhaps oak leaves or crushed lotus petals? The bitter-sweet perfume tickled Telamon's nostrils and stirred his memory. What was it? And then he remembered, even as Olympias shifted her gaze and stared directly at him. One glance from the dark-green eyes of this serpent woman, the Witch Queen, and Telamon recalled her visits to the academy at Mieza. It was her scent! He recalled Olympias crouching down before him, running her finger down his cheek, asking him if he truly loved her precious Alexander.

A phrase from Euripides' *Bacchae* caught Telamon's eye: it ran along the wall just behind the throne: "*Dionysus deserves to be honoured by all men. He wants no one excluded from his worship.*" Olympias shifted on her throne and looked behind her.

"I had the painters put that there," she said. "Do you believe in it, Telamon? Don't you think everyone should drink the sacred wine?" She turned to face him squarely. "The sacred blood of the gods, the juice of the crushed fat grape. Are you a follower of Euripides, Telamon? Or just an admirer of his works?"

"I much prefer Aristotle's treatise on drunkenness."

"Ah, Aristotle." Olympias laughed. "That elegant, spindle-shanked fop! So, you don't like wine?"

"I didn't say that, my lady."

The queen continued her teasing. "In Book Six of the *Iliad*, Homer claims wine revitalizes the body."

"In the same book he also says it drains your strength."

"It does not become me," Olympias murmured, quoting from the *Iliad*, fingers tapping the arm of her throne, "to rage relentlessly on."

"In which case, my lady, perhaps you would tell me why I am here."

The humour drained from the queen's face. She tapped her sandalled foot and, picking up a bracelet, slid it on and off her wrist.

"Did you miss the groves of Mieza, Telamon?"

"I missed my friends."

"Did you miss my son?"

"My lady, you have my answer. I missed my friends."

Olympias laughed abruptly. Telamon started as one of the pitch torches, fixed on the wall to his left, flared out and died. Olympias jabbed a finger.

"So, why are you here?"

"Because you summoned me."

"No, why are you in Pella?"

"I have been since autumn."

Olympias, as if bored with this conversation, rose, stepped off the dais and walked towards him.

"Philip's dead. My husband, the king."

"I know, my lady."

"I crowned his killer."

"I know, my lady."

"I am not saying I killed him." Olympias walked round and stood behind Telamon.

"Of course not, my lady. You wouldn't hurt a fly."

Olympias laughed again and poked Telamon in the shoulder. He shifted uneasily. The chair seat was made from interlacing thongs which cut through the thin cushion. He stared down at the mosaic of the floor – not a very good one, a red-haired Dionysus bestride a goose. The god reminded him of a drunk who had tried to attack him in an alleyway. Where was it? Memphis or Abydos? Telamon couldn't recall. He was more concerned with curbing his fear. Olympias was like a cat who'd caught a bird. She did not mean him ill, at least not now. She wanted something. He half-suspected the truth. Only if he refused would the danger emerge. If Olympias wanted him dead, his head would have left his shoulders as soon as he set foot in Pella. Of course, her darling Alexander would have left strict instructions: somewhere in Olympias' perfume-filled quarters stood a silver-gilt casket kept secure with three locks; only Olympias held the keys. In that casket would be a scroll of parchment, listing the names of those Alexander had warned his mother not to touch. He was sure his name would be on it. Alexander never forgot his friends, not even those who disagreed with him or decided to walk different paths.

"I remember you, Telamon. You and Alexander hunting hares among the tombs at Mieza. Do you remember them? The grey slabs, the long grass? Swarms of butterflies, the silence broken only by a buzzing of bees? You always wore large sandals! You seemed to swim in them."

Olympias crouched down, whispering in his ear. Telamon smelt her strange perfume.

"Dark-faced, dark-haired Telamon. Always studious. I remember you picking up a bone a dog had unearthed from a grave. You and Alexander argued whether it was from the leg or the arm."

"It was from the leg, my lady: a femur. I was right, your son was wrong."

"You didn't like killing, did you? Remember when Ptolemy caught a baby thrush and said he would sacrifice it on a stone, you cried so Ptolemy let it go?"

"Your memory fails you, my lady." Telamon was aware that Olympias had stepped away. "Your son Alexander intervened. He punched Ptolemy on the nose, so he dropped the baby bird and it flew away."

"Ah yes. Now look at you, Telamon." Olympias walked around and stood before him, fingers to her chin, tongue clicking. "Telamon garbed in the tunic and mantle of a physician. Let me study your symptoms. Let me judge your appearance."

She stepped back as if assessing his worth. Telamon held her gaze.

"You are taller than I expected." Her voice was a whisper. "Black cropped hair." She paused. "How old are you, Telamon?"

"Twenty-six."

"And you already have grey hairs. Just a few, but they make you look distinguished. Doesn't Hippocrates, in his 'Corpus', say a physician must instil confidence in the patient? You make me feel confident, Telamon! Your face is dark, sallow with deep-set eyes. What colour are they?" She peered closer. "Light green, a little like mine. You have your mother's short nose. Your upper lip is thin but the lower is more generous. Your moustache and beard are well clipped." She put her head to one side, a gesture which acutely reminded Telamon of Alexander. "A scholar's face, secretive but not sly. Solemn-looking but, I think, Telamon can laugh! The ladies like you. So, Telamon, what is your life?"

"Medicine, my lady."

23

"And your wife?"

"Medicine, my lady."

"And your pastimes? Medicine, my lady," Olympias answered for him, mimicking his voice.

She came and stood over him. Telamon glimpsed one of the Foot Companions move slightly sideways as if to keep him in full view.

"You've been everywhere, Telamon. Let me see: Cos, Samos, Chios, Athens, Memphis, Abydos, Thebes in Egypt . . ."

"Even Tarentum in southern Italy." Telamon finished the list for her.

Olympias tapped the ring on the physician's left hand, displaying Aesculapius and Apollo, the healer.

"So, you do really believe in the gods, Telamon?"

"If gods do deeds of shame, the less gods they are."

"Is that one of your aphorisms?"

"No, my lady, Euripides."

"Ah, he who talks of deathless consciousness. Do you believe in life after death, Telamon?"

"The other life is a fountain sealed," Telamon quoted from Euripides. "This life has problems enough."

Olympias' eyes rounded in amazement. "You, a physician, do not like life? You have nothing but medicine? No ambition? No patron? No desire to improve your station. Why are you so sad, Telamon?"

"As the poet says, my lady: 'Our sweetest songs are those which tell our saddest thoughts.'"

"You *do* like Euripides." Olympias walked back and sat on the edge of the dais, hands resting on her knees. "Of all my son's companions, Telamon, I liked you the most. Do you know why? Because you posed no threat. You didn't want to be a general. You didn't want to be a soldier. You didn't want to strut around. I wager you are a lady's man. Did you have a wife in Egypt?"

"Just a lover."

"And she died?"

"A heset girl in the Temple of Isis. A priestess, my lady. A soldier abused her, she sickened and died. I was absent at the time."

"And the soldier?"

24

"A Persian officer. I killed him."

"How did you do that?" Olympias' head turned to the side, a smile on her lips. "Did you poison his wine? Stab him in the back? Or hire an assassin?"

Telamon kept his face impassive. Olympias stamped her sandalled foot.

"Are you ready to tell me? How did you kill him?"

"I met him in a wine shop just off the Avenue of Sphinxes in Thebes. I cursed him. He drew a sword and lunged at me. I learnt a lot in the groves of Mieza."

"Ah yes, Black Cleitus, my son's sword-master."

"The officer wasn't very good. His sword missed me. My dagger struck home. A clean cut straight to the heart."

Olympias sighed and got to her feet. "And so you came home?"

"I had no choice. The Persians would have crucified me on the walls of Thebes."

"And how is your mother? And your brother's widow and child? A sprightly boy, I hear."

Olympias had that chilling, sombre look. Telamon felt the sweat break out on the palms of his hands. Olympias had delivered her threat. Just her words, the way she emphasized "sprightly" while her eyes remained hard and brooding.

"Well!" She clapped her hands and returned to her throne. "You have the reputation for being an outstanding physician, Telamon." She eased herself down. "Tell me, what's the difference between spotted hemlock and water hemlock?"

"They are deadly poisons. Spotted hemlock leads to paralysis. Water hemlock provokes convulsions. Both bring about death."

"Is that from observation?" Olympias queried.

"No, Plato's description of Socrates' death. The philosopher was given spotted hemlock in his wine."

Olympias, lips pursed, nodded as if she were a scholar listening to a teacher.

"And you've viewed the corpse?"

Telamon recalled the ghastly house of death: the white, liverish flesh of the old man sprawled naked like a lump of meat on a slab. Olympias turned to the officer standing beside her.

25

"He did study the corpse? Closely as instructed?"

"As instructed, my lady."

"Well." Olympias turned back to Telamon. "Tell me what you know of that corpse."

"He was one of your retainers, my lady, he worked in the palace."

"Of course!"

"I would say a shoe-maker."

Olympias smiled.

"I could tell that," Telamon continued, "from his hands. They smelt of leather and tannin. Slight abrasions scored the fingers where he held the needle. His spine was a little curved from bending over his workbench. The muscles of his wrists and arms were well developed but his paunch and spindly legs show he was a man used to sitting down."

"Very good!" Olympias breathed.

"The corpse was slightly swollen." Telamon warmed to the task. "Putrefaction had set in early."

"And the cause of death?"

"Poison!"

Olympias threw her head back and laughed. "You are not going to accuse me!"

Telamon gazed coolly back. No, he thought, I wouldn't do that. Olympias, Witch Queen! Mistress of the poison! Telamon idly wondered how many potions, elixirs and antidotes her secret store-chests contained. He recalled the story of how Alexander's half-brother had been born hale and hearty, a sturdy rival to her son until Olympias had decided to feed him a certain food. The boy had recovered but spent the rest of his life wandering the palace, a veritable idiot and a powerful warning to anyone who challenged the rights of Olympias and her beloved son.

"I traced the poison," Telamon declared. "The right leg was swollen, the blood had turned to pus."

"How did he die?" Olympias insisted.

"I have heard of it happening before. A needle slipped, went into his leg. The wound was very small and closed immediately. The poor shoe-maker thought he was safe but the needle was

26

tainted and his blood became poisoned. He would have suffered pains in his head, tightness of the jaw, high fever, delirium. Death would have followed shortly afterwards."

"And what would you have done?"

"Why, my lady, opened the wound, drawn out the needle, then slit the leg."

"What for?"

"To pour in a mixture of honey, salt and wine. The stronger the wine the better. Not the light wine of Olympus or Athens but the strongest I could find; a deep, dark purple. Such an infusion would have cleansed the wound."

"How?" Olympias leaned forward genuinely curious.

"I don't really know, nor does anyone. Wine, honey and salt contain properties which cleanse the flesh and kill pus."

"I must remember that. So, you don't believe the production of pus is good? Hippocrates believed it was, as do my physicians."

"They are wrong." Telamon kept his voice confident. "Pus must be cleansed and not allowed to settle in the body. A wound should always be drained."

"And you can do that?" Olympias asked.

"It's possible. I've seen it done in Egypt – not only a wound, my lady, but even pus from a lung."

"And the bandage?"

"Clean linen, not tied too tightly. This allows the wound to breathe. Tighten the bandage and it seals the putrefaction in."

"And if that didn't work?"

"Then, my lady, I would have amputated the leg, about three inches above the knee. I would have given the man a heady wine laced with an opiate – this prevents convulsions and shock."

"But he would have bled to death."

"In Italy, my lady, I saw a surgeon do the same to a soldier's leg. He had received a poisoned arrow in an ambush. They used small clamps to seal off the blood, they then cauterized and bandaged the stump."

"My son will find this interesting," Olympias whispered almost to herself.

"Your son, my lady? He has left for Asia; his armies gather at the Hellespont."

Olympias clapped her hands. "Clever boy, Telamon. And you are to join him."

Telamon bit back his anger.

"The army gathers at Sestos," she continued. "You will join my son."

"Will, shall, must, my lady? I am free born, a Macedonian!"

"Nobody's free, Telamon. We all have duties, impositions and tasks, Telamon."

Olympias got up, rubbing her hands together. She stepped off the dais and walked towards him. She crouched down, no longer the queen but more like a mother pleading for her son.

"I trust you, Telamon, gold and glory aren't your concern. My son is surrounded by traitors, assassins, spies."

"Including your own?"

"Including my own."

"But I am not your spy."

"No, Telamon. You can't be bought, bribed or sold. I have read your treatise on poisons. You do have affection for Alexander. You will protect him not because I ask you, but because you want to."

"Alexander has asked for me?"

Olympias nodded. "He's heard all about you, Telamon. He insisted that you join him. Where else can you go?" Her eyes and voice became pleading. "You don't like Macedon! Athens perhaps? No Macedonian is welcome there. Or the Persian Empire? Asia, Egypt, North Africa? But there are warrants out for your arrest, Telamon, that Persian officer was highly placed. Think of the opportunities," she urged, "to heal, to mend."

"And if I don't go?"

Olympias got to her feet and walked slowly back to her throne. "I can't guarantee anything, Telamon." She paused and looked at the heavy-beamed ceiling. "This is where my rival Eurydice hanged herself!"

"Are you threatening me?"

"No, Telamon, I promise you. If you join my son, your mother, your brother's widow whom I know you like, and her sprightly little boy will always be safe. They will be my friends and I shall be their protector."

"Against what?"

Olympias spread her hands. "Accidents, unfortunate mishaps."

Telamon sighed and plucked at a loose thread on his cloak. He'd ask his mother to look at that. The fear had passed – the threat was clear. Telamon got to his feet and walked to the door. The officer on guard drew his sword. Olympias must have made a sign because he re-sheathed it.

"Where are you going, Telamon? You can see how much I love you. No man ever turns his back on me."

Telamon turned. "Why, my lady, I'm off to pack. It's a long journey to Sestos."

Olympias grinned and, going back to the table, sorted among the jewels. She plucked up a leather bag of coins and tossed it to Telamon who caught it deftly.

"That's for your journey, physician!"

Telamon undid the cord and, turning the bag up, emptied the golden coins onto the floor where they clinked and rolled.

"As you said, my lady." He let the leather bag fall. "For neither gold nor glory! Perhaps, on this occasion, I'll take the glory. The gold," he gestured, "you can have."

He walked towards the door. The guard opened it.

"Goodbye, Telamon!" Olympias called. "Tell my son his mother loves him."

Telamon, tense with rage, was already walking along the stone vaulted passageway to the pool of light at the far end.

Prologue III

The young woman was running. She did not know where or why. She stopped and peered back along the dusty trackway, which was fringed by whispering oak trees. She was sure the Furies, like screeching eagles, were plunging to drag her back to the terrors from which she had escaped. She paused and looked down at her gown, torn and bloodstained; her feet were scarred and bleeding. The blow to her head seemed to have changed everything. The oak trees moved like a reflection in running water. Sounds came from afar. She stumbled on, aware of the pain in her back and shoulders. She touched her face and winced at the bruises round her mouth. "A sweet-faced wench" was how one of the sailors had described her. Sailors? The young woman paused. That was something she *did* recall, the sea voyage, the little fishing craft. She was sitting there with other women and the escort the village headman had sent with them. They had been frightened but happy. The other girl was a stranger, more knowledgeable. Why had they been taken? Some story from deep in the past? The young woman looked through the gap in the oak trees. The snow-capped mountain in the far distance, was it Olympus? Was she going to the home of the gods? She crouched down on the dusty trackway. Why was she here? Something about Cassandra and reparation for a hideous murder, a priestess killed, blood screaming to the heavens for vengeance.

The young woman got to her feet and stumbled on. She rounded a bend and the oak trees gave way to a broad, windswept plain. The glint of a river caught her eye. Those sprawling ruins at the top of the hill. Wasn't that the sea she could hear crashing against the rocks? Why was she here? What had happened? She closed her eyes and swayed backwards and forwards on the balls of her feet. She had been wearing a garland like the other one. They had been laughing and talking but after that they were in darkness, those sinister, masked figures crowding round them. She remembered her companion turning to run, the club smashing into the side of her head, the blood spurting out through the poor girl's nose and mouth. Hands had seized her violently, tearing at her clothes. She'd started to run, hitting the side of the cave, falling on her face. Bruises, the hard pebbles marking her soft body, but she had reached the mouth of the cave and it was dusk – that's why they had gone there in the first place, drawn by the sight of fire and the cooking smells.

The girl began to shake. She couldn't stop trembling. Her bowels felt loose and she wanted to retch. Somehow or other the ruins before her were familiar. Wasn't that where she was supposed to be going?

She left the trackway and stumbled forwards. A bird circled overhead. Its cry reminded her of the call of a ghost. She paused and looked up at the sky. Was she home? Back in Thessaly? Would she eat and drink? And was the sun setting because it was evening again? And when darkness came would those hideous figures appear? She stumbled and fell, scuffing her knee. She got up and walked on. She was aware of broken walls, crumbling gateways. Suddenly a man appeared, small, squat, bald except for a circlet of black hair which looked like a wreath on his head. He had bright eyes and a snub nose. He spoke to her but she couldn't understand. She didn't like him. He had a greedy, salacious look and kept wetting his lips like one of those sailors. He drew closer.

"What is it, my dear?"

Now she could understand his harsh guttural tongue.

"Why are you here?"

She opened her hand. He glimpsed the small ivory owl kept

32

there. Now she realized why her fingers had been so clenched. She used to wear the owl round her neck on a chain.

"Athena's owl!" the man exclaimed. "You'd best come with me."

He grasped her by the hand. She had no choice but to follow as he led her through the ruins. Other people appeared, crowding round her, mouths moving, but she couldn't hear their voices. In front of her rose a small temple, steps leading up to it. Columns fronted a porticoed entrance. Soaring above it all was the helmeted figure of Pallas Athena. She recognized that – she had been told about the goddess. The man led her in. Inside it was dark but sweet-smelling. She crouched down, the floor was cool. She was aware of columns and statues. Three women hurried towards her. The man was summarily dismissed. She was taken down a passageway into a small room warmed and scented by a brazier. The woman who sat down on the stool opposite, was she the goddess? Chestnut hair, a beautiful face, wide-spaced, sea-grey eyes, smiling lips, her eyes anxious, brow furrowed. She touched the young woman's face, murmured something and gently took the owl from her hand.

"What is your name? Tell me who you are." The grey eyes were now crinkled in concern. "You are one of the maidens we expected, aren't you? My name is Antigone, priestess of this temple. These are my two assistants, Selena and Aspasia."

The names and faces meant nothing to the young woman. She began to tremble again. She stared round wildly. She would have got to her feet but one of the helpers kept her down and a goblet was held to her lips.

"Drink!" a voice ordered.

The young woman obeyed. The cup was drained and she was falling again, but not into sleep – back to that hideous nightmare and the sombre gloom of Hades.

Chapter 1

"When the next campaigning season started, Alexander left Antipater in charge of affairs . . . and marched for the Hellespont."

Arrian, *The Campaigns of Alexander*,
Book I, Chapter 11

T he time had been chosen by Aristander, soothsayer and keeper of the king's secrets: the rising of the star Arcturus in the forty-second year of the Olympiad. Alexander of Macedon stood in the middle of a circle of twelve stone altars erected in honour of the gods of Olympus. The sacred ring topped a small hillock a few miles from the city of Sestos, overlooking the steel-blue, fast-moving currents of the Hellespont.

Despite Aristander's preparations, the auspices were not good. A cold evening mist curled in from the sea, a sombre cloud which threatened to shroud the fires which flickered on eleven of the altars. Alexander lifted his hand. The trumpeters raised their salpinxes and blew a long, deafening blast which carried across the water and back over the Macedonian camp, which seemed to stretch to the far horizon. All now fell deathly silent. The troops, congregated around the hill, stared up at the sacred place where royal bodyguards protected the place of sacrifice. Those who had arrived first peered through the stockade, eager for a glance of their king. Alexander of Macedon, garbed in the full dress armour of a commander of the Royal Brigade, waited patiently, head slightly tilted back, staring up at the dark, forbidding clouds which hid the dying sun and threatened to obscure the paltry light of moon and stars. A gloomy, windswept night was promised.

Around Alexander were grouped his companions. There was tall, dark-haired Hephaestion with his sharp, sombre face, moustache and beard: some whispered how Alexander's "shadow" looked more like a Semite than a Macedonian. Next to him Ptolemy, sunburnt, clean-shaven, hair cropped. A cast in his right eye, together with his broken nose and slight harelip, gave him a perpetual sneering look. Then there was Nearchus, the small Cretan, concerned with the catapults, mangonels and other machines of war. Finally, Seleucus, tall and thick-set with heavy-lidded eyes, who dreamed of becoming an Asiatic potentate.

On the left of their king was a group of priests, led by the balding, spindle-legged Aristander with his bulbous eyes and ever-dripping nose. He looked the part everyone assigned him: warlock, magician, seer and fortune-teller. A priest who knew the secret rites and had been despatched by Olympias so that his mastery of the black arts could assist her son. They all watched him as the milk-white bullock with gilded horns, a garland of flowers round its neck and carefully drugged, plodded into the sacred enclosure. The royal page leading it stopped before Alexander. The king, using a small knife, sliced some of the hairs from between the horns and, going up to one of the altars, sprinkled these over the flames. Aristander handed him a gold goblet of Chian wine. Alexander poured this onto the fire and stepped back. The bullock was led closer to the altar where no fire burnt. At Aristander's signal, the priests grouped round it. One raised the ceremonial axe and brought it down in a slicing cut, striking the bull expertly at the back of the neck. It bellowed with fear and its forelegs crumpled beneath it. Another priest, straddling the animal, pulled back its head and, in one deft stroke, drew a scythe-like knife across its throat. The bull's bellow was echoed by the bystanders, even as its lifeblood gushed into the silver bowl to be taken up to the sacred fire.

Alexander watched carefully. As he did so, the Delphic Oracle came back to haunt him: "*The bull is prepared for sacrifice. All is ready. The slayer awaits.*" Words which prophesied his own father's death. Had Philip been sacrificed? Had his mother Olympias been the priestess? And why had the sacrifice taken place? To protect Olympias or Olympias' beloved son? And was he innocent of

36

his father's blood? Or would Philip's shade come wandering back from Hades to mock and taunt him in the early hours of the night?

The priests had now lifted the bull's carcass onto the altar. Alexander tried to dispel his gloomy thoughts as the priests cut open the belly. He pulled up the hood of his war cloak and lifted his hands in prayer to Zeus the all-seeing. The bull's entrails slopped out. A sudden horde of flies, noisy in their buzzing, came to hover over the pool of blood. A bad sign. Alexander's heart skipped a beat. Were they sent by the Furies? A sign of impending displeasure and punishment by the gods? Of all of them? Or just one? Apollo perhaps? Hera? Or Poseidon whose permission Alexander needed to hurl his arms across the Hellespont. Surely the other signs would be good? The bull had been carefully chosen, Aristander given strict and secret instructions. The king recalled the letters he had received from Olympias. Was all this the workings of a god or the machinations of men? Every prince was surrounded by traitors and assassins, but to fail now, even before he started?

Aristander, his arms deep in the bull's belly, groped and seized the still warm liver full of the bull's rich lifeblood. He placed it on the altar and stared down; turning to his master, he shook his head slightly. Alexander had his reply. The auspices were not good. The liver was still vital but he could tell by Aristander's lopsided smile that it was blemished, unacceptable to the gods. Alexander pushed back his hood and grasped Hephaestion's arm.

"Useless!" he whispered. "It's sullied, tarnished! I give it to the gods and the gods send it back. Tell the assembled men, the signs are still not clear enough."

"And?" Hephaestion asked.

"Oh, clear up the mess!" Alexander snapped, and walked off.

He left the sacrificial enclosure, walking down the avenue between the troops. He tried to smile and was relieved when his parasol-carrier, hurrying behind him, tripped and fell to the amusement of the soldiers.

"A good sign!" Alexander shouted, helping the man to his feet. "The gods know I need no protection! I have you and I have them. What more does Philip's son need?"

His words, carried and repeated, were greeted with roars of

approval. Alexander walked on. He felt a sudden chill down his left side and paused. Was that his father? A ghost? A premonition? Alexander felt vulnerable. He had walked from the sacrificial enclosure – no one was here to protect his back. On either side were his Macedonian pikemen, but any one of them might be an assassin. Alexander resisted the urge to hurry. Instead, he crossed over to a group of Thessalians and began to tease them about their long hair, recalling their exploits during previous campaigns. Some Alexander recognized by name and asked about their families, all the time fending off the same questions. When would they march? When would they cross the Hellespont?

"We will march soon enough," Alexander reassured them, hiding his own unease. "And believe me, within a year you will all be clothed in silk. You will feast on gold and silver cups and platters while the ladies of Persia cater for your every need."

"Every need?" one wit retorted.

Alexander pointed a finger at the speaker and winked playfully. "In your case, there may be one or two exceptions!"

A roar of laughter greeted his reply. Alexander passed on. He heaved a sigh of relief as he reached the royal enclosure, ringed by carts and the trophies set up to commemorate former victories, guarded by an elite unit from the Royal Brigade. Alexander had a few words with the captain of the watch and passed through. In the centre stood an altar, strewn with wet, bedraggled flowers. Alexander went across and, picking up a wild lily, crushed it between his fingers. Hadn't Olympias, or was it Aristotle, warned him about the juices of this flower? Wasn't it poisonous or . . . ? Alexander looked towards the royal pavilions set up in the shape of a "T". The crossbar was his council chamber, the upright his personal quarters. At the entrance thronged a group of physicians. Perdicles the Athenian, tall, broad-browed, his black hair cropped close. Slanting eyes, a thin nose above prim lips. Next to him, Cleon of Samos: small, blond-haired, moon-faced and fussy, a man of secrets, close to Alexander's right hand. Leontes of Platea, brown as a berry with mischievous eyes and a slobbery mouth which seemed to ever hang open. Finally Nikias – where was he from? Ah yes, Corinth. Dry-eyed, dry-faced with a dry wit. A shock of unruly grey hair crowning an old man's face, furrowed and deep-set. The physicians were exchanging hot words with the officer who blocked their entrance – they didn't realize Alexander had arrived until the soldier came smartly to attention.

"Is he here, sire?" Perdicles called. "We heard a rumour . . ."

"*You* heard a rumour and *I* know the truth," Alexander teased. "Yes, you may meet him, but not now."

He winked at Cleon and pushed by them into the first part of the tent, the waiting chamber, where the royal pages lounged. Alexander handed his cloak to them and lifted the partition which led to the inner chamber containing his table, chairs, treasures and personal possessions. The pageboy, tending an oil lamp, spun round.

"Get out!" Alexander ordered.

The boy, wiping his hands on his tunic, hastened to obey. Alexander caught him by the shoulder and spun him round. He stared down at the smooth, olive-skinned face.

"You are a good boy." Alexander smiled. "I am just tired. Tell the others to keep quiet."

Alexander ignored Telamon whom he'd glimpsed sitting on a stool to his far left between two coffers. Instead he went across to the desk and sifted among the papers which littered it.

"The secretariat is always busy."

"Aren't we all?" Telamon coolly replied.

Alexander glanced at him sharply and began to undo the straps of his corselet.

"Oh, for the love of Apollo, or whatever god you believe in, Telamon! Don't sit there. Come over and help an old friend."

Telamon obeyed and, crouching down, unloosened the strap just beneath the armpit.

"You've changed," Alexander commented.

"So has the world, sire."

Telamon undid the strap, narrowing his eyes as he loosened the buckle.

"You've been out in the sun too long, Telamon. Your eyesight is not so good."

"Just the same, sire – near-sighted."

39

"You used to call me Alexander."

"And a lot more, sire," Telamon quipped.

"How's Mother?"

"Deadly as ever."

"Did she threaten you?"

"No, just those I love."

Alexander took off the corselet and threw it on a stool. "They are safe. Don't worry about her, Telamon. Your name and those of your family are on my list."

Alexander unloosened the war kilt, sat on a stool and undid his marching boots, then removed the sweat-soaked tunic. He stood naked except for a loincloth and spread his hands.

"Do I pass muster, physician?"

Telamon studied the rosy-white skin marred by old wounds and bruises, the darkened areas burnt by the sun. Alexander's legs and thighs were thick and muscular, his stomach flat.

"A healthy mind in a healthy body, eh, Telamon?"

"The body passes muster, sire."

Alexander's smile faded. He crossed to the chest, took out a white purple-edged tunic and pulled it over his head.

"You haven't changed at all, Telamon – tart and cynical as ever."

"Life is short, science so long to learn," Telamon replied. "Opportunity is elusive, experience is dangerous, judgment is difficult."

"Euripides?"

"No, sire, Hippocrates."

The king walked across, hand outstretched. Telamon clasped it. Alexander pulled him close.

"I wish you'd come sooner," he said fiercely. "As Euripides says, 'The day is for honest men, the night for thieves.' Do you still enjoy the playwright, Telamon?"

"One of his phrases in particular," Telamon replied. "The sacred fragment: 'Those whom the gods wish to destroy they first make mad.'"

Alexander felt his erstwhile friend tense as if expecting a blow. The king kissed him gently on the cheek and stepped back.

40

His head went to one side, his finger close to Telamon's face. "I wanted you here, because I need you. Because I trust you. However, if you don't want to be here, I can fill your purse with gold and send you back."

"I'd love to accept." Telamon smiled. "But I can't for two reasons. First, there is no going back. Second, you have no gold left."

Alexander grabbed him by the arm. "But I *do* have work." He glanced towards the entrance to the tent, face solemn, eyes worried. "Some men in this camp, Telamon, wish me dead. Others want to see me fall. I have just sacrificed the third bull in two days, the prime cullings of my herd. Like the rest, its liver was blemished. I don't know which is going to run out first: bulls for sacrifice or my patience with the gods." He paused. "There's something else I want to show you."

Alexander slipped on a pair of sandals. He tapped the leather satchel which Telamon had slung over his shoulder. "You brought your medicines?"

"A soldier carries a sword, a physician his potions."

"You may need them."

Alexander lifted the tent flap and they went out through the antechamber into the cold night air. They were immediately surrounded by the other physicians – Telamon knew them of old. Perdicles grasped his arm, his face bright with pleasure.

"I heard rumours but I didn't think you'd come."

The others would have joined in but Alexander called across a guards officer to be an escort and they set off through the gloom, walking carefully between the tents and pavilions, wary of the guy ropes and tent pegs. Some tents were large, some were small but placed close together – not only for security, but to prevent a night attack. Enemy infantry or cavalry would find such narrow alleyways as great a hindrance as any ring of guardsmen.

"What are you smiling at?" Alexander asked, ignoring the chatter of the other physicians behind him.

"Our youth." Telamon smiled back. "Black Cleitus taking us out into the hills, showing us how and where to pitch camp. By the way, where is the great brute?"

41

"In Sestos buying wine. You'll sup with me tonight, Telamon?"

Alexander paused as a cowled figure stepped out of the darkness. The officer half-drew his sword but relaxed as the man pulled back his hood.

"Our man from Tarsus!" Alexander exclaimed. "The tent-maker. Is all ready?"

The tent-maker nodded.

"And the fire?" Alexander asked.

The man shook his head. "I don't know. All I can say," he added mournfully, "is that one good tent has been demolished. Leather and cord are very precious."

"I know. I know." Alexander waved him away. He grasped Telamon's hand as they used to do when they were boys. "It was your tent," he whispered. "You have one for yourself. Both chambers went up in flames, only the poles and cords remained. It's a good job you were not in it."

"An accident?"

"Perhaps," Alexander replied.

Telamon glanced away. The cold night breeze chilled the sweat from his brow. He was tired after his long journey from Macedon and he idly wondered why his tent had burnt to the ground. Such fires were common but usually caused by someone being careless inside. He was about to ask further when Alexander stopped before a large, square-like tent, its roof rising to a peak. It had a cloth front, the rest consisting of stretched leather skins lashed to poles and kept taut by ropes and pegs. The guardsman outside lifted the flap. Alexander led Telamon in, the other physicians following behind.

The tent was not divided into two, but stretched like a small hall. A capped brazier stood in the centre. There were woollen rugs strewn on the ground, cushioned seats and polished small tables. At the far end were beds, coffers, chests and a high-backed chair and stools around a trestle table. A young woman, dressed in a simple dark-red tunic, sat at the table staring vacuously before her. Three women, talking quietly among themselves at the far end of the tent, rose and came forward. All three were dressed in the light-blue tunic and mantle of priestesses of Athena. Their leader carried a white, crooked shepherd's staff. A small bronze owl of Athena hung from a chain round her neck and her rings were emblazoned with the same symbol. Her two companions were mere striplings, dark-haired and pale-faced. The priestess, who introduced herself as Antigone, was striking in both looks and poise: sea-grey eyes in a long olive face, high cheek-bones, full red lips. She fleetingly reminded Telamon of Olympias and seemed unabashed in Alexander's presence. He paid her every courtesy, bowing slightly and spreading his hands like a suppliant in a temple.

"Why, my lord," Antigone's voice was soft but vibrant, "you promised to bring a physician, but not a gaggle."

She ignored Perdicles and the rest, and coolly studied Telamon with a slow appraising look, searching his face as if she were trying to recall him. Alexander made the introductions. Telamon felt slightly embarrassed and overawed – he wondered if Antigone was truly curious about him or quietly mocking.

Antigone stretched out a hand for Telamon to kiss. He did so. Her fingers were long, cool and perfumed.

"You look tired." Antigone clasped his right hand, her thumb gently stroking his wrist. "I know you, the famous physician!"

Telamon, embarrassed, looked at Alexander who was thoroughly enjoying his discomfort.

"Antigone, priestess of Athena," Alexander declared. "Serves the goddess at their temple in Troy. She has crossed the Hellespont to greet me. Honour enough! She also brought guides."

"Guides?"

Alexander made a cutting gesture with his hand. "I'll tell you later. First, the patient!"

Antigone stood aside. Alexander ushered Telamon towards the table.

"My lady, perhaps you can tell our physician the young woman's story."

Telamon stared down at the doll-faced, empty-eyed girl who still sat, lips soundlessly moving. Now and again she blinked or pulled a face and flinched as if from some unseen enemy. Telamon felt her pulse. The blood beat quickly through her wrist. He stared into her eyes: her dark pupils were enlarged and her breathing was shallow.

"She is in a trance," he declared. "But one brought on by fever."

He gazed up at Antigone. The priestess was playing with one of the heavy rings bearing the owl of Athena.

"Who is she? One of your temple maidens?"

Alexander sat on the edge of the table, arms crossed, staring down at the floor.

"She is what is left of a legend, Telamon. The curse of Cassandra!"

"Cassandra raped by Ajax after the fall of Troy?"

"The warrior," Alexander agreed, "took Cassandra prisoner and ravished her. The legend developed that his descendants, the hundred noble families of Locri in Thessaly, had to pay reparation. Cassandra, the prophetess, had been sacred to Athena. The hundred families were to send two maidens a year to serve in the goddess' temple at Troy."

"But that's legend!" Telamon protested.

"It was until about five years ago. My father Philip wanted to make his landing at Troy successful. He wished to appease Athena, so he persuaded the Thessalian chieftains to reinstate the practice. Every spring two maids were to be taken across to the Hellespont, landed on the shore and told to make their own way to Troy. At least, that's the theory."

"Aspasia and Selena were the first." Antigone gestured at her companions. "None of the rest ever arrived. I wrote to Philip myself but he could do little – the western shore of the Hellespont is ravaged by brigands and outlaws. Two maidens would fetch a high price in the slave markets."

"It's barbaric!" Telamon exclaimed.

"It's happened before," Alexander explained. "This year was no different."

Telamon glanced at him quickly. Was Alexander lying? He caught the glance between the king and the priestess, a faint smile as if they were fellow conspirators.

"The practice will end now." Alexander sighed. "We have no further need for sacrifices. This unfortunate was found wandering on the outskirts of the ruins at Troy."

Telamon studied the girl's head, sifting her luxuriant hair. He felt lumps, a healing scab. Her face had been carefully painted to hide the fading cuts and bruises. He ordered a lamp to be brought closer.

"We have examined her," said Perdicles, coming forward with the other physicians.

"She's witless," Cleon lisped.

"There's nothing we can do," Nikias declared gently, "except hand her back to her family."

Telamon, crouching by the girl, grasped her hand, which was cold and clammy. He pressed his ear against her chest and, gesturing for silence, picked up the quick heartbeat.

"I can cure her," he declared.

Leontes guffawed. He came and stood behind the girl, glaring down at Telamon as if he was responsible for the young woman's injuries.

"Are you a miracle-worker, Telamon? Will you smear toad fat on her skin and perform a dance round her?"

"I'll make you eat the same fat!" Telamon snapped.

Alexander snorted with laughter and stood up. "Nothing worse than a gaggle of physicians arguing over a cure," he taunted.

"I'll not argue." Telamon got to his feet, face flushed with anger. "I have seen such trances before. They are brought on by a deep terror."

Alexander apologized with his eyes. "What do you recommend?"

Telamon cupped the girl's chin in his hands, turning her head. "What is it?" he asked softly. "What are you frightened of?"

"The darkness."

The woman's lower lip trembled. Her voice was guttural but Telamon could understand her tongue. During his exile he had worked for a while in Thessaly.

"What about the darkness?"

"Furies lurk deep inside. Monsters, they coil like snakes up my skin." She pressed her hand against the side of her face. "And the screaming. That and the spurting blood. A monster's claw stretches out to catch me. And the . . ." She closed her eyes and sniffed. "The pit, grotesque sights, foul smells."

45

She lapsed into silence, staring down at the tabletop.

Telamon took the satchel off his shoulder and undid the buckles. He searched among the phials carefully placed in the small pockets and straps within. He took one out and squeezed the girl's hand.

"I am going to put you to sleep," he said. "And you will sleep for a long, long time."

"What will that do?" Alexander asked, curious.

"It will allow the body and mind to rest. Free the phantasms in her soul. Sometimes she will awake screaming but go back to sleep again."

"A woman's remedy," Leontes muttered.

"No, far from it." Telamon pulled out the stopper and sniffed it carefully. "In fact, it's a soldier's remedy. My lord," he turned to Alexander, "you have met soldiers whose wits have been turned by the shock of battle?"

"Lunatics," the king agreed. "Not fit for anything."

"They are lost in the maze of their terrors," Telamon explained. "They go round and round searching futilely for the way out. Sleep escapes them and the faster they walk, the more desperate they become and the worse it gets."

"I have heard of this," Perdicles broke in. "They call it the sleep of Aesculapius, the dream of forgetfulness."

Telamon agreed. "I have seen men sleep for weeks, sometimes months, that's all they do: sleep, eat and drink."

"Are they cured?" Leontes didn't sound so arrogant now.

"In some cases yes. In one or two I admit . . ."

"Sleep is the brother of death," Antigone broke in. "They never regain consciousness."

"Precisely, my lady. Now, if I could have some wine?"

Antigone went deeper into the tent. She brought back a goblet emblazoned with Athena's owl and filled it with wine. She tasted it and, winking at Telamon, passed it over as if it were a loving cup. Telamon sipped the wine and sniffed: it was rich and dark.

"From the vineyards of Chios," Antigone explained.

Telamon tasted the wine again. He quietly resolved that if he was involved in Alexander's madcap campaigns and the killing and wounding began, such wine should be preserved to ease pain and cleanse wounds. Watched by the others, he poured the powder into the wine and stirred it with an ebony stick taken from his satchel. He picked the goblet up and tried to make the woman sip. She refused.

"Let me try," Antigone declared, taking the cup.

Telamon moved away. Antigone sipped the wine to give reassurance. She tried again but the patient recoiled, shaking her head. The priestess put the wine back on the table. Others also tried, but failed. Telamon crouched down, turning the woman's face gently with his fingers.

"Close your eyes," he urged. "Think of going home."

A faint smile appeared on the young woman's lips.

"This wine will take you home. It's magic wine, it will make you better."

Telamon took the cup from Antigone, and this time the girl sipped. Telamon placed the goblet down before her.

"We can do no more," he said.

Alexander was impatient to go. Antigone murmured something about a funeral. Telamon placed the phial back in his medicine satchel and did up the buckles. They all made to leave the tent.

At the entrance, Telamon stared back. The young woman was now holding the cup between her hands, staring into the wine as if it contained the waters of Lethe, the river of forgetfulness.

"Will she drink it?" Alexander asked.

"She'll drink it," Telamon declared. "And fall asleep like a child with her head in her hands. Or she might go back to bed."

He gazed around the deserted tent and smiled to himself. Even here, in this military camp, he could tell this was a place of women: cleaner, fresher, the little items placed here and there, the tidiness. He recalled Analu's sun-filled chamber in the temple of Isis and his smile disappeared.

"Will she be safe?"

"She will be safe," Alexander assured him. "The tent coverings are tied tight — not even a worm could crawl underneath. The entrance is guarded."

They joined the rest. Perdicles and the other physicians were muttering among themselves. They raised their hands, shouting farewells. Alexander turned to talk to Antigone. The royal body-guard now circled them, fierce and sinister in their Corinthian helmets with starched, horsehair plumes running from the crown of their helmets to hang down between their shoulder-blades. In the darkness they looked like creatures of the night, faces almost hidden by the broad nose and cheek guards. They stood silently, their presence only betrayed by the chink of metal.

"I want you to come with us, Telamon!" Alexander called across. "I must pay my respects at a funeral."

"What is this funeral?" Telamon asked, pulling his cloak tighter against the cold night air.

"My lady Antigone," Alexander said, grinding the heels of his sandals into the rain-drenched earth, "brought me scouts from across the Hellespont. Once we have reached Troy, we will march down the coast, keeping in contact with our ships. You have crossed the Hellespont?"

Telamon nodded. He recalled the open windswept plains, the dark forest of fir and oak, the rushing rivers, a landscape gouged by deep ravines.

"A place of ambush," he said.

"Father said the same." Alexander peered up at the sky. "We will go along the coast, Telamon, and strike inland. I don't want to be ambushed."

He grasped the priestess' hand. Behind Antigone her two acolytes stood like shrouded statues.

"My lady brought me scouts led by Critias, a former soldier in the Persian army. He knows the lie of the land, the location of the wells, where rivers can be forded, which ravines and gullies can hide an enemy. Critias will draw maps and his men will guide us. They will be our eyes and ears."

"And this funeral?" Telamon insisted.

"The Lady Antigone arrived with these guides some days ago. Yesterday evening one of them was found on the rocks below the cliffs, his corpse drenched by the sea."

"An accident?" Telamon couldn't make out Alexander's face in the darkness but he sensed his uncertainty.

"No, a dagger thrust between his ribcage, up to his heart. He must have been dead before he fell to the rocks."

Alexander abruptly marched away. Antigone came up beside Telamon as he began to follow the king.

"The king has great trust in you, physician." She walked elegantly, her hand resting on his arm. Telamon was pleased by her touch. Antigone reminded him of Analu: her serenity, the laughter in her eyes, her blunt speech and lack of guile.

"Do I know you?" he asked.

"Perhaps you do, Telamon. A traveller once came to our temple from lands further east across the Hindu Kush. He was a Brahmin, one of their holy men. He claimed we were all trapped on the Wheel of Life and came back to it time and again."

"The teaching of Pythagoras?"

"Something similar," she agreed. She dug her nails gently into his wrist. "Perhaps we met before, Telamon. They say that when we come back, the souls are the same but the relationships different. Perhaps, last time, I was your sister?" She laughed softly. "Or your mother?" She leaned closer and whispered in his ear: "Or even your lover?"

For the first time since he had arrived in Sestos Telamon laughed. Alexander looked over his shoulder but walked on. The royal enclosure still lay quiet. On leaving it the smells of the camp greeted them: woodsmoke, burnt peat, the stench of wet leather and horse dung. News of the king's arrival spread. Men left camp fires to toast him with their beaker cups, but the ring of bodyguards kept such well-wishers away. They made their way up between a row of tents and stopped before one. Telamon recognized the usual sleeping place for a detachment of eight soldiers. A makeshift brazier blazed in front of the entrance. On either side of this, pitch torches sputtered in the wind. From a rope hanging above the entrance to the tent hung a water stoup, the symbol of mourning, so that visitors who came to visit the dead might, on departure, cleanse themselves of pollution.

The tent was guarded. A sentry lifted the flap and Alexander entered. The makeshift funeral bier stood in the centre of the tent. The corpse lay in a circle of vine branches, feet towards the door. A slave stood by the head, waving a spray of myrtle to keep away marauding flies. Around the low-slung bier crouched the other scouts. They were all garbed in dark clothes, a sign of mourning. Their hair was freshly shorn, their faces covered in white chalk and garish streaks of paint. They made no attempt to rise as the king came in and their accusing glances showed that they blamed Alexander for their companion's death.

A burly, thick-set man, better dressed than the rest in tunic and mantle with a white cord round his waist, greeted them. He had deep-set eyes and weatherbeaten cheeks; his white hair was close-cropped like a soldier's. He grasped Telamon's hand.

"I am Critias." His light-blue eyes were friendly. "You must be Telamon – the king said you would come."

Telamon didn't understand why Alexander should be telling anyone about his arrival. He muttered his condolences and stared at the corpse, which was swathed in bands of linen and covered with a makeshift pall. Alexander demanded a cup of wine. He took this, stood at the head of the bier and dramatically lifted the cup like a priest making an offering above an altar.

"I have prayed," he declared in a strong voice, "that this man's shade will not be troubled in his journey across the river of death. I will supply the honey cake to satisfy the hunger of Cerberus. I will pay for Charon's ferry and I, Alexander of Macedon, swear that I will seek justice for his blood. I pledge this in the presence of the priestess of Athena and my vow is sacred!"

Alexander's gaze shifted. Just for a moment Telamon glimpsed his sardonic humour. "My own personal physician, Telamon, son of Margolis, a Macedonian by birth and upbringing, will investigate the cause of this man's death."

Alexander lowered the cup, took a deep gulp and passed it to the first mourner. While the cup was passed round, Alexander produced a purse, shaking out silver coins which winked in the light of the oil lamp. He placed these at the side of the corpse's head.

"My lord." An officer, ignoring the obsequies, had raised the tent flap. "You'd best come quickly!"

Alexander strode out. Telamon, Critias and the priestess followed. Alexander took the officer to one side, an arm across his shoulder, listening carefully as the man whispered in his ear. The king snapped his fingers at Telamon and hurried off. They reentered the royal enclosure. The flap to Antigone's tent was pushed back, the entrance thronged by soldiers. Telamon followed Alexander as he thrust his way through. The young woman they had left sitting at the table now lay slumped on the floor in an untidy heap. Perdicles and Leontes sat on stools staring down at her.

"Is she dead?" Alexander demanded.

"Poisoned," Leontes replied, glaring spitefully at Telamon.

Telamon ignored him and hurried over. He picked up the wine cup. It was empty. The young woman lay in a huddle and yet, even as he felt her arm, Telamon recognized the stiffness was unnatural. He pulled the corpse over. Her face was a livid white with strange blotches high on the cheeks. Telamon searched for a blood pulse but it was futile. The skin felt cold and clammy and the rigidity of her muscles was testimony enough. He stared pitifully at the half-open eyes, the lids slightly purple as if the blood was bursting to break through. Her lips were bloodless, almost white, her jaw firmly clenched.

"What is it?" Alexander whispered.

"Poison." Telamon got to his feet and rubbed his face. "She has been poisoned. Socrates' death, some potion like hemlock. Paralysis, tightening of the limbs, an inability to breathe."

"Your first patient here," Leontes murmured.

Telamon picked up the cup and sniffed at it. "Someone must have come into this tent after we left."

"That's impossible!" the captain of the guard protested. "I have spoken to the sentry. Look around you. No one has been in here! The guard heard a movement, followed by a clatter. When he lifted the tent flap, the young woman was sprawled as you find her."

Telamon went across and examined the wine jug, but it was only pretence, a way to hide his confusion at the speed and cunning of the assassin.

Chapter 2

"Alexander was asked: 'Where, O King, is your treasure?' 'In the hands of my friends,' he replied."

Quintus Curtius Rufus, *History*,
Book 2, Chapter 3

"Are you sure it's poison?" Perdicles asked.

Telamon sat in his colleagues' tent and shook his head disbelievingly. Alexander had left, ordering the corpse to be removed, shouting that Telamon's new tent, close to his, was to be prepared. Antigone's two companions, Selena and Aspasia, agreed to dress the body so it could be taken out with the guide's corpse to the large funeral pyre built on the cliff top. Telamon scrupulously checked the wine, the cup and the tabletop but could find no trace of any noxious powders. The goblet had been drained; the odour of wine and the opiate was so strong it masked anything else. He glanced across at Perdicles. The Athenian stared sadly back.

"It's hardly a good introduction, is it?" Telamon murmured. "Leontes has it right: my first patient here dies within the hour. But how?" He got to his feet and strode round the small tent. "The priestess poured the wine. I saw her carry the cup. Others touched it but, if there had been any powder from a hidden ring or secreted in the palm of a hand, it would have been noticed. Yet she's dead." He whirled round. "Are you sure no one entered that tent after we left?"

Perdicles shook his head. "The king himself questioned the guard. The young woman just sat there, drank the wine and mysteriously died. How much spotted hemlock would it take?"

53

Telamon pulled a face. "Poisons are like wines, they have different strengths. But a few grains, not much more than your fingertip, if it was pure ground powder. Spotted hemlock, well, as you know, it freezes the limbs. The victims can't breathe. They choke to death very quickly. Of course," he added wistfully, "the opiate I gave would only heighten the effect."

He came and sat down on the small leather chest which Perdicles had mockingly introduced as "his finest chair".

"It could have been suicide," the Athenian remarked.

"No." Telamon, restless, got to his feet. "Antigone answered that. She offered to have her tent searched. Moreover, where would a poor distracted thing like that have the wit and cunning to find such a powder and then use it? She was terrified but not suicidal." Telamon beat his hand against his thigh. "We questioned everyone! I sipped the wine. Afterwards the victim sat in a closely guarded tent, its leather sheets lashed tightly together. Only a ghost could get through that."

"Have you ever dissected a corpse?" Perdicles asked.

"On a number of occasions in southern Italy. In this case it wouldn't prove anything. It would simply confirm our diagnosis. The poor woman has suffered enough. Alexander will have to explain it to the family."

Telamon was angry. He had been depicted as a fool, slyly and subtly threatened. He went deeper into the tent. Cleon lay fast asleep on his cot bed snoring like a pig. Telamon sat down on the other bed. He removed Perdicles' heavy woollen cloak, which was spattered with mud along its hem, and picked at the fat barley husks stuck to the wool. He stared moodily down at the mud-caked sandals thrown into a far corner. He rolled a barley husk between his fingers. Perdicles, rather agitated, came and sat down next to him. The Athenian gestured across at Cleon.

"I envy you, you have a tent to yourself. I share with him. I've never seen a man sleep for so long, like a babe without a care in the world."

Cleon rolled over on the bed and squinted at both of them.

"I heard that. If you'd drunk the wine I drank . . ." He stretched. "Ah, the sleep of Dionysius!"

Telamon wiped his fingers on his robe.

"Why are you here, Telamon?" Cleon asked sweetly. "With your marvellous reputation and strange cures? Why don't you just bugger off and leave us all alone?" He pulled himself up. "By the way, I've heard your theory about bandaging."

"Why am I here?" Telamon snapped, ignoring the jibe about his medical skill. "I am beginning to ask myself that. I don't really know."

They heard shouts at the entrance to the tent. A pageboy came bustling through with all the arrogance of a successful general. He sketched a bow and pointed at Telamon.

"Your tent is ready, your baggage is stowed and the king wishes you to join him at supper. You'd best come now!"

"How can I refuse?"

Telamon got to his feet and followed the page, deliberately walking like a woman, swinging his hips, tunic flouncing above his bottom. Cleon called out something sarcastic about having friends in high places; Telamon ignored him. Outside, the camp was coming to life. The routine tasks had been completed, pickets set up, patrols despatched, sentries and guards in position. Loud neighs from the horse lines carried through the clang and clatter of the small smithies where the armourers, sweaty and black-stained in the light of their fires, worked late into the night. The army had finished its evening meal, the air carried the scent and flavours of different foods. Soldiers were returning to their units to sleep or sit chatting round the camp fires. Telamon heard a mixture of different tongues: the leisurely drawl of Greek mercenaries, the high-pitched chatter of Thessalian horsemen. Orders were being posted up, officers shouting for men, trumpets braying. They entered the royal enclosure. The page gestured at a large box-like tent with dyed cloths hung over the leather sheets.

"That is yours," he declared hoarsely. "You'll find everything there."

He sauntered off into the darkness. A guard lounged outside warming his hands over a dish full of charcoal. He smiled and nodded as the physician walked by him and around the tent. It was very similar to the one where the young woman had been murdered. He lifted the drape and studied the leather sheets beneath. These were pulled tight, the holes along the edges reinforced with rings. Twine, or cord, looped through them, kept the leather lashed smartly to the ash poles, at least a dozen along each side. The knots were tied expertly like those on a ship's rigging. Telamon crouched down. The base was similar, the holes larger for the guy ropes, tied tight to pegs driven into the ground. Telamon pulled at the bottom of the sheet, taut as a bowstring.

No one, he reasoned, could get under this, and it would take an age to undo the cord. Surely someone would have noticed? Then the assassin would have to kill, leave, and re-tie the sheets with the same knots used by the tent-riggers.

"Is everything all right, sir?" The guard was on his feet, staring curiously at him.

"Everything's fine." Telamon grinned through the darkness. "Where are you from, soldier?"

"Father owns a farm just outside Pella. I am one of the Foot Companions. I'll be here for four hours, then I'll be relieved."

Telamon thanked him, lifted the flap and went inside. The tent was divided by a cloth into a living chamber and sleeping quarters. Telamon was grateful at Alexander's thoughtfulness: woollen coverings lay strewn on the floor; the camp bed had a feather-filled mattress and bolster; chairs, coffers and stools stood about. There were four oil lamps, one of them lit, and even a sealed jug of wine and an earthenware goblet. Telamon heard a sound and glanced round. The pageboy stood in the entrance, a red ribbon round his black, curly hair.

"What do you want?"

"To serve you, master." The page gazed cheekily back.

Telamon moved across to his travel bags which had been placed against a chest. He crouched down and examined the buckles. They were loosened – someone had been through them. Telamon glanced at the pageboy.

"Piss off, boy! I don't like people with noses bigger than their brains! I'll find my own assistant."

The page flounced out. Telamon heard the guard laugh. He went and sat on the edge of the bed. Why had Alexander, he wondered, brought him here? What on earth did he want with him? And, more importantly, why had he truly come? He got up, filled the goblet with a mouthful of wine and rinsed his mouth out. He returned to the bed and dozed for a while. He was roughly awakened and found himself staring up at the sly, watery-eyed face of Aristander.

"Ah." Telamon rubbed his eyes. "The keeper of the king's secrets, seer of the future . . ."

Aristander gestured to the servants behind him. "Fresh water! Up you get! You've got to change and be in the royal pavilion within the hour!"

Aristander swept out. Telamon watched him go. Had Aristander given instructions for his possessions to be searched? He sighed, got to his feet, washed his hands and face, rubbed oil into his hair and beard and dressed in his best tunic and mantle. He kept his marching sandals on but carried his slippers. A page, waiting outside, led him across to the royal pavilion.

The banquet had already begun, the guests lying on long low couches, small tables set before them. The pavilion was long, poorly lit but rich with a perfume which mingled with the less pleasant odour from the earthenware oil lamps. Alexander lorded it from a lion couch at the top of the pavilion. In the shadows behind stood two guards officers.

"Welcome, physician." Alexander gestured with his cup. He turned to his companions. "All hail to Telamon!"

The toast was taken up with a roar. This was one of Alexander's famous drinking parties. Only the closest and dearest were invited to lounge drunkenly on couches. This time, however, an exception had been made. On Alexander's left the priestess Antigone, lying like a queen, sipped carefully from a goblet. She winked slyly, telling the physician that she was the only sober person present. Next to her was Hephaestion, and then Ptolemy with his mistress, a Greek prostitute who insisted on dying her hair a deep red. Seleucus, already deep in his cups bawled at Nearchus and Aristander. The king's sword-master, Telamon's former tutor at the military academy, was also present: Black Cleitus, with his dark, lined features and cropped head, the sword slash which had taken out his right eye making his face look twisted. Alexander loved the sword-master, the king's personal bodyguard, dearly. Black Cleitus' sister had been Alexander's wet nurse.

"You haven't changed at all, Telamon!" Cleitus' one eye glared.

"You look as ugly and dangerous as ever!" Telamon shouted back.

Cleitus, who always insisted on wearing his black cloak lined with bear fur, threw his head back and bellowed deeply, wiping his mouth on the back of his hand.

"You are late, Telamon," he jibed. "Still frightened of swords, are we?"

"Aye, just as frightened of you, if the truth be known!"

Ptolemy giggled noisily. Black Cleitus glared at the physician.

"And d-d-do you, do you still st-stutter, Telamon?"

"Only when I meet someone as ugly as you."

Cleitus would have lurched to his feet but Alexander clapped noisily.

"Telamon, join me! Come!"

Alexander sprang to his feet swaying slightly. He gestured to the couch on his right. A pageboy led Telamon round. Alexander clasped the physician's hand, then pulled him closer, kissing him on each cheek.

"Watch your tongue!" he warned. "They are all deep in their cups. I am not as drunk as I pretend." He laughed, pushed Telamon away and returned to his couch.

Telamon made himself comfortable and stared round. Most of the royal companions looked as if they had come straight from the drill ground, except for Alexander who was as clean and tidy as ever. His blond hair, carefully combed and oiled, was parted down the middle, the fringe lying flat against his sweat-soaked forehead. He was dressed in a snow-white, knee-length tunic edged with purple. He had gold sandals on his feet and the rings on his fingers glinted in the light. Telamon stared at the beautiful amethyst hanging on a silver chain round the king's neck.

"A present from Mother," Alexander explained. "She says if I put it into wine, it will show if there's poison."

"I could have used it earlier," Telamon retorted.

"Mother sent messages," Alexander continued blithely. "She wasn't too happy with her conversation with you. But, there again, as the poet says: 'The only joy of a woman is to have her sorrows ever on her lips'." He toasted Telamon with his cup. "Let's thank the gods Mother is far away, eh? I love her dearly but her moods change as quickly as she moves her eyes."

"What are you whispering about?" Ptolemy called over. "Telamon, where have you been? Why did you leave the groves of Mieza? Why didn't you grow up with us all and become a warrior? Wouldn't you like to be a warrior, Telamon?"

"Wouldn't you?" Telamon retorted.

Ptolemy would have replied but the servants bustled in. The meal was not a banquet – nothing more than a drinking party. The food was second-rate: barley broth, pilchards, black pudding and roasted hare with fairly hard bread and unripe fruit looted from the local orchards. Cleitus protested loudly at the foul Euboean wine, so Alexander ordered it to be replaced with Thasian. Olives and nuts were served. The fruit girl also handed each guest a wreath of myrtle. She then took out a flute, struck up a tune and Ptolemy led them in a raucous sing-song. Telamon glanced across at Antigone. She lounged gracefully, ignoring Cleitus' lecherous glances, like an elderly aunt indulging a group of rowdy young boys. Telamon nibbled at the food and drank the undiluted wine. Antigone smiled at him; he toasted her back. Alexander was shouting something down the tent. Telamon seized the opportunity to whisper across to the priestess.

"Be careful what you drink," he urged. "These parties go on until the early hours."

"I heard that," Alexander said, falling back on the couch. He called across a servant. The large ceremonial goblet on the table in front of him was filled with wine. Alexander shouted for silence, calling upon the god of good fortune. Alexander grasped the goblet and spilled a few drops of wine on the floor as a libation. He drank as the rest chanted a verse and then the "cup of kindness" was passed round. This was the signal for the serious drinking to begin. A huge mixing bowl was placed in front of Alexander – a gorgeous piece of Samian ware depicting a horde of satyrs chasing anxious

59

maidens. The dice were brought. Hephaestion won, throwing two sixes and a three, and he now took command as Lord of the Feast.

"Two and one," he said.

The measure was decided for the evening. Two stoups of wine for a portion of water were poured in the mixing bowl. The cups were filled. Hephaestion gave the toast and Telamon, like the rest, emptied his in one gulp. This was the signal for the guests to relax and talk among themselves. Alexander, however, took out a dagger and tapped it against the mixing bowl, the sign for silence.

"I welcome my friend, Telamon," he began. "And the Lady Antigone, priestess of Athena, from her temple at Troy. When the auguries dictate, the crossing will take place. The main army will meet General Parmenio at Abydos. I will first march south to Elaeum."

"What's there?" Ptolemy called.

"The tomb of Protesilaus."

"And who's he?"

"Telamon?" Alexander asked.

"The first Greek killed in the Trojan War."

"Clever bastard!" Ptolemy bawled.

"We will cross to Troy," Alexander continued matter-of-factly. "Make sacrifice and organize the army into battle array. We will then march south following the coastline. Critias is drawing his maps and, thanks to the Lady Antigone, we have guides enough."

"And when will all this happen?" Seleucus drunkenly brayed.

Ptolemy paused from nuzzling the neck of his mistress, and the whole tent fell silent.

"When?" Alexander queried, turning his head sideways. "Why, only when the sacrifices are pure and the gods accept our gifts."

"But it will be summer soon," Ptomely protested. "The wells and rivers will dry up. What if Darius and that bastard Memnon refuse to meet us in battle?"

"What if? What if?" Alexander turned ugly. He glowered around. "We know the Persian fleet is putting down a revolt in Egypt. What if the stars fall from heaven? Or the sea begins to boil? Haven't you forgotten the signs? The night I was born the Temple of Artemis at Ephesus was consumed by fire. I intend to spread that fire to the ends of the world."

Alexander was singing the same hymn of glory as he had as a boy, and it always entranced them. Even the cynical Black Cleitus was listening intently.

"How did Socrates describe us Greeks?" Alexander asked the throng. "We sit like frogs croaking round the pond." He laughed. "Well, the frogs are loose. We'll march to the edge of the world and bring it under the sway of Macedon." He lifted his cup. "To glory!"

They replied with a roar. Alexander, as if tired, lounged back on the couch and winked at Telamon.

"Do you think I'm telling the truth?" he whispered.

"Aristotle said truth was only an idea which can be divided and pared down. When you reach the part which is indivisible, you have arrived at the truth."

Alexander glared back. "What are you saying, Telamon?"

"I keep asking myself, sire, why I am here? But, of course, the real question is why are *you* here?"

"Do you believe I am the son of a god, Telamon?"

"If it makes you happy, sire."

Alexander pulled himself back up on the couch. "Do you *believe*?"

Telamon noticed how the contrast between the king's eyes was now quite definite: the left a deep blue, the right a dark brown. His face was slightly flushed, lips purple-stained as if he had supped deep of blood.

"Don't you believe Olympias conceived me by a god?"

"If she believes that, sire."

"Alexander! My name is Alexander!"

The king looked round. His companions were staring at him. He tapped the end of his nose. "Continue with your talking. Well, Telamon?"

"If you believe that, Alexander, and Olympias believes the same, then that's your truth. Philip believed differently. Is that why we are here, to prove that you are a god? Or that you are a better man than your father? Or is it for glory? Or what I heard travelling here, to bring the whole world under the sway of Greece?"

"I don't know," Alexander murmured. "I just don't know." He

paused, sipped at his wine and smiled. "You never married, Telamon?"

"We have a great deal in common, Alexander."

"Sleep and sex," Alexander slurred, "remind me that I am mortal."

He pulled himself further up the couch, his face still full of contention. The physician studied his boyhood friend. You are a leopard, he thought, a master of ambush. Your moods are as shifting and as sudden as your mother's.

"I asked for you, Telamon . . ." Alexander paused to reply to one of Ptolemy's jibes. "I asked for you," he repeated, lounging back, "for many reasons." Alexander's face softened. "Do you remember when we were boys at Mieza? Cleitus would kick us out of bed long before first light. What did he say?"

Both chorused the call Cleitus would make. "A run before breakfast gives you a good appetite while a light breakfast gives you a good dinner!"

"What was that?" Cleitus called down the pavilion.

"Go back to your wine, old man," Alexander retorted. "Telamon and I are making up for lost time."

Alexander held his cup out for a servant to refill, reminding him of the measure to be used.

"I've drunk too much wine," Alexander continued. "Do you remember, Telamon, a white marble statue glistening in the early morning sun? The inscription carved on the plinth, how did it go? 'I AM AN IMMORTAL GOD, MORTAL NO MORE'."

"Is that how you see yourself?"

"Never mind that!" Alexander snapped. "We'd pray, wouldn't we? To god the father, to his son, born of the horned servant." Alexander closed his eyes. "May they guide and protect us all the day long." He opened his eyes. "I was happy then. I was free. I was the beloved son of the king and his wife. It was all a stage," he murmured. "And, as I became older, the shadows stretched across the stage to engulf me. Mother and Father closed in. First in small things. One day at Mieza I was riding a horse; it vaulted a wall. There was a slave girl carrying grapes. She was using her tunic as a basket; long golden legs and hair the colour of ripe corn. I teased and I flirted with her. We lay together in the cool shade of a holm oak tree."

"Oh, I remember this," Telamon replied. The wine had made him relax and the memories came flooding back. "The wood nymph . . . ?"

"That's right!" Alexander agreed. "The wood nymph! She was a beautiful girl. We lay on a bed of crushed grapes. The next day I went looking for her but someone had told Mother, hadn't they? The girl had been sold and Olympias informed me that I'd probably encountered a wood nymph, a gift from the gods. Do you know, Telamon, I believed her." Alexander's face turned ugly, a far-away look in those strange eyes. "That was Mother's first real lesson: there was only to be one woman in my life and that was Olympias. She began to sing her siren hymn, of how I was sacred, chosen by the gods. How Hercules and Achilles were my ancestors. Of course, I thrilled to this. The second verse was more cruel: that, perhaps, I was not Philip's true son but the offspring of a god. I was confused. Do you remember how sad I became, Telamon?"

"I told you to speak with Aristander."

Alexander laughed abruptly. "Out of the pot into the fire, eh? Aristander of Telemus." He turned and toasted his keeper of secrets who was lounging morosely at the far end of the tent. "He hummed the same song as my mother, but he told me the hard truth." Alexander glanced down, and when he looked up his eyes were full of tears. "He said that Philip and Olympias loved each other to distraction. When they first met on the island of Samo-Thrace, Philip believed he had been visited by a goddess; that he would never love another woman." Alexander sighed. "Of course, Philip drunk was different from Philip sober. He'd mount a goat, and probably did when he was drunk. Olympias never forgave such infidelities. You remember, Telamon? When we were boys and visited Pella, you stole into Olympias' bed chamber?"

Telamon repressed a shiver: sometimes his own nightmares came creeping back.

"Your mother's room was full of ivy," he said quietly. "There was a vine tree embedded in the outside wall with twisting branches of luxuriant leaves."

63

"And the snakes?" Alexander asked. "The snakes curling in and out? No wonder the story spread, how Olympias lay with a snake, a disguise for the god Apollo. She began to hint to Philip that I was not his true son; he retaliated with more women. Yet I did love him. The day I tamed Bucephalus," he went on, referring to his beautiful black warhorse which took its name from the brilliant white blaze on its forehead, "Philip hosted a banquet and toasted me. 'Here, he proclaimed, is my son the horse tamer!'" Alexander blinked quickly. "I have never been so proud in my life. He made me drink wine. I begged him to remain faithful to my mother. He became angry so I retorted: 'The way you sire bastards I'll have no kingdom to inherit!'" Alexander leaned over and grasped Telamon's tunic. "He grabbed me like that, and pulled me close. 'If you are half the man I am,' he replied, 'you'll win your kingdom *and* keep it!' Of course, Mother heard all about it and took me into her confidence. She described how, when I was conceived, the night wind rushed through her room, the very stars were dimmed while the house was rocked by thunder and lightning. Mystical flames filled her bed chamber, and so on and so on." Alexander rubbed the side of his face. "Mother against Father, Father against Mother. Philip was a good general. He decided to take Olympias literally. If I was not his son he would marry again. So he wooed Attalus' brat. He divorced Olympias and gave Eurydice a son. Only the gods know how the battle would have gone if he hadn't been killed."

"Were you guilty of that, Alexander?"

The king glanced away. "No, no, I don't think so."

"And Olympias?"

"I'm not too sure. I thought that was finished." Alexander continued softly, "The Persians claim I did kill Philip. They argue no son could kill his true father so ergo, Philip is not my father. So, I am both a usurper and a bastard."

"But that's your enemies," Telamon reassured him. "You are Captain-General of Greece, holy vengeance against Persia."

"I am still Alexander!" The king's reply came as a hiss.

He would have continued, but the noise in the tent died as Ptolemy sprang to his feet and shouted: "Let's play kottebos!"

A servant brought a pole and drove it into the ground in the centre of the couches. A plate was balanced on top. Ptolemy stumbled to his feet. He drunkenly toasted his companions.

"Here is to my love!" he bawled, draining his cup and throwing the dregs in the direction of the plate. When he missed, he loudly cursed and slumped back on his couch. Others staggered to their feet to hoots of derision. Antigone lay quietly, lolling against her couch, eyes half-closed. Telamon couldn't decide if she had been trying to listen to their conversation or was studying these wild Macedonian chieftains.

"I am still Alexander," the king continued. "Philip's dead and Olympias is back in Pella but their spirits haunt me. Olympias told me before I left that I must go to the Oasis of Siwah in the Egyptian desert where Amun-Zeus would reveal the true secret of my parentage."

"And Philip's ghost?"

"Ah, the man of iron. Sometimes I have nightmares about him. I am back on the battlefield at Chaeronea. The dead are piled high. The Sacred Band lie like a row of felled corn. The place is littered with shields and spears. The cries of the dying are shrill as night birds. An army of dead hoplites confront me, dressed and armed in their great plumed helmets, corselets, shields and spears. Their eyes and mouths are filled with blood. They stand between me and Philip. I fight through them." Alexander waved his hand. "I lay to the left and the right, pushing with my shield, thrusting with my sword. Eventually I am through, but Father's gone."

"Only nightmares . . ."

"No, no, listen."

Alexander swallowed hard, his face heavily flushed, eyes glittering. Telamon noticed how his brow was soaked in sweat. Is this man sane, he wondered? When he had first arrived, Alexander had reminded him of his boyhood friend. But now? Was that only a mask he wore? Alexander clinked his goblet against Telamon's.

"You are secretive as always, Telamon. I want to tell you why you are here. I am surrounded by enemies, by traitors, by spies."

As if on cue Telamon glanced around. Ptolemy, ignoring the raucous noise of his companions, was staring across at them, a heavy-lidded glance, slightly mocking, as if he knew what Alexander was saying but didn't care.

"Listen!" Alexander stretched across and clutched Telamon's arm. "Darius and Memnon. I know their tactics."

"You have a spy close to them?"

"Of sorts. The Persian king will not challenge my crossing of the Hellespont. He hopes to draw me into his vast territories, exhaust my army, starve it, surround and kill it, but that's for the gods to decide. What concerns me is the spy they have close to me. Is it you, Telamon?"

"Nonsense! I wouldn't be here if you hadn't sent for me!"

"Why did you send away that page?"

"I don't like pretty bum boys. I'll choose my own assistant, as I do my friends."

"Get someone you trust," Alexander ordered. "Have you been down to the slave pens? We still have a few Thebans left to sell. You may find someone there."

"You were talking of a spy?"

"I don't know who it is." Alexander shook his head. "The only name I've been given is Naihpat."

"Naihpat?"

"Nonsense, isn't it?" Alexander made a face. "Naihpat – Apollo knows what it means." He pointed down the tent. "I have my keeper of secrets, Darius has his: a mysterious figure called after one of their gods, Mithra." Alexander stretched out his hand, fingers curled. "How I would love to trap him and all his secrets: all those in Greece who furtively received Persian gold. I'd show no mercy, Telamon. I'd crucify them all."

"Who's your spy?" Telamon asked abruptly.

"Well, I think it's Lysias, one of Memnon's cavalry commanders. He sent me a secret message: he wants to meet me at Troy."

"For what purpose?"

"I don't know. He simply asked to meet me there and then tell me why."

"So, what do you fear, Alexander? Secret assassination? Betrayal?"

"No, I fear Philip."

"He's dead!" Telamon's voice rose.

"No, listen. Do you remember that line?" Alexander screwed up his eyes, a favourite gesture when he was a boy at the academy. "The one from Book Nineteen of the *Iliad*. How does it go? 'The liver was plucked from its place and, from it, the black bile drenched the front of his tunic.'"

"What has that got to do with Philip?"

"Do you remember the Delphic Oracle?" Alexander asked. "'The bull is prepared for sacrifice, all is ready, the slayer awaits.' Father thought it was a reference to the Persian Empire; only after his assassination did people realize it was about him." Alexander paused. "I need a pure sacrifice, Telamon, before I order my troops to embark. Every bull I sacrifice is tainted. The portents augur badly, so we shelter on this headland and my army waits."

"Ignore the signs!" Telamon snapped. "Bring your fleet in and sail!"

Alexander shook his head. He put the wine goblet on the ground and, crossing his arms along the headrest, leaned his chin on his wrists, studying Telamon intently.

"Look around, physician mine. Is anyone watching us? Do you think anyone can hear?"

Telamon obeyed. Seleucus was now talking to Antigone. Aristander was feeling his crotch; the prostitute and Ptolemy were embroiled in some argument. Servants had now withdrawn, the flute girl had disappeared. Through the half-lifted tent flap, the physician could make out the shield and spear of a guard.

"Do you remember that scout whose corpse is to be consumed by fire?" Alexander continued. "The one who was found on the rocks below the cliffs? The only people who know the truth are Critias and Aristander. The rest think his death was simply the result of a camp fire brawl. The dagger was still embedded in the guide's body, in his hand a small scrap of parchment." Alexander's gaze never wavered. "The dagger was winged, of Celtic origin." Telamon flinched. He didn't know whether it was the cold night breeze or Alexander's soulless eyes. "The same sort of dagger," Alexander whispered, "which killed my father."

"But Pausanias was a madman! We all know the story,"

Telamon comforted. "Such daggers can be bought in any market-place."

"Can they really, physician? And what about the piece of parchment thrust into the dead scout's hand? A note bearing a message: '*The bull is prepared for sacrifice, all is ready, the slayer awaits.*' Do you realize what is happening, Telamon? Is father going to stop me?"

"Don't be ridiculous. You are as superstitious as an old woman."

Alexander moved his arms and smiled, his face transformed. "I am glad you came back, Telamon." He beat his first against his chest. "Olympias, Philip and all the might of Persia will not stop me. *Nothing* will stop me!"

"Is that why you levelled Thebes?"

"Just before you left Mieza," Alexander replied, "we fought with wooden swords. I kept lashing out until Cleitus intervened."

"You apologized. You talked of a red mist before your eyes."

"That's what happened at Thebes." Alexander bit his lip. "People should know when they are defeated. Time and again Thebes would meddle, conspire, start whispering campaigns throughout Greece. I remember standing before the Electra Gate watching the Sacred Band deploy. We drove them back. The red mist came down. I thought: this time, this time, I will settle matters once and for all. Never again would Thebes challenge Macedon. I gave the order, 'Take no prisoners! Leave not one stone upon another!'" He smiled crookedly. "Apart from the temples and the house of the poet Pindar. We killed all their fighting men. I took thirty thousand slaves and made a fortune out of their sale." He lifted a hand. "Never again will Thebes challenge me!"

"But someone is?"

"Yes."

Alexander coughed and swung his legs off the couch. He sat, speaking over his shoulder at the physician.

"And so we come to why you are here."

Alexander put the wine cup on the table. Telamon glanced down: the edge of the rug covering the ground near the king's couch was deeply tinged with wine. Alexander had indeed not drunk as much as he pretended. He had taken sips, the occasional gulp, but a lot of the wine had been secretly poured out.

"Look around you, Telamon. My hungry companions, they all want to be kings and princes and ride through Persepolis in glory. As long as I am faster, stronger, fiercer, more cunning, more fortunate, I am safe. As long as the pack feeds well, I'll be their leader. The same goes for the boys outside. They don't really want to leave the black soil of Macedonia but they dream of the soft, plump women of Darius' harem, of digging their arms elbow-deep into caskets of pearls and precious gems. If I realize those dreams, I am their king, their god-saviour. They wouldn't care if I proclaimed myself to be Apollo incarnate."

"You have Hephaestion, a true friend."

"Yes, I have Hephaestion, and I have Telamon. I thought long and hard about you. The day you left Mieza, riding behind your father, going down that white dusty trackway, the cypress trees on either side whispering goodbye. All Telamon wanted to be was a physician – not women, glory or gold. That's the first reason you're here."

"And the second?"

"In all my days, Telamon, I never met a pair of eyes like yours, sharp as a falcon's! You used to sit staring, missing nothing. There's the man I want, I thought: it's time Telamon came home. I heard about your little trouble in Egypt. The Persian territories are closed to you." Alexander shrugged and pulled himself up on the couch. "You can't go to Persia. No Macedonian is welcome in Greece, not really, so why don't you join your friends? Mother's threats helped you along the way. You are here, Telamon, because there is nowhere else to go and, above all, you are curious. Your curiosity would get the better of you. What better place to learn your trade and improve your skill? Before the year is out you will have patients enough." Alexander stretched across and tousled Telamon's hair. "But really, I want you to be my eyes, Telamon. I want you to dig out this spy Naihpat. I want to know how that young girl and the scout died."

Seleucus called something across to them.

"Shut up!" Alexander bawled back. "I am talking!" He turned

back to Telamon. "Do you remember Homer's *Iliad*? You used to quote it line by line. I still keep a copy under my pillow. How many wounds does Homer describe?"

"One hundred and forty-nine."

Alexander snapped his fingers and smiled. "How was Eurypylus wounded?"

"By a poisoned arrow in his leg: the arrow was removed, the poison sucked out."

"By whom?"

"Achilles' great friend, Patroclus, in Book Eleven. He washed the wound with warm water, then smeared it with the bitter-sweet root of some plant."

Alexander drew closer. "No one else knows this," he hissed. "I have had two messages left scrawled on a piece of parchment. The first is from Book Nineteen of the *Iliad*: '*The day of your death draws near.*'"

"And the second?"

"From Book Twenty-one, slightly changed: '*Die an evil death till all of you pay for the death of Philip.*'"

Chapter 3

―――――◦◦◦◦――――――

"From Darius, the King of Kings, to his satraps . . . this
thief and robber, this deformed man, Alexander, capture
him then."

The Ethiopian version of
The History of the Pseudo-Callisthenes

T he Persian war galley had left its escorts after passing Chios on
the port side, cutting its way through the Hellespont, taking
advantage of the spring haze and welcoming the darkness. It was a
flagship from the imperial fleet, its pine hull painted a blood-red
just above the water-line, black beneath the taffrail. On either side,
just under the bronze prow, a leaping panther glared; next to it, the
painted all-seeing eye – a talisman to fend off ill-luck. Memnon and
his captains stood in the stern, which was carved in the shape of a
beautiful white conch shell. The sails had been furled, the masts
taken down, the war colours hidden away, the lanterns and lamps
dimmed. Even the master oarsman muttered his words in a whisper
as the great trireme coursed through the water to take up station off
the city of Sestos. Memnon was confident that they would not be
noticed. The starlit sky was fast clouding over and the mist was a
welcome ally, every so often shifting like a curtain being pulled
aside. The keen-eyed lookouts, high on prow and stern, could
make out the lights of Alexander's Macedonian camp. Memnon
stood listening to the water lap against the hull. The banked oars
stretched out like great arms waiting for the order. The captain and
his officers were vigilant for any danger, be it a sudden shift in the
wind or an approaching ship.

"I don't want to be driven back on the rocks," the captain, a native of Memnon's Rhodes, whispered in the general's ear for the umpteenth time.

"The gods are with us," Memnon remarked restraining an urge to scream abuse at the man. "All will be well."

Memnon went and stood by the side and stared out across the water. No fishing smacks or boats. Alexander was confident that the Hellespont was free of any hostile shipping. Memnon smiled to himself. To a certain extent he agreed with Darius' tactics. Why not make Alexander feel more confident, that he was protected by the gods? Yet Memnon didn't believe in the gods – only in the power of his own arm and cunning. Arsites, the satrap of Phrygia, did not know he was here. Memnon had the use of certain ships and the Rhodian had decided to take matters into his own hands. Diocles, his mute servant, came and stood beside him. He placed his hand over his master's, a sign that he wished to speak. Memnon glanced pityingly at him. Diocles was still suffering from sea-sickness: eyes and nose running, stains of vomit round his mouth.

"What is it?" Memnon asked slowly.

Diocles made signs with his fingers.

"Do you think there's a traitor among us? I can't believe, Lysias . . . !"

Memnon made a cutting movement with his hand and stared out across the slopping water. From somewhere beneath the decks a man shouted, but the sound was muffled. Memnon stood and listened to the beat of the great warship: pine timbers straining against the pitch, the creak of oars. The ship rose and fell in the quickening current. Now and again a steersman would issue an order, passed down to the rowers manning three banks of oars; some would then dip gently, keeping the trireme on course. Memnon's had been buffeted, driven off course. He still couldn't accept that Lysias had been a traitor. He had so much to lose. Yet Darius had been insistent. Memon thought of the hideous Tower of Silence, soaring up to the sky, the Persian dead, wrapped in their shrouds, hanging from the rafters. In the centre a cage where Lysias had been placed, without food and water, to await a long and painful death. Memnon quietly prayed Lysias would meet it with courage, hanging there between heaven and earth, the dead all around him.

Diocles touched his hand. More signs. "I know. I know," Memnon replied. "Arsites and Darius claim there are more spies among us. I don't believe that." Memnon peered closer as his manservant made urgent movements with his fingers. Memnon shook his head; he couldn't understand. Diocles repeated the gestures.

"Yes, you are correct. Neither Darius nor Arsites know about this. They want . . ." Memnon kept his voice low. "They want the wolf to enter their sheep pen. I prefer to kill it before it ever approaches." He smiled thinly. "A slight change of plan."

"A sign, sir!" The captain came over, pointing into the darkness. "There, sir. North-west of us!"

Memnon gazed through the misty darkness. The sea-bank shifted and he glimpsed the lantern gleam.

"Are the men ready?"

The captain nodded and walked away. Memnon touched Diocles' cheek and walked along to the prow where the signals were being answered by a leadsman with a shuttered lantern. A fishing smack drew closer. Memnon could make out a steersman, another man under the loose sail and a third on the prow. The fishing smack chose its course carefully and nestled just under the prow of the trireme. Grappling hooks were thrown up. The fishing smack was held secure at the end of straining ropes, while fighting to stay clear of the oars jutting out above it.

"For Apollo's sake!" Memnon breathed to the captain. "I don't want it to become entangled! One of Alexander's captains might decide to take a midnight cruise."

"We'll hold it firm," the captain reassured him.

Memnon turned at the sound of steps. Five men emerged from below. Each carried a bundle in one hand, armour in the other. They were dressed simply in tunics, cloaks and marching boots. Tawdry jewellery, bracelets, rings and necklaces glittered in the poor light. With silver pendants hanging from their earlobes and their hair cropped close, they appeared to be what they pretended to be: hoplite mercenaries looking for a master. Memnon clasped the hand of their leader, Droxenius.

"You know what you have to do? And what to say?"

73

"We are soldiers from Argos," Droxenius replied. "We are mercenaries coming to take the drachmae of Alexander of Macedon. We travelled over land. We have arms but no master. We have seen service in Lydia and further north. We thought of joining Memnon at Rhodes. But," Droxenius touched his groin, a sign to fend off ill-luck, "we think he'll lose. When money and luck run out, so does a mercenary."

Memnon laughed softly. "What happens next," he ordered, "is up to you. Choose your time and place and strike immediately. If you escape you'll have wealth beyond your wildest dreams. Don't be taken prisoner. If you die and find yourselves in the Fields of Elysium, be comforted. I will make the sacrifice and treat your friends like mine." The cold night wind whipped Memnon's cloak. "You have one task and one task only: the execution of Alexander of Macedon. You claim to come from Argos but, in truth, you are of Thebes. Remember what that city was and the ruin Alexander has made of it." He walked closer to the group, studying each of their hard, set faces. "Each of you has a blood feud. The shades of your kinsfolk, mothers, fathers, brothers and sisters, scream for vengeance against the tyrant! Strike hard! Strike fast!" He lifted his hand in salute. "Then run like the wind!"

He clasped each of their hands. They moved to the prow and, helped by members of the crew, clambered down the ropes into the fishing smack. Droxenius went last. Just before he went over the side, Memnon caught him by the shoulder.

"No one knows you are coming. Spies can be as thick and fast as flies on a dog's turd. Your task is to kill Alexander, but be wary. If you can, try and find a person called Naihpat."

"And if we do?" Droxenius searched Memnon's face. "Do we kill him?"

"No." Memnon shook his head. "But, if the gods are fortunate, on your return, tell me who he is."

Droxenius nodded. The fishermen were calling through the dark. Memnon could feel the swell of the rising sea as the fickle tides of these waters changed. Droxenius clambered down. Memnon passed his bundle over the side. The grappling hooks were removed. The captain rapped out an order, the trireme moved gently backwards, the master oarsman carefully directing certain rowers. The warship fought against the swell of the sea, allowing the fishing smack to turn and head into the misty darkness.

Droxenius sat in the stern and studied the three fishermen. Memnon had explained they had been bribed to come out at night, to obey the lantern summons and take certain men ashore. The fishermen had been well paid by Memnon's agents, and had been promised even more once the landing was completed.

Droxenius braced himself against the pitch of the small craft. After the safety and warmth of the trireme he felt as if he had been thrown onto a raft in a turbulent sea and left to fend for himself. Nevertheless, the fishermen knew their task. At first there was nothing but the pitching sea. Orders were rapped out. Droxenius, through the darkness, could make out the faint outline of the sheer white cliffs and the sandy pebbled beach of a narrow cove. The fishing smack kept on course until the shallows scratched and beat at the hull. Two of the fishermen jumped out, urging Droxenius and the others to join them. The mercenaries obeyed. They pulled the fishing smack up the pebbled-strewn beach. Droxenius made sure everything was unloaded and carried up onto the dry sand. He stared up at the sky – it must be long after midnight and a lengthy journey still awaited. He stared along the cove. If treachery had been planned it would happen now. Some movement, a glint of armour, the neigh of a horse . . . All lay silent. One of the fishermen plucked at his arm, holding up his hand.

"Ah yes!" Droxenius smiled. "Payment! Lads!" he called softly through the dark, "our ferrymasters want gold and silver. Give them what I do!"

Droxenius' sword leapt from its scabbard – one quick thrust deep into the fisherman's stomach. The fisherman, his face a mask of surprise, gaped at this brutal, blood-choking parry.

"I am sorry," Droxenius whispered. He put his hand behind the man's neck and pulled him deeper onto the sword. "It's better this way!"

His companions were dealing with the other two fishermen, both of whom had been caught by surprise. In a few heartbeats all three lay dead on the beach. Droxenius rapped out orders. The corpses were bundled aboard the fishing smack. Two of Droxenius' men, stripped naked, pushed the boat back into the bobbing waves, unfurled the sail and allowed the wind to carry them out a little distance. From where he stood Droxenius heard the fishing smack being deliberately holed, timbers being wrenched apart. He kept looking over his shoulder at the cliff top and prayed their luck would hold. Yet, why should Alexander be sending out scouting parties? When Droxenius glanced back across the sea the fishing smack was already sinking. His two men, expert swimmers, left it to its fate, slipped into the water and swam ashore.

"There will be no trace," one of them declared, shaking off water like a dog. "We lashed the corpses to the boat. Weeks will pass before it's found."

Droxenius urged them to dress. Once all was ready, the group of assassins slipped like hunting dogs into the darkness.

Darius, King of Kings, would have been pleased at the chaos and death which now threatened to engulf Alexander of Macedon, feasting with his companions, apparently oblivious to the dangers around him. The scouts whom the priestess Antigone had brought were also falsely comforted. They had paid their last respects to their dead companion. Alexander himself had saluted the corpse, provided Charon's fee as well as the food to feed the hideous dog Cerberus. Now the scouts sat round their fire on the edge of the Macedonian camp, enjoying the wine and food the king had provided for the wake. They now dismissed their companion's death as an unfortunate accident. The camp was full of brigands, thieves and prostitutes. Perhaps he had just been unfortunate – after all, their dead comrade had the reputation of being a lecher.

"Like a goat on heat," one of them joked. "Perhaps there was a quarrel over a woman, a game of dice or knuckle bones."

Death was never far away. Everyone knew the dangers which threatened. With such thoughts and words the scouts comforted themselves. A group of hardy peasants from the Ionian coast, they were already discussing among themselves what they would do with the silver and gold Alexander of Macedon had promised. The priestess Antigone had assured them in no uncertain terms: "No fighting, just march and guide Alexander's army south. In return, more gold and silver than you would earn in a thousand lifetimes." Cunning farmers, they had weighed up all the possibilities. They prided themselves on being of Greek stock. They didn't like the Persians with their haughty ways and flowing robes, their arrogant faces and dark eyes, their clicking tongue which they could never understand.

"It will be easy," their leader Critias had declared. "We'll take Alexander south and collect our reward. What happens then is for the gods to decide, not us!"

They had all agreed.

"Where is Critias?" one of them blearily shouted. "He should be here sharing the loving cup!"

"Oh, he's becoming too high and mighty for us now," another replied.

They all nodded in agreement, faces flushed, eyes gleaming. The rich wine Alexander had supplied was making itself felt; old tensions and rivalries were surfacing. They had always regarded Critias as rather high and mighty, a Greek with a shadowy past and a little learning. He had promised to draw maps for Alexander, showing the location of wells and springs so that men on horses would not burn under the strengthening sun.

"He should be here," Lascus, the biggest and burliest of them, bawled. He stretched across, took a piece of soft charcoaled fish and thrust it into his mouth, chewing noisily. Lascus just wished they would make the crossing. He wanted to go home. He wanted his villagers, especially the women, to see him in all his glory. Hadn't Alexander promised them a spear and sword to keep and take home? Lascus picked up the pewter jug and, ignoring the protests of his companions, drank straight from it.

"What do you think of our chances, Lascus?" a companion called.

"Easy as sowing corn!" the boaster replied, lowering the jug. He stared drunkenly round the camp fire; all his companions' faces were smeared with fat. It had been months since they had drunk and eaten so richly. Lascus felt his stomach curdle – he must gulp water before he fell asleep, otherwise he would wake up with his head thick and ringing.

"I'll tell you what will happen." Lascus smacked his lips. "You've got to think of what the Persians will be doing."

"What happens if they burn the land?" someone shouted. "It's been done before!"

Lascus winked drunkenly. "I don't think so. They know about the Macedonians. And so do I. I've watched them drill. They love flat ground. I've been down to the slave pens. I talked to a red-haired bitch who had been captured at Thebes." He gestured with his hands. "Big tits she had. Pity about her face," he added. His remarks were greeted with applause and lewd suggestions. "I'm going to go back there," Lascus declared.

"But what about the Macedonians?"

"Well, I talked to this red-haired bitch. Do you know what she calls herself? The same as that goddess, the one Antigone talks about — Cassandra. I don't think that's her real name."

The questioner, however, was glaring across at Lascus, teeth bared like a dog.

"As I've said. I've watched the Macedonians drill. They broke the Theban army in front of the main gate. They used the walls of a city as a smith would an anvil. They hammered and pushed them back. They found a gate open, Alexander and his horde poured through. The Persians won't be trapped like that. Alexander may know his army, but we know our country."

His remarks were greeted with nods and grunts of approval. The guides recalled the terrain where they had been reared: dusty plains, copses of woods, steep hills and deep ravines, rushing streams and rivers still full from the winter snows.

"The Granicus!" one of them called out.

"Ah yes, the Granicus."

Lascus recalled the tumbling river, its steep scrub-covered banks. He would have words with Critias about that. Lascus' stomach heaved. He muttered something, got to his feet and staggered off into the darkness. He remembered the instructions they had been given. The camp marshals had been most clear about them: "Urinating and defecating must take place well away from the camp!"

Lascus stumbled around the sleeping forms of the soldiers, past dying camp fires. At one point he was stopped by a guard. Lascus pointed at his groin. The man hawked, spat and let him by. Lascus made his way to a clump of trees. In the far distance he could make out the lights of Sestos and wondered whether he should visit there. He paused as he heard a sound behind him. He stared back towards the light of the camp. The ground was broken and uneven here. In places he could make out rocky plinths covered with moss. Critias claimed an old city once stood here. Lascus made a face in the darkness. What did Critias know? He stood and relieved himself noisily and turned to go back towards the camp. He glimpsed the shape flitting towards him, a racing, moon-dappled shadow. Lascus stared. Before he could recover, the figure was on him. A sharp burst of fiery pain shot through his side. He tried to defend himself but death had been so fast, like an arrow through the dark. Lascus stumbled forward. The pain was so intense. He scrabbled at the wound and the winged hilt of the Celtic dagger thrust deep into his side. Lascus fell to his knees quietly cursing his own stupidity. An owl hooted from the trees. Lascus the guide, the would-be hero, collapsed to the ground, eyes staring sightlessly as the scrap of parchment was thrust into his now numb fingers.

The feasting in the royal pavilion had grown raucous. A quarrel had broken out between Seleucus and Ptolemy over the reputation of a certain lady they both loved in Macedon. Hephaestion lay back on the couch, smiling blandly to himself. Alexander, unaware of the tension, ignored his guests, deep in conversation with Antigone. Telamon felt his eyes grow heavy. He was determined that he would not be carried off to his tent, as Ptolemy had jibed, "Like some boy after his first drink". He felt a gust of cold night air. One of the royal bodyguards entered the tent. Alexander rose from his couch and they had a whispered conversation, which Aristander joined. The king sauntered over to Telamon and kicked the foot of the couch.

"Aristander would like a word with you."

"What about?" Telamon asked crossly.

"Poison." Alexander grinned and moved on.

The king's keeper of secrets was already at the tent flap beckoning him urgently. Telamon joined him outside, where the chilly night air sobered him up.

"What is it?" he demanded.

"Come with me, Telamon. You are in no danger. I assure you."

They walked a few paces when Telamon heard a sound and whirled round. A group of burly mercenaries was following them, Celts not Greeks, all dressed in a motley collection of armour: leggings pushed into boots; leather corselets over tunics; helmets shaped in the various forms of wild animals. Their leader wore a leopard skin over his shoulder and carried a shield emblazoned with the all-seeing eye, Aristander's personal emblem. Their swords were drawn and two carried pitch torches. Telamon stood and watched them approach. The Celts were huge men, at least two yards high. Their hair, plaited with gaudy ribbons, fell down to their shoulders. Their helmets hid the upper part of their faces, luxuriant beards the lower.

"Ah my pretty boys!" Aristander sauntered back, using a tooth-pick to clean his painted nails. "Aren't they pretty boys, Telamon? My personal bodyguard! A dozen of the brutes." He simpered. "Lovely lads who eat me out of house and home. Aren't you, my lovely boy?" Aristander asked the leader.

The man replied in broken Greek, his light-blue eyes glaring ferociously at Telamon in the torchlight.

"No, no, you naughty boy!" Aristander slapped the brute playfully on the hand. "Telamon's not my quarry, he's my friend. Aren't you my friend, Telamon?"

The physician stared back.

"Aren't you?" Aristander stamped his foot.

"If you say so."

"More importantly," Aristander wagged his fingers in the leading brute's face, "he's the king's friend, he's Alexander's physician. He's not a traitor." Aristander stepped back and looked lovingly at the collection of armed rogues. "Do you know what I call them, Telamon? My chorus. I teach them songs. Right, lads!" Aristander stood like a stage manager. "Let's have the Hymn to Apollo!"

Telamon gazed in disbelief as the Celts, oblivious to their surroundings, intoned the well-known hymn:

> Apollo, Lord of Light!
> Golden opponent of ever-lasting night!
> God's own son!
> The Golden One!
> All hail to Apollo!
> King of the Sun!

The singing was throaty and out of tune. Somewhere from the royal enclosures a voice shouted, "Shut up, you noisy bastards!"

The leader of the bodyguards shouted something filthy back. Aristander tapped Telamon on the shoulder.

"You are not going to believe this. They just love Sophocles and Euripides!" He turned back. "Right, lads, the Theban Chorus!"

Like children before a schoolmaster, the Celts, still glaring at Telamon, intoned the famous speech from Sophocles:

> In Thebes, city of sun,
> The gracious voice of God is heard.
> My heart is riven with fear.
> Terror at what shall be said.
> Oh healer of Delos hear,
> Fear is upon us. What shall you do?
> Things new, or old as the circling year?
> Speak to us daughter of precious hope.
>   Come, deathless word!

"That's enough!" Aristander bawled. "Good lads!" He sniggered. "When we return to Athens we'll put the play on, whether they like it or not. Well, come on, the night may be young but I'm not!"

Aristander strode away. Telamon followed, all around him the silent yet menacing mercenaries. They left the royal enclosure and went through the sleeping camp, across the picket lines and up the hill to the place of sacrifice where Alexander had laid out twelve

81

stones to the gods of Olympus. Aristander went and leaned against one of the altars. The bodyguard made to group round.

"Not too close! Not too close!" Aristander said sweetly. "By Charon's bum!" he whispered to Telamon. "They don't smell too sweet; they have quite an aversion to bathing."

He issued orders and the pitch torches already there were lit, bathing the eerie place of sacrifice in the light of dancing flames.

"Why do you think I've brought you here, Telamon?"

"To see a play?"

Aristander giggled behind his hand. Telamon wiped the sweat from his brow and pulled his mantle closer. The breeze was strong, cold, with the salty tang of the sea. In the distance the crashing of the waves against the rocks echoed like faint thunder. Aristander followed his gaze.

"I don't like the sea, Telamon. I'll be glad to be across it. Alexander thinks the Persian fleet is in Egypt, anchored in the delta. I am not too sure. If they came back and challenged our crossing, I'd pray for another Salamis, only the gods would know what could happen then. How did you find our noble lord?"

"Much the same. A little more confused."

"Very good." Aristander wagged a finger and gazed across at his bodyguards who were crowded around a makeshift fire.

"Alexander is confused and not confused. Do you want the long, boring, diplomatic explanation or the short, blunt one?"

"My balls are beginning to freeze, Aristander."

Again the snigger. "Alexander's mind? Well, he can think of three or four things at once. He's the glory of Greece. He wants to emulate his father and he wants to conquer to the rim of the world. You know that, Telamon, but his army doesn't. We are going to march to the very edge of existence: that's Alexander's dream."

"And how many will be killed?"

"That could be construed as treason. Men die anyway."

"So they'll understand it's for the honour of Macedon – or is it the glory of Alexander?"

Aristander faced Telamon squarely. He was no longer the fop with a painted face and fingernails; his face was lean and hungry, his eyes hard, mouth firm.

"Alexander is a god," he hissed, "in mortal flesh. He is surrounded by traitors and by those who wish him ill. In my view there are four people, four walls protecting Alexander. Olympias, Hephaestion, Aristander and, I think, *you*, Telamon. So, please don't disappoint me!"

"Alexander is much loved by his troops."

"That's because he's victorious. Shall I tell you something, Telamon? We are going to cross to Asia. Alexander will seek out the Persian army and utterly defeat it. It's either that or face annihilation. There is no compromise, no question of doubt."

"So, why doesn't Alexander just cross?"

"He strives for glory but the auspices *must* be right. He wants to cross as Alexander, without Olympias riding his back or the shadow of Philip walking by his side. Everything conspires against him. Earlier this morning Alexander sacrificed a bull to Zeus. I chose that bloody animal myself! Yet the liver was tainted and the signs were bad. We have the death of the guide and that young woman. Alexander has also told me about the messages left, the quotations from the *Iliad*."

"How often do they come?"

"Ever since we arrived here, usually brought by a tinker or pedlar. Letters arrive every day from this person or that. Mercenaries swarm in looking for employment, it's only a matter of time." Aristander looked wistfully out towards the sea.

"Before what?" Telamon urged. "Aristander, don't be so mysterious! I am freezing!"

"I'll soon warm your blood! I'll soon warm your blood!"

Aristander walked away and came back. Telamon felt a little nervous. Despite the wine and his trust in Alexander, the physician was wary of this keeper of secrets, this creature of Olympias with his shifty eyes and sinister reputation.

"It's no great secret," Aristander declared. "Darius wants Alexander to cross so he can crush him, but there *must* be assassins here, paid by men, or women, who simply want Alexander dead!"

"Here in the camp?" Telamon demanded.

"Oh yes, here in the camp! Even drinking companions cannot be trusted. Have you heard about Seleucus? His mother also claims he was begotten by a god. Ptolemy hints that Philip was his real father while Nearchus will always follow the strongest."

"Why tell me all this here?"

"Because you know things others don't about Alexander: his dreams, his mind, and the demons which haunt his soul. As I said, he's confused by the sacrifice and the constant whispering campaign. Alexander seeks battle. A great victory against Persia will mean vindication by the gods. I have spoken enough. Stay there!"

Aristander sauntered off. Two of his bodyguard leapt to their feet and hastened back to the camp. Aristander beckoned Telamon over to warm himself by the fire.

"Well, well." Aristander stretched his hands out, his cruel face lit by the dancing flames. "Lovely boys!" he breathed.

They reminded Telamon of a pack of wolves ready for the hunt.

"Right, lads!" Aristander clapped his hands. "Let's have Creon's speech from Sophocles' play. We'll begin together, halfway through. It's a pity my dwarf Hercules isn't here. Ah well! I'll lead off." And he began: "No wound strikes deeper . . ."

The rest of the bodyguards joined in:

> Than love that has turned to hate.
> This girl's an enemy: away with her!
> Once having caught her in a flagrant act
> The one and only traitor in our state
> I cannot make myself a traitor too.
> So she must die . . .

Telamon listened attentively as the barbarians shouted the lines, eager to please the little man sitting on his right. Aristander gestured for silence.

"I taught them Greek myself. I am very proud of the boys, so is Hercules. Don't you want a bodyguard, Telamon? In this place of curling snakes someone should watch your back."

"I have my own thoughts on that."

"Good!"

Aristander turned away and began to sing under his breath one of the mournful songs of his Celtic bodyguard. They all joined in and were still singing when the other two returned escorting the physician Leontes and the young pageboy who had offered to help Telamon. Both looked heavy-eyed and anxious. Aristander made them join the circle. Leontes squatted down and stared beseechingly across at Telamon.

"I am sorry to disturb your slumbers," Aristander began sweetly. "Tell me, Leontes, do you like my friend Telamon or are you jealous of him?"

"I know little about him. What is this? You have no right!"

"I have every right."

Leontes scratched his nose. The blinking of his eyes increased.

"Did you set fire to Telamon's tent?"

"Of course I didn't!"

"But you have been to his new one tonight? Haven't you?"

Leontes let his hands come up beseechingly.

"True or false?" Aristander demanded. "You sent my friend a flask of wine. Good Chian in a lovely vase, black and red Samian ware, its top sealed. Are you always so generous to those you don't like?"

Telamon's heart skipped a beat.

"Shall I go and fetch the wine," Aristander continued, "and make you drink it?"

"What's this, Leontes?" Telamon demanded.

"He sent you a gift," Aristander explained. "It contains a potion: henbane, belladonna, spotted hemlock, watered hemlock, snake venom?"

Leontes would have sprung to his feet but the bodyguard forced him to stay still.

"If you don't tell me," Aristander whispered, "I will lose my temper!"

"It has the juice of senna."

"Ah! To drain the bowels? To make my friend Telamon spend all day over the privy? Why did you do that, Leontes? The army cooks," he sniggered, "would do a better job. What else?"

Telamon stared in disbelief.

"Do you have spotted hemlock among your powders?"

"I have a little."

85

"Did you give some to that girl? The one found wandering outside Troy?"

"I did not! I did not! I never touched the cup!"

"True, true," Aristander agreed. "At least, I think you didn't."

Leontes looked pale, haggard. "I resent Telamon. I thought I'd play a trick."

"How much senna?" Telamon demanded. "You stupid bastard, Leontes! You know it can do great damage."

"There's nothing like watching physicians debate," Aristander mimicked Alexander. "But the night is growing on and I am growing tired. Let's move to other matters, Leontes. I have been through your possessions. Who gave you the golden darics in the pouch hidden beneath your bed, dug into the ground? You gave one to this page."

The young man, who had been sitting as immobile as a statue, started in alarm.

"I have been across the Hellespont," Leontes spluttered. "What I have, I earned well."

"What as?" Aristander demanded. "A physician or a spy? Did you know Lysias?"

"Who?"

"You do know Memnon the Rhodian? The Greek traitor in the pay of Persia?"

"I have met him."

"But not his companion Lysias? Did you know Lysias wished to meet Alexander at Troy?"

"I, er . . . everyone knows."

"Everyone doesn't! Tell me, Leontes," Aristander got to his feet and stretched his arms, "have you met Arsites the satrap? We are going to ravage his territories in the very near future." Aristander pointed. "His lands lie just across the Hellespont."

"Yes, I have met him on a number of occasions, but from afar."

"Um." Aristander crouched down. "I think you are lying, Leontes. Why did you join the army? Write to the king offering your services?"

"I knew his father."

"Or was it because of the man you killed in Athens? The

powerful corn merchant? You mistook a simple fever for something more serious and overdosed him."

"That was a mistake. I had to flee."

"Do you know anyone called Naihpat?"

"No, no. What are you talking about?" Leontes spread his hands. "I played a joke on Telamon, I admit. A stupid one."

"Yes, and you bribed a royal page to help you. Do you know Alexander received a secret warning about you, Leontes?"

The physician groaned, fingers to his mouth.

" 'Trust not Leontes', that's all the letter said. So, what do we have here?" Aristander jabbed the air with his finger. "Telamon's tent was burnt, I think by you. That young woman whom Alexander wished to question dies mysteriously of spotted hemlock. You didn't tell us you had spotted hemlock in your medicine chest. You seem to have met Memnon and Arsites. You have golden darics, the coin of Persia, hidden away. You send tainted wine to the king's personal physician and friend. You bribe a royal page. You are the subject of a mysterious warning to the king. You are a traitor, Leontes!"

"No, no, that's a lie!"

"I'll tell you what." Aristander rubbed his hands together. "You shouldn't really be here, Leontes. It's time you went home."

Aristander turned to the leader of his bodyguard and spoke in a tongue Telamon couldn't understand. An order was rapped out. The men either side of Leontes dragged him to his feet.

"What are you going to do? Telamon, please help me!"

Telamon seized Aristander's arm but he shook him off.

"Oh, by the way," Aristander pointed to the page, "you may leave now. If I find you in this camp within the hour, I'll have you crucified. Go on! You have an hour! If I ever see you again, you'll die!"

The page jumped to his feet and ran off into the darkness. Aristander gestured to the bodyguard.

"Do as I say, take him home!"

Leontes struggled and screamed but was held fast. Telamon made to rise but a muscular hand gripped his shoulder and the physician watched helplessly as Leontes was dragged out of the sacrificial circle, past the altar to the edge of the cliff. The guards gave him a push. Leontes' scream echoed through the night as he tumbled to the sharp rocks below.

"He might have been innocent!" Telamon whispered.

"No man is innocent," Aristander murmured. "And I did promise him that he would go home!"

Chapter 4

———◆◆◆———

"Philip said: 'My son, seek a larger empire for Macedon is too small for so vast a spirit.'"

Quintus Curtius Rufus, *History*,
Book 1, Chapter 4

T elamon spent a restless night, his sleep plagued by nightmares. He was standing on a black beach, a red sea before him, dark rocks jutting up. Sinister shapes came and went. He was not pleased to be shaken awake by Aristander, smiling down at him.

"Sweet Apollo!" Telamon rolled over on his side. "My nightmares have come true!"

"Come, Telamon," Aristander was abrupt. "We have business. The king is insistent."

"The king is insistent!" Telamon pulled himself up. "Last night, Aristander, you took a man to the top of the cliffs and threw him off."

"Did you drink his wine?" Aristander asked sweetly.

"No, I threw it out."

"And if you had drunk it?"

"My bowels would have been liquid for days, maybe weeks."

"Look." Aristander crouched down, imitating Alexander, head slightly to one side. "I should have had Leontes crucified. He might have killed you. He would have certainly weakened you. Soon, Telamon, we will cross the Hellespont. We may win or we may lose. If the latter, we will have to evacuate fast and you know what happens to the weak in any retreat? Do you want the Persian immortals to play games with your head? Or to spend the rest of your life hacking rocks in one of their silver mines?" Aristander pressed his point. "Leontes acted suspiciously. I have been through his belongings. He did have hemlock powder, Persian gold and, more importantly, carefully hidden away, letters of accreditation from the Persian satrap Arsites. So, do not mourn for Leontes. No one is going to miss him. Now get up, we have business to do!"

Aristander slipped out of the tent. Telamon groaned. The chorus had apparently joined their master and were chanting verses from Aristophanes' *The Birds*.

"I don't believe this," the physician murmured to himself. Here he was in an armed camp surrounded by murder, summary execution, treachery and plotting. No one appeared to be what they claimed. Aristander was standing outside in the warm morning air praising his gaggle of cutthroats on their knowledge of an Athenian play. Telamon sighed and washed hurriedly. He rubbed some oil into his beard and hair, put on a tunic and a pair of stout marching sandals, grabbed a mantle and joined Aristander.

"The beautiful boys", as Aristander called them, greeted him like a long-lost brother, no longer with solemn stares but with bear-like hugs. Telamon's face was pressed against leather and fur which gave off the pungent odour of kennels.

"You see, Telamon." Aristander spread his hands. "They love you. They see you as their friend." He talked excitedly to the chorus. The leader strode forward and, crouching down, clasped Telamon's hand in his.

"Don't pull away!" Aristander warned. "They are pledging loyalty to you."

"Why? Because I am your friend?"

"No." Aristander grinned. "Because I told them you are their physician. Come on now!"

Telamon stared round. Members of the royal bodyguard thronged the enclosure, dressed simply in cloaks and causias – flat broad-brimmed hats. They were arranged so that no one could move from the enclosure without being challenged. It was strangely quiet. Despite the strengthening sun and the refreshing morning breeze, which every soldier welcomed, no fires had been lit, no cooking smells sweetened the air.

"They are all sleeping," Aristander whispered, but his eyes had a guarded, secretive look.

"And Alexander?" Telamon asked.

"Alexander sleeps. His justice doesn't."

Beyond the royal enclosure the camp had been roused and cooking fires lit to heat a gruel made of barley or wheat. The more fortunate had strips of dried meat and quarter-masters walked around with deep baskets full of dark rye bread which, together with flagons of wine, they distributed to the troops for their morning meal. Different odours, sights and sounds greeted them, more like a market-place than a military camp. Peasants and hucksters had swarmed in from surrounding villages to sell their wares of food and drink, over which swarms of flies noisily buzzed. An enterprising barber had set up a stall beneath a tree – he offered to cut hair and beards, and oil them with the perfume of almonds and sesame seeds. A group of soldiers were haggling with a whore, only to break off and mock an Athenian dandy, an exquisite sight, his cheeks rouged, his long hair anointed, combed and dyed. He wore an enormous onyx ring on his hand which he kept flashing about as he minced with all the elegance of a female dancer in his high-heeled boots as he trailed his embroidered cloak in the dust. Telamon watched him go, his lover following behind him, both impervious to the insults of the soldiers.

"The men should be careful," Aristander whispered. "Athenian hoplites may dress and act like ladies but they are skilled swordsmen, quick to take insult."

Telamon drank in the sights. He had arrived just before dusk but now he could see the extent of Alexander's camp, though little of its order or organization. Different units merged with other brigades. Some of the men had tents, others had set up makeshift bothies of branches and bushes. Women and children sauntered about, eager to buy up the fresh fruit – grapes, pomegranates, huge pumpkins and cucumbers. Pastry cooks sold cakes flavoured with honey and wine. Local fishermen offered conger eels and dried fish, smelling of pickles and sour wine. One enterprising merchant had set up a cheese stall where the whiff of garlic was off-putting but at least covered the stench of rancid cream. Hucksters and pedlars

91

offered needle and thread; sweating bakers worked over the makeshift army ovens; blacksmiths set up their forges and lit charcoal braziers, blowing the flames with bellows; soldiers clustered about with pieces of armour and equipment to be repaired.

"If we were attacked?" Telamon murmured.

"We won't be," Aristander replied, stepping round a pile of horse dung. "But, if we were, you'd be surprised."

At last they reached the edge of the camp, which was not so chaotic. Lines of infantry in helmets, carrying shield and sword, guarded the perimeter. Aristander and Telamon, accompanied by the bodyguard, passed through them. Here, in the open rough grassland, the cavalrymen were drilling their horses, running them up and down, exercising them gently. A fine dust swirled about and the morning air rang with shouts, exclamations and the heart-catching drumming of hooves.

"Where are we going?" Telamon asked.

Aristander continued on across the scrubland into a cool cypress grove. Telamon was surprised to find Antigone and her two helpers there. The priestess sat on a rock, her two companions like guardians on either side. Beneath a tree Perdicles and the other physicians looked wide-eyed and anxious. In the centre of the grove, grouped round a corpse covered by a horse blanket, stood Critias and the guides. They stepped aside as Aristander arrived. Telamon glimpsed a hand and leg jutting out from beneath the blanket, which Aristander pulled aside. Telamon stared down at the murdered guide: a burly man, head flung back, eyes staring sightlessly up at the sky. One arm was stretched out, the other almost touching the Celtic winged dagger thrust deep into his left side. The stench of death and corruption, the iron tang of blood, mixed with urine, fouled the air.

"Why are we all here?" Telamon asked, crouching down, though he suspected the answer: the winged dagger, the piece of parchment rolled into the dead man's hand. He plucked this out and gave it to Aristander. "I know what it says," he declared. " 'The bull is prepared for sacrifice. All is ready. The slayer awaits.' "

Aristander squatted beside him and unrolled the parchment.

"If I didn't know you better, Telamon," he whispered, "I'd have

92

you arrested. Just like Philip's death, yes? A Celtic winged dagger thrust up into the heart, the words of Delphi. And another guide has been killed."

Telamon scrutinized the corpse. He stared at the liverish face and smelt the mouth: the tang of wine was still strong. He felt the legs and arms – ice-cold.

"He's been dead for hours?" he asked Aristander.

"Yes, one of the dawn patrols found him. I had his body brought here. It's not good for the troops to see a corpse being carried through the camp." Aristander smirked. "It doesn't do for morale."

"Why have you summoned the other physicians?"

"Because I am getting suspicious, Telamon," Aristander retorted. "You've heard the old proverb, 'One rotten apple . . .' The guide was apparently killed when we were feasting last night. I know that the high priestess Antigone was with us and never left. I also heard her ask one of the servants to check on her two companions. He reported they were fast asleep and the guard outside their tent said they had never stirred. We know where Alexander's friends were, so that leaves our noble physicians!"

"But why them?"

"Why not?" Aristander jibed. "They all know the details of Philip's death. They can write, most of the army can't, and they must know the value of the guides."

Aristander got to his feet and led Telamon across to the priestess. She seemed none the worse for the drinking and late night, and got to her feet as they approached. The rest of the guides came trailing behind. Aristander shouted at them to stand back. The chorus stepped in between their master and the now agitated yet sleepy-eyed guides.

"Good morning, Telamon." Antigone grasped the physician's hand and squeezed it gently.

"My lady, it's good of you to come," Aristander apologized. "But I needed you here. You hired these men?"

"At Alexander's insistence," she declared, her eyes never leaving Telamon.

In the morning light Antigone's full beauty was more apparent. Telamon couldn't decide whether her skin was really ivory or a very pale olive. He stood entranced by her full red lips, high cheek-bones and those exquisite sloe eyes with their dreamy grey gaze; her fine plucked eyebrows and her thick, rich hair, peeping out from beneath her pale blue veil. Her perfume was fragrant, every movement delicate and feminine.

"My lady, are you sure we haven't met?" Telamon teased. "You stare as me as if we had. I wonder why a woman such as yourself serves in a dusty temple at Troy?"

He gazed quickly at her two companions, like peas in a pod: dark skins, black hair, ever watchful eyes. They giggled at Telamon's compliments and glanced shyly away.

"Don't you know?" Aristander made to explain, but Antigone held up her hand.

"Don't you know?" She picked up the question herself. "I am of pure Macedonian blood. A kinswoman of Philip and a distant relative of Alexander himself. My life has always been dedicated to the goddess. Why Troy?" She shrugged prettily. "Why not?" She leaned closer. "I have served at Eleusis, even Athens. I went to Troy because Philip asked me. If you want to know what happens in the market-place, Telamon, stand in the centre."

"Philip was a cunning fox," Telamon murmured. "Everyone passes through Troy."

"Yes they do." Antigone laughed softly. Looking past Telamon, she stared at the corpse sprawled on the dew-fresh grass and her smile faded.

"These men are Alexander's eyes!" she snapped. "I chose them carefully. They exchanged bread and salt and swore a most solemn oath before the Great Lady in my temple. I brought six and now only four remain."

"Will they desert?" Aristander whispered.

"It's possible," the priestess agreed. "From now on I'll have their tent guarded. Now, sirs," she clutched the folds of her mantle, "I have done what I can. I have reassured them that all is well, that they are safe, that this is the work of a traitor. The rest I leave to you. Oh, by the way.' She pulled up her cowl. "Your physician friends?" She indicated with her eyes. "They seem nervous, agitated. One of their number is gone."

Aristander stood aside to let her pass.

"Don't worry, my lady. He decided to go home."

Antigone nodded at Telamon and, escorted by her two companions, walked across the glade. She stopped, one hand on Critias' shoulder and whispered something. The man nodded and the priestess disappeared among the trees.

"You like her, don't you, Telamon? Yet she's vowed to the life of chastity."

"Didn't you know?" Telamon retorted. "So am I."

Aristander chuckled and led him across to the guides grouped around the corpse. He questioned them closely: their story was simple and straightforward. The dead man was Lascus, rough-mouthed but a good companion. He had been eating and drinking with them the previous evening and left the camp fire to relieve himself. He never came back.

"We thought he'd gone to bed," one of them declared. "Back to the tent or fallen asleep on the grass. It was only when Critias roused us this morning . . ."

"We returned to the camp fire," the map-maker explained, clearly agitated. "The guards were there. They said they had found a corpse. I sent for Aristander and the corpse was removed here."

"Where were you last night?" Telamon asked.

"Who are you to ask?" Critias snapped.

"He has every right!" Aristander gestured with his hands. "Don't be obstinate, Critias, just answer the question."

"I never left my tent. I was busy with maps. Ask the guards!"

"We will!"

Critias glared at Aristander.

"And the rest of you?" Telamon asked.

The guides clustered together, a group of frightened peasants, now bitterly regretting ever leaving their villages and crossing the Hellespont. They all confirmed each other's stories. Lascus had left and no one had followed him. Most of them had drunk so much they couldn't even remember what had happened at the end of the evening's carousing.

"The king didn't promise this!" one of them protested. "We were offered arms and gold."

"Every hero must face danger," Aristander jibed. "In future do not wander off by yourselves. Keep close. The king will have your tents guarded."

"That's not good enough . . ." one of them complained, but his protest died under Aristander's glare.

"You may leave!" Aristander ordered.

The guides, grumbling among themselves, slouched off into the trees. Perdicles got to his feet and came across.

"My companions and I . . ." he began.

"You and your companions can shut up and stay there!" Aristander clutched Telamon by the wrist. "Come. I'll show you where the corpse was found."

They left the group of physicians in the grove. Aristander walked over to where a soldier stood leaning on his spear in the rough gorseland between the picket lines and the grove. He stood aside as they approached. Aristander pointed to the crushed grass, the dark stain still visible. One of the cavalry men came thundering too close and Aristander shouted at him to stay clear. Telamon crouched down and stared at the bloodstain. He caught the smell of urine and glanced back towards the camp.

"How closely guarded are the picket lines?"

"We are not in enemy territory," Aristander explained, "so not intensively."

"Lascus," Telamon pointed back towards the camp, "was drunk, his belly and his bladder were full. He was a stranger, wary of giving offence, so he came here to relieve himself. He was probably grateful for a walk in the cold night air. He staggered out, relieved himself and was promptly murdered."

"But how? The assassin couldn't guess that Lascus would come here."

"Much simpler than that," Telamon explained. "The assassin knew the guides would be eating and drinking their fill at the funeral feast. It was only a matter of time before one of them left, as Lascus did. All he had to do was wait, follow and strike."

"But you've seen the guide," Aristander objected. "A burly, thick-set man. He could defend himself."

Telamon shook his head and got to his feet. "Not really. He was very drunk. Think of him out here, Aristander, away from his home on this windswept gorse under the night sky, the darkness all around him. You've been drunk, haven't you? Lascus comes out here to relieve himself, swaying backwards and forwards on his feet, half-asleep . . ."

Aristander shrugged in agreement.

"The fleet-footed assassin," Telamon continued, "slips quietly through the darkness. One good thrust and Lascus is no more. I've seen assassins do the same in a busy market-place."

Aristander scratched his head. "Do you know, Telamon, the news will spread. If I was one of those guides, I'd forget all about gold and glory and desert at the next possible opportunity."

"How valuable are they?" Telamon asked.

"Think of us, Telamon, as lost in a great forest which sprawls on every side: pathways, groves, marshes and swamps. Once we cross the Hellespont that's what we face. We are in Persian territory and they know their own land. They can move armies and keep us confused. That's before we come to the question of wells, rivers and streams, where it's best to ford and where not." Aristander coughed and waved his hands to clear a cloud of dust stirred up by the horsemen. "I have other matters to attend to." He jabbed a finger back at the grove. "Question your physician friends. They already know about Leontes. Let that be a warning!"

Gathering his cloak around him and shouting for his "beautiful boys", Aristander strode away. Telamon watched him go, the chorus grouped around him. Telamon could never understand Alexander's close personal relationship with Aristander. No matter what happened, Aristander never changed. Telamon racked his brains. The soothsayer had been brought to the Macedonian court by Olympias. Did he know something about her? Was he just an extension of the witch Queen's brain which teemed like a box of snakes? Leontes' execution the previous evening had been so summary. Did Olympias want her precious son to cross the Hellespont? Was Aristander involved in some shadow play? Telamon crouched down and looked at the stain on the grass again. "And what should I do?" he murmured.

He was caught up like a player edged onto a stage. He had no choice but to perform his role. If he left the camp, Alexander would pursue him. The Persian territories were closed, as were Greece and Macedon. He sighed and got to his feet. "Whether you like it or not," he whispered to himself, "this is your home and the task must be done."

He walked back into the grove. The physicians still sat talking quietly beneath the trees. Perdicles had set himself up as their leader and spokesman. A more frightened, woebegone bunch Telamon hadn't seen for many a day. Nikias had even been sick, brought on by fear and tension. Cleon just sat sullen and withdrawn. Telamon crouched down.

"You heard what happened to Leontes?"

"His corpse has been brought up," Perdicles declared. "Aristander told us we could burn it later today with the other two cadavers." He smiled briefly. "You can throw on some incense and toast him with a cup. Aristander claimed it was an accident – Leontes 'went for a walk' and slipped." Perdicles gazed accusingly at Telamon. "What really happened?"

"The sharp, brutal truth? He was thrown over, found guilty as a spy."

Cleon groaned and lay back on the grass staring up at the branches. Nikias leapt to his feet. Telamon stared hard at Perdicles. Ever since Leontes' death the previous evening he had been reflecting on what he knew. It was time, as well as his duty, to warn this sly-faced Athenian of the dangerous path he was treading.

"He probably deserved it," Perdicles declared. "Did he murder that young woman?"

Telamon shrugged. "Everything's possible." He sat, and listened to the chatter of the birds. Now and again his gaze shifted back to the camp beyond the trees, from which the clamour was increasing as the Macedonian army faced another day, digging pits, foraging and drilling.

"You should all be very careful," Telamon warned. "We are physicians, we wander across frontiers into this city and into that. All of us have sat at the feet of Persian masters and taken their gold. All of us must answer the question of why we are here."

"You know why!" Cleon shouted from where he lay in the

grass. He pulled himself up, wiping his mouth on the back of his hand. "The same reason as you, Telamon: we are good physicians but landless men, we have nowhere to go. The same is true of many in Alexander's army. Aristander himself dare not stay in Macedon, the generals hate him. The camp is full of soothsayers, cunning men, mercenaries, scribes, priests, grooms and cooks, all hiding here because they have nowhere else to go."

"And there will be Persians," Telamon warned. "More precisely, Persian traitors. Others, more dangerous, have a foot in both camps. If Alexander wins they'll hail him to the skies. If he loses, they'll flee like the wind. Before that, if the money runs out."

"It already has!" Perdicles snapped. "Oh, we've got a tent and food but when are we going to be paid?"

"If you have Persian darics," Telamon warned, "I'd get rid of them as soon as you can. I wager an obol to a drachma that Aristander has been through all your possessions."

"Poor Leontes!" Cleon moaned. He scratched the side of his cheek and stared across the grove. "I had to flee Corinth," he added mournfully. "The jealousy of others. Two things this world hates: a physician who fails and a physician who succeeds." He got to his feet. "Will Alexander sacrifice again? I hope to Hades he does so we can all piss off and leave this benighted place! If I had the money I'd go into Sestos, get drunk and find the fattest whore I could lay my hands on!" Cleon walked over to the corpse. "Only the gods know who did that! Come on, I haven't yet broken my fast!"

Telamon would have asked Perdicles to stay but his attention had been caught by a swift blur of colour in the bushes a few feet to his left. At first he thought it was a bird, but the bushes shifted again. Telamon was sure he glimpsed a small hand, the glint of a ring. The physicians wandered off. Telamon sat, cross-legged, watching them go. He felt hungry and tasted the acid at the back of his throat, regretting the extra cups of wine he had drunk the previous evening. Telamon realized he was being watched, but the spy could only leave when he did. Telamon just hoped the secret watcher was as hungry as himself.

"You can stay there for a while," he whispered, and began to list what had happened since he had arrived in the Macedonian camp.

He chanted the first five letters of the Greek alphabet: "Alpha, beta, gamma, delta, epsilon." So, what do we have? he reflected. Alpha: my tent was burnt down before I even arrived. Why? There was nothing in it. Was it an accident? Or was it linked to these mysterious events?

Beta: that young woman, the Thessalian, the sacrifice to Athena. What had happened to her, so hideous she had lost her wits? Antigone had apparently taken good care of her, brought her across so Alexander could question her. But why? Telamon rocked backwards and forwards. Probably because it wasn't safe to leave her in Troy – her attackers might search her out and kill her. Yet, in the end, she had been murdered. But how? Telamon closed his eyes. He thought of that cup full of wine. Several people had touched it but he was sure he had seen no one put any powder or potion in it. Nevertheless, the young woman had died. Telamon opened his eyes and beat his fist against his knee. But how? That tent was sealed and guarded. And why kill her? Because she might regain her wits?

Gamma: the deaths of the two guides. Telamon could under-stand how vital they were to the Macedonian army. Whoever was killing them wished to blind Alexander so, when he crossed the Hellespont, he'd wander about or, better still, stumble into an ambush. Last night's killing was eerie. Telamon could visualize it. A drunken oaf, ungainly on his feet, attacked swiftly and ruthlessly in the darkness. And the previous death? Who had lured the guide to the cliff top, then stabbed him? As far as Telamon knew, that scout hadn't been drunk. A young, vigorous man, he could defend himself, yet he had gone to his death like a lamb to the slaughter.

Delta: whoever was behind all this knew Alexander's mind. The use of the Delphic Oracle, the winged Celtic dagger. Both were aimed at provoking memories, stirring the guilt in Alexander's soul, playing upon his superstitions. If all this became public knowledge, it would affect the morale of his army. Was this the work of the spy Naihpat? The one who kept sending Alexander quotations from the *Iliad* about the imminence of his death? Whoever Naihpat was, be it an individual or a group, they were achieving considerable success. Alexander was edgy, superstitious and fearful. He had lost that confidence which so marked him out.

Finally, epsilon: the sacrifices. Telamon smiled to himself. He had suspicions about that, but when should he confront the person responsible? He stared out of the corner of his eye at the bushes. He got to his feet and walked slowly over.

"Haven't you ever read Aristotle?" he shouted. "Particularly his *Ethics*? Marvellous quotation! How does it go? That famous verse from Chapter Four? Ah yes." Telamon stared at the bush. " 'The man who is angry on the right grounds, with the right people, in the right manner, at the right moment, for the right length of time is to be praised.' I am angry. I also agree with Aristotle's line from his *Metaphysics*: 'All men naturally desire knowledge.' But what I can't understand is why they have to hide in bushes to achieve it. If you keep hiding there I am going to become angrier by the moment. I don't like to be spied on."

The bushes swayed. A large head popped up: black cropped hair with the ugly face of a satyr, bulbous eyes, squat nose and a mouth like a landed carp. The head rose a little higher revealing thick-set shoulders.

"Oh, for Apollo's sake, stand up!" Telamon exclaimed. "And come out!"

"I am standing up!"

The dwarf pulled the bushes aside and stepped out. He grinned maliciously at Telamon's surprise. He was barely four feet high, what the Greeks call a "grotesque". Small and squat with dumpy legs, his head was almost as big as his body. He was dressed in a dark-green tunic tied round the middle by a cord. There were marching sandals on his small, fat feet. A bracelet circled one wrist and tawdry rings shimmered on his fingers. Telamon stared at him curiously.

"What's your name?"

"Hercules."

"Oh, the great hero." Telamon recalled Aristander's whisperings the previous evening.

"The one thing I can do is listen." The voice was surprisingly deep, the tone cultured. The dwarf's angry eyes studied Telamon

101

from head to toe. Telamon's memory stirred. He crouched down and poked the little man in the chest.

"Hercules! I remember you. You're one of Aristander's creatures, that's right!" Telamon recalled the groves of Mieza, Aristotle's academy of young Macedonians. "Olympias came to visit us. She arrived in a chariot, dramatic as always, Aristander in attendance. You were walking with him, hand in hand. We thought you were his boy."

"I am." The dwarf's head jutted forward. "I'd be grateful if you didn't crouch down when you talk to me."

Telamon murmured an apology and got to his feet.

"What are you doing here, spying on me?"

"I wasn't spying on *you*, I was spying on the physicians. I spied on Leontes: that's how Aristander my master knew about the gold as well as the wine he sent to you. If it wasn't for me, you'd be spending all day on the privy."

"But you stayed?"

"I had to, hadn't I? I thought you'd leave with the rest."

"How did you learn about the wine?" Telamon asked. "And Leontes?"

"I hid under his bed."

"So you can steal in and out of tents as well!"

"Only when people are careless."

"And what did you learn from our physician friends?"

"They're stupid and frightened. Perdicles needs watching." The dwarf's face was transformed by a smile, head coming up, eyes sparkling. "Aristander trusts you!"

"And Perdicles?" Telamon asked.

"He said something remarkable. He doesn't think the army will move or the fleet sail. He was comforting that idiot from Corinth. He should keep his mouth closed." Hercules' broad face had turned ugly. He looked at Telamon. "I had to stay in the bushes. I thought you were going to remain here all day."

"Well, I'm not." Telamon stretched out his hand. "I'm going back to camp. You can come with me. I want to break my fast and consult with my fellow physicians."

Hercules grasped Telamon's hand and they made their way out

of the grove, across the wasteland now thronged with cavalry. As they entered the bustling camp, Hercules squeezed Telamon's fingers and slipped away into the crowd.

Cleon was outside Perdicles' tent, feeding his face with bread and olives. Perdicles was inside, squatting on the ground, studying a manuscript, muttering to himself. He glanced up as Telamon entered.

"What's troubling you? I saw the way you were looking at me in the grove."

Telamon squatted down, so close that Perdicles snatched the manuscript away and rolled it up.

"If you get any closer, Telamon, people will start talking."

"Do you have any barley husks?" Telamon asked.

"What?"

"Barley husks."

"What do I want with barley husks?"

"That's what I keep asking myself," Telamon replied. "Why should an elegant, Athenian physician have barley husks clinging to his cloak? And why should his sandals be coated with mud and have similar husks clinging to them? Where are they now? Was it mud or the manure of some bull? And why did you become so agitated when I noticed all this?"

"What are you talking about?"

"You know full well, Perdicles. You have been wandering round the sacrificial pens where the bulls are prepared for offering. You plod through the mud and pick up some of the prime barley husks which must be fed to the animals. What did you use? Yew leaves, crushed and powdered? Not enough to kill the animal but certainly enough to turn his entrails a peculiar colour. No one would suspect. You could even claim an interest in bulls and bullocks. How you like the animals! No one would suspect, because no one would see anything wrong. But I saw something wrong last night: barley husks on your cloak, a pair of sandals, thrust away, still caked with dung."

The arrogance drained from Perdicles' face. His eyes slid to the corner of the tent where his sandals and cloak lay.

"You haven't got time for that," Telamon said. "Perdicles, how long have we known each other? Years? Our paths cross and cross again. What are you involved in? You don't give a whit for any city or any kingdom. What does it really matter if Macedon or Persia wins? Why are you hiding here, Perdicles? Some angry husband? Someone who can whistle up bully boys?" Telamon touched him gently on the nose. "You are a very good physician, Perdicles, but you have two weaknesses: someone else's pretty wife and the lure of gold."

Perdicles swallowed hard and sat back on his heels.

"If Aristander knew," Telamon continued in a whisper, "Leontes would not be the only physician to walk on air. I may be wrong but barley husks still cling to your cloak. Aristander will ask questions." Telamon spread his hands.

"What do you want?" Perdicles gasped.

"The answers to two questions. First, why? Second, when will it stop?"

"Stay here." Perdicles got slowly to his feet. "No, don't worry, I'll answer your questions, but I need someone else."

Telamon sat on a stool. He heard Perdicles angrily telling Cleon to stay outside the tent and mind his own business. For the first time since he had arrived in the Macedonian camp, Telamon quietly confessed to a sense of smug complacency.

"Not everything's a mystery," he murmured.

He sat listening to the sounds of the camp. Then Perdicles returned, followed by a hooded figure. The cowl was pushed back and Ptolemy's monkey-like, lazy-eyed face smiled down at him.

"Well, well, Telamon, no wonder Alexander hired you. He said you had the eyes of a hawk."

Ptolemy still looked as if he was suffering from the after-effects of the previous night's drinking. He snapped his fingers. Perdicles hurried across with a camp stool. Ptolemy sat down and rubbed his eyes.

"What do you prescribe for a hangover, Telamon?"

"First, don't drink. Second, if you do, eat well and for the rest of the day drink plenty of water, making sure it's fresh."

Ptolemy smirked. "You're not much of a soldier, Telamon. Do you remember that day I fought you out in the groves of Mieza?"

104

"Why, do you wish to continue it?"

Ptolemy's face grew hard. "The sacrificial bull? Perdicles likes gold."

"So he did it at your orders?"

"I like victory, Telamon." Ptolemy took a deep breath. "You've seen Alexander's army: a small fleet and about thirty to forty thousand men. Across the Hellespont Darius can muster over a million. Memnon alone can whistle up a force of Greek mercenaries almost equal to ours."

"So you don't think Alexander should cross?"

"Not yet. We need more ships, more men, more treasure. The Persian fleet is safely off the delta. One day it will return." Ptolemy leaned closer, wine fumes on his breath. "Think of what might happen, Telamon. Alexander crosses the Hellespont and is ambushed. He struggles back to the coast. News comes pouring in that Greece, led by Athens, is in revolt. The Persian fleet, reinforced by Athenian triremes, patrol the straits." His hand came out like a claw. "We need to clear the Persian fleet from the sea. We should wait till autumn, maybe even till next spring."

"And so Alexander will do what Ptolemy wants?" Telamon retorted. "That's really the crux of the matter, isn't it? Ptolemy, who believes he is Philip's son, that he is a better general than Alexander!"

Ptolemy's gaze fell away.

"Tired already, Ptolemy, of playing second flute? If Alexander heard of this, he'd send you back in chains to Pella."

"But he won't, will he? Do you know why, Telamon? Because you are not only a good physician, you are also a prig! You never did like telling tales. Also, the next time Alexander sacrifices, the auspices will be untainted, most favourable." He stretched out his hand. "Do you agree, for old times sake?"

Telamon clasped Ptolemy's hand and nodded. Ptolemy got to his feet, kicking the stool away.

"I am in your debt, Telamon, for the first time in my life. Oh, Perdicles," he grasped the physician by the shoulder and pulled him close, "you won't babble, will you?"

Perdicles shook his head, his face full of fear.

105

"Otherwise . . ." Ptolemy moved round the tent. He paused, hand on hip, and stared back over his shoulder. "A pity about poor Leontes, wasn't it?"

And, laughing to himself, he lifted the flap and went out. Telamon would have followed but Perdicles called out his name.

"What is it?"

"Be careful," the Athenian warned.

"Oh, don't worry." Telamon smiled. "I've already decided on that."

Chapter 5

———◦◦◦◦◦———

"Thebes, itself, taken by storm was sacked and razed. Alexander hoped that so severe an example would terrify the rest of Greece into submission."

Plutarch, *Lives*, Alexander

T elamon sat outside his tent on a camp chair. He found the heat and bustle of the camp offensive. The weather was getting warmer, the sun stronger by the day. Unless Alexander moved soon, a paralysis would spread through the army. Desertions would increase and, if the royal treasury was empty, the army would melt away like snow on a hill. The physician walked to the flap of the tent and pulled it back to let in some air.

The guard, lounging outside, lifted his head from the bowl of gruel he was stuffing into his mouth with his fingers. "I brought you some food, sir. You'll find it within."

"Thank you."

The food lay on top of a chest covered by a linen cloth. Telamon pulled this off to reveal some rancid cheese, some rather rotten fruit and freshly baked bread. The beer in the jug was a local brew, rather watery but tasteful. Telamon broke his fast. He felt dusty, sweaty and tired. He wondered what Alexander would decide. On his return, Telamon had been surprised to see the royal bodyguard in full dress armour and wondered if some crisis had arisen.

A shadow darkened the entrance to the tent. The dwarf Hercules swaggered in.

"Nomalet."

"Pardon?"

"Nomalet." The dwarf grinned. "I am skilled in that, putting names backwards."

"Very good, Selucreh," Telamon responded in kind.

"I like letters you see." Hercules came forward. "I like playing with them. Some names are difficult to reverse, aren't they?" He stopped and stared down at the platter. "Do you want those cherries? I've had little doof this morning."

"Doof?"

"Food." Hercules popped a cherry into his mouth and chewed noisily.

"You seem to have taken a liking to me," Telamon remarked, "but you're not here to share my food, are you?"

"Aristander wants you now, with your medicine." Hercules took another cherry. "And, when my master says 'now', he means now!"

"Well, don't let's keep him waiting."

Telamon pushed the platter away. He'd plucked up his leather satchel and was out of the tent before Hercules caught up. The little man slipped his hand in his.

"My master's name is difficult to reverse."

"As far as your master is concerned," Telamon retorted, "it's always hard to tell which is the back and which is the front."

"I could put that more cruelly," said Hercules.

"What's happening?" Telamon asked.

"I don't know."

They made their way through the narrow avenues between the tents into a large space before the royal pavilion, full of royal bodyguards. The soldiers stood in serried ranks before the entrance, dressed in breastplates of purple bronze with coloured kilts and greaves. On their heads were old-fashioned hoplite helmets, the nose and cheek guards almost hiding their faces. Each carried a spear and their rounded shields, propped against their legs, displayed the charging lion of Macedon. They stood silent, impervious to the heat and dust. Officers patrolled backwards and forwards. Light armed troops stood along the sides of the pavilion. Telamon and Hercules were only let through when the dwarf gave the password for the day.

Aristander was waiting in the antechamber. He grasped Telamon by the arm and virtually pushed him into the king's personal quarters, leaving the dwarf behind. Alexander was sprawled on his bed and Hephaestion, anxious-faced, sat on a stool beside him. The tent smelled sour. Alexander was still wearing the tunic from the previous night's banquet, which was stained with wine and food: His face was pale, eyelids half closed and fluttering.

"Has he been poisoned?" Hephaestion whispered hoarsely.

Telamon noticed the vomit stains around Alexander's mouth. Aristander came to stand behind him.

"How long has he been like this?" Telamon asked, lowering his leather satchel to the floor.

"He woke this morning a little thick-headed," Hephaestion replied. "He took no food but sat back on the bed. He has vomited. I cleaned him up."

"Alexander! Alexander!" Telamon shook the king's shoulder. Alexander's eyes flew open and stared unseeingly at Telamon. The contrast in colouring was very marked, the pupils greatly enlarged.

"I am going to examine you," Telamon explained.

Alexander tried to speak but gagged and shook his head. Dispensing with ceremony, Telamon felt Alexander's hands and feet. They were cold, but his neck and chest were warm. He felt the king's stomach, kneading the hard muscles with his fingers. He couldn't detect any lump. Alexander winced and forced a smile.

"What are my symptoms, physician? Have I been poisoned?"

"You've drunk too much," Telamon retorted, "but it's not that, is it?"

"Then what?" Aristander asked sharply.

"Can you stand up? Can you walk?" Telamon asked Alexander.

"I feel so tense," the king confessed. "I am frightened that if I stand I will fall. My throat is dry, my belly feels as if I have eaten sour grapes." He groaned and held his head. "While this throbs like a war drum."

"What did you dream about?" Telamon asked.

"Good old Telamon, always the mind, never the body!" Alexander scoffed. "I had my dream again. I was back at Chaeronea, charging the Theban phalanx on Bucephalus. They had my father surrounded. I was cutting through them but it was like slicing at the sea. I made no headway. I kept waking up and going back to sleep again. I thought I had drunk too much, then, this morning, another warning."

Aristander dropped a small scroll into the physician's lap. The parchment was coarse; the writing could have been anyone's – neat letters, carefully written to disguise the sender's hand, three quotations from the *Iliad*. The first was from Book Nine: "*Can you not understand how the power of Zeus is no longer with you?*"; the second was from Book Eleven: "*You will bring glory to me and your life to Hades*"; and the last was from Book Nineteen: "*We are the Furies who, from underground, revenge dead men.*"

"How did this come?" Telamon asked. "Aristander, guards stand outside, you have spies hiding in the grass and behind bushes. You are supposed to be keeper of the king's secrets."

Alexander laughed sharply. Aristander looked uncomfortable. "The scroll was fastened with twine," he explained. "It was dropped at the feet of a guard at the gate of the royal enclosure. The man did not see who brought it. He picked it up and brought it to me."

"And you showed it to Alexander?"

"Of course. I keep his secrets, not mine."

Telamon got up and bent over Alexander.

"My lord, sit up!"

Alexander made to refuse. The physician beckoned to Hephaestion and they both dragged Alexander to a sitting position, arranging the feather-filled bolsters behind him. Telamon was pleased to see a little colour return to Alexander's cheeks, and his breathing was no longer so sharp and shallow.

"What's wrong?" Alexander croaked, not meeting Telamon's eye.

"You know what's wrong."

Telamon grasped Alexander's wrist and measured the quick pulse.

"You know all the tricks, don't you, Telamon?"

"I know *you*, Alexander. You are having a panic attack brought on by wine, nightmares and threats."

"Alexander doesn't panic," Hephaestion declared.

"Alexander has, does and will." Telamon smiled across at the king's friend. "His muscles are all tense, his breathing is shallow. He's fearful. The wine makes him unsteady. His mind is troubled; this sparks deep anxiety, his body responds. It's like pouring salt into a wound. I have good news for you, Alexander." Telamon just hoped his lie would hold. "I, too, dreamt last night. I was wading through the Hellespont: on the far side stood a man dressed in full armour. As I drew closer, the warrior took off his helmet, with its great horsehaired plume, black as night. It was your father. He was gesturing at me, shouting, 'Why doesn't Alexander follow?'"

Aristander spluttered; Telamon held Alexander's gaze.

"I told him about the sacrifices. Philip replied: 'Tell my son to search the countryside for a pure white bull. Let it be taken by trusted guards and held by them until the moment of sacrifice. Tell him to pay no heed to warnings or whispers of the night!'"

The change in Alexander was marked. He was no longer dull-eyed or white-faced. He leaned forward and grasped Telamon's hand.

"Are you sure? You are not lying?"

"It was but a dream, my lord, but find this animal, perform your sacrifice, embark your army!"

Alexander lay back against the bolsters.

"In the meantime," Telamon continued drily, "I wish you to sleep. Aristander? A little wine."

The keeper of secrets brought a small goblet over. It reminded Telamon of the cup the young woman had drunk from the night before. Telamon quietly promised himself to revisit Antigone's tent. He opened his leather satchel, took out some of his precious poppy juice, and added a tincture to the wine. He stirred this and held it to the king's lips.

"Think of Persia," Telamon whispered. "Think of glory! Free your mind of dark images – drink!"

Alexander obeyed, swallowing the contents in one gulp. Telamon sat by the bed holding his hand. The king wished to continue the conversation but his body began to jerk, his eyes grew heavy, his head went to one side and he fell into a deep sleep.

"And when he wakes up?" Hephaestion asked, as solicitous as any mother.

Telamon studied the dark, bearded face of Alexander's friend. A simple soldier, he reflected, totally unswerving in his loyalty and affection. Alexander's bosom friend, his nurse, his guide who would agree with anything the king said. In many ways Hephaestion looked very like Alexander's father, Philip.

"When he awakes," Telamon sighed, "he will feel much better. A little heavy-eyed, but the pains and the anxiety will have gone. He might sleep for hours. Give him nutritious food to eat, not fruit but bread, dried meat. No wine, but pure water!"

He refastened the buckles on his leather satchel and left. Aristander followed him into the antechamber.

"Alexander believes you. Do you know that? When he wakes up, he'll say Telamon told me the truth because Telamon doesn't have dreams: he doesn't believe in the gods."

"Then we have something in common, don't we?" Telamon replied.

For the first time since they had met, Aristander laughed.

"Last night the king also gave me a message for you, physician. You need a helper. He mentioned the slave pen where we still hold captives from Thebes. There's not much left, but you can have whoever you want." Aristander brought out from beneath his cloak a small seal – a piece of hardened wax with the king's stamp upon it.

"Show that to anyone who challenges you."

Telamon took the seal and stared at it.

"Keep it safe," Aristander warned.

"These messages?" Telamon asked, pocketing the seal. "The quotations from the *Iliad*?"

Aristander pulled a face. "Parchment like that can be bought throughout the camp; the ink is common, the letters deliberately formed well. It could be anyone. The guard doesn't know who brought it. It simply lay at his feet, that's the usual way people present petitions to the king."

"Yes, but this person knows both the *Iliad* and Alexander's soul."

112

"As do you, Telamon. You recognized his anxiety attack, the sudden panic."

"Few people do," Telamon replied. "I was with him when he had his first attack at Mieza. Nearchus, Alexander and I had a wager – who could swim the fastest across a river." Telamon sighed. "Like the boys we were, we stripped naked and jumped in. The river was deeper, faster flowing than we thought. Nearchus swam across, as did I. Alexander turned back. It's the only time I have ever seen him refuse to meet a challenge. He swore us to keep it secret. Nearchus was very good about it, he said he only did what any water rat could do."

"Nearchus is no threat," Aristander agreed. "But others could see this anxiety as a weakness."

"I just see it as Alexander," Telamon replied. "He's anxious and confused: he doesn't know whether to move to the left or the right. However, once he's made up his mind, he'll go like an arrow to the mark and he'll take us all with him. To glory or to Hades!"

Hercules was waiting for him outside.

"What's the matter? What's the matter?" He clutched at Telamon's robe.

"The king is well and the king is sleeping," Telamon loudly replied, so everyone around could hear.

He made his way through the line of guards. Cleitus and Seleucus stood, heads together, talking quietly. Ptolemy winked slyly at him.

"Where are you going?" Hercules demanded.

"To see the priestess Antigone."

"Ah, she's another one whose name is hard to turn round. A kinswoman of Alexander, you know? She knew Philip well. He said he'd trust her with his life. Why are you seeing her?"

"About a murder."

Telamon walked quickly through the narrow avenues between the tents and pavilions. The soldier on guard outside Antigone's tent let them through. The priestess sat on a chair examining a piece of needlework. Selena and Aspasia crouched on the ground before her, busy with needle and thread. Antigone put the piece of cloth down and rose as Telamon entered.

"You've seen the king?"

"I've seen the king. He sleeps well."

Antigone raised one eyebrow. "And your visit here? To check on our health? We are hot, bothered by the flies."

"I would like a cup of wine."

Antigone stared at Hercules. "You seem to attract all manner of creatures."

The dwarf made a rude sound. Antigone turned away.

"Can I have the cup the woman drank from last night? The one who died?"

"Certainly."

Antigone went deep into the tent and brought back the cup, half-filled with wine.

"I have added some water but it's not as strong as the king drank last night."

Aspasia fetched a small stool. Telamon thanked her and sat down. He drained the wine and examined the cup carefully.

"Don't worry." Antigone had picked up her tapestry and smiled at him from under her eyebrows. "I cleaned it myself."

Telamon turned and pointed to the table. "She was sitting there. You brought the cup across. I put the potion in. What happened then?"

"You drank it, I drank it," Antigone replied. "You placed it on the table. People were milling about."

"I saw it move," Aspasia spoke up, her voice low. "A hand picking it up, moving it closer, but I cannot remember whose."

Telamon examined the cup carefully. It was made out of precious metal, with a silver frieze on the outside depicting a young woman holding a bulbous-eyed owl. The stem and base were also of silver, the inside brightly polished. Telamon handed the cup back. He had thought that by revisiting the tent his memory might be stirred, but there was nothing. He made his farewells. Hercules, who had been virtually ignored, followed him out into the sunshine.

"Where to now, physician?"

"The slave pens."

"I'll show you."

Telamon would have preferred to go by himself, but Hercules insisted on taking his hand and leading him out of the enclosure. The clamour of the camp greeted them. Telamon could see the men were restless. No longer soldiers, they had stripped themselves of any fighting equipment, eager to find any shade against the sun and while away the time in games of knuckle bones and dice. The only men wearing any armour were anxious-eyed officers who strolled around, eager to intervene in any fights.

"You can see the danger, can't you?" Hercules declared.

They stopped to take directions and found the slave pen near the horse lines. A soldier, dressed in a leather corselet, helmet beside him, slouched before the main gate. He got to his feet as Telamon approached.

"I'm only new here," he called out, putting up his hands. "Yet I have my orders. This is my first task. Get your own whores, the slaves are for sale not for use!"

"Shut up! You don't know who you're talking to!" Hercules growled.

"I told you I was new," the soldier muttered. He scratched his black beard and wiped the sweat from his brow. He had a cruel, lean face, with one eye permanently half-closed by a scar which cut diagonally across his brow to just beneath his ear. Telamon showed the royal seal. The soldier studied it curiously and handed it back.

"Where are you from?" Telamon asked.

"Argos." The fellow grinned, his sharpened dog teeth giving him a wolfish look. "My name is Droxenius. We arrived this morning. We made our mark and we've taken our drachma. This is my first duty, guarding slaves. Is the king well?"

"None of your business!" Hercules snapped.

Telamon let go of the dwarf's hand. "You can leave. I want to be alone."

Hercules backed away, making an obscene gesture with his middle finger at the guard as he left.

The slave pen was a great wicker-work cage. Droxenius slipped off the latch and, with a mocking gesture, ushered Telamon forward.

"There's not much and the smell is rich."

Telamon stepped inside. The guard was right. The pen stank like a pigsty. At the far end clustered a huddle of broken, pathetic people, dark-eyed and thin-faced, like shades from Hades. These were the remains of Alexander's conquest, the fruit of his great victory over Thebes. Men and women, bereft of their families, now facing a life of abuse and slavery. Telamon looked to his left where there was a row of water jars; one, covered by a cracked board, must be the privy. The stench was sickening. Flies buzzed, but not a sound came from the slaves. All eyes on Telamon, they watched like ghosts from the shadows thrown up by the wicker-work cage. Telamon counted. There were at least forty. One person caught his eye, just a blur, a woman with red hair, bright-eyed, not dulled like the rest. She was wearing a dark-green, stained tunic and hid behind two old men. Somewhere in the group a woman abruptly wailed. Telamon decided that, whatever happened, something had to be done for these wretches. Most were old: they would fetch little in the slave markets and, if they continued here or followed the army, they'd be dead within months.

"I can do something for you," Telamon declared, though even as he spoke his words sounded hollow, and drew no reaction from the huddled group.

"I'll get better food and water. This is a pig pen." Telamon's voice faltered. "Is there anything else?"

"You could jump off the cliffs!" a woman's voice shouted.

Telamon was sure it was red-hair. For the first time since he had entered, the group moved. Telamon heard a low laugh.

"You could jump off the cliffs!" the voice repeated. "And take all Macedonians with you!"

Telamon curbed his temper. "I'm here to help. I'm a physician."

"Then heal yourself!" the voice retorted.

"I need a helper, an assistant. Is there someone here who knows anything about medicine?"

"No, just the lack of it!" the voice answered.

"I'm looking for a helper," Telamon repeated. "The person I choose, or who volunteers, will be free!"

Dull eyes stared back. An old man clambered to his feet and spoke with a Doric accent.

"I used to be, er, I *was* a physician."

An old woman gently seized his hand and pulled him back down again.

"Is there anybody else?" Telamon called out.

Silence. He sighed, turned on his heel and walked back to the gate.

"You are probably looking for me?"

Telamon turned round. The young, red-haired woman was now standing in front of the group. Telamon walked back. She was of medium height with strong legs and arms and lean-bodied. The red hair was like some sort of halo, as if she had combed it with her fingers, her one link with ordinary life. Her eyes were slightly sloe-shaped, green and defiant in a strong though not pretty face. Her skin, roughened by sun and wind, had a yellowish tint from months of malnutrition; her hands were filthy and mud caked her left arm. She followed Telamon's gaze.

"Some of the soldiers wanted to have fun," she declared. The strong chin came up, lower lip jutting out. She turned her head slightly sideways. "But they didn't force me. No one has forced me. I tell them that I am dedicated to the Lady, the war goddess Athena."

"And are you?"

"Once." Her gaze didn't waver. "That's how I survived. I was a helper, an assistant, in the Temple of Athena at Thebes just near the Cadmea."

Telamon nodded. Now he understood. When Thebes had been razed, Alexander had spared the temples.

"And how were you caught?"

"I was stupid enough to go looking for a friend. I told the soldiers who I was but they didn't believe me."

"Where are the salivary glands?" Telamon abruptly asked.

"At the root of the tongue."

"What drives the blood?"

"The heart."

"How do you take a man's pulse?"

"By pressing your fingers gently against the throat or the wrist."

"If I offered a patient root of fennel and parsley soaked in sweet white wine, of which two cupfuls should be drunk with water each day what would his ailment be?"

"I would say the patient had something wrong with his bladder."

"Very good!" Telamon smiled. "And if there is giddiness in the head, heaviness in the brows, singing in the ears, tears in the eyes, failure in the sense of smell and swelling of the gums?"

"I would say the man was suffering from a chill and his nose will run with phlegm. A boiled concoction of hyssop is recommended on an empty stomach. Mustard and warm honeyed water to swallow and gargle."

Again Telamon agreed.

"And if a woman is pregnant? And she has sudden and severe shrinking in the breasts or belly in the seventh or eighth month?"

The woman blinked and glanced away. "Then she is a very lucky woman, physician: her foetus is dead and will not be born into this place of horrors!"

"You have read the work of Hippocrates?"

"Of course. I learnt his herbal remedies as well as his lists of symptoms and signs."

Telamon nodded. In his journeys round Greece and Egypt he had encountered women such as this. Temples, like that of Athena in Thebes, were places of healing and, by custom, could not turn anyone away. Those who worked in them often became more skilled and efficient than many so-called physicians whose knowledge of the body was more theory than practice.

"If I agreed, would you take me?" The woman's voice was harsh. "Will I be free?"

"You will be free."

"You'll write a document saying that?"

"Signed and sealed."

The woman's eyes grew watchful, her face wary.

"You look a typical physician," she jibed. "Clean, neat, orderly, precise. I would say a dull face, apart from the eyes. A man who likes to control his passions, yes? He has been hurt but likes to hide it. That's why you've come here, isn't it? You want a stranger, someone you can trust, because you find trust very difficult."

Telamon clapped his hands mockingly.

"And what's stopping me," she continued, "from cutting your throat at night and fleeing?"

"You could do that," Telamon declared. "And then the Furies would pursue you."

She laughed and shook her head. "I don't believe in them."

"You'd be a stranger: poor, vulnerable, wandering the wasteland. You've made a calculation. You've decided that you'd be better with me than to stay here or go elsewhere. Am I right?"

The woman licked her lips. "I'd love some water, fresh and clean." She jabbed her thumb over her shoulder. "And these poor worms. I've been with them for months. I can't just walk away."

"Oh yes you can. In the months ahead you will walk away from many things." He paused. "I can't make any promises but I'll see what I can do. Are you coming or aren't you? The stench in here is terrible!" Telamon swatted a fly.

"Lead on master," she taunted. "Shall I walk behind or in front of you? Or trot beside you like a good dog?"

"My name's Telamon. Where you walk, how you walk, is your own concern."

The physician went to the gate and lifted the latch. As they left, the soldier turned his face away, hawked and spat. Telamon shook his head and walked on.

"What's the matter?" asked red-hair. "You seem puzzled."

"Nothing," Telamon mused. "I'll show you in a minute."

They left the dusty enclosure and re-entered the camp. They had hardly gone twenty paces before the catcalls and jeers began.

"Aye, red-hair!" a soldier called, lifting his tunic and exposing his genitals. "Do you fancy a sausage?"

"No, thank you, I only eat big ones!"

The retort provoked roars of laughter. They wound past the dusty tents and bothies. Groups of soldiers huddled over games of dice or shared jugs of wine. A contortionist, a young woman, her body thin-ribbed, was performing an exotic dance to the sound of a flute and drum. The soldiers clapped and, as Telamon and his companion passed, they invited the woman to join in. Telamon grasped her wrist and was pleased that she didn't pull away.

119

"What's your name?"

"Cassandra."

"That's not your real name, is it?"

"Cassandra was a prophetess of woe," she declared. "That's my name now and always shall be. It's the only . . ." she pushed her face closer, ". . . it's the only one I shall answer to."

Telamon flinched at her stale smell and she pulled away. "I've tried to keep myself clean, but this tunic is my only one. I haven't washed for months. When they took us from Thebes they allowed us to wade through a river – my last bath!"

"What can you do apart from medicine?" Telamon asked.

"I can sing and dance."

"Just answer the question!"

Cassandra smiled, eyes full of mischief. "I can do medicine, prepare herbs and poultices. I can cauterize a wound. I have stitched flesh."

"And veins?" Telamon asked.

"On two occasions only, but I failed. The man bled to death. His leg had been crushed under a cart, one of the temple physicians removed it."

"The age-old problem," Telamon agreed. He was aware of soldiers gathering round, peering at Cassandra.

"A silver piece, sir!" one of them shouted. "A silver piece and let me borrow her until the morning!"

Telamon held up the royal seal. Muttering and cursing, the soldiers melted away. Cassandra stared and gaped open-mouthed.

"You are a royal physician? One of the Horned Devil's company?"

Telamon pressed a finger against her lips. He had heard the remark made of Alexander before, either because of the way he swept his hair forward or the helmet he wore, carved in the shape of a ram's head.

"I'd be careful what you say, Cassandra. Keep your eyes open and your mouth shut!"

She pulled her face away. "That's good advice for a young woman. Now you tell me. Why were you puzzled back at the slave pen? You strode away shaking your head."

"Every soldier we passed," Telamon replied, walking on, "has whistled, catcalled, made an obscene gesture or offered to get between your thighs. The one at the slave pen just looked away."

"Perhaps he likes bum boys," Cassandra murmured. "A lot of soldiers do. A sweet pair of buttocks and they are in Elysium. You're not like that, are you, Telamon?"

The physician ignored her and stood aside as a groom leading a frisky warhorse came down the narrow trackway. He then walked on quickly, forcing Cassandra to hurry to keep up with him. The guards let them into the royal enclosure. Again came catcalls and whistles. Ptolemy came swaggering up.

"Home comforts, eh, Telamon?"

"General Ptolemy, this is Cassandra. A temple helper from Thebes."

Ptolemy looked the woman up and down. Cassandra noisily cleared her throat. Telamon shoved her away.

"Jealous already?" Ptolemy shouted.

Cassandra spun round, her eyes blazing with fury. "I am not your dog! Why did you do that?"

"You were going to spit!" Telamon hissed.

"He led the attack on Thebes," Cassandra retorted, eyes blazing with fury. "Gods, I thought I'd never be given the chance to slit so many throats. I hope he falls ill."

Telamon pushed her into his tent, ignoring the whistle of the guard outside. He walked quickly to his chest, flung it open and took out a dagger. Cassandra stood her ground as he pressed the tip against her throat.

"Do you want to die?" Telamon asked. "Because the way I am offering you now is quick. Ptolemy would have you crucified. Would you like that? On the cliff tops?" He turned the dagger over and presented the hilt to her. "Or, if you want, you can cut your own throat. I promise I'll see to your ashes."

"I'd like some water."

Telamon went to a water jar, picked up the ladle and filled an earthenware pot. Cassandra drank greedily and poured the dregs over her face.

"Will you behave?" Telamon insisted, stretching out his hand.

121

"I am a stranger," he continued, "but we could become friends. I swear on my father's life, by my father's soul, by heaven and earth, by all that's supposed to be sacred, you have nothing to fear from me. I don't want you as a bed companion or as a slave but as a helper. If that doesn't suit you, think of us as two soldiers, back to back. I protect yours, you protect mine."

Cassandra grinned. "I've heard some proposals in my life, but that's the best." She kissed his hand.

"Good! Now." Telamon pointed around. "This is where you sleep. I'll have another cot bed moved in. You can prepare my food or I'll prepare yours. Check everything you eat and drink – that includes the water I have just given you. Keep things tidy. If I do not, tell me. You don't hawk or spit in here, clean your nose or ears, or any other orifice of your body. If you wish to go to the privy the guard outside will guard you. Now, you stink!" He went back to the chest and drew out a small phial. "This is a sort of perfume, I use it myself." He grinned. "As you know, Hippocrates advised physicians to smell fragrant."

He seized Cassandra by the elbow and she didn't resist as he led her out of the tent. The soldier scrambled to his feet. He was a tall, raw-boned man with watery eyes and ever-gaping mouth, but quick in his movements.

"Do you like being a soldier?"

"Why yes, sir."

"Do you want plunder?"

"Who doesn't?"

"And you wouldn't like to be crucified?"

The man's mouth gaped even more.

"What's the matter?" he stammered.

Telamon patted Cassandra on the shoulder. "This is Cassandra, my assistant and my friend. She stinks."

The soldier sniffed. "I know that. She's worse than a cow."

"I'm not interested in your sex life," Cassandra interrupted.

The soldier threw back his head and laughed.

"You will take her to the stores," Telamon ordered. "She will need cloth – tunic and a mantle." He held his hand up. "Two changes, marching sandals and a dagger."

"Who'll pay for all this?"

Telamon handed over the royal seal. "The king."

The soldier took the seal and kissed it.

"You'll also get a piece of linen," Telamon declared as he pushed the small phial into Cassandra's hand. "This young woman will go down to the beach, she will strip naked," he ignored Cassandra's gasp, "and swim in the sea. She'll wash herself and, while this goes on, you will keep your back to her. One peep and you'll be digging latrines for the next month."

The soldier mockingly waved Cassandra forward. "If the lady wishes?"

Telamon watched them go, then went back into the tent. He took a jug of water, slightly salted and distilled with herbs, brought it out to the mouth of the tent and washed his hands and face. He went back in again, gazed around to make sure all was well and lay down on the bed. He felt hungry, slightly tired. Half-listening to the sounds of the camp, his mind drifted. He was sure he had made the correct choice. There was something about Cassandra. She was calculating, probably devious – she had to be, to survive, but she was no fool. If she could curb her tongue and hide her real feelings . . . ?

Telamon drifted into sleep. When he woke, Cassandra was sitting on a stool at the foot of the bed staring at him, a dagger in her hand. The physician pulled himself up.

"Were you just thinking about it?"

The woman had tied her thick red hair behind her. Her face was scrubbed clean, hands the same, nails neatly pared with the dagger. She was dressed in a brown tunic with a cord round the middle. On her feet she wore stout marching sandals.

"Who are you?" Telamon asked. "I'd like to bind you by an oath."

"Where's my letter of liberty?" she retorted.

"I'll have a scribe write it. Oh, by the way, where's the seal?"

Cassandra undid the small wallet tied to the cord round her waist, took out the seal and handed it over.

"I'll have the letter drawn up," Telamon affirmed. "And keep it safe. Do you believe in the gods, Cassandra?"

She shook her head. "I never did. When Thebes was sacked, any doubts disappeared. It was terrible, hideous, the streets were packed with soldiers. They were butchers, moving from house to house. In some places the blood ran ankle-deep. I left the temple and went out to the portico. All I could see were shields and swords. A sea of helmets. Iron, flashing in the sun, drenched with blood. They moved among the citizens like butchers among lambs. No one was spared; then they burnt the city. The smell of burning flesh was everywhere. Everything you ate or drank tasted of it, all for the glory of Macedon!"

"Thebes shouldn't have rebelled."

"I can tell from your eyes you don't believe that! The Macedonian wanted to make an example. He wanted to terrify Greece. Alexander is a great killer. He's a blood-supper!"

"You'll not say that in his presence."

"No, but I'll say it in my soul for as long as I live!"

Chapter 6

"To Philip succeeded his son Alexander, a prince greater
than his father in both virtue and vice."

> Marcus Junianus Justinus,
> *History of the World*, Book 9, Chapter 8

Hercules wandered into the wood – that's what he called it,
though it was really just a clump of trees a good mile away
from the camp. He stared back in the direction he had come. The
ground dipped and rose, the view obscured by clumps of trees,
bushes and wild grass. Very few people came here; the area was
dotted by quagmires and marshes, swamps and morasses, and the
camp heralds had proclaimed these to be dangerous after two
archers had been drowned. Hercules, however, wanted to be
alone. He studied the ground underfoot carefully – it was hard,
sun-baked. Hercules knew the signs to watch for, the fresh sprouts
of vivid greenness. Such a spot lay just within a stone's throw,
where the grass thrust up long, willowy and fresh. The dwarf liked
to be alone. The camp jarred his nerves and, though his master was
powerful, Hercules was the butt of many jokes. "Come here, boy!"
a soldier would shout. "I have a job for you!"

Hercules took the small wineskin he carried over his shoulder,
pulled back the stopper and let the raw juice run into his mouth.
Maybe he'd get drunk, sleep it off and wander back to camp in the
evening. Hercules was full of self-pity. He liked palaces, their
shadowy, shiny passageways, the doors and windows he could
creep through, the keyholes and cracks he could listen at. But, out
in the open, in a smelly camp, what use was he? Tents were difficult
places to listen at, he always had to be careful. If someone glimpsed

125

his shadow going down the sides of a pavilion where he had no right to be . . . The dwarf sat down on a stone and picked at a scab on his chin. Aristander had been angry with him.

"Find out this! Find out that!" he had screeched. "You are supposed to be my little cat, Hercules, yet you've found nothing!"

"That's not true!" the dwarf had shouted across the deserted grove. "That's simply not bloody true!"

He had tried to listen but it was difficult; he'd been lucky with Leontes. Hercules had crept into his tent and, when someone had come in, slipped beneath the cot bed – which was when he had found the gold darics and the incriminating letters Leontes carried. Hercules sniffed. If the truth be known, many in the Greek camp had seen some sort of service in Persia. Mercenaries were arriving every day, not to mention the gaggle of camp followers attracted by the prospect of easy plunder. Soothsayers from the mainland, Scorpion-men from Egypt, quacks and leeches, professional beggars and cunning men.

"They all swarm in like flies on a cow pat," Hercules murmured mournfully.

He had made the same point to Aristander as his master had dressed in the evening in his gold wig and woman's dress – "The keeper of the king's secrets' little secret", as he called it. If the king didn't need him, Aristander would paint his face and rouge his lips, don a wig and a woman's soft tunic and mantle. He particularly liked the thick-heeled shoes of the hetaerae, the courtesans of Athens, with their bracelets and rings. A strange one Aristander! His master hinted that he controlled the black arts and could summon up demons, but Hercules didn't believe that. Aristander was the master of illusion. The dwarf was always frightened that his master would lose interest in him and recruit another spy. He'd even glimpsed more dwarfs amongst the newcomers. Hercules had warned against these arrivals from across the Hellespont, but his master had been dismissive.

"Just because you've been to Persia," Aristander had squeaked in that high falsetto voice he cultivated on such evenings, "doesn't mean you are a traitor." He'd poked his servant in the chest. "Your job, mannikin, is to discover traitors. I want to know why

126

the sacrifices aren't perfect and, above all, who is slaying our guides."

Hercules had his orders. He had gone out like a rat nuzzling among the rubbish. So far he had caught only little prey like Leontes. If he had his way Hercules would arrest all the physicians. The dwarf hated them. They always regarded him as a curiosity, a freak. Well, those physicians had better watch their mouths! They were only here because Alexander had ordered them to be and because there was nowhere else for them to go. Telamon was different. Hercules took another swig of the wine. He liked Telamon: distant, rather cold but still kindly, a man who talked to him as if he was a man, not some object of ridicule.

Aristander thought differently. His master had waggled one painted fingernail at him. "Believe you me, Hercules," he had whispered, clutching the dwarf by the shoulder, making him sneeze at the perfume which billowed from the costly woman's robe, "Telamon is a very dangerous man."

"And why is that, master?" Hercules sometimes felt the keeper of secrets liked to be a new Socrates, with his constant question and answer.

"Because Telamon is not frightened of Alexander." Aristander flounced onto the couch. "And, more importantly, he's not really frightened of me. Two good reasons, and I'll give you more. Telamon doesn't believe in the gods."

"Or the black arts," Hercules added cynically.

Aristander had slapped him for that.

"If he doesn't believe in the gods, little man, how can he believe that Alexander is the son of a god destined for glory? Finally," Aristander had added, "Telamon thinks for himself. Oh, I know all about him. What he sees he believes and what he believes he always analyzes."

"Why did Alexander invite him back?" Hercules had asked.

"Oh, don't be stupid! It's obvious. Telamon can't be bribed. If he gives his word he'll keep it. He's a friend from youth and, above all, he'll tell Alexander the truth and, as we have discussed before, that can be very dangerous."

Hercules breathed in deeply, savouring the fragrance. He already felt heavy-eyed. "Why did Telamon leave Mieza?" he demanded.

Aristander, slouched in his favourite feminine pose, elbow resting on one arm of the couch, fingers splayed, imitated the elegant, dismissive gesture of a courtesan.

"That, my little dwarf, is something I would love to know. He was the son of one of Philip's captains, a favourite called Margolis, so Telamon joined Alexander out at Aristotle's school in the groves of Mieza. Aristotle!" he snapped. "That arrogant, spindle-shanked philosopher. Anyway, one day Margolis arrived and took his son away, and that was the end of it."

"How old was Telamon then?"

"Slightly older than Alexander. About fourteen or fifteen. Even Olympias doesn't know the truth. She nagged Philip but he wouldn't say."

A twig snapped. Hercules whirled round. He put the wineskin on the ground and felt for the long dagger sheathed at his belt. He peered into the green darkness. A prickle of fear chilled the sweat on his back. Had he been followed from the camp? Yet no one followed Hercules. Perhaps this was different? Perhaps those he had been questioning? A bird fluttered. Hercules sighed and returned to his reverie. His master wasn't pleased. Hercules had been ordered to find out as much as he could about Telamon, but the physician was as wary as a cat, sly as a mongoose. He wouldn't chatter or gossip like the rest, and he'd soon sent that page packing. Hercules had tried to ingratiate himself but Telamon had made it very clear he was his own man. He had even gone into to the slave pens alone, and found that red-haired wench. Hercules' hands stole to his crotch. She looked big and beefy, and that was another thing Hercules missed: the ladies of the court who, under the influence of wine, could be free with their favours. Aristander had warned him to keep away from the camp followers.

"They've got every disease under the sun!" he'd declared. "I don't want you bringing their filth in here!"

Aristander loved to ape women but was shy of them, and Olympias terrified him. Olympias! Hercules often tried to put her name backwards. What was it, ah that's it, SAIPMYLO. It didn't make sense! Hercules loved this game. He'd turned his attention to the spy Naihpat. Put round the other way, the name became Taphian. Now where had he heard that before?

He took another swig of wine. If he could discover the identity of this traitor, his master would reward him, forget his curses and blows, perhaps even give him money to visit a pleasure house in Sestos. Hercules licked his lips. Naihpat, Taphian. What did they mean? The dwarf could read and write but ever since his master had bought him out of an acting troupe most of his education had been listening at other people's doors and windows.

The birds chatter disturbed him. Some creature scuttled across the ground, a blur of quick-moving fur. If the truth be known, Hercules concluded, I am drunk. He heard a sound behind him but delayed looking round in order to restopper his wine. Then he looked over his shoulder. The net was already snaking out. It fell, covering the dwarf. The more he struggled the more the weights took effect and enmeshed him in the coils. Hercules staggered to his feet and tripped over. He glimpsed a shadow and screamed as the club fell, smashing the side of his skull. He was still screaming as he slipped into unconsciousness. The assassin kept bringing the club down, reducing Hercules' skull to a mass of bone, blood and brain.

Cassandra tied the bandage round Telamon's wrist.

"I disagree." He undid it. "It's too tight. It interferes with the flow of blood and does not allow the wound to breathe. If it hasn't been cleaned properly, it will also seal the putrefaction in. How many times would you change it?"

"Once every two days." Her green eyes crinkled with amusement. "Are you going to tell me that's wrong?"

"For a simple cut, no, but for a wound? I would change the bandage, if possible, at least once a day, perhaps even twice. I'd clean it with a mixture of heavy wine, salt and honey."

Despite her calloused fingers, Cassandra's touch was soft and gentle. Since her outburst against Alexander, Telamon had gently diverted the conversation, interrogating her closely on her knowledge of medicine.

"You've learnt a lot," he complimented her.

"I would have learnt more if Alexander hadn't burnt Thebes."
She shrugged. "Now it looks as if my education will continue. Are
you sure you don't want me as a bed companion?"

Telamon gently chucked her under the chin. "If I say yes, you'll
say no. If I say no, you'll protest."

"Well, aren't I pretty? I'm not saying I want to be, but aren't I
pretty?"

Telamon studied her strong face, washed clean but still chapped
by the sun and wind; slightly sallow, the cheeks a little sunken from
malnutrition.

"You are comely," he replied. "You look as if you need proper
nourishment. Did your family die in Thebes?"

Cassandra plucked at her red hair. "I didn't have any family. I
was left as a foundling on the steps of Athena's shrine, the usual
practice. The temple guards thought I was the daughter of a Celt,
possibly one of the mercenaries the city hired. My mother may
have been the daughter, or wife, of some respectable Theban
merchant." She glanced at Telamon from under her eyebrows.
"You are going to laugh! I was a cuckoo's egg laid in someone's
nest. If my skin had been swarthy and my hair dark, that's easy to
hide. A number of men aren't quite sure who their father is. And, I
suppose, an equally surprising number of women. However, in a
city of dark-haired people, a lusty brat with a pale face and a fuzz of
red hair is difficult to explain away."

"It's a wonder you weren't exposed," Telamon said. "Temple
guardians aren't the most kindly of people."

"I had a small owl pressed into my little fist," she explained. "A
similar amulet round my neck, so the guardians knew I had been
dedicated to Athena; that applied to a number of us. Most of the
others ran away as soon as they could."

"But you?"

"Where could I run to? I was considered a freak. Everybody
knew, when . . ." she paused.

Telamon was sure she was going to reveal her true name.

". . . Even when I went to the market-place," she continued
off-handedly, "the urchins would follow, calling out names."
Cassandra picked up the bandage and rolled it up neatly. "Anyway,

I liked the temple. I had a chamber, a change of clothing, good food and the gratitude of patients. I enjoyed my work. I very rarely left Thebes and, if it hadn't been for Alexander, I would have probably died there, either of old age or boredom. And you, master?"

"Telamon. My name is Telamon."

"Yes, master."

"Well," the physician sighed. "I might as well tell you before Ptolemy makes it up. My father was a brigade commander in the Foot Companions. His name was Margolis. He was tall with hair as black as a raven. He was one of Philip's drinking companions, a ferocious warrior, brave in battle. Philip sent his son Alexander to the groves of Mieza, a quiet, rustic idyll where he would receive military tuition from Cleitus and the best education Athens could offer from the philosopher Aristotle." Telamon paused. "Certain companions were chosen to go with him. I was one of them. I went for three years. I didn't want to leave my mother." He sighed wistfully. "I was the only son, or I was at the time. I was to be both a scholar and a warrior, so half my life was pleasant. I was very good at my studies. However, when it came to swordplay, how to thrust a dagger, the best way to hold a spear or lunge with a lance, I was fairly useless."

"You were a coward?"

Telamon scratched his chin. "Yes, you could say that. I didn't like being hurt. I couldn't see the point of hurting other people. I much preferred to sit at the feet of Aristotle and ask him what came first, the day or the night? Why does the sun rise in the east and set in the west? Was the world a dish hung between heaven and hell? Who were the gods?"

"And were you good at that?"

"Aristotle said I had a masterful eye for symptoms."

"What did he mean?"

"He would make me study something then tell him what I had learnt just by close inspection. Why do a clump of trees lean to the left rather than the right? Was this the work of the wind? Or the branches searching for the sun? If a horse galloped in a certain way gathering its forelegs or turning its head to one side, what did it mean? Then he'd turn on the servants. Why did such a person screw his eyes up? What could I tell from that woman's hands?" Telamon laughed softly. "I enjoyed it. Aristotle didn't know much about the human body but he pretended to. He was puzzled by how the blood flowed. Was it controlled by the brain, the heart or some other bodily humour?"

"And Alexander?"

"He protected me on the parade-ground and, in turn, I'd help him with his studies. We both read the *Iliad*. Alexander is still obsessed with it," he added drily. "I loved the poem, the way the gods become involved in human affairs. Alexander was fascinated by my theory that Homer must have been a physician because he described wounds very accurately. We used to stay up half the night under the stars, discussing the different combats.

"Alexander's mother stuffed his mind with stories about how Achilles was her ancestor and, therefore, his. Alexander began to think he *was* Achilles, an immortal man-god, the world's greatest warrior. I, of course, was cast in the role of Patroclus, Achilles' lover and companion."

"Were you lovers?"

"Oh, we embraced, sat arms linked or walked hand in hand. I always thought it was slightly ridiculous. I told Alexander I wasn't his Patroclus but that one day he'd find him."

"And now he has, in Hephaestion?"

Telamon agreed. He clicked his tongue.

"So why did you leave?"

Telamon blinked. "Try as I might," he murmured, "every time I describe it – and you are the second woman I have told – my eyes fill with tears. The army had returned to Pella, my father with them. Another of Philip's great victories! Now, usually my father would come galloping out to Mieza, great war helm on, cuirass and kilt gleaming in the sunlight. On that occasion, he didn't. I was on the parade ground, fencing with wooden swords when this man appeared, his hair and beard long. He stood staring at me, arms hanging by his sides, fingers curled. He was dressed like a peasant in a tunic, a cord wrapped round his middle. 'That's your father!' one of my companions shouted. At first I couldn't believe it. I dropped my sword and shield and ran over. He grabbed me and clutched me to him. He looked different, he smelt different, eyes and face were sad. I panicked. Was something wrong with Mother? With my baby brother, my sister? He just held me away, eyes searching every inch of my face. 'There's nothing wrong, Telamon,' he whispered. 'You are coming home.'"

"Was there anything wrong?"

"No. We owned a farm outside Pella, the earth was good and rich, but my mother was as wary as I. She explained how Father had returned dressed in a simple tunic. He'd handed his weapons, his armour and horse back to Philip. He vowed he would never kill again and left the palace. Philip thought he had been injured, a blow to the head. He came down to visit us, Alexander with him. I heard their voices raised in argument. Philip, however, loved my father. He said he wouldn't interfere in his decision. If there was anything he wanted . . . but my father never asked. He became a farmer again, interested in crops and animals. Once I found him with a new-born lamb. He was sitting with his back to a wall cuddling the lamb, tears streaming down his face." Telamon shook his head. "That's the way he became. My father wouldn't kill anything. He stopped eating meat. Oh, he'd allow us to slaughter for the feasts but he'd never touch the meat himself. He never talked about the army. He wouldn't have swords or shields in the house. He never visited the temples but went out and stood among the barley, raised his hands and, for all I know, worshipped the sky."

"You never found the reason why?"

"Never. Something had happened which changed his life. He never spoke about it. 'Macedon has become the temple of war,' he once said. 'You, Telamon, must never be a soldier.'" The physician smiled. "On that we agreed. I wanted to study medicine. Father put his wealth at my disposal. I visited all the great medical schools: Athens, Corinth, the island of Cos. During my studies both my father and brother died. By then I had drifted from my family."

Telamon paused as he heard noises from outside; the bray of a trumpet, the shouts of an officer, a burst of laughter. "I became a traveller thirsty for knowledge, like a farmer sifting corn, winnowing the false from the true, learning as much as I could about the human body." He smiled thinly. "In doing so I learnt little about the human soul. I drifted like a feather in the wind till I visited Thebes in Egypt." Telamon shook his head. "A place of wonder, Cassandra: temples and statues soaring up to the sky; obelisks gold-plated to catch the sun. The great sprawling necropolis, the houses of life in the temples. I learnt a great deal about medicine. I also met the great love of my life." He saw the surprise in Cassandra's face. "Oh yes, I have loved and been loved: her name was Anula, she was a temple girl, a heset!"

"Was she beautiful?"

"Egyptian handmaidens shave their heads. She always wore an oil-drenched wig bound by a beautiful silver filet. A gold gorget circled her throat, made of cornelian, studded with precious jewels. She could sing and dance, Cassandra. She bubbled with laughter." His voice grew harsh. "I had to be with her all the time and she with me."

"She died?"

"No." Telamon sighed. "She was murdered. I killed the Persian officer responsible. I fled to Cyprus – that's where Olympias' agents picked me up. They said I was needed in Macedon, so home I came. I travelled light." He gestured to the side of the tent. "My medicine bag, a chest or two of books and manuscripts, what clothing I could buy." He leaned across and tugged Cassandra's hair. "Oh, by the way, I pay you by the month – that's if we survive. If we meet the enemy and we win, that's good. If it looks as if it's defeat, well, one thing we have in common, Cassandra, are a good pair of legs: we run!"

She burst out laughing. "And you came here because Olympias asked you?"

"No, I came here for a number of reasons. I had nowhere else to go. I was curious about Alexander and, to be perfectly honest, I was curious about my father. I would like to know what happened. I'm waiting for Alexander to tell me."

Telamon whirled round at a clash of armour. The tent flap was lifted aside. Alexander entered. He clapped his hands, staring around, grinning from ear to ear.

"I've come to thank you, Telamon. I slept like a baby." He came over and pushed Telamon down as the physician made to rise. "Well, what do you think of your patient?"

Alexander had changed. His golden hair had been clipped and oiled; he smelt fragrantly of some perfume. He was dressed in a white tunic, edged with gold, which fell beneath his knees, and marching sandals; on his left wrist was a silver bracelet, embossed with the pythoness; rings glittered on his fingers. He dug his nails into Telamon's shoulder.

"Your dreams were correct, Telamon? You weren't lying, were you?" He bent down. "You saw Philip? He told me to cross?"

Telamon nodded.

"And the bull? The sacrifice?"

"Pure white," Telamon replied. "It must be guarded carefully."

"I have already got Ptolemy on to it." Alexander tapped Telamon on the shoulder and turned to Cassandra. "And this is your red-hair? She looks strong enough."

"What shall I do, your majesty, kneel?"

Telamon closed his eyes. Alexander chose to ignore the sarcasm. He cupped Cassandra's chin in his hands. She stared fiercely up at him.

"You are from Thebes, aren't you?" He made a face. "That was a lesson in hubris. I lost my temper, but they were bound by oaths."

"Would you keep an oath to a conqueror?" Cassandra retorted. "What's left of Thebes live like pigs in that pen."

Alexander moved his head sideways and studied her closely.

"What's your name?"

"Cassandra."

"Ah, the prophetess of doom. Is that your real name?"

"It's my name."

"You remind me a little of Olympias, my mother. What shall I do with you, Cassandra, eh? Smack your face for being insolent?"

Telamon caught his breath. Alexander was glowering at Cassandra.

"Return you to the pig pen? I'll tell you what I'll do." His voice dropped. "Aristander!" he called out over his shoulder.

The keeper of secrets hurried in, a small wicker basket in his hands. Alexander's eyes never left Cassandra's face.

"Open the basket, Aristander!"

The lid was removed.

"Show Cassandra what I have brought."

Aristander pushed the basket closer. Alexander let go of Cassandra's face. Cassandra picked out the items: hair brooches in the shape of silver grasshoppers, an ivory comb, a gold embossed hand-mirror, a small jug with a sealed stopper.

"It's a mixture of musk and frankincense," Alexander explained. "My presents to you, Cassandra. I've brought nothing for Telamon." He smiled lazily at her. "You do have a tart tongue! Aristander, go down to the pig pen, give each of the prisoners a silver piece, some bread and meat in a napkin. They can wash themselves in the sea. One tunic," Alexander emphasized the points on his fingers, "one mantle, one pair of sandals and a walking cane each. Tell them they are free, they can go where they want."

Cassandra still stared defiantly. Alexander went to touch her again but she flinched. The king patted her on the shoulder.

"I know how you feel. I always kept to the blind side of my father." Alexander was full of nervous energy. "The sacrifice will go well," he declared, as if reassuring himself. "I have told the camp marshals to clear out all undesirables."

Telamon, distracted, sniffed hard at an acrid odour seeping into the tent.

"I know," Alexander murmured, "they are burning the dead – not only those who have been murdered. We have sickness in the camp, it's time we moved. But, Telamon, I wish to reward you; don't we, Aristander? We are going for a picnic, just a few of us. The Lady Antigone has agreed to be my guest. My cooks have been busy: light wine, strips of roast duck, some fruit and freshly baked bread. We'll leave the stench of this camp. Just you, Telamon. Cassandra has had her reward."

The king wouldn't brook a refusal. He strode out of the tent gesturing at Telamon to follow.

"These murders?" Cassandra whispered.

"I'll tell you when I return."

Telamon followed the king out into the sunlight. Hephaestion

136

was there along with Antigone. The king donned a military cloak, its hood pulled up.

"I don't want to be noticed," he declared. "The grooms are waiting."

They left the royal enclosure. Just by the entrance Alexander's pages helped him arm: a baldric with an ivory-handled sword and dagger in their silver-edged sheaths. Hephaestion did likewise. Alexander tossed a sword belt to Telamon.

"For cutting wood," he teased.

They entered the camp proper. It was now well past midday and most of the men were resting, seeking shade from the burning sun. A stiff sea breeze helped, though it also brought a sickly, sweet smell and wisps of black smoke from the funeral pyres blazing along the headlands.

Alexander moved quickly down the narrow trackways, through the picket lines to the clump of trees where Telamon had met Aristander earlier that day. Here, royal grooms milled about holding the horses. Alexander's was a beautiful bay with a silver-studded harness and a gleaming, soft saddle-skin of leopard fur. Hephaestion rode a similar horse with burnished reins, caparisoned with a snow-white soft lamb-skin. A gentle palfrey was provided for Lady Antigone, whom Alexander gallantly helped up. Aristander had what he called a "sorry-looking nag". Telamon was given a vigorous two-year-old which Alexander nicknamed "Thunderbolt". Telamon looked askance. The animal was beautiful, black as night with silver-studded reins of the same colour and a thick red saddle-cloth.

"I'm not a cavalry man."

"He's a good horse." Alexander offered the reins to Telamon. "My gift to you."

Telamon accepted and, helped by a groom, eased himself into the saddle. The animal was surprisingly docile and well trained. It snickered and shook its head. Telamon leaned down and patted its neck.

"That's the way," Alexander agreed. "Never ill-treat a horse."

Hephaestion was summoning up the bodyguard – two cavalry officers from the Companions Brigade, dressed in grey-purplish tunics, white cuirasses and leather kilts of the same colour. Purple bands circled their waists – the regimental colour. Each wore a Boetian helmet and was armed with a sword and a small spear.

"Is that enough protection?" Aristander asked.

Alexander looked over his shoulder. "I want to attract as little notice as possible. They'll do." He mounted and gestured for them to move off.

Hephaestion led the pack pony laden with provisions. He and Alexander were laughing about something which had happened earlier in the morning. The king acted as if he had risen fresh as a bird – no reference was made to his sickness or panic attacks. They left the busy outskirts of the camp. The trackways and adjoining paths were thronged with pack ponies and marching men. Of course, the king was recognized; the men stood aside and either clashed sword against shield or raised spears in salute. Alexander was in a good mood, stopping now and again to talk. When he recognized individuals he called out their names, asking about their family and what they hoped to achieve.

Antigone drew alongside Telamon and pushed back her hood. She looked even more beautiful, the wind catching her reddish hair, eyes sparkling, face bright with excitement.

"It's good to be away from the camp, Telamon. I understand you have been busy. The king needed medicine and you have also found yourself a companion."

"There was nothing wrong with the king which a good sleep wouldn't cure," Telamon replied.

"Look, a good sign!"

Hephaestion pointed to the sky where an eagle circled on the breeze, searching the heath below for prey. Aristander agreed. He tried to deliver a lecture on why eagles brought good luck but no one really listened. Hephaestion was having trouble with the pack pony. Alexander was teasing him.

"If you can't control that, how can you lead a brigade?"

Hephaestion replied with an obscenity. Alexander laughed and turned away, pointing out the different sights.

"Good country!" he called over his shoulder. "At least for hunting. Look at the different types of tree: holm, oak, ash, laurel and fir." He pointed to the copses which dotted the rolling grasslands. "A few more streams and rivers and you'd think you were back in Macedon."

Telamon recalled the plains, the rushing rivers, the marshes and dark rich forests of his homeland. He shook his head.

"The plains of Thrace," he whispered, "will never make me homesick."

Nevertheless, the countryside was pleasant, dotted here and there with the occasional farmstead, though most of the peasants had fled to the town at the approach of Alexander's army. Now and again the trackway was shaded by the lines of fir trees which was a welcome relief from a sun Telamon found difficult to bear. He regretted his haste in leaving the camp and not bringing the flat rounded hat many of his countrymen wore against such glare.

"What made Alexander do this?" he asked Aristander, who sat slumped on his nag beside him, lost in thought.

"His excellency," Aristander sardonically replied, "has always been impetuous." He glanced over his shoulder at the two cavalry men chattering like children behind them. "I just wish he had brought more guards."

"The camp is close by," Telamon replied. "We are in no danger here."

Aristander shook his head. "A king is never safe," he said. "I'm also concerned about my dwarf, Hercules. He's been gone for hours. You saw him this morning, Telamon? When you went to the slave pens to choose that red-haired bitch?"

"Cassandra. My friend and assistant is known as Cassandra."

"And mine is Hercules, who seems to have disappeared," the keeper of secrets snapped. "We all have better things to do than jolt along the road like a gaggle of country bumpkins. My lady," he called across to Antigone, "the guides, they are still anxious?"

"With two dead, their bodies consumed by the funeral pyre, of course they are. They also feel as if they are no longer trusted."

"Ah! You mean the Thessalians who now protect them?"

"Or guard against desertion."

Aristander shrugged. "The same thing," he murmured, gathering the reins. "We are all in this dance together, surrounded by men of war." He urged his horse forward to ride alongside Alexander.

"Why did you come?" Telamon asked Antigone. "Why didn't you just wait for the king to cross the Hellespont?"

"I am a Greek by birth." She smiled. "By upbringing and by education. I am also a distant kinsman of Alexander." Her smile widened. "I knew his father well. No, no," she held a hand up, gesturing daintily, "not like that! Philip often crossed the Hellespont to inspect the troops and establish his bridgehead. I'd met him before: due to his influence I was given the Temple at Troy. Of course, everyone comes to Troy, including Philip. This was, oh, five years ago. He bought me my two Thessalian handmaidens, Aspasia and Selena. Philip came to visit me, worship and talk. Oh, how Philip talked! How he would march to the rim of the world and make it ring with his achievements. He just prayed that a second Homer would recount his exploits."

"Did he ever tell you why?"

"Philip was a boy in a man's body," Antigone replied. "Just as bad as Alexander." She lowered her voice. "He saw himself as the great hero. The new Agamemnon who'd face as many adventures as Odysseus. I used to tease him that he wanted to put as much distance between himself and Olympias as possible. He never took offence." She shook her head and stared out across the heathland. "He was generous to a fault. You've heard the story about Chaeronea?" She didn't wait for an answer. "Philip smashed the combined armies of Greece and got drunk. He began to dance across the battlefield. An Athenian captive, Demades, shouted that Philip was acting like a barbarian, showing ill respect for the dead. Any other king would have taken Demades' head. Philip sobered up. He apologized for his actions, released Demades, loaded him with riches and sent him back as his envoy to Athens."

"You're talking about father again?" Alexander had been listening to their conversation, despite the clatter of the horses and the muttered conversation of his companions. "Did he charm you as well, Antigone?"

"He charmed everyone," she replied. "He used to take me sailing in a fishing boat. He'd catch supper as well as cook it."

140

Alexander shrugged noncholantly and rode back to Hephaestion.

"But Alexander isn't Philip," Telamon whispered. "Why have you come?"

"I brought the guides. I also brought information. Above all, I brought myself, a sign of good luck." She drew closer. "Believe me, Telamon, Alexander is going to need all the good fortune the gods send him."

"The Thessallian maidens who were killed, outside Troy, why did Philip reinstate the practice?" Telamon asked.

"I wanted more companions," Antigone replied. "I told you how I gathered information. Aspasia and Selena question travellers, especially from the Persian court. Philip intended the Thessalians not only to be good companions for myself but to listen and report back."

"Are you a Macedonian spy, my lady?"

"I am priestess of Athena." Her eyes were laughing. "Of course I am a Macedonian spy, and the Persians can't touch me. If anyone wishes to contact Alexander, or the cities of Greece, then they come to Athena's temple at Troy."

"Were you surprised at one of Memnon's generals approaching you?"

"Ah yes, the renegade! He has a Master of Horse, Lysias, who, I think, wished to change sides? He was to meet Alexander at Troy. However, I brought a change of plan. Lysias has been betrayed, probably by the spy close to Alexander."

"Do you suspect who this spy might be?"

"No one does," Antigone replied briskly. "Whoever it is has been active for some time. Philip was plagued by the same traitor. The king cannot decide whether it is one person or two. It could even be a group."

"What of his companions?" Telamon enquired, intrigued at such deep treachery.

"Rumours abound. Some people whisper Aristander. I have even heard the name Olympias."

"Olympias?"

"She hated Philip towards the end. She has deep reservations

141

about her son's campaign. So do others. Look around you, Telamon: the physicians you rub shoulders with, Alexander's drinking companions. You've heard of Parmenio?"

"Alexander's general in Asia, the commander of the bridgehead."

"Do you know how many times he tried to hire scouts? At least five. He failed. On one occasion he mistakenly hired men in the pay of Persia and had to retreat in the face of Memnon's forces." She pulled at the reins. "Oh no, the signs are not good. Not everyone wants Alexander to march to the rim of the world."

Telamon leaned down and patted his horse's neck. The situation was becoming clearer. He recalled Ptolemy's clever face and the frightened eyes of Perdicles. Had he made a mistake this morning? Had Alexander simply been the victim of heavy drinking and poor dreams? Or some subtle poison? Telamon gazed up at the sky. For the first time since he had arrived he quietly wondered whether the world his father had rescued him from was about to close in and trap him for good.

Chapter 7

"Memnon the Rhodian, famed for his military competence, advocated a policy of not fighting pitched battles . . . whilst, at the same time, sending naval and land forces across to Macedonia and transferring the impact of war to Europe."

Diodorus Siculus, *Library of History,*
Book 17. Chapter 18

Droxenius and his four companions were sweat-soaked. They jogged under the sun, carrying their full armour across their shoulders. Now they stopped beneath a fig tree. Droxenius took off his tunic and the rest did the same, relaxing in the shade, turning their wet bodies to catch the cool breeze. Dressed only in their loincloths, sandals on their feet, armour and weapons piled around them, they shared out their coarse bread and rough wine. Droxenius himself broke the bread, dipping it into the small mound of precious salt poured out on a broad leaf. He lifted a piece of bread and saluted his comrades.

"To the death!" he murmured.

"To the death!" they chorused back.

They finished the bread and salt, drained the wineskin and threw it away. Then they gazed up towards the sun and listened intently as their leader intoned a hymn to the all-conquering, ever-victorious Apollo. Droxenius drew his sword and held it up so that the blade flashed in the sun. Then he lowered it and stared round, sad-eyed.

"If any one of you wishes to leave . . ."

"You've had our response," one of them replied, snatching up clumps of grass and drying his skin. "Either victory or death!"

"Very good." Droxenius smiled. "Let us reflect for a few minutes."

He got to his feet and walked to the edge of the shade. The mercenary captain's mind was full of memories and images. Ghosts thronged round him: his sweet-faced wife, his sister and brother, the grizzled features of his grandfather; their house, near the Cadmea in Thebes, with its whitewashed walls, courtyards and blossom-filled orchards – nothing more now than a mass of ash and cinders. He and his companions had taken the most sacred oath by earth and sky, fire and water, to avenge such destruction. Even though he only had revenge to live for, Droxenius found it hard to imagine death on a day such as this. The spring grass of the heathland stretched before him, burnt a dull yellow by the sun, its carpet of hyacinths and crocus a sea of orange and blue petals. The spreading trees, the tamarisk with their vivid buds, the different greeness of the willow and elm, all invoked memories of happier days.

One of his companions came up behind him. "We are most fortunate. How did you know?"

"The tyrant is impetuous," Droxenius replied, not turning round. "It's Alexander's one weakness. He's done it before, galloping off into the unknown with a few companions. Some people say it's a gesture of friendship. Others say he must escape to think. Whatever, now is our chance, our opportunity. We shall never have it again." He gazed up at the sky.

"If we are victorious?" his companion asked.

"We'll make our way down to the coast," Droxenius replied. "Steal a boat or capture a fishing smack and go back to claim our reward. But enough said."

They returned to their companions and armed for battle. They put on their tunics, and over these the corselets of plated bronze. Each helped the other, bringing the two halves of the corselet together, fastening the laces, securing the shoulder clasps, then tying the brace around the middle to hold the armour together. They stepped into their war kilts which fell in a fringe of thongs down to their knees, and fastened on their sword belts. Sandals were secured, padded bronze greaves fastened to protect their legs.

They picked up their round shields, slipping their arms through the thongs, weighing the shields carefully, making sure the straps held. They stood in a circle. Droxenius stretched out his hand and his four companions covered it with theirs.

"It is to be done," Droxenius whispered. "So let's be at it!"

They picked up their great Corinthian helmets with their stiffened plumes, each dyed a different colour. These now transformed their appearance, making them look like gods of war made flesh. The heavy helmets covered their ears and most of their faces were hidden by the broad noseguard which came down to the upper lip. Droxenius turned his shield and stared at the face of the gorgon emblazoned on the front.

"If only," he whispered, "if only that face would turn my enemies to stone!"

He drew his sword. The rest did likewise and, following their leader out of the shade, made their way across the heathland. Using bushes and trees as cover, they slunk like wolves towards Alexander's bodyguard.

Telamon sat beneath the outstretched arms of an oak tree. He stared at the brook bubbling and gurgling a few feet away. They had taken off their sandals, washed their feet and slaked their thirst. Hephaestion had shared out the food. Aristander was sulking, still protesting that he couldn't see the point of it all. Antigone and Telamon nibbled on the last of the cheese, lost in their own thoughts. Alexander and Hephaestion sat, like two boys, heads together. The king was issuing instructions on what had yet to be done. Telamon decided to ignore Aristander and leaned back against the tree.

"Do you hear that?" Alexander called out. "Hephaestion said we've only supplies for another thirty days, then we'll have to start living off the land."

"I've got worse news than that," Telamon said, not even bothering to open his eyes and swatting at an annoying fly. "If we stay much longer, my lord, the camp will become polluted. The cesspits will overflow. In the quickening heat disease will soon spread."

"The sacrifice must be made!" Aristander insisted. "We must be gone!"

Telamon stirred. He had heard a sound from behind the brow of the hill where the royal bodyguard had remained. Was that a scream? A clash of metal? Hephaestion and the rest ignored it but Alexander turned, staring up like a hunting dog, muttering something under his breath. Telamon was sure it was a curse. Aristander caught Telamon's agitation.

"What is it?"

Telamon got up and walked round the oak, staring up the hill. He glimpsed movement; his throat went dry. Five figures appeared on the ridge. For some reason he immediately thought of an extract from Homer's poem: the surprise of the Trojans as Achilles ceased sulking in his tent and advanced towards them. For a while the five figures stood there, sinister and black against the skyline. Hephaestion jumped to his feet.

"Maybe they're a party from the camp?" he declared.

Telamon glanced to where the horses were hobbled, harnesses and saddles removed.

"Don't even think of it," Alexander murmured, wiping the sweat from the palms of his hands on his tunic. "The horses will panic, and we'll have to ride up hill. They'll be more of a hindrance than a help!"

Telamon looked over his shoulder. Antigone hadn't said a word. She just stood, owl-eyed, white-faced, lips moving soundlessly as if muttering a prayer.

"They're not from the camp," Telamon declared. "I don't think they bring fresh wine and bread. The two bodyguards must be dead. They've come to kill us."

The five figures moved, not at a charge but leisurely, carefully. The breeze brought the clink of armour and the chilling, shuffling movement of their sandalled feet through the grass. All five were armed like hoplites. They wore no cloaks and advanced as a group only a few inches apart. The sun glinted on their drawn swords and the shields held up against their chests.

"They're mercenaries," Alexander murmured. "Notice the way they're dressed, the old-fashioned helmets, the way they carry their shields, not too high, not too low, bodies slightly turned, ready to bring their shields together against a slew of arrows."

"This is not a drill ground!" Aristander exclaimed. "We should have brought bows and arrows, more bodyguards."

Alexander smiled, balancing on the balls of his feet.

"We could outrun them," Hephaestion suggested.

"You, I and, perhaps, Telamon, yes," the king said. "But Aristander, Antigone? Anyway, Alexander of Macedon runs from no one."

Telamon was drenched in sweat; his throat was dry. He remembered the blade he had drawn in the wine shop at Thebes, the way he had plunged it so quickly, so effortlessly into that Persian officer. Could he do the same again? Despite his fear, he was fascinated by Alexander's reaction; the king was enjoying himself, relishing the prospect of combat.

"What do we do?" Hephaestion murmured.

The five hoplites were still advancing slowly at a measured pace. Telamon could make out glinting eyes, bearded faces. He caught their stench – sweat and leather – and wondered who had sent them.

"We have to fight." Alexander walked away and drew his ivory-handled sword from its scabbard. He picked up his mantle and wrapped it round his left arm. Hephaestion and Telamon did likewise.

"Aristander," Alexander ordered, "take Antigone across the brook. Make your way along to the horses. If this goes the way it shouldn't, do your best!"

"I can fight," the priestess declared. "I have a dagger."

"Then say your prayers that you don't have to use it on yourself!" Hephaestion joked.

Alexander walked out of the shade of the oak tree to the feet of the hill. "Hephaestion, you take the left! Telamon, the right!" he ordered. "Do exactly as I say. We must stop them before they reach the bottom of the hill. If they stand on the incline they'll feel unsteady."

Alexander walked briskly forward, sword hanging down by his side. Telamon paused to wipe the sweat from his hands. He picked his sword up and followed suit. Alexander chose his position: the oak tree behind him, Telamon on his right, Hephaestion on his left. He stood, one foot forward, swinging the sword backwards and forwards. Telamon looked over his shoulder. Aristander and Antigone were across the brook. The five mercenaries seemed a little disconcerted by Alexander's confidence. The leader stopped. He and his companions found it difficult to gain a secure footing on the steep incline of the hill. They stood in a silent line. Telamon studied each of them. From the way they walked, their battered armour, the way they held their shields up, bodies slightly turned, swords out before them, he recognized veterans who had sold their swords all round the Middle Sea.

"Fellow Greeks! Gentlemen!" Alexander called out. "What business do you have here? Are you from the camp?"

Their leader, his plume dyed a blood red, stepped forward. Telamon could make out a bearded face, glinting eyes; he also glimpsed a scar which jogged his memory – he recalled the soldier lounging near the slave pen earlier that day.

"By what name are you called?" Alexander demanded. "Why are you here?"

"My name is Droxenius," the leader replied. "We are not from your camp but from Thebes."

"Ah!" Alexander gave a deep sigh. "And the blood of your kin is on my hands?"

Droxenius nodded.

"And have you come for yourself, or were you sent?"

"We bring messages from General Memnon."

"Ah, the Rhodian renegade?"

"To the Macedonian murderer!"

"And you are no better," Alexander retorted. "Assassins on a warm spring afternoon."

Droxenius brought his sword up in salute. "We give you fairer warning than you gave our kinsfolk in Thebes."

Behind them Telamon could hear Aristander's wails and protests. He felt as if he was dreaming. The shaded oak, the grassland, birdsong, clear and fluted; the smell of wild flowers and, mixed with it, the stench of war, leather and bronze, blood to be spilt, scraping steel, men grunting and cursing as they struggled for life. Everything his father had tried to protect him from. The cloak round his left arm grew heavy. He turned sideways. Alexander had his head slightly to the left, studying Droxenius as if he recognized him. The mercenary captain now stepped back to join his comrades. Alexander remained motionless. The man on Droxenius' right whispered something. Droxenius turned his head.

"Now!" Alexander shouted, leaping forward.

Telamon, surprised, followed suit. The mercenaries, too, moved, taken off their guard, but then Alexander turned abruptly, tugging at Telamon's cloak. Telamon fled, following Alexander back under the shade of the oak tree, across to the edge of the brook. The mercenaries, taken by surprise, also charged but the steep incline and the force of their run unsteadied them. One missed his footing and slipped, another had his helmet caught in the overhanging branches of the oak tree. Their line broke up.

"Now, Telamon! Now, Hephaestion!" Alexander urged. "Stand and fight!"

The king's face was rigid, slightly pale, eyes gleaming. Telamon had no choice but to obey. Alexander and Hephaestion swept forward with Telamon behind. Their enemy was disorganized. Alexander confronted his opponent, then moved swiftly to the right, bringing his sword down, gashing the exposed flesh between helmet and corselet. Hephaestion crashed into his opponent's shield, sending him reeling back, stumbling to the ground. Hephaestion thrust his sword deep under the kilt, up into the groin, leaving his adversary screaming and squirming. Alexander was leaping forward to take care of the man who had injured his ankle when he had slipped. Hephaestion turned to face Droxenius while Telamon spread his feet and confronted the mercenary whose helmet had been caught in the branches of the oak tree. He'd now freed himself and edged forward, shield up, sword flickering like the tongue of a snake. Telamon desperately tried to recall the skills he had learnt on the drill ground at Mieza. Alexander had turned the odds, but Telamon daren't ask for help. Hephaestion was clashing his sword against Droxenius' shield. Beyond the oak tree, Alexander was involved in the hand-to-hand struggle with the fallen mercenary. Telamon's opponent was a grizzled veteran, his hair, moustache and beard an iron-grey, small black eyes, a swarthy face criss-crossed with scars, mouth slightly open to reveal missing teeth and blackened stumps. The insignia on his shield showed a Cretan bull-dancer. The mercenary moved the shield carefully, a smile on his lips. He was aware of Telamon's nervousness and lack of skill.

"Are you the lady in the group?" he whispered. His accent was harsh.

Telamon didn't reply. He edged forward; his opponent stepped back.

"Come on, pretty lady!" the man hissed.

Telamon loosened the cloak on his arm, a trick taught him by Black Cleitus. The mercenary came charging in. Telamon stepped to one side and threw the cloak at his opponent's face. The man went by, clawing at the cloth. Telamon swung back his sword and struck, eyes half-closed, at the man's head. The sword bit deep, shuddered and slipped from his hand. His opponent turned. Telamon stood helplessly, but one glance showed the mercenary was past help. Blood was pouring out from an ugly, bloody rent from his ear down to his chin. The mercenary swayed, slightly drooping to one side. He coughed. Blood spurted out of his nose and mouth. His sword slipped from his hand. He slumped to his knees and, with a groan, fell sideways to the ground.

Telamon picked up his sword. Alexander was kneeling beside his opponent, wiping his blade on the grass. Droxenius and Hephaestion were still locked together. The mercenary captain had dropped his shield. Hephaestion had lost his sword. They stood like two hideous lovers in a deadly embrace, grunting and gasping as they pushed and shoved. Hephaestion was determined to shake the sword out of his opponent's hand. Alexander walked leisurely across. He came up behind Droxenius, moved to one side and, before the mercenary captain even knew what was happening, thrust his blade deep into the man's side, through the gap where the two pieces of corselet met. Hephaestion shoved him away. Droxenius staggered back and fell to his knees. Alexander, still holding his sword, grasped the horsehair crest and roughly pulled the helmet off. Droxenius was now lost in his own world of pain. Strange sounds came from the back of his throat.

"Droxenius," Alexander murmured as if the man was his friend. The dying man's head came up. Alexander swung his sword which made a silver arc as it scythed the air and decapitated the mercenary clean at the neck. The head bounced along the ground. Blood gushed up from the still erect torso, bubbling like water from a fountain. Alexander kicked the corpse to one side and walked back towards the brook. Telamon fell to his knees and, though he tried, couldn't stop being sick, vomiting up what he had eaten and drunk. He felt cold; his body shook as he stared round at the sprawling corpses, his own opponent staring sightlessly at him. The mercenary whom Hephaestion had struck in the groin lay moaning in a widening pool of blood. Hephaestion went over and knelt by him. Telamon turned away as he heard a blade slice through soft flesh followed by the man's last, blood-filled sigh. The man's helmet still swung from an oak branch. In the long grass sprawled the blood-spotted corpse of Alexander's other victim. Telamon became aware of Hephaestion beside him, of his cloak being draped over his shoulders, a wineskin pushed towards his mouth.

"Go on," Hephaestion murmured. "Drink, Telamon. Trust me." He crouched down. "Even though I am not a physician."

Telamon drank.

"That's enough." Hephaestion took the wineskin away and helped Telamon to his feet.

They walked back to the brook. Aristander and Antigone were seated in front of Alexander, who had washed his hands and was enquiring solicitously if all was well. He winked at Telamon and patted the ground beside him.

"Sit down, sit down! It will pass."

Telamon obeyed. The wineskin was handed round. Hephaestion and Alexander chattered like boys. Antigone was pale-faced, shocked by what she had seen. Aristander was full of protest.

"Why didn't we bring Black Cleitus or more bodyguards?"

Alexander, still full of the joy of battle, wiped the sweat from his arms. "If I go somewhere, must I take half of Macedon with me?" He lifted his face and hands to the sky. "I give you thanks, Father

151

Zeus, for the favours shown to your son. I shall sacrifice and sacrifice again in thanksgiving. I take this as a sign of your good-will." He lowered his hands and bowed his head.

Telamon closed his eyes. Alexander was happy, not only because of his love of battle, of conquest and victory – he had looked for a sign and one had been provided. Telamon opened his eyes and stared at the king who sat, head bowed, lips soundlessly moving. Had Alexander hoped for this? Had he deliberately come out into the open countryside looking for some sign, some mark of divine approval? Aristander was correct, even here in Thrace. Alexander was among his enemies, men who would take his head and earn a vast reward from his many enemies, both at home and abroad.

Telamon shrugged off the cloak. "I feel better now," he said. He felt warm, slightly sleepy, and the nausea had faded.

"Are you wounded?" Alexander asked.

"Just my dignity."

Hephaestion shrugged. "Then it's a question of 'Physician, heal thyself.' "

Telamon got to his feet and walked back across the battleground. The corpses were now stiffening, the pools of blood congealing; black clouds of flies hovered. He wanted to escape, and was halfway up the hill when the king caught up with him.

"Don't take offence at Hephaestion's teasing." Alexander slipped his arm through Telamon's. "You did well, physician. A warrior who killed his first man in battle."

"And I hope the last." Telamon paused. "Why did you come out?"

Alexander's face was now wrinkle-free, smooth – a face from the past. His strange eyes were open and clear. Telamon noted the laughter lines round the mouth, the tousled red-gold hair, that sweet body perfume Alexander always exuded, whatever his exertions.

"You were looking for a sign, weren't you? You must have known assassins in the camp watch your every movement?"

"My life is in the hands of the gods, Telamon. I have a destiny to fulfil." Alexander's voice was matter-of-fact but steel-hard. "If all the hordes of Persia had marched down to that brook, I would have

152

still escaped unscathed. You dreamed right, physician, my fortunes *have* changed." He squeezed Telamon's arm. "You brought me good luck. You have every right to wear a silver crown. You fought beside your king and gained *aristeia*." He saw the puzzlement in Telamon's eyes. "Courage in battle. Now, while Hephaestion collects the horses, let's see what happened to the poor bastards who were supposed to be my bodyguard."

The two cavalry men lay sprawled in the grass just over the brow of the hill. A pool of blood was already congealing, a feasting ground for flies. One man hadn't even had time to draw his sword – he had been killed instantly by a blow to the neck. The second lay a few yards away, sprawled on his back, eyes gazing sightlessly up at the sky, one hand near a terrible rent in his throat.

Telamon pointed down the hill to the long waving grass. "They must have been sleeping, poor bastards! Droxenius and the rest crawled up like cats. It never pays to be a soldier and sleep in open country."

Alexander took the sashes off both men – the insignia of their regiment.

"They don't deserve these. Men who guard me shouldn't sleep!"

"Does that include me, Alexander?"

The king started walking down the hill, indicating Telamon to follow.

"Telamon, the spy in my court buzzes like some angry, invisible bee which stings then flies away. Well, whoever it is, they've stung enough and stung too deeply. If Aristander can't catch them, you must!" Alexander grasped Telamon's hand, squeezing his fingers tightly. "I can hire more guides, but we've already lost the best."

"Do you think the spy arranged this?"

Alexander pulled a face and stared down towards the road. "Perhaps. My life rests in the hands of the gods, but I remember the proverb, 'The gods help those who help themselves.' Fortune can be a capricious bitch!"

"The dead?" Hephaestion called out as he and the rest clustered on the brow of the hill.

"Leave them!" Alexander shouted. "We'll go back to the camp and send out scouts."

"Shall we gibbet the mercenaries?" Aristander shouted.

"No. They were warriors. Take their arms, set them up as a trophy before the altar outside my tent. Now, I'm thirsty and, I'm sure, Ptolemy is waiting with good news."

The royal pavilion blazed with the light of oil lamps set along the tables as well as those which hung on silver chains from the poles across the roof of the tent. The air was hot, sweet with perfume. Telamon wondered how long this celebration would last. Around the tent Alexander and his personal companions sprawled. They feasted and toasted each other with wine which contained very little water. The king had changed into a gown of purple edged with gold, a silver wreath upon his head. He insisted that Hephaestion and Telamon wear the same. Outside the tent, as he had come in, Telamon had glimpsed the trophies – the pile of armour taken from the mercenaries surmounted by the helmet of Droxenius. Their former wearers were now nothing but ash, burnt on the great funeral pyre Alexander had set up along the seashore.

Antigone offered Telamon a bowl of fruit. "The king is in good humour."

"He has good cause to be," Telamon replied. "He sees his deliverance as a smile from Zeus."

"And, of course, Ptolemy's find?"

"Ah yes," Telamon agreed.

Ptolemy had found a pure white bull. This had been taken out to the place of sacrifice overlooking the sea. The king had gathered his bodyguards around him. The fires had been lit, incense burnt, libations made, but Alexander left nothing to chance. Before the sacrifice began he ordered Aristander to scrawl on his right arm, and keep it hidden, a phrase from the *Iliad*: "*The Gods find favour with thee*".

The bull had been led out, its throat cut. Aristander had found the auspices to be most favourable. He'd wept with joy as he wiped the blood from his arm and showed the priests, as well as those around them, the mysterious message scrawled along his arm.

Alexander had been hailed with a paean of praise and the clash of arms. The king had mounted his black warhorse. He'd addressed his troops in short, fiery, passionate sentences which were relayed by heralds carrying their white wands of office.

"The gods have signified their approval!" he shouted, his words carried by the breeze. "The glory of Olympus is around us! The path to Asia lies open. We shall all ride like kings through Persepolis!"

His words were greeted by the fierce Macedonian war cry, "Eynalius! Eynalius! Eynalius!" and the clash of arms.

On his return to the royal enclosure, Alexander had been beside himself, and his jubilant mood affected the whole camp. The army secretariat, headed by Eumenes, was already busy with muster rolls, carefully scrutinizing all new arrivals. The marshals received fresh orders to clear the vagabonds and beggars, the whores and other itinerants from the camp. Men were organized back into their own units. The camp perimeter was reinforced. The long-awaited proclamations had been issued: within two days the army would embark; the fleet was ready. Within the week they would be in Asia.

Telamon gazed round the tent. Alexander had proclaimed this was the last night they would feast and celebrate. The king staggered to his feet, the loving cup grasped in both hands. He stared round at his companions: Ptolemy, Hephaestion, Seleucus, Amyntas, Cleitus and the new addition, his father's favourite general – the grizzled-haired, scarred-faced Parmenio. He had established the bridgehead in Asia and was responsible for mustering the fleet which would transport the army across the Hellespont.

"You have eaten and drunk well!" Alexander shouted. "My cooks have filled your bellies with the richest of foods!"

Shouts of approval greeted this. The royal kitchens had been both busy and generous: fresh plaice cooked in vinegar, olive oil and capers; shellfish; wild pig highly flavoured with herbs; fruits, nuts and pastries coated with thick honey. The wine had flowed like water. It had affected everyone; gleaming eyes in flushed faces gazed back at Alexander.

"I've filled your bellies!" the king shouted again. "But I promise you, I'll fill your hearts with glory and your purses with Persian gold!"

Again roars of acclamation. Telamon looked to his left. Antigone was staring at Alexander, eyes glittering, lips wet, mouth half open. She, too, had drunk deeply, exchanging many a toast with the king, greatly honoured at the respect Alexander had shown her. It was very rare for a woman to attend such feasts.

"We will fight, and we shall win!" Ptolemy shouted.

"Where is Aristander?" Antigone asked.

Telamon shook his head. The soothsayer had returned to the camp furious. He had put on a brave show for the sacrifice. Afterwards he had retreated to his tent to sulk and worry over the non-appearance of his dwarf.

"What was that? Who's missing?" Alexander held his hand up to silence Ptolemy's shouting. He stared around, swaying on his feet. Telamon wondered if he was truly drunk or just pretending.

"Is our keeper of the king's secrets still angry with me?" Alexander slurred. "Because he nearly felt cold steel? Go and get him, Telamon." He put the wine cup down and clapped his hands. One of the bodyguards stepped out of the shadows from behind the couch. Alexander took his shield and sword, clashing the blade against the rim. He began a shuffling dance and the others followed suit, leaping to their feet, taking shields and swords from the guards. They joined Alexander in his war dance. They climbed over couches, moving to the centre of the room, standing in a ring, beating sword against shield. They moved in and out, shouting the Macedonian battle cry.

"Just like Philip," Antigone whispered. "Steel and blood, the prospect of glory." She nodded at the dancers, now creating their own ominous music.

Telamon, glad of an excuse to leave, nodded to Antigone and slipped down the side of the tent and out into the cold night air. For a while he stood, allowing the breeze to cool his face and neck. In the far distance the bells of the guards tinkled as each was handed from one guard to another – a system set up by Alexander to ensure that the perimeter was sealed and no guard slept.

Telamon made his way to Aristander's tent. Its entrance was

guarded by members of the chorus who greeted Telamon like a long-lost brother, though they were reluctant to let him through.

"On the king's orders!" Telamon snapped.

"Oh, let the boy through!" Aristander's voice cooed.

The tent flap was lifted. Telamon stepped inside and stopped in surprise. Aristander was by himself, lying on a couch surrounded by small oil lamps. The soothsayer was almost unrecognizable: his face was heavily painted and rouged with rings of black eye kohl; his lips were carmine red, his fingernails a deep purple. He was garbed in a woman's black and gold tunic with a white mantle over his shoulder. He lay propped up on the side of the couch, one hand elegantly holding a silver-chased goblet, the other hovering over a dish of ripe plums.

"Come in, boy!" Aristander whispered.

Telamon sat down on the proffered stool. If he hadn't been so surprised he would have burst out laughing, but the hard look in Aristander's cruel eyes kept his face impassive.

"A man has to relax at the end of the day," Aristander lisped. "And what better than to relax as a woman? I was so frightened, Telamon. Those horrible men and their hideous swords. Why didn't Alexander bring a larger bodyguard? And why didn't he let me take my lovely lads? The chorus would have made short work of them! Would you like some wine? You can watch one of their performances. They're very good with Aristophanes' *The Birds*."

"Aristander . . ."

"No, call me Narcissa!"

"Aristander," Telamon continued, ignoring the look of annoyance he received, "the king wants your presence in his tent. He knows you are sulking."

"Well, he will have to wait, won't he? I'm still upset. I'm very worried about Hercules. He's always here at dusk. I have no one to serve me." Aristander lurched forward. "You do like me, Telamon?"

"Why does the king trust you?"

Aristander waggled a finger. "That's what I like about you, physician, you are so blunt and honest. By a horse's tits, what you see in Telamon is what you get! To answer your question, boy: the king trusts me because . . ." he waved a hand airily, ". . . because he trusts me. I know secrets. I discover his enemies. I destroy them."

"You're not doing a very good job with Naihpat."

"No, I am not. It's like trying to catch a mist."

"How long has Naihpat existed?"

"About four years, perhaps five."

"And you have no clue?"

"None whatsoever."

"Why is the spy so dangerous?" Telamon asked.

"The Persians know secrets," Aristander replied. "They soon discovered Philip's plans about Asia. Parmenio found it hard, almost impossible, to establish a bridgehead. He didn't fare too well against Memnon, who drove him back."

"So it must be someone close to the Macedonian court?"

"Clever boy!"

"And there have been murders before?"

Aristander's lower lip trembled. "Some people believe so, yes," he lisped. "That's right. Some people believe that Philip was murdered at Naihpat's instruction and that of Mithra, his master."

"But that was the madman Pausanias, one of Philip's former lovers, abused and buggered by some of Philip's friends."

"He was an ideal choice," Aristander retorted, smiling slyly. "It's easy to turn a madman's wits, sharpen his desire for vengeance."

"So it wasn't Olympias?"

"I didn't say that," Aristander snapped. "There are as many theories about Philip's death as there are hairs on a bear. Believe me, Telamon," Aristander removed the blond wig and threw it to the floor, "I have searched for Naihpat. Here and there like a dog snouting round a farmyard. I used to suspect Naihpat was in the pay of the Athenians, but I've bought Athens – I haven't discovered anything there. No, he's Persian, body and soul. His job is to keep Macedon from crossing the Hellespont. That's why those mercenaries were sent today. Why the guides have been murdered. And poor Hercules . . ." Aristander's voice quavered.

"Did your dwarf discover something?"

"Perhaps. Hercules slid like a shadow round this camp. Very

interested in your physician friends he was." Aristander lowered his head and smiled. "Particularly Perdicles and his relationship with General Ptolemy. Do you know anything about that?"

Telamon gazed coolly back.

Aristander leaned forward. "You have doubts, don't you? About those mercenaries, the ones who tried to kill us today?"

"I have been thinking." Telamon gazed round the tent. He wondered what Cassandra was doing. He had hardly had a chance to talk to her since his return. He had found his quarters clean and tidy, and Cassandra had even claimed she had found fresh herbs which would be useful.

"And what has my good physician been thinking?"

"That the guides were killed by Naihpat. Apollo forbid, even your dwarf Hercules, if he got too close! But the mercenaries? I'm not too sure."

Aristander swung his feet off the couch and sat up. He began to strip the necklaces and bracelets from round his neck and wrists.

"I am intrigued, Telamon."

"The Persians wish Alexander to cross into Asia," Telamon continued. "That's obvious – the king himself has told me that. If Darius wished, he could whistle up a fleet of warships, or worse land an army in Thrace. He *wants* Alexander to come to Asia to be defeated, to be captured, disgraced and killed. If Naihpat is his spy, he will be following Darius' orders: confuse Alexander, frighten him, blind his army, but let him come on."

Aristander got to his feet. He took off the woman's dress, exposing his scraggy body, which he quickly hid beneath a dark-green tunic with a gold cord round the middle.

"I see what you are saying, Telamon. Very good! This afternoon those bastards said they had been sent by Memnon; they probably were. Which means – and Alexander would be interested in this – there's tension between Memnon and his Persian masters. When Darius hears of what happened he will be furious. The gap between Memnon and Darius will grow. You know the Persians, Telamon, they don't like Greeks." Aristander sat back on the couch, tapping his fingers against his mouth. "Can I be the one who tells Alexander this?"

159

"Be my guest," Telamon said. "It's your conclusion."

"Memnon has estates not far from Troy." Aristander clicked his tongue, a gesture he'd copied from Olympias. "I'll tell Alexander those estates must not be touched. Let's see if we can deepen the divide between Memnon and his masters even further. Come here, my lovely lads!" he bawled.

The chorus trooped in. Aristander demanded water and a towel to wash his hands and face.

He smiled as he washed his hands. "Oh, by the way, Telamon, don't tell anyone what you've told me tonight, especially not Ptolemy. He likes nothing better than to . . ." Aristander paused at the sound of voices outside the tent. Cassandra pushed her way in, red hair all tangled, her broad face heavy with sleep.

"They said I'd find you here," she gasped.

"What is it, girl?" Aristander demanded.

"Critias the map-maker: he's been found murdered in his tent!"

Chapter 8

"Alexander was eager for action and opposed to any delay."

Diodorus Siculus, *Library of History*,
Book 17, Chapter 16

"The killer left a message," Alexander declared quietly. "The usual threat: 'The bull is prepared for sacrifice. All is ready, the slayer awaits.'" He waved the piece of parchment between his fingers.

"Where was that left?" Telamon asked.

"On the floor beside him."

Telamon crouched down: the blood from Critias' side had congealed on the ground. The knife was thrust in almost to the hilt. Telamon eased it out with a sickening plop and examined it carefully. Just like the other: a bronze blade with a hardened wire handle, shaped in the form of a wing on either side.

"I have already made enquiries," Aristander declared. "Those daggers can be bought in any market-place. The Celts fashion them in their smithies and export them south."

Telamon weighed the dagger in his hand: light, easy to carry with a wicked point and sharp, serrated edges, it would slip easily into a man's flesh, cutting off his life flow. He put the weapon down and, on hands and knees, crawled round the chair and table.

"What are you doing?" Alexander taunted. "Sniffing for a scent?"

"This is how the corpse was found?" Telamon got to his feet.

"As you see it," Alexander replied. "The guard became suspicious. He heard no noise and wondered if all was well. Critias

161

usually went for a walk or sent for some wine. A garrulous man, he liked to talk. When the soldier lifted the tent flap that's all he saw; the oil lamp still burning and Critias slumped over the table. The pool of blood, glinting in the light, attracted his attention."

"Call him in!" Telamon demanded.

Aristander brought the sentry in: a burly Macedonian plough boy with a shock of black hair; unshaven, eyes red-rimmed with tiredness.

"Come on, sit down beside me," Alexander invited. "You are in no trouble. You farmed land outside Pella, didn't you?"

"No, my lord, further south."

"Ah yes, yes."

For a while Alexander chatted about crops, the richness of the soil, the difficulty in clearing trees so the land could be ploughed. Then the king gestured to the corpse.

"Did you often talk to him about Macedon?"

"My lord, we talked about everything. Sometimes Critias would invite me in, other times he'd come out."

Two of the oil lamps flickered out. Aristander went and brought replacements.

"And tonight?" Telamon asked.

The guard heritated.

"Answer his question," Alexander insisted gently.

"I felt bored. The night wore on. I lifted the flap. Critias was asleep at the table, head on his arms."

"So, he was asleep?"

"Oh yes, this was between the first and second watch. Critias often did that, then he'd wake up. As we went into the third watch, I lifted the tent flap again. I saw the blood and raised the alarm. Those physicians were not far away, drinking wine around a fire, chattering like a group of crows. One of them went to rouse you, sir." He pointed at Telamon. "But the red-haired woman said you were at the feast."

"I can vouch for that," Alexander declared with a lopsided grin. "I was the only sober one there."

"Did anyone leave the feast?" Telamon asked.

Alexander shook his head. "Some of them couldn't even hold a cup, never mind a dagger." He grasped the guard by his shoulders and squeezed tightly. "You look sleepy-eyed. Could someone have slipped by you?"

The soldier would have jumped to his feet but Alexander kept him seated.

"Don't lie man!"

"I never lie, to you. I'd take an oath on my mother's soul. My lord, I sit, but I cradle my lance across my lap so it stretches across the tent flap. No one came through that entrance. Even if I had dozed off – and I didn't – an intruder would have tripped over my lance. Anyway, the tent flap was tied down. Critias did that against the night breeze. Whenever I opened it I had to unloosen the knots."

Alexander gave the man a coin, patted him on the head as he would a dog and dismissed him. Telamon got to his feet and stared down at the chair.

"What intrigues you so much about that?" Aristander queried.

"The corpse hasn't been moved, has it?" Alexander asked. He joined Telamon. "That's what puzzles you?"

Telamon said nothing. He pulled the corpse from the chair and laid it gently on the ground. He then moved the chair.

"Look at the indentations. They're firm and quite deep. Critias must have been sitting here for hours; this is where he was killed. What intrigues me is not only how the assassin entered but that death must have been instantaneous."

"Critias was asleep?" Alexander queried.

Telamon pointed to the empty goblet. "In a wine-soaked dream," he murmured, "a man's sleep becomes deep. My lord, if I may?"

Alexander gave him a guarded look but nodded. Telamon guided him to the chair and sat him down.

"I suspect the assassin came behind Critias, who was fast asleep." Telamon, using his fingers, pressed Alexander's throat. "His throat was cut and the dagger thrust deep into his side."

"Wouldn't Critias start, scream awake?" Aristander queried.

"The assassin simply lifted Critias' head, put his fingers across the mouth and cut the throat from ear to ear. He placed the head

163

gently down, thrust the dagger into the corpse and left the warning on the ground beside him."

Alexander agreed. "I have done the same against enemy sentries, and they have been awake. Critias died without even realizing it."

Telamon turned to the table. It was littered with scraps of parchment: inked drawings now obscured by the encrusted blood.

"Where are his maps?"

Alexander walked across to a small coffer, light-brown and made of Lebanese cedar. He undid the clasp, pushed back the lid and cursed.

"Ash!" he exclaimed.

"Impossible!" Aristander cried.

"There were at least seven maps here," Alexander declared. "Critias was going to hand them over once we had crossed the Hellespont."

Telamon grasped the casket. Grey-white ash fluttered like feathers to the floor.

"They were here tonight," Alexander declared. "I visited Critias. He showed me them. I was asking about the route south from Troy. He described in detail what fords exist."

Telamon peered at the inside of the coffer which was slightly stained by the ash but not singed or burnt.

"What is this?" Aristander whispered. He snatched the casket from Telamon. "We have a casket containing maps and scrolls, wrapped up and tied in ribbon. Their author is stabbed and the maps are turned to ash without the wood being burnt." He waved the box in his hand. "My lord, I am a soothsayer. No account of this must be published." His voice dropped to a whisper. "The men would talk about fire from heaven, the anger of the gods. All the good of our sacrifice would be undone!"

"It's impossible!" Alexander seized the coffer, searching with his fingers before giving it to Telamon: the wood felt cold and smooth.

Alexander paced up and down, beating his fist against the palm of his hand. "Telamon, you are supposed to have the eyes of a hawk! Aristander, you are keeper of the king's secrets. Yet I am attacked out in the open countryside, my map-maker is murdered and all his work is reduced to feathery ash!"

Telamon did not answer, but carefully inspected every panel of the tent. All the leather sheets were pulled taut and fastened expertly into the holes. None of the lashings were loose or looked as if they had been interfered with. Telamon excused himself and went outside. A crowd had gathered. He recognized Ptolemy who looked remarkably sober. Antigone stood shrouded in a cloak next to a worried-looking Perdicles. Telamon fended off their questions. He walked around the outside of the tent but could detect nothing untoward. The guy ropes were undisturbed, attached to wooden pegs driven deep into the ground. He tugged at the panels but they were too tight for anyone to raise and creep under. He re-entered the tent. Alexander was still fascinated by the coffer. Aristander stood with hands hanging by his side. His woebegone expression showed Alexander had made some cutting remark. Telamon studied the tent again: the corpse sprawled on the ground, ghastly in the light of the flickering lamps; the pool of blood on the table; the winged Celtic dagger; the mound of feathery ash; and the crumpled parchment which had carried the warning.

"What's the noise outside?" Alexander demanded.

The tent flap lifted and Ptolemy led Antigone and Perdicles into the tent.

"What's the matter?"

Ptolemy gazed around, taking in the scene. "Another corpse, eh?"

Alexander's expression wiped the sneering smile off Ptolemy's face. Antigone crouched beside Critias. She cupped his face gently in her hands and murmured a prayer.

"Don't ask," Alexander murmured, "for I don't know. I cannot say what has happened here!"

Antigone stared at the ash on the ground, a worried expression in her eyes.

"My lord," she whispered, "Critias' death is a blow."

"It is to be kept silent," Alexander ordered. "That includes you, Perdicles. Anyway, what do you want? Why are you here?"

"Cleon's gone."

"What!"

165

Telamon walked over. "Cleon?" He recalled the bland, fat face, the tousled blond hair.

"He's taken his baggage with him," Perdicles confessed. "His medicines and his manuscripts. All packed and gone!"

"Since when?" Alexander demanded.

"Since early this evening. He was seen down near the horse lines." Perdicles shrugged. "He hasn't come back!"

"Gone!" Alexander exclaimed. "Without my say!"

"He was a free man," Ptolemy drawled. "He had his own horse. Like any of us, he could come and go as he wished."

"Not from this camp!" Alexander seized Ptolemy's shoulder and swung the general round. "You are not as drunk as you appear to be, my friend!"

Telamon decided to intervene before a quarrel broke out. "My lord, if I could have a word?"

Alexander cleared the tent, including Aristander, who threw dagger glances at Telamon.

"What is it?" Alexander snapped.

"You have everybody and anybody in this army," Talamon declared. "You hired physicians for your own use and those of your entourage."

Alexander nodded briskly.

"I know why you summoned me, but the rest?"

"Leeches and apothecaries!" Alexander shrugged. "Well, you can hire them by the cart-load. Good physicians are rare. You might not like your colleagues, Telamon, but you share a lot in common. You are all skilled. You are all landless and, above all, you have nothing to lose by coming with me. Mother prepared a list, your name headed it. The same goes for the rest. You all have little secrets which Mother got to know." He laughed sharply. "You have all done business with Macedon and you are all rather unpopular in other places." Distracted by the dagger, Alexander picked it up from the table, shaking off drops of blood. "You also share one great flaw." He stared at Telamon from under his brows. "Physicians, like philosophers, are well-known for travelling. All of you have been across the Hellespont. You have done business with both Greeks and Persians. You could all be in the pay of the enemy.

166

Leontes certainly was. Now it looks as if fat, fluffy Cleon had a foot in either camp."

"But why did he leave now?" Telamon was suspicious of Alexander's careless attitude.

"What do you mean?"

Outside the babble of voices rose. Aristander's high, squeaky tones were quite distinct.

"Why should Cleon leave now?" Telamon insisted. "Could he be the spy Naihpat?"

Alexander screwed up his eyes. "It's possible. He, like the rest, served with my father. He had been hired as an army physician. He'd know a few of our secrets. I am never too sure if Naihpat is substantial or a shadow but, true, Cleon could have poisoned that girl and killed those guides."

"If I understand correctly," Telamon said, "Cleon fled before the sacrifice, so he doesn't know we are about to cross the Hellespont; nor can he be implicated in Critias' murder. Perhaps Cleon just became tired or bored or . . . ?"

Alexander leaned forward. "Or what?"

"Apparently he left camp after we returned. Perhaps Cleon was Naihpat or Naihpat's messenger? He scurried away to tell his masters how the assassination attempt failed. That would be of interest, a matter of urgency, to them."

Alexander got up and put an arm round Telamon's shoulder. The physician smelt the wine on his breath.

"You won't leave me, will you, Telamon?"

"As you've said, I have nowhere to go."

"Aristander is out of his depth here." Alexander took his arm away. "He's used to scurrying around palace corridors. Very good at spying on others but not so skilled at catching those who spy on us. That's your job, Telamon." Alexander pointed at the corpse. "I want this Naihpat trapped." He drew a deep breath. "This has gone on long enough. Critias' body can be burnt. Tomorrow the whole army will drill. Lazy bastards, I'll give the likes of Ptolemy something to think about!" And, punching Telamon gently on the arm, Alexander left.

Aristander came bustling in. Telamon scrutinized the tent once more and, ignoring the keeper of secrets' bitter litany of moans, slipped out into the night, where he stood staring up at the stars.

"Something's very wrong," he whispered. "How could Cleon leave like that?" He rubbed his eyes as if he could wipe away the tiredness. And Alexander? Was there something false about his anger at Cleon's sudden departure?

On the breeze came the ringing of the sentries' bells followed by the blast of a trumpet marking the passing of the watches in the night. Telamon walked to the edge of the royal enclosure and glimpsed pinpricks of torchlight as officers made their rounds. The guard, resting on his spear, told him how the soldiers were being prepared for the drill the following morning, repeating Alexander's sentiment – that it was time for all those lazy bastards to show their worth!

Telamon walked on. He watched a group of officers from the shield-bearer's regiment carry away Critias' corpse covered by a blanket. He made his way back to his own tent. Cassandra had brought in a small cot bed. She was sleeping in the far corner. Telamon was amused at the way she had moved his bed to the opposite corner. He took off his sandals and tunic and, using some of the precious salt, cleaned his teeth. He washed his hands and face in the water bowl and sat on the edge of the bed drying himself carefully, thinking about what he had seen and heard.

"How goes the mighty physician?" Cassandra's voice was muffled. "Another murder? Will you tell me what is going on?"

"I will tell you what is going on," Telamon replied, lying down on his bed and pulling up the coarse blanket, "when I know myself. Tell me, is Cassandra your real name?"

"Is Telamon yours?"

The physician didn't answer. His mind, full of images of hoplites, swords and raised shields, slipped into an uneasy sleep.

He was roused before dawn by the roar of trumpets and the shouts of officers. Men were being roughly awakened and called to arms to assemble around their officers and standards.

"What's happening?" Cassandra called out sleepily. "It's so lovely to sleep in a bed again. You can come over here if you want!"

"You don't really mean that," Telamon murmured. "Our Captain-General is about to parade his forces. Nothing like manoeuvres to keep the men happy. There'll be knocks, sprains and bruises to tend afterwards. I suggest you go back to sleep."

Telamon stared at the rim of light round the flap of the tent and thought once again about the events of yesterday: the bloody struggle down near the brook; Alexander, resplendent in his purple cloak, white cuirass, gold-fringed war kilt and silver greaves, hands extended, beseeching the intercession of Zeus; the drunken banquet which had followed; Critias sprawled in his own blood, the gaping wound in his neck like a second mouth. Telamon tried to drift into sleep but the bustle from the camp grew louder. A group of royal pages decided to play a ball game where two sides fought for the prize just outside the tent. Telamon groaned. He threw back the blanket, got up and staggered to the tent mouth. The guard on duty agreed to bring him some water and, if he could find any, watered beer and food. The sun had risen but it was almost hidden by the clouds of dust raised by the marching men, which billowed about on the morning breeze. The soldier thanked the gods that he was on sentry duty and was only too happy, as he said, "To fetch and carry". Telamon, using a polished piece of metal, carefully shaved his face, clipped his beard, then washed. He found a clean tunic and put it on, fastening the leather belt round his waist.

"Cassandra, I'll wait for you at the tent mouth!"

Telamon went and sat there, watching the pages in their white tunics run backwards and forwards. Behind him, Cassandra rose and prepared herself. She came and stood beside him, a hand resting lightly on his shoulder.

"I'm ravenous, Telamon. I am so hungry I could eat one of those pages!"

The guard came back with two bowls of oatmeal flavoured with milk and honey. From beneath his cloak he brought out two small bread rolls and a piece of cheese wrapped in a not too clean piece of linen. "I stole these from one of the royal cooks. It's the best I could find." He roared at the pages to piss off and, when they wouldn't, Telamon shouted across that they fetch a jug of beer. At last one of

169

them insolently agreed. He sauntered back and placed it at Telamon's feet. More trumpet calls. The pages hurried off. Telamon and Cassandra withdrew deep into the tent where he informed her sharply and succinctly about the murders. She listened carefully.

"There's always blood." She shrugged. "Wherever Alexander goes, bloody, sudden death follows. The solution, however, to all this is simple. The assassin wishes to frighten our great conqueror and blind his army when it lands on the Hellespont. You should thank the gods; you were lucky to escape yesterday."

"I think I met Droxenius, their captain," Telamon replied. "He was near the slave pen when I first met you." He described the mercenary, and Cassandra agreed.

"Poor bastard!" she said, wiping the bowl clean with her finger. "He was probably searching for any survivors from his family. I remember him: a scar across his face. I couldn't decide whether he looked fierce or sad. Well, now he's gone." Cassandra sighed. "As we'll all be, soon."

Telamon offered the beer jug to her. Cassandra took a generous swig. "You've got sharp eyes and quick wits."

"How do you think these people were murdered?" Telamon asked.

Cassandra pulled a face. "The first guide, perhaps he was just taking the sea air. The second one was drunk."

"And Hercules?"

"Oh, Aristander's dwarf? I heard about him, creeping like a snake from one tent to another. Perhaps he saw something he shouldn't. It's easy to hide a corpse in the sea or in the woods and marshes around here." She smacked her lips. "Critias' murder is different, a real mystery. A man sitting on his chair, the only entrance guarded, his throat cut, a knife thrust into his ribs, his maps burnt but the casket which contained them unscorched. No wonder the Macedonian is angry. Soldiers are worse than sailors when it comes to superstition. I never met one I have tended who hasn't worn an amulet or a charm." She raised her head at a long shrill trumpet blast. "But these matters don't concern us, master. Or should I say, Telamon?" She grinned. "Alexander is sur-

170

rounded by traitors. I would wager a gold daric to a jug of wine that the Persians have more spies in this camp than hairs on my head. Apparently your colleague, Cleon, was one of them." She got up and went and stood at the mouth of the tent. "Have you ever fought, Telamon?"

"Never in a battle."

"I saw fighting once," she said. "When Alexander attacked Thebes. The Sacred Band made its last stand outside the Electra Gate. I disobeyed the priest's order and went on the top of the wall. I have never seen anything so fierce. Row after row of armed men and those terrible pikes . . ."

"Sarissas," Telamon corrected her. "They are at least eighteen feet long."

Cassandra came over and knelt beside him. "What is it about Alexander's army? What makes them so victorious?"

Telamon fetched the shield the quartermaster had given him – a round circle of bronze with a leather lining and straps. Its shining surface was emblazoned with a charging bull.

"Very fearsome!" Cassandra teased.

"The Greek army," Telamon explained, thrusting his arm through the shield straps, "always fight with the shield on their left and the spear in the right hand." He tapped his chest. "They usually wear a corselet or cuirass front and back, a leather fringed kilt to protect the groin and marching boots with soft leather linings, held in place by straps over the sole and heel. The cavalry wear these or heavy sandals. Sometimes the infantry fight bare-footed. They have a sword strapped under their left arm, usually a dagger on their right. On their heads they wear the large hoplite helmet with its broad ear- and noseguards and its horsehair plumes, though these are becoming old fashioned."

"They wear different ones now."

"Yes, the Boetian helmet, really a leather or bronze cap, open at the front, with a ridge to protect the cheeks as well as the nape of the neck."

"Or the cock-crested one, the Phrygian? But what makes *Alexander's* army so different?"

"In the past the hoplites used to advance," Telamon explained.

171

"Both armies would meet, and push and shove. Now, if you were carrying this shield, Cassandra, which way would you move?"

"To the right."

"Why?"

"Because my left side is guarded by the shield so I'll naturally seek the protection of the shield wearer to my right."

"Good!" Telamon took the shield off. "Philip of Macedon and Alexander changed all this with three basic ingredients: surprise, shock and the sarissa. Philip used to lecture us when he came to the groves of Mieza. 'What's the use of wearing a heavy helmet?' he'd bawl. 'If you can't see or hear anything it's not much protection. The same goes for shields and breastplates against a long pike which is why Philip introduced the sarissa. Now." Telamon got to his feet and pulled Cassandra to hers. "You are a Macedonian soldier. You are carrying a small shield on your left wrist but also grasp an eighteen-foot pike, fashioned out of cornelian wood or elm, weighted with a heavy butt. How many hands are you going to need?"

"Two! Now, the front line I understand. But where do I rest such a long spear if I'm in the second?"

"On the shoulder of the man in front."

"Ah, I am beginning to see. If thousands of men marching with these pikes lower them . . . ?"

"Precisely," Telamon agreed. "You engage the enemy long before he can close with you. It's like walking straight into a huge porcupine or hedgehog. What's the use of your petty lance, then? Your bronze shield or helmet?" Telamon recalled his own excitement when Cleitus used to drill them. "Can you imagine, Cassandra, thousands of sarissas coming straight for you, held by trained men marching swiftly? What would you do?"

"Break and run."

"That's what Macedon's enemies do. Yet, there's more to it than that. Philip realized the value of cavalry. He used infantry and cavalry together to hit the enemy, cause confusion and create an opening for his phalanxes of pikemen to sweep in."

"What's all this business about moving to the right, then?" She cocked her head sideways. "Do you know, Telamon, it's the first time I've seen you excited. You're really a soldier, aren't you?"

172

Telamon shook his head. "No, I am not. I just admire the awful beauty, the breathtaking terror as well as the bravery, courage and passion of the fighting man. Come, I'll show you about moving to the right."

They grabbed their mantles and left the tent. The dust was now settling. The sun was higher and the cool dawn breeze had dropped. They took directions from a guard and made their way through the almost deserted camp. The only people who remained were marshals, slaves, servants, the occasional sick or injured soldier and the scribes from the different secretariats. In the far distance clouds of dust rose, muffling the shrill of trumpets and the roar of men preparing for battle. They left the camp, skirting the place of sacrifice, and joined the rest of the spectators on the brow of a low hill which overlooked the windswept plain Alexander had chosen for the manoeuvres. Even Telamon caught his breath as he gazed at the magnificent sight below: the entire Macedonian army in full battle array, its long line stretched a few yards from the cliff edge into the far distance. The army now stood silent. Each unit had found its place. Telamon pointed out Alexander on Bucephalus, resplendent in his purple cloak and grey-purple cuirass, a magnificent war helmet on his head, galloping up and down the battle line. He raised his sword and the entire line clashed arms and a blood-chilling war cry echoed liked thunder, an awesome paean to the Macedonian god of battles.

"Eynalius! Eynalius! Eynalius!"

Once he had completed his ride, escorted by his personal companions, Alexander slowly made his way back. The dust was now settling.

"Right!" Telamon grasped Cassandra's shoulder. "The heart of the Macedonian army are the Companions, regiments of infantry and cavalry."

"I see those," Cassandra said. "They're the ones with the purple cloaks, sashes of similar colour round their waists."

"These are Macedonians," Telamon explained. "They wear plain, bronze Boetian helmets. You can make them out, the rim above the forehead, round over the ear and along the nape of the neck. This allows them to see and hear clearly. White feathers, or plumes of horsehair, distinguish the officers. They wear corselets or cuirasses which are deliberately moulded to protect the muscles of the body. These are reinforced by a belt and shoulder guards. They carry small shields and a lance; a sword on the left side, sometimes a dagger on the right."

"And the different saddle-cloths?" Cassandra asked.

"Again the colour of the regiment. Purple and yellow, red and gold. The principal officers usually have the pelt of some animal: leopard, jaguar or panther."

"Won't the enemy notice them in battle?"

"Philip said the same," Telamon agreed. "His armour was often shabby, his saddle-cloth more of a blanket than anything else. Philip was brave but he didn't like to be noticed." Telamon shook his head. "Alexander and his personal companions take great pride in not only leading but being *seen* to lead. Personal courage is the order of the day."

"And the other horsemen?" The dust clouds wafted aside. "Oh look! Those!" Cassandra pointed to both wings of the army where squadrons of horse could now be seen, their riders wearing strange helmets. Some wore simple armour with shield and lance, others were heavily armoured, their shoulders draped with the furs of wild animals.

"Thracian and Thessalian regiments," Telamon explained. "Alexander's allies."

"So, those are the ones," Cassandra whispered under her breath. "The survivors of Thebes talked of wild monsters on horses."

"May the gods help any who fall into their hands," Telamon agreed. "They are brave but ruthlessly savage. Rumour has it that they practise cannibalism." He glanced quickly at Cassandra. She was sweating, breathing quickly – the sight of this army evoked memories. He decided to continue. "The cavalry are organized into squadrons. Each has two hundred men with a leader and trumpeter. Four squadrons make up a brigade. Two brigades constitute a regiment. In turn, a number of these form a phalanx. The principal squadron are the 'royals' who always take up their position on the right, the place of honour. This is where Ptolemy and the rest now stand. They enjoy the title of royal bodyguards, no more than seven or eight of them; they act as Alexander's generals and overall commanders."

"And the cavalry units out in front? The ones with light shields and spears?"

"Oh, they are the *prodromi*, the scouts. They fan out before the army. They depend on local knowledge – that's why Alexander hired Critias and those guides. Scouts are useful in open deserts or wide plains but, in unknown territory, it has been known for unwary scouts to lead their army into an ambush."

Cassandra pointed to the extreme right flank of the army, grouped behind the royal bodyguard – a mass of archers, slingers and lightly armed footmen, with others who were heavily armoured with ornate, plumed helmets.

"You'll find the same on the left," Telamon explained. "More mercenaries: Cretan archers, Agrianian footmen, slingers. All the mercenaries around the Middle Sea are flocking in to take Macedon's promises of Persian gold. However, the main army is in the centre, Macedon's backbone. Come!" Telamon led Cassandra further along the brow. They stopped and studied the deep lines of footmen, their great sarissas held up.

"They are so lightly armed!" Cassandra exclaimed.

"There are two types," Telamon explained. "First, the phalangists – they wear nothing but a tunic, boots and the flat hat or the *causia*. Their real weapon is the sarissa. On either side of them stand the guard's regiments, the ones who wear the Phyrgian helmets with a cockscomb crest."

"And the different colours signify different regiments?"

"Correct." Telamon smiled. "Those who wear plumes or feathers are the officers. The guardsmen wear corselets, greaves and helmets. Their task is to protect the vulnerable flank of the phalangists. The infantry are divided into units. The smallest is a file of sixteen men; a company includes thirty-two files; three companies make up a battalion; two battalions equal a regiment. Like the cavalry, they each have different colours, not to mention the trumpeters – these are trained by the army secretariat in an array of calls. Notice how the royal trumpeters are never far behind Alexander. Each call means different orders:

ground arms, shoulder arms and so on – that's what's going to happen now."

All along the battle line trumpets were braying. Each unit received the call and passed it further along. Telamon, who had seen this happen time and time again, felt his heart skip a beat, his heart beat faster. The battle line began to extend. The cavalry on the flanks were now moving forward, some of the infantry regiments with them, so the whole formation took the shape of a bull's horn. Behind the cavalry massed the light armed infantry – mercenaries, slingers and footmen. The real marvel was the core of the army: the Foot Companions and guards regiments. As if controlled by some huge invisible hand, they rapidly formed different shapes, from deep order to long files of men, then moved into close order where each section of the infantry became a rectangle of bristling spears, four across and sixteen deep. The trumpets brayed again, and the regiments assumed a different battle order: small phalanxes or squares of men, eight across and eight deep. The trumpets shrilled a different call: the phalanxes clustered together again.

"Now you see it," Telamon observed. "Units and regiments forming to become one huge phalanx."

Again the trumpets rang out, a long, blood-tingling blast. The Macedonian war cry shrilled through the air, sending the birds whirling in the sky. The phalangists began to advance slowly. The front ranks brought their sarissas down, facing out; those behind them came down at an angle.

"Cassandra!" Telamon urged. "Imagine yourself as a Persian cavalry man or Athenian soldier. You have infantry regiments menacing your front; the cavalry squadrons, supported by light infantry and auxiliaries, pounding your flanks. You can't engage with the enemy in front because their sarissas are three times as long as your spears. You try and hack the sarissas with your sword, but you find it difficult because of the men around you. The sarissas draw closer . . ."

He paused. The phalanx quickened its pace and the beat of thousands of sandalled feet produced its own sombre, warlike rhythm. A shrill call of trumpets rang out. The huge phalanx in

176

the centre was now moving faster while the cavalry on the wings broke into a trot. Telamon could only imagine the terror, the fear of an enemy facing such a foe.

Cassandra broke his reverie. "I can see it works here, on the flat plains of Chaeronea, or before Thebes. What happens if they're on a river bank or wooded hilly country?"

"Ah!" Telamon shook his head. "That's where Philip and Alexander come into their own."

His words were drowned by the blast of trumpets. The whole battle line ceased its advance, coming to a halt as if one man. Officers shouted and a great cheer went up.

"The king's congratulating them," Telamon explained. "But, to answer your question, shock and the sarissa are powerful weapons. Finally, don't forget Alexander's great talent – that of surprise."

He was about to continue when he heard shouting behind him. He looked over his shoulder. Aristander, Antigone and Selena were hastening towards them, ringed by the chorus, who were carrying a makeshift stretcher containing a corpse covered by a blanket. Telamon hastened down. Antigone's face was wet with tears and Selena seemed to be in a trance.

"It's Aspasia," Aristander explained. "She was found dead in the woods."

Chapter 9

———◦◦◦◦———

"Aristander . . . told Alexander that he had no cause for alarm."

Arrian, *The Campaign of Alexander*,
Book I, Chapter 2

They were soon joined by the other two physicians, Perdicles and Nikias, who had also been watching the manoeuvres. Perdicles pulled back the blanket. Cassandra gasped. Even Telamon, used to death in all its forms, felt a stab of pity. The young woman was covered in thick mud, the green slime of the swamp clogging her mouth, nostrils and eyes. Selena was sobbing loudly, supported by Antigone. The priestess' grief was all the more telling because of her silence, tears streaming down her face. The corpse attracted the attention of others. Aristander used the chorus to form a protective ring round the makeshift stretcher.

"Not here," Telamon declared.

"You can use my tent," Perdicles offered.

They left the drill ground, the air ringing with the shouts of officers and the brassy calls of the trumpets. They entered the camp and reached Perdicles' tent. The chorus stood on guard outside. Perdicles helped Antigone and Selena to stools. Telamon, Nikias and Aristander examined the corpse. Jugs of water and rags were brought. The young woman's cadaver was stripped of its mantle. Telamon noticed the jewellery still on her neck and wrists, the rings on her fingers – these, too, were removed. Aspasia's mouth, ears, nose and eyes were cleaned and the rest of her body washed. Her skin was still soft, the limbs supple. She looked as if she were asleep, except for the half-open eyes and gaping mouth.

"She died quite recently," Telamon commented. "Wouldn't you agree, Perdicles?"

"Within the last three hours, certainly."

"How?" Antigone demanded.

"My lady, you must know more than we do," Telamon replied.

"Where was she found?" Perdicles asked.

"She went out this morning," Antigone said, her eyes dull from weeping, her voice matter-of-fact. "She took a large basket to collect some flowers and herbs. She walked over to a copse of woods about two miles from the camp."

"Why didn't someone go with her?" Perdicles demanded.

Antigone smiled softly. "Aspasia was safe," she murmured. "She's a handmaid of Athena. No soldier would ever dare raise his hand to her. She received nothing but respect."

"True," Telamon agreed. "Her corpse shows no mark of violence; none of her jewellery was taken."

"She shouldn't have gone!"

They all whirled round. Selena, her face disfigured by weeping, had gouged her nails deep into her cheek; the blood trickled down to stain her woollen white robe.

"She shouldn't have gone!" she repeated, glaring at them. "She was my friend!"

Selena staggered to her feet, her body trembling with rage. She stamped her foot, eyes blazing, mouth opening and shutting, but in her hysteria only managed a strange gargled sound at the back of her throat.

"I will take care of her." Antigone walked across and put her arm round the young woman's shoulders, muttering quietly to her in a tongue Telamon couldn't understand. The priestess glanced across and smiled weakly. "It's Phyrigian, the ancient tongue of Troad, the area around Troy. I will see her safe."

They left the tent. Telamon continued his examination.

"What did happen?" he asked.

"From what I can gather," Aristander replied from where he stood turning over a manuscript on a small chest beside Perdicles' bed, "the young woman went to collect flowers and herbs. She

180

went into the wood carrying a basket. You're the expert, Telamon, that's the best place to collect herbs, isn't it?"

"True," the physician agreed absentmindedly. "A shady dell or fertile grove. I've been to such places myself. Plants are well watered, stronger, more varied."

"Perhaps she saw something?" Aristander continued. "A herb or flower she wanted. She must have stumbled and fallen into a marsh." He pointed to the mud-stained clothes piled on the ground beside the corpse. "Perhaps her own clothes became wrapped round her face and legs. You can imagine how it was – the more she struggled, the worse it became."

"But shouldn't her body have sunk to the bottom?"

"No," Aristander disagreed. "She was light, not weighted with stones or armour like a soldier."

"How was she found?" Cassandra asked.

The soothsayer looked curiously at her, not expecting questions from a woman.

Telamon repeated the question. "How was she found, Aristander?"

"Since yesterday I have been more vigilant regarding the king. I have sent out squadrons of light horse to scour the countryside. Alexander wishes to sacrifice another fresh young bull. I want to make sure that there are no more surprises lurking in the undergrowth. I still have hopes of finding Hercules." Aristander brushed a tear from his eye. "Anyway, a sharp-eyed cavalry officer noticed a blur of colour in the woods. He and his colleagues dismounted and went into the trees. They saw a basket lying on its side and Aspasia's body floating on the nearby surface of a marsh."

"Could someone have ambushed her?" Perdicles asked.

Telamon gestured at the corpse. "I doubt it, there's no mark or bruise on her."

"Well, it's a strange thing," Aristander declared. "The cavalry have scoured those woods. True, they didn't venture in too deeply because of the marshes and swamps, yet they were sure no one else had been there. Another patrol saw the young woman walking across the heathland into the woods. They were resting their horses. They greeted her, she replied. No one followed her in."

Telamon checked the young woman's hands. "I would agree with that, were it not for this." He pointed to the knuckles of Aspasia's right hand, which were slightly grazed, and to the nails of two of her fingers, which were broken.

"And look at this." Cassandra pushed back Aspasia's night-black hair.

Telamon studied the slight bruising in the centre of her forehead.

"It's nothing remarkable," Cassandra observed. "The knuckles of one hand are scratched, two fingernails are broken, and the bruise on her head is slight."

"So she wouldn't have lost consciousness as a result?" Aristander asked.

"No, it's nothing but a bump, though it's fresh: it occurred just before she died."

"What do you think happened?" Nikias asked. The superstitious physician had kept well away from the corpse. Telamon understood why – Aspasia had been a handmaiden dedicated to Athena.

"What I suspect," Telamon replied, getting to his feet and staring down at the corpse, "is that Aspasia went out to collect flowers and herbs. True, she may have been murdered, or she may have been attacked, but I don't think so. Aspasia was a stranger here. She forgot the warnings about the marshes. She saw a plant or herb she wanted, put her basket down and, in her excitement, hurried forward. She was caught in a quagmire. She would have cried out but she stumbled and fell on her face into the marsh. She may have grazed her hand and bruised her forehead. She panics and breathes in, tries to scream – in doing so she sucks more mud into her mouth and nostrils. Death would follow very quickly. The poor woman suffocated." Telamon tapped Cassandra on the shoulder. "She's a priestess and will have to be prepared for burial. Gentlemen, Cassandra should do that. No offence must be given. I am sure the Lady Antigone would agree."

Nikias was only too pleased to get out. Aristander said he wished to talk to Perdicles, and they sauntered out of the tent. Telamon sat on the stool just inside the entrance to catch the breeze which still carried the sound of trumpets and shouted orders from the drill ground.

"What shall I do, Telamon?" Cassandra asked.

"Bathe her, clean her body. Scrutinize it for anything suspicious. Take one of Perdicles' blankets and wrap it round her. When you have finished, tell Antigone. See if you can discover more details about what happened this morning."

Telamon watched a cloud of dust blow across the front of the tent. "In this heat her corpse must be disposed of quickly, certainly within an hour or two."

Cassandra became busy. More water and rags were brought. Telamon went to his own tent and returned with some spices and a small phial of perfume containing myrrh and frankincense.

"I see no mark," Cassandra declared, combing the dead woman's hair.

"Was she a maiden?" Telamon asked.

"Well, she's not a soldier," Cassandra teased.

"A virgin?" Telamon snapped.

"Yes and no." Cassandra glanced up. "Her hymen was broken but that was some time ago. There's no sign of any sexual interference."

She gently caressed the dead girl's feet and muttered something under her breath.

"What was that?" Telamon asked.

"The fragrant dew falls on roses and the May flower fields are covered in bloom."

"You are a poet?"

"I wish I was," Cassandra replied. "Lines from Sappho, a fitting elegy for this young woman." She smiled at the surprise on Telamon's face.

"Are you a follower of Sappho?"

"Well, what do you think, master?" Cassandra stared at him, hard-eyed. "Do you recall that famous passage from Aristophanes' *Lysistrata*?"

Telamon shook his head.

Cassandra sprang to her feet like an actress on a stage, hands extended. Telamon laughed as she minced up and down the tent, imitating the high-born ladies from Aristophanes' satire.

"Anything you want," Cassandra quoted from the play. "If I had to, I'd walk through fire. I'd do anything rather than give up penises. Lysistrata dear, there's nothing like them."

"But you don't believe in that?" Telamon chuckled. "You wouldn't agree with the author of *Women's Diseases*?" Telamon closed his eyes as he recalled the line. "Women who have intercourse with men are healthier than women who do not."

"No, I wouldn't agree with it," Cassandra retorted, going back to the corpse. "A man would say that, wouldn't he? And what do you believe in, master, or should I say, Telamon? Would you agree with the murdered Agamemnon when Ulysses visited him in Hades: 'There is nothing more deadly on earth than a woman'?"

"Well, he would say that, wouldn't he?" Telamon mimicked. "After all, he was murdered by his wife!" He came and knelt beside the corpse. "She was beautiful." He looked at the full breasts, narrow waist, broad hips and long slender legs. "Do you think she was a follower of Sappho? After all, her hymen had been broken."

"Possibly." Cassandra shrugged. "What does your famous Aristotle write in his tract *On the Diseases of Women*, that the hymen can be broken by other, violent activity? I doubt if Aspasia had a man; there's certainly no sign of her having conceived."

"Have you ever fallen in love, Cassandra? Lain with a man?"

Cassandra's face softened. "I have met people I have loved," she replied enigmatically. "But marriage, childbirth? Never! A troupe of players once came to our temple. They performed Euripides' *Medea*. I always remember the line, delivered by Medea herself: 'I would rather stand three times in the battle line than give birth to a single child.'"

"Are you frightened of the pain?" Telamon asked, curious at the direction this conversation had taken.

"No." Cassandra got to her feet. She poured water into a bowl and washed her hands. "Why should I bring a child into this world of blood, peopled by men like Alexander, Philip and Ptolemy?"

She came over to him, wiping her hands on one of the rags. Telamon couldn't decide whether she was angry or on the verge of tears.

"I have heard the rumours, Telamon," she whispered, leaning down. "Within weeks Alexander will be in Asia. Just think of the blood which will flow. Death by the sword, by fire." She gestured at the corpse. "Or by stupid accidents like this."

They left the tent. Telamon summoned two guards. He ordered one to stand over the corpse and the other to fetch Antigone.

"Where are we going?" Cassandra asked.

"I want to see the place where this young woman died."

Telamon sought out Aristander. Within the hour a young cavalry officer led them out of the camp, across the sun-washed heathland and into the cool darkness of the trees. The officer briefly explained what had happened, and his account agreed accurately with Aristander's. Telamon thanked him and the officer left. The physician and his companion sat in the shade of an oak and stared across the clearing.

"It's easy to see how the accident occurred," Cassandra declared. "Bushes, trees, clumps of long grass. Look at the flowers, Telamon, they're like beacon lights drawing you in. You put your foot wrong and, for the unwary or inexperienced, you're up to your waist in mud before you even know it!"

"And you saw no other marks or bruises on her?" Telamon asked.

"Why do you ask?"

Telamon shook his head. "The basket's gone."

"That was probably returned to Antigone. What are you implying?"

"I've been recalling my geography," Telamon declared. "I've been to the Troad on two occasions. There's not much there, just ruins – tombs on the promontory, windswept plains and, in the distance, the wooded slopes of Mount Ida. Troy and all its glory have gone. When you travel south you enter a different country. You could easily get lost there." He sighed, got to his feet and helped Cassandra to hers. "More importantly, a small army like Alexander's could be ambushed. To put it bluntly, it seems that anyone who could help Alexander through such countryside is being slain, knifed or, as in this case, drowned and suffocated in mud."

"But it was an accident," Cassandra protested.

"A philosopher once claimed there's no such thing as an accident . . ."

"Telamon! Telamon!" a voice roared.

The physician seized Cassandra's hand. They made their way back through the trees to where the leader of Aristander's chorus stood like some great bear in his fur-lined cloak. In one hand he held his grotesque boar's head helmet, in the other his dagger. He pointed this at Telamon.

"You are to come to the king. He wants you."

"And you can put that away!" Cassandra declared sharply, eyeing the dagger.

The leader of the chorus just stared at her.

Cassandra advance threateningly. "Go on!' Put that ugly dagger away! You're only showing off. This is the king's friend. He'll come because he wants to!" She glanced over her shoulder at Telamon, raising her eyes in exasperation. "One thing I've learnt about the Celts, they are great liars and they love drama."

The leader of the chorus sheathed his dagger. He now stared devotedly at Cassandra as if she were some long-lost empress.

"Well, come on, you great hunk of flesh!"

The leader of the chorus snapped to attention and bowed. He strode off across the heathland, Telamon and Cassandra hurrying to keep up with him.

The army manoeuvres had now finished and the men were marching in units back into the camp. Discipline was now relaxed – helmets off, with slaves and servants to carry spears and shields. A cavalry unit thundered by, raising clouds of dust and greeted by catcalls and jeers from the foot soldiers. The leader of the chorus elbowed his way through the press. Instead of taking them to the royal enclosure, he led them across the camp to where the hospital tents had been erected next to a small brook. So far these had only been used for minor injuries and ailments yet, even as they approached the main tent, Telamon heard hideous screams. Royal footguards thronged the entrance; the inside, poorly lit by oil lamps, smelt sour. The king and his companions were holding a young cavalry officer down on a trestle table. They were spattered with blood, pools of which had formed on the floor to the right-hand side.

"May Apollo be thanked!"

Alexander, still in his full purple-grey dress armour, greeted them. His hair was soaked in sweat. He loosened the cloth around his throat and used it to wipe sweat from his arms. Ptolemy, Hephaestion and the others clustered about, distracted by the moans and screams of the patient. Alexander pushed Telamon forward.

"He fell off his horse," the king explained.

Telamon looked at the man's hand, a mangled lump of flesh. "A horse kick?"

"No. The horse just stood on him," Alexander replied drily. "Telamon, I know your skill. What can you do?"

"You have other physicians, my lord. If you want to test me, just say."

Alexander ignored this. "What do you recommend, Telamon?"

"Has he had an opiate?"

"He's had nothing."

Telamon turned and grasped an orderly by the arm. "I want the strongest wine you have with some poppy powder – you know what that is?"

The man nodded.

"Cassandra, go back to my tent, bring my medical satchel and the small coffer of cedar wood embossed with a silver snake. One of the king's men will go with you."

Alexander turned and snapped his fingers. Cassandra left escorted by two officers. The orderly brought the wine and the poppy powder. Telamon mixed this and, telling the officer's companions to hold him tight, forced the wine between the man's lips.

"Drink!" he urged, ignoring the frantic look in the man's eyes. "Drink and you'll know peace."

"I'm going to die," the man gasped, blood bubbling on his lips from where he had bitten his tongue. His face was ashen and sweat-laced.

"You are *not* going to die," Telamon replied. "Not yet. Drink this and you'll know peace. Just for a short while fight the pain and drink the wine."

The man obeyed. Again the cup was filled and more powder added. The patient became sleepy-eyed, drowsy; Telamon kept

187

him awake, slapping his face until he drained the second cup. At last the man lay silent.

"The river of Lethe," Alexander murmured. "The waters of forgetfulness!"

"Poppy seed and heavy wine," Telamon replied caustically. "And it won't last long. The pain will bring him back to consciousness."

"I want to see this but I'm hot!" Alexander lifted his arms and a page ran forward to unstrap the cuirass. "What are you going to do, Telamon?" Alexander looked as if he had forgotten all about the army. Once more that insatiable curiosity which had so plagued Aristotle at Mieza was to the fore. "What will you do?"

Telamon ignored him. He picked up the victim's lolling arm and placed it gently on the table. He carefully examined the shoulder, forearm and wrist. He lifted the mangled hand. The patient stirred. Telamon crouched down and examined the hand. The fingers were mangled, bloody shreds of skin and bone.

"I'll have to amputate," Telamon declared. "Here at the wrist, and I'll have to do it quickly."

The orderly forgot who was present. "Can you do that? He'll bleed to death."

"If I don't," Telamon replied, "within hours the hand will be infected, the poison will spread, his arm will swell up and he'll die in agony. I'll need some fire in an earthenware bowl, hot water and fresh bandages. You have those?"

"Do it," the king urged.

The orderly obeyed. For a while all was confusion. Telamon had the tent cleared except for Alexander, his companions and the orderly. Cassandra returned. Telamon urged her and the orderly to wash their hands thoroughly. He opened his medicine satchel and took out his instruments: a small, sharp saw, a set of pincers, small bronze clamps, needles. He cauterized these above the fire.

"Why are you doing that?" Alexander demanded.

"I am not too sure," Telamon replied. "I witnessed a similar operation in Syracuse: fire is a great cleanser. Anything which touches an open wound should be cleaned."

"Will he die?" Alexander patted the shoulder of the young officer who was already beginning to stir.

"He could do," Telamon declared. "It's easy to remove the hand – a butcher could do that with a cleaver. It's the bleeding and bandaging which counts." He gently touched the unconscious patient's face. "And if the bleeding doesn't kill him, the shock to his mind might. I can give no guarantees. Cassandra, are you ready?"

Telamon took some powders out of his satchel and mixed them with a goblet of wine.

"More poppy seed?" Ptolemy asked, the cynical look gone from his face.

"No, no, something more powerful. White mandrake, given in the proper quantities, really is the water of forgetfulness."

Telamon forced the wine between the patient's lips, pushing open the mouth and arching back the head to ensure that the officer, who was now beginning to rouse from his drug-filled sleep, swallowed the potion. He drained the cup. Telamon pronounced himself satisfied and stood back.

"Cassandra, I am going to take the hand off at the wrist but before this I am going to apply tourniquets above the wrist and elbow. Just before I start cutting, you must tighten the tourniquets as firmly as you can. I will then cut. The blood will seep out. If fortune favours us, the flow will be slight. As I cut, the veins will become obvious. I hope to be able to either knot these or clamp them. Once the damaged hand is amputated, the clamps must be swiftly removed so that surtures can be made."

Cassandra glanced fearfully at him. "Can you do that?"

"I will do it," Telamon affirmed. "I will also use a rasp to smooth down the bone. The stump must be washed." He turned to the orderly. "I want the heaviest wine and the strongest vinegar. And whatever honey you can find. I will also try to cauterize the stump." He smiled at Alexander. "And our king will have learnt something."

The cavalry officer was now fully unconscious, head lying back though even now he stirred. Ptolemy offered to help in applying the tourniquets while Alexander gripped the patient's shoulder.

"He should lie still," Telamon advised. "But it is not unknown for pain to bring a patient back to consciousness."

Telamon washed his hands, picked up the small saw and ran its blade through the flame. He closed his eyes and murmured a short prayer that he would recall everything he had seen and read. He made the first cut. Ptolemy and Cassandra kept the tourniquets tight. Telamon worked as fast as he could. It did not take long to remove the hand. He quickly applied the small clamps and used the rasp to make the bone ends as smooth as possible. The blood flow was slight. Telamon worked quickly with the surtures.

"Why the speed?" Cassandra whispered.

"The blood flow must not stop for long," Telamon replied. "The tourniquets will have to be released."

At last Telamon pronounced himself satisfied. The blood flow had fallen to a mere trickle. The clamps and surtures held and the stump was liberally washed with a mixture of wine, vinegar and honey. Telamon shook his head at Alexander's spate of questions.

"They all contain properties," he explained, "which ward off infection. The stronger the wine and vinegar the better."

"I thought you had to wait for the pus?" said Ptolemy.

"The Egyptians disagree." Telamon wiped the sweat from his cheek with the back of his wrist. "They claim a wound doesn't in itself contain putrefaction, but that it comes from the air and from dirt. The cleaner a wound is, the better."

He took a knife from his chest and held it above the flame. Once it was hot to the touch, he carefully pressed it against the exposed flesh. The cavalry officer stirred, whimpering in his drug-filled sleep. Again Telamon applied the knife, careful to avoid the places where he had inserted the surtures.

"The stump is level and clear."

Telamon applied more wine, vinegar and honey and carefully wrapped the stump in linen bandages.

"Shouldn't they be tighter?" Alexander asked.

"What I do, many don't," Telamon responded. "In Syracuse a physician told me to allow the wound to breathe while, at the same time, being protected. Healers in Egypt agree with this."

At last the bandaging was finished. Telamon instructed the orderly on how the wound was to be inspected morning, noon and night, washed in the prescribed mixture and bandaged with clean cloths. All the used dressings should be burnt.

Telamon felt the pulse in the officer's neck.

"Good!" he declared. "The beat is regular and strong."

"And the mandrake?" the orderly asked.

"No more of that. Heavy wine and poppy seed." He pointed to the gory mess around the table. "Have the patient removed to cleaner quarters. These should be cleansed thoroughly with water, salt and vinegar." He glanced at Alexander. "My lord, I am finished. I have done what I can."

Telamon walked out of the tent. Alexander followed him.

"I understand you saw the manoeuvres." Alexander tapped a sandalled foot. "The army is ready!"

From somewhere across the camp a great cheer went up.

"They have seen the fleet," Alexander remarked. "One hundred and sixty triremes. Parmenio will lead the troops across the straits."

"And us?" Telamon asked.

"We'll make our own voyage." Alexander smiled. "A pilgrimage, a little way south, then across to Troy." He stamped his foot and looked up at the sky. "I understand there has been another death, Telamon. You may have saved that soldier but the spy seems to do what he wants in my camp."

"We have no evidence of murder. It could have been an accident."

Alexander turned to face Telamon squarely, a cynical look in his eyes. "I trust you, Telamon," he murmured. "But I don't trust everyone." He clapped his hands for his bodyguard to approach. "Clean yourself up, physician. You did well." He poked Telamon in the chest. "Aristotle would have been proud of you. Let's hope your king will be!"

Spinning on his heel, Alexander sauntered off, one arm round Hephaestion's waist, the other grasping Ptolemy's shoulder.

"Schoolboys," Cassandra whispered. "They are like boys playing a game."

"They are not schoolboys," Telamon replied. "They are warriors with a hunger for blood, glory and marching to the rim of the world. They see it as some kind of game, a deadly one. These killings might end," he continued, taking Cassandra's arm, "when we cross the Hellespont."

"*One* type of killing," Cassandra corrected.

"Yes, you are right. Once across the real bloodshed will begin."

"Where are we going now?" Cassandra asked.

"I want to visit Antigone, pay my respects."

The priestess was in her tent. Selena lay sleeping on one of the cot beds. Antigone was packing her possessions. She was still pale-faced, her eyes red-rimmed with weeping. She wore a simple peasant's tunic, her lustrous hair hanging down to her shoulders. She smiled at Cassandra but her eyes hardened at the sight of Telamon.

"I am grateful for what you did for Aspasia." She gestured at the tent flap. "It's too humid to keep the corpse here. The king is most generous." Her voice was tinged with sarcasm. "He will arrange for the burning. The funeral pyre will be lit just before we leave tomorrow morning."

"Tomorrow morning?"

"Not by sea," Antigone explained. "Alexander's had an attack of superstition. The rest are crossing the Hellespont but Alexander is going south to the Elaeum peninsula. You know who's buried there?"

"Protesilaus," Telamon replied. "The first Achaean killed in the Trojan War. They say his ghost still haunts the tomb."

"Alexander and his household – and that includes you, Telamon – will sacrifice to placate his spirit. Alexander does not wish to die on his first day in Asia."

"But you will be happy to return to Troy?"

"I will be happy to go home."

Telamon looked down at a tied bundle of clothes on a stool.

"Aspasia's," Antigone explained. "She was like a child, excited at the thought of going home. She'd packed everything in preparation."

Telamon moved the bundle and sat down on the stool. Antigone stood over him. She was so close he could smell her perfume.

"I'd offer you some wine, but I don't have any."

"Where are they from?" Telamon asked, glancing at the sleeping Selena. "Selena and Aspasia?"

"They are Thessalians but I regard them as kin." Antigone stared at Cassandra who'd wandered to the entrance of the tent.

192

"How long have they been with you?"

"Four or five years. The first offerings from Thessaly. King Philip chose them and paid for their passage to Troy."

"So why did you come? I mean, here? To this place of war?"

"I've told you. Alexander ordered me." She smiled. "Well, I *wanted* to come. It's years since I met Alexander and I had to bring the guides as well as the hapless Critias."

"Will the guides desert?" Telamon asked.

Antigone pulled a face. "Possibly. They are frightened men. They believe they are marked for death. Aristander is keeping a close eye on them, when he is not mourning that dwarf."

"Did you know Hercules?"

"A busy little fly, Telamon. He irked the soldiers, Ptolemy especially. Hercules had some nasty habits, including watching people make love. It's not a trait which endears you to others."

Telamon got to his feet and walked over to Selena. He pressed his hand against her cheek, which was warm and rather flushed.

"Perdicles gave her a sleeping draught," Antigone explained. "She'll be all right in time. I never thought she'd become so hysterical. She and Aspasia were very close. I tutored both in the mysteries."

"These maidens, the ones from Thessaly who were supposed to make their way to your temple at Troy. How many were killed?"

Antigone narrowed her eyes. "Philip reintroduced the custom, punishment for the Thessalian tribes he defeated." She laughed sharply. "Philip didn't believe in the gods but he did believe in luck. He knew one day his army would sweep through Troy. He wanted to please every god, including Athena."

"And all these maidens were murdered?"

Antigone smiled. "You misunderstand. We don't know if they ever came. No," she corrected herself, "we know about the last two. After all, I brought the survivor to Alexander myself, but the others?" She shrugged. "More rumour than fact."

Cassandra called from the entrance of the tent. "Telamon, there's a messenger."

A pageboy entered the tent.

"Your presence is required," he declared pompously. "The king is in council."

"Both of us?" Antigone asked.

"Both of you, but not her." He thrust a thumb over his shoulder. "Not the red-haired mare!"

Cassandra lunged at him, but the boy was too quick. He dodged her swinging hand and, bellowing with laughter, ran from the tent.

"What Alexander wants, Alexander gets!" Antigone murmured. She gestured at Selena. "Tell the king I'll be there shortly. I want a guard posted."

Telamon made his excuses and left.

"What do you make of her?" he asked Cassandra once they were out of earshot.

"A devout priestess, furious at the death of her handmaid. You can tell that from her tone, the way she holds herself."

"Go back to our tent," Telamon urged. "Alexander has the bit between his teeth – we'll strike camp at dawn." He indicated the rising noise and bustle of the camp. "And keep well away from them. They'll be celebrating."

Cassandra stepped away, waggling her fingers. "Oh, don't worry. You keep forgetting, Telamon, I have seen how Macedonians celebrate!"

In the royal pavilion Alexander, washed and changed, was kneeling on the floor, his generals around him as they sifted maps and muster rolls, passing documents from hand to hand. The king raised his head as Telamon came in.

"We'll be leaving tomorrow, Telamon. At dawn." Alexander winked. "I want you with me, for two reasons. First, I wish to sacrifice a bull at sea, my offering to Poseidon – it had better be acceptable. Second, and this is no great secret, I suffer from seasickness. I want you close by. I don't want the lads seeing Alexander of Macedon vomiting his guts out."

"In all things a true descendant of Achilles."

"In all things," Alexander quipped. "Achilles come again! Now, Telamon, sit down. We leave tomorrow. I want you to make sure that all's well with that bloody bull. No mishaps." Alexander gestured across at Parmenio. "You will make the crossing from Sestos to Abydos and march south. We'll meet on the plain of Troy. You'll bring everything with you, the siege equipment and carts."

"And then?" Ptolemy asked, gnawing at a piece of meat.

"It will be dusty marches and hard rations," Alexander declared abruptly. "We'll seek out the Persian army, bring it to battle and utterly destroy it. The sooner the better! Ah, my lady."

Alexander rose to his feet as Antigone, dressed in her priestess' robes, entered the pavilion. Alexander kicked Seleucus with his foot, forcing a space. He brought across a stool and gallantly gestured for the priestess to sit.

She smiled. "I am not a soldier, Alexander."

"No, my lady, but you are the priestess of Troy." Alexander's face burned with excitement, eyes sparkling so much Telamon wondered if the king had a slight fever. "Achilles lies buried near your temple, does he not?"

"On a promontory overlooking the sea," she agreed. "To the west of the city."

"And your temple possesses his arms?"

"Yes, they were dedicated there by Agamemnon."

"Impossible!" Ptolemy broke in. "They'd be rusted, rotten!"

"They have been well preserved," Antigone retorted. "Hidden in tar-covered sheets. I will show them to you."

"I claim them as Achilles' descendant," Alexander declared. "As Captain-General of Greece, as the vengeance of Zeus against the pride of the Persians!"

"You are all-powerful!" Antigone raised her voice as she echoed the words of the Delphic Oracle. "You are all-powerful, Alexander of Macedon!"

"In return," Alexander proclaimed, "I'll dedicate my own arms to Athena. Ask her blessing on this sacred expedition!"

Alexander's excitement was infectious. No longer nervous, or wary of crossing the Hellespont, he was now filled with dreams of glory, believing himself to be the reincarnation of Achilles, the chosen one of the gods. He sifted maps backwards and forwards, giving each of his commanders precise instructions, curtly dismissing any threat from the Persian navy. Wine was poured and served; the discussions became more heated and excited. Alexander proposed to rebuild Troy, to glorify the temple of Athena. He broke off and grinned at Telamon.

"You can go now."

Telamon got to his feet. Antigone also made her excuses and rose.

"You are walking back to my tent?" she asked.

Ptolemy muttered some salacious remark. One of his commanders, Socrates, burst into raucous laughter which Alexander stilled with a glance. Telamon ignored them and made his way out, Antigone resting on his arm.

"It will be good to be home. They say the weather will be fine. If only Alexander could break free from his superstitions."

"He is agitated," Telamon agreed. "These murders and constant references to his father – his nerves have become fretted, wary of this and that. Alexander wants a battle. He needs further signs from the gods. He wants to placate all the shades and ghosts which prowl his dreams. My lady, one question? These maidens from Thessaly? You once described yourself as a listening-post for Macedon?"

"True. They were to help me."

"And Aspasia and Selena?"

Antigone stopped near the pathway leading up to her tent. "The same!" She leant over and kissed Telamon on the cheek. "But now, perhaps, we will not be needed."

Telamon bade her goodnight and leisurely made his way across the royal enclosure. Cassandra sat outside his own tent talking to the guard. He stood for a while watching them, and then heard screams, shouts and exclamations. He hurried back towards Antigone's tent. She was kneeling outside. She had torn her gown and picked up dust to throw over her head. Telamon pushed her aside and went in. Selena lay on the ground, blood trickling out of her mouth, her eyes sightless in her pallid face. In her side, thrust deep, was a winged Celtic dagger.

Chapter 10

"Alexander passed the Hellespont and, at Troy, sacrificed to Athena, and honoured the memory of the heroes buried there, especially Achilles."

Plutarch, *Lives*, Alexander

"**P**oseidon, all mighty, Lord of the Waves! Master of the Storm! Rider of the Winds!"

Telamon braced himself against the sway of the warship and stared across at the sixty triremes escorting Alexander's flagship *The Lion of Macedon*. Its sails were now furled, the anchor stones piled high in the prow. The sea breeze was fresh and salty; the sunlight, beating down on the deck, shimmered on the gilded statue of Athena which jutted out on the prow. All around them clustered the fleet, or at least those triremes which had not joined Parmenio in the transportation of the rest of Alexander's army to Abydos. Black, slippery as eels with the red eye painted just beneath their prows, the war fleet clustered like a wolf pack, prows stretching out to the distant shore of Asia. Telamon held on to the taffrail.

"One sacrifice after another, eh?" Cassandra whispered into Telamon's ear.

He agreed. Yesterday Alexander had left his main army and marched south to the Elaeum promontory where he had offered sacrifice and paid libation to Protesilaus. Afterwards they had embarked. Now, with the coast of Asia in sight, Alexander was determined, seasickness or not, to sacrifice to the gods. Telamon watched anxiously as the snow-white bull, heavily sedated, was led along the deck. The priests moved forward, incense was sprinkled, the tuft of hair between the bull's horns cut and sprinkled into the bowl of fire on the makeshift altar just beneath the prow. The bull struggled slightly. Telamon and the others, a few yards behind Alexander, held their breath.

"Oh, gods!" Ptolemy murmured. "The last thing we want is a bull running amok!"

The priests held the animal's head back. Aristander, using a *kopis*, a curved sacrificial knife, expertly sliced the bull's throat. The bull's dying bellow was greeted by shouts and exclamations as its hot, gushing blood was caught in a silver bowl. Alexander, garbed in full dress armour, a purple-grey cloak hanging from his shoulders, a laurel wreath on his head, finished the sacrifice amidst gusts of incense and the sweet spices of myrrh, frankincense and cassia. The deck ran with blood. Marines and sailors dabbed their fingers in it and ran a line across their foreheads, eager to take part in this successful sacrifice to the gods. The butchers were now cutting the dead animal up, slicing it expertly while sailors armed with leather buckets of sea water began to wash the deck. Alexander turned to face his household. Eyes gleaming, he lifted his hands.

"We have paid sacrifice, the gods have answered, victory will be ours!"

A trumpet rang out. Somewhere deep in the trireme a drum began to beat. The oars were lowered. Alexander's purple ensign was raised. The fleet of war triremes and escorts surged forward towards the shore of Asia.

"He should have been an actor," Cassandra murmured. "He loves every second of it, doesn't he?"

The other commanders were clustering round Alexander to convey their congratulations. Signals were exchanged with the other ships which now closed in. The air was filled with the sound of trumpets and drums. Standards were raised, the infectious excitement spread. Men clustered on the sides and in the prow, eyes searching for the harbour of the Achaeans, the place where Agamemnon and his army had landed to plunder and burn the fabulous city of Troy.

Cassandra, standing behind Telamon, was irrepressible. "I heard an interesting tale, about the lover Leander who used to swim from Abydos to his paramour, Hero, in Sestos. She was a priestess of Aphrodite and used to guide him in with a lamp."

"What happened?" Telamon asked. He didn't turn round. He was watching Alexander instructing the captain.

"One night a mist fell. The lamp was obscured. Leander drowned and Hero committed suicide."

"Can someone swim the Hellespont?" Telamon asked.

"It's only four thousand yards, and has been done. The sailors call it a river rather than a sea. They say it's rich with fish but I don't think Alexander would give much time to that. Look there!" She pointed through the early morning haze and the physician made out a jutting promontory.

"Sigeum," she explained. "The cliff tops of Troy."

"Where Achilles and Patroclus lie buried?"

"It's also the place, where Agamemnon lit his first beacon fire to inform his wife Clymnestra that Troy had fallen. Little did Agamemnon know that Clymnestra was plotting his murder. Ah well," Cassandra sighed. "Do you think the Persians will be waiting for us beyond the cliff tops?"

The physician shook his head. He watched the oars rising and dipping to the steady beat of the steersman's drum. He braced himself as the ship gathered speed.

"The Persians will not meet us. They want the vastness of their country to swallow us up, like a bird does a gnat."

"And will it?"

"Perhaps we will become like Xenephon," Telamon said. "Marching backwards and forwards."

"How will we get home?"

Cassandra wasn't worried but she was trying to make this stone-faced physician anxious. She was fascinated by him. A man who hid his feelings; a physician who could save life; an exile who was patronized and befriended by a king. Telamon the cold who, at times, could be so kind.

"I don't think we will ever go home."

A seagull skimmed down in front of the prow. Telamon recalled a story told by his father of how seagulls were the souls of dead sailors.

"If Alexander is victorious he will march to the ends of the earth," he said.

199

"And if he is defeated?" Cassandra asked.

"The Persian ships will prowl these waters and those of us who escape will have to follow Leander's example and swim for our lives." He paused. "We'll find Troy deserted, though, and Alexander can play Achilles to his heart's content."

Telamon walked away. Antigone was sitting under a leather awning in the stern. The priestess looked calm and composed, slightly pale-faced, hands on her lap, eyes closed, apparently lost in prayer. Telamon glanced across at a nearby ship, low and black in the water, its prow, in the shape of a griffin, cutting through the sea. Alexander had been furious at Selena's death. The murder of a servant of Athena was bad luck; her death was kept secret, her corpse burnt the same night. Both Aristander and Telamon had been loudly berated for making little progress.

Alexander had summoned them and listened, grim-faced, to their accounts. Behind him stood Ptolemy and the two physicians, Perdicles and Nikias. All three seemed to enjoy Telamon's discomfort.

"What is it?" the king had yelled, his face flushed with anger. "Is this killer some angel of death? Can he sweep through my camp and touch with black, feathery wings anyone he wants? Are you behind these deaths, Aristander?"

He had accused and taunted until his temper exhausted itself. Then he had waved his hands in disgust and strode away. If he had meant to frighten Aristander he was successful. The keeper of secrets volubly protested but, as he quietly confessed to Telamon, he could see no logic, no explanation in Selena's death. Antigone had been distraught but eventually composed herself. The guard on duty at her tent loudly protested his innocence.

"The lady priestess left," he had said. "Now and again I raised the tent flap. I peered in. The young maiden was fast asleep on the bed with her back to me. I saw nothing wrong. No one approached the tent."

Telamon had examined the place of murder. The tent had only one entrance and, as with the other deaths, it would have been impossible for any assassin to creep either through or under the tent awnings. Selena had been brutally and skilfully murdered, the dagger expertly slipped under her ribcage up into her heart. Her corpse had been cold, the blood congealed. Telamon reckoned the woman must have died at least an hour, even more, before she was found. The guard had described the discovery of the body. Lady Antigone had arrived at the tent. He had lifted the flap for her and they had both seen the corpse sprawled on the floor. Selena's robes were soaked in blood, as were the linen sheets and the straw-filled mattress. There was no sign of any struggle, of any resistance. Only the horror of death, the gaping, blood-soaked mouth, the half-open eyes, the cruel dagger and, beneath the bed, a small scroll bearing that telling message, as usual, the words slightly changed: "*The bull is ready for sacrifice, the slayer awaits, all is prepared.*"

Telamon, accompanied by Aristander, had questioned both Antigone and the guard closely: their story agreed. Selena had been asleep when Antigone left the tent. No one had approached the tent. When the priestess returned, the corpse lay sprawled inside. The guard couldn't recall when he had last peered in.

"I was reluctant to." He smiled nervously. "I mean, she was a temple maiden. I didn't want to be accused of prying."

Telamon rubbed his eyes and broke from his reverie, wiping the light sea-spray from his face. He had seen something yesterday which had intrigued him. Yet his mind was tired. He could not recall the details. It was like staring at a manuscript – he could recognize the words but not make out their meaning. He started at a shout from the watch on the prow. The cliffs of Rhoeteum were in sight, along which lay the famous harbour of the Achaeans. Alexander now took the helm and his flagship sped like an arrow towards the shore. The leadsmen in the prow swung their ropes weighted with stones; anxious orders were passed. The thudding below decks ceased. Only one bank of oars was used and the other ships hung back. Telamon sensed the excitement: this was Asia, the fabled Troy, the treasure house of Persia!

Alexander, helped by the helmsman, guided the prow in. Orders rang out: the oars came up, the keel juddered as the trireme scraped the sandy, pebbled bottom and slowed down. Alexander surrendered his post to the helmsman and ran along the deck of the ship. Hephaestion was waiting in the prow, javelin in hand. Alexander grasped this and flung it with all his might. The javelin arched in the air and plunged into the soft sand of the beach, to the cheers of the crew which were taken up by those in the watching ships.

"I receive Asia," Alexander cried, "as a gift from the gods! My spear-won prize!"

Roars of approval greeted this. The ship's keel now dug deep, its prow juddering as it left the water, slicing through the soft, pebbled sand. The ship finally came to rest, water lapping around its stern, lifting slightly on the sway of incoming waves. Alexander, dressed in the gorgeous panoply of a fully armed warrior, drew his sword, leapt from the prow and marched like a conquering hero up the beach to reclaim his spear. He grasped it and returned, arms lifted, spear in one hand, sword in the other, appearing to be what he wanted to be – the new Achilles, the god of war, the Captain-General of Greece coming to claim his own. Such dramatic gestures evoked further cheering. The clash of arms echoed around the small cove, sending the sea birds up screeching. Alexander's captains carefully scrutinized the cliff tops but no one appeared to oppose them; no cavalry or javelin men, no swirl of a Persian cloak or glitter of a standard. The coastline was empty! The rest of the fleet swept in. Masts were lowered, oars lifted. Two ships came to grief on submerged rocks but there were no losses: men, animals and baggage were safely brought ashore.

Scouts were sent out. The fire in the earthenware pots was brought up, and camp fires lit. Some enterprising souls had caught fish on the voyage and these were soon being grilled above the flames. Alexander allowed his men to recover from any seasickness while the triremes were prepared for sea again, awaiting a change of wind. A trumpet sounded and the marshals moved through the camp proclaiming that the foragers had returned and no enemy was to be seen.

"It's a good job," Ptolemy observed as he led Alexander up the winding path to the cliff tops. "The gods be praised! A group of women, armed with distaffs, could have held us off."

Telamon was glad to leave the beach. He relaxed as he gazed over the tree-filled, windswept plain leading up to Troy. The landscape was deserted as if sleeping under the hot sun. Nothing but grasslands, olive groves and oak trees. Plants and flowers, some of which he didn't recognize, were fresh in their brilliant spring blossom. Now he was away from the sea he could make out the snow-capped, cloud-free summit of Mount Ida, dense forests on either side, the glint of a river and the occasional black smoke from some lonely farmstead.

Alexander was excited, walking up and down, quoting lines from Homer's *Iliad* and pointing out different locations around them. At last Hephaestion persuaded him to relax and take off his dress armour. Horses were brought and, protected by a screen of scouts, Alexander led his army along the white, dusty trackway through the trees, across the heathland, up the brooding hill and into the ruins of Troy. As they approached peasants appeared, bringing gifts of bread and fruit, or just stood wide-eyed, full of curiosity. Alexander greeted them as if he were their saviour and they raised their hands and gave a desultory cheer.

At last they reached the outskirts of the ruins – the foundations of thick walls, avenues, broken gateways, pillars and mounds. In some places the ruins were hidden by dense clumps of grass or thick green moss.

Alexander loved it. Pointing to the distance, he indicated the River Scamander and the reputed place where some duel from the ancient war had been fought. Troy itself was disappointing, little more than a village of makeshift houses and huts set up among the ruins. Telamon couldn't distinguish anything heroic, Homeric or dramatic but, like the rest, he kept his own counsel as Alexander, quoting the *Iliad*, chattered on.

At last they reached the town square, fringed by ruins and dilapidated houses. Some inhabitants spoke a coarse Greek, and were more interested in what they could sell than in the arrival of the army. Alexander dismounted and, going back, helped Antigone do likewise. He snapped his fingers and beckoned Telamon over.

, "Are you sure you are well, my lady?"

Antigone, dark-eyed and pale-faced, lips pressed into a bloodless line, nodded and pulled the cowl of her mantle over her head.

"Is there anything Telamon can do?" Alexander asked solicitously.

Again the shake of the head. Alexander would have continued his questioning but a group came out of a side street, led by an old priest, staff in one hand, a pot of glowing incense wrapped in a rag in the other. Behind him a boy tinkled a bell. The strange procession wound its way across the square to be greeted by murmurs of laughter from Alexander's entourage – soon silenced by glares from the king. The local headman came forward carrying a tawdry cushion bearing a laurel wreath daubed with gold paint. The headman bowed to Antigone. Blinking his bleary eyes, he attempted a speech but his tongue seemed too big for his mouth. Telamon suspected that he had prepared for this occasion by drinking as much wine as his fat paunch could hold. The man swayed dangerously on his feet. Hephaestion pushed his way through. Antigone spoke sharply. The man shoved the cushion in Hephaestion's direction. The king's friend took the gilded wreath and held it up as if it was the diadem of Asia, before placing it carefully on Alexander's head. The king pressed it firmly down and remounted his horse. Encouraged, the townspeople, peasants and farmers drew closer. Alexander drew his sword and declared how he had come to free them from the tyranny of Persia, to restore democracy and free all peace-loving Greeks. The towns-people, led by their headman, gave a faint cheer. Ptolemy and the rest kept their heads down, shoulders shaking. Telamon had to glare at Cassandra, who was feverishly gnawing her lip. Even Antigone wore a supercilious smile. Alexander, however, was lost in the glory of the moment.

"My lady, your temple." He gestured at the narrow street from which the procession had come. "We shall worship there!" Alexander tugged at his reins and, with Antigone beside him, rode up the cobbled, narrow street. Here and there were houses, in other places the moss-covered ruins of walls and fallen palaces. It was difficult to visualize the glory and pride of Priam's court or the gold decorated chariots of Hector thundering through such ruins. The narrow street debouched into a square which housed a busy market-place, the stall owners doing frenetic trade with the peasants and farmers. The air was rich with the smells of horse dung, spices, cooking food and rotting fruit.

Alexander made a sign: the herald lifted his trumpet and gave three shrill blasts. The market fell silent. All eyes turned to the mouth of the street. Alexander dismounted and, while grooms hurried to take the horse's reins, solemnly led his party across to the temple of Athena – a small, dingy place with crumbling steps leading up to a colonnaded portico; above this, a tympanum depicting Athena as a warrior. The doors of this shadowy place opened to reveal temple helpers making hasty preparations. One was still sweeping the steps, so sudden and unexpected was Alexander's arrival.

Antigone walked before the king. The townspeople greeted their priestess with cheers and clapping; Alexander took this as a gesture of support for himself. Telamon and others followed him up through the antechamber and into the long, rectangular-shaped shrine, with a row of transepts on either side and, at the far end, a soaring statue of Athena armed with helmet, spear and shield.

Alexander quickly burnt incense before the statue, more interested in the tarred, heavy leather bags which hung on either side. At Antigone's insistence, the temple helpers took these down, undid the cords and drew out the most impressive-looking armour. The weapons were a sharp contrast to their dingy surroundings. A gold, muscle-shaped cuirass with silver-embossed straps and shoulder guards; greaves, their insides padded with soft leather, the outsides silver and gold-rimmed; a red war kilt over a white cloth background, each leather strip embossed with silver roundels. The shield had a soft leather inside with silver straps, its five-layered surface of beaten gold with a large silver medallion in the centre displaying the severed head and whirling hair of the Medusa. The splendid helmet was Corinthian with a silver horsehair crest, its broad ear- and noseguards of costly dark red leather rather than metal.

"The weapons of Achilles," Antigone announced.

Telamon and the rest gazed in disbelief. The armour was precious, undoubtedly the work of a craftsman. The priestess, despite her own grief, caught their suspicions, though Alexander was fully convinced. Telamon wracked his memory: according to the *Iliad* the god Hephaestus had fashioned these weapons, after the death of Patroclus, as Achilles prepared to fight his dramatic, vengeful duel with Hector.

Ptolemy was sceptical. "These weapons are supposed to be hundreds of years old! They look as if they were fashioned yesterday!"

Telamon quietly thanked the gods that Cassandra wasn't present
– her loud, hooting laugh could have cost her her head. Alexander
apparently didn't hear what Ptolemy had said, he was so engrossed,
while Antigone chose to ignore the cynical mutterings of the royal
companions.

"These are yours, Alexander," she proclaimed, her voice low
but carrying. "Captain-General of Greece, descendant of Achilles!"
She turned to the rest as if to quell their doubts. "All I can say is
what I know. These weapons have been kept hidden, handed on
from one priestess to another." She smiled thinly. "True, they have
been repaired, refashioned, rebuilt, but they are still the weapons of
Achilles."

Alexander was already trying them on. The helmet was a little
too large and he muttered something about wearing a hood
underneath. The cuirass fitted snugly. Alexander lifted the shield
– it caught the light streaming through the narrow windows and
shimmered like a silver coin. Alexander's face was flushed, his eyes
vivid, already lost in dreams of being the new Achilles. He
absentmindedly thanked the priestess and vowed to dedicate his
own armour to Athena. He also promised to rebuild a new temple
and refound Troy in all its glory.

Seleucus hid his giggles while Ptolemy raised his eyes heaven-
wards. Antigone withdrew into the shadows and Alexander took
over as the king-priest. His own armour was brought and placed at
the foot of the statue. More incense was burnt and, dressed in his
new finery, Alexander swept out of the temple.

He insisted on visiting all the shrines of Troy. A makeshift altar
was set up in the market-place. Alexander sacrificed to Zeus, god of
the enclosures. Similar offerings were made to Apollo, Athena and
Hercules. He visited the place where Achilles' son slit Priam's
throat and made further expiation. The troops he had brought
were now forgotten. Hephaestion had quiet words with Ptolemy,
and General Socrates was despatched to arrange an encampment.
Led by Alexander, the royal court spent the afternoon visiting
every site in Troy. Merchants, shopkeepers and would-be guides
were all swept up in Alexander's fervour. Excitement grew at his
lavish generosity. All the storytellers, minstrels and confidence

tricksters of the small town flocked like flies to a piece of raw meat, each eager to tell their tale.

"My lord, this is the gate through which Hector drove his chariot."

"My lord king, this is the place where Hector died."

"At this spot, my lord, Ajax violated Cassandra and committed suicide."

Alexander drank it all in as if it was the sweetest wine. One enterprising shopkeeper, however, went too far. He thrust a battered lyre, strings broken, into Alexander's face.

"My lord, this is the instrument which Paris used before the golden-haired Helen. Remember," the shopkeeper added, "Paris' name was also Alexander!" The king glowered at him and thrust him aside.

Telamon's mouth grew dry with dust, his legs ached. He grew tired of having to recall lines from the *Iliad*. He tried to slip away but Alexander grasped him by the arm and dragged him back as if he secretly suspected Ptolemy and the rest were quietly laughing at him.

With the physician on one side and Hephaestion on the other, Alexander never stopped to eat or drink. He seemed oblivious to the strong sun, the dust, the clouds of flies or the need to rest. Verses from the *Iliad* tumbled from his lips. His only concession to the growing exertions was to take off Achilles' armour. He carried the shield while the rest was distributed among the others, Telamon included. Round and round the hill of Troy they went. At last they reached the wild, clover-coloured heathland which stretched to the promontory to the west of Troy overlooking the sea. Here Alexander paused and, at Ptolemy's insistence, watered wine was served in chipped goblets.

Telamon cleaned his throat and mouth and glanced around. Only a few of the king's companions remained, carefully shadowed by a well-armed group of royal bodyguards. The rest had slipped away. Telamon smiled quietly at how Aristander seemed to have made himself invisible. Alexander blinked and wiped the sweat from his face.

"I thought there was more," he murmured, his strange, rather protuberant eyes studying Telamon. "I've always thought of this.

As a boy I dreamt every night that one day I would march in glory to Troy." He took a deep breath. "But, now, I am tired."

Ptolemy cheered under his breath.

Alexander thrust his goblet into Telamon's hand. He took off his cloak and tunic, his sandals and loincloth and stood naked before them. His body was covered with a dusty sweat, yet he was oblivious to any embarrassment.

"Bring me oil! A garland of flowers!" he ordered.

A guard hurried off and brought back the items. Alexander was limbering up like an athlete. No one dared ask why. Ptolemy glared at Telamon.

Alexander turned round. "I am going to run. Haven't you read the *Iliad*? How Achilles and Patroclus hunted wolves naked?"

He pointed to two soaring mounds, a short distance apart, on the promontory.

"The graves of Achilles and Patroclus," Alexander announced. "Hephaestion, will you accompany me?"

"We'll all go," Ptolemy said. "You're going to race, aren't you?"

"Yes, as a tribute to my ancestor," Alexander agreed. "As the heroes did in Homer's time."

He took the flask of oil from the guardsman who put the flowers down on the ground beside him. The rest stripped off like athletes preparing for a race: Ptolemy, short, squat and wiry; Hephaestion, dark and thick-set; Seleucus, light and podgy.

"It's like Mieza!" Alexander declared. "We'll race again as we used to at dawn. Thank god Cleitus isn't here, eh? He'd make us run till we dropped."

"I thought they were buried together," said Telamon.

Alexander's expression became angry. "Who are?"

"Achilles and Patroclus. Do you remember the last book of the *Iliad*?" Telamon closed his eyes and quoted the verse: " 'Therefore let one single vessel, the golden two-handled urn, the one your mother gave me, hold both our ashes.' Aren't they Achilles' words? And in the *Odyssey*, when the wanderer visits Agamemnon in Hades? Doesn't Agamemnon describe how Achilles and Patroclus were buried together? So why are there two burial mounds?"

Alexander gripped Telamon's wrist and nipped the skin. "Perhaps they are, and the other mound was raised as a memorial. Anyway," Alexander glanced out of the corner of his eye at his companions, "we shall race and I shall win."

Telamon and the rest of the retinue watched in bemusement as Alexander, fleet as a hare, raced across the heathland, ploughing his way through the long grass, crushing the bright red poppies. Ptolemy and the rest followed, laughing and shouting, arms flailing, hair flying. They shoved and pushed, but no one overtook Alexander. The figures faded into the distance. They reached the mounds and went round each three times. Telamon could make out Alexander climbing each mound to pour the oil and lay the flowers. Then they raced back. The bodyguard cheered.

Telamon decided he had had enough and made his way back into the town. He found himself in the market square and went around looking at the stalls. All of the food had already been purchased by the quartermasters. The physician stopped at a stall, its one-eyed owner shouting the prices. Telamon studied the vases and boxes.

"The work of local craftsmen," One Eye declared. "Are you a soldier, sir? No, you cannot be . . ."

"I am a physician. I always look for boxes to carry instruments, phials, potions." Telamon, curious, picked one up.

"A few obols, sir, less than a drachma," One Eye declared.

Telamon studied the box closely. "This is the work of a local craftsman?"

"I'd like to say no, sir, but I can see you are sharp. Yes, a carpenter with a small homestead outside Troy. He sells to me, I sells to you."

Telamon paid. He took the small box and made his way back up to the temple. There was no sign of Antigone. The old man who guarded the door was slack-mouthed and dreamy-eyed. He told Telamon that the priestess' house lay in a small garden beyond. The porter got to his feet. Did sir want to be shown around?

Telamon thanked him but said he'd go by himself. For a while he wandered round the temple, but it was like many others he'd visited. The air was still sweet with the incense Alexander had used. The king's armour had been removed, as had the tar-covered cloths. Telamon stood underneath the statue and gazed round. He found it difficult to imagine a woman as graceful and dignified as Antigone serving in a shrine like this. He returned to the ante-chamber. Before he left, the porter unlocked a small coffer and took out a thick scroll.

"Place your name, sir. Inscribe your name, sir, and win the favour of Athena."

Telamon recognized the ritual. He didn't want to give offence so he handed the man a coin. The porter lay the leather-backed scroll on the ground together with an ink horn and goose-quilled stylus. Telamon undid the scroll and wrote the date and his name. Curious, Telamon pushed the scroll back, unrolling it across the floor. He noticed there had been few visitors in the previous months, but one name caught his eye: "Cleon". Telamon also recognized Philip, Alexander's father, and another name, crudely etched.

"What's the matter, sir?"

"Oh nothing, nothing." Telamon got to his feet and the porter re-rolled the scroll. Telamon walked out of the temple. The sun was beginning to set and the breeze blew cooler. Telamon strode down the side of the building. The priestess' house lay behind a courtyard wall; he could see the red tiled roof. He stopped at a gate and gently pushed it open to reveal a small garden with a fountain, in the shape of a nymph, at the centre. Antigone was sitting on a bench with her back to him. He was going to call her name when he saw her shoulders shake and realized she was crying. He did not wish to intrude so he closed the gate and returned the way he had come.

Telamon strolled across the town, through the ruined gateway and down the grassy hillock. Alexander's small army lay camped on the plain below. Typical soldiers, they had made themselves as comfortable as possible. Some had erected tents. Others, less fortunate, had stripped the trees to build makeshift bothies. General Socrates had set up a closely guarded picket line. Telamon was challenged on a few occasions but was recognized and let through. A Thessalian who remembered seeing Cassandra escorted him to the gate of the royal enclosure. He found his tent, Cassandra sitting outside chatting to the guard. She squinted up at him.

"I thought you'd sailed back. Come in!"

She lifted the tent flap. Inside it was comfortable and tidy.

Cassandra had turned a chest into a makeshift table. There was bread, cheese and meat, two cracked jugs, one full of water, the other of wine, and a small bowl of fruit.

"I've been waiting for you."

She placed an oil lamp in the centre of the table. Telamon washed his hands and face.

"We should dine together," Cassandra declared. "The physician with his helper."

She had washed and even put some paint on her face. Her thick red hair was gathered behind and tied with a bronze clasp.

"Where did you get all the food?"

"You gave me some money. I bought some, the rest I stole, like everyone else in this camp. Where's our conquering hero? Strutting round Troy with that ridiculous helmet in his hand?"

Telamon grinned and picked up a piece of cheese. It tasted fresh and tangy. "You should watch your mouth."

"And you should watch your head. Alexander of Macedon is volatile, and cunning with it. He's told you off, hasn't he? The murders? A guard overheard it."

Cassandra half-filled a cup with wine, added some water and handed it to him.

Telamon sipped from the cup. "There's no logic to this. Here we have Alexander of Macedon preparing to invade Asia. He's read everything he knows about Troy. Yet he has to hire guides."

"I thought that was strange," Cassandra replied. "Didn't you?"

"Not until today. It was when the trireme beached." Cassandra made to speak but he raised his hand. "Didn't you notice how Alexander rode directly inland? He never used those guides. Moreover, when we arrived at that ruined place . . ." Telamon paused at the blast of a trumpet. "May the gods be thanked!" he breathed. "The king's returned! Anyway, Alexander reaches Troy and walks around as if he was born here."

"That's what I am trying to say. I've been wondering about these guides. When we watched the army manoeuvres you pointed out the scouts, the light horsemen. I've just seen some of them return from scouring the countryside – they didn't need guides. More important, I went across to the royal pavilion."

"Oh no!" Telamon groaned.

"Well, I offered to help them put the pavilion up, carrying chests and coffers. I met the secretary of the army, what's his name?"

"Eumenes."

"He was carrying scrolls. I had a quick look at one of them."

Telamon rolled the cup between his hands.

"It was a map. I saw the city of Ephesus, another place, Miletus. All the western sea coast of Asia with the offshore islands. The map was very accurate. Eumenes kept it in a coffer. I was very sly, wasn't I?"

Telamon stared in disbelief. "But, but . . . !" He felt a twinge of annoyance at the gleam in Cassandra's eyes.

"What you are trying to say, learned physician, is that if Alexander has scouts and very accurate maps, why should he need Critias and those guides? Why was one murdered on a cliff top? The other out in the darkness? Who did kill them? And Critias? I know his death bothers you. I wonder . . ." Cassandra crossed her arms and hugged herself. "That little runt who disappeared, Aristander's creature Hercules. Did he find something?"

Telamon stared bemused at her. "God in Hades!" he breathed.

"It's all a lie, isn't it, Telamon?"

"I went to the temple. I saw Cleon's name, the physician . . ."

"The traitor?"

"Yes. As I walked back," Telamon stretched out his cup to be refilled, "I began to reflect. Cleon was small and fat. He wasn't a very good horseman yet he managed to ride out of Alexander's camp and not be caught. I mean, if Alexander wanted, and Aristander was keeping an eye on those physicians . . ."

"You don't think Cleon escaped at all, do you? You suspect he's dead?"

"He could be," Telamon murmured. "Or, there again, Alexander could be playing a subtle game. Cleon is simply a part of it, as are we all."

Chapter 11

―――――◄◦◦◦►―――――

"The views of Memnon the other Persian generals scarcely examined. They abruptly terminated the discussion."

Quintus Curtius Rufus, History, Book 2, Chapter 4

Dascylium, the lakeside fortress of Arsites, satrap of Phrygia, was an oasis of green coolness. Its soaring walls and towers were surrounded by rich meadows and game reserves where rare birds and animals thrived. It was a veritable paradise, a pleasure park with its garden terraces, palm groves, shaded walks, canopied bowers and leaping fountains. Both inside and outside the wall of this fortress lagoons glinted in the sunlight, rich and well-stocked with fat carp and other fish. Small woods of holm, oak, ash and fir served as hunting reserves, specially cultivated for the satrap's pleasure. Usually Arsites and his court would lounge out under the sky, feasting and drinking but, on that fateful day, the parklands were empty, silent except for the screech of the brilliantly plumed peacocks on the freshly watered lawns around the castle walls.

Inside, in the dimly lit audience chamber, Arsites and his court met Memnon the Greek. The Rhodian mercenary, dressed in a simple plain tunic, ignored the gorgeous wall tapestries decorated with the fantastic shapes of exotic birds and animals. He lounged, ill at ease, on the golden encrusted banqueting couch and glared at the small acacia-wood table before him, piled high with iced fruits and long fluted goblets emblazoned with silver tigers and filled to the brim with chilled white wine. Memnon had eyes only for Aristes, dressed in his exotic robe of honour over a light golden blouse pushed into trousers. He wore purple and silver slippers and a tight-

213

fitting conical hat, a *kulah*, fringed with ribbons at the back. Arsites' face was rouged, his lips painted, fingernails the colour of henna. His ringleted hair, beard and moustache gleamed with precious oils.

A group of women, Memnon considered. He tried to control his irritation and knew such a judgment was unfair. Arsites and his companions, sprawled on couches around the room, might dress like courtesans but they were brave warriors, eager to bring Alexander to battle. Indeed, that worried Memnon more than anything else. He looked to his right where Cleon, the blond-haired, empty-faced physician, recently arrived from Alexander's camp across the Hellespont, slurped noisily from a goblet. Memnon glowered at him in distaste. Shifting his gaze the Rhodian glimpsed the smiling face of his servant and henchman Diocles who warned him with his eyes, as he had before the banquet, to restrain his temper and not bully Arsites, Mithridates, Niphrates and the rest.

"You are well, General Memnon?" Arsites leaned over and plucked a grape from the bowl in front of him.

"I am well but busy."

Memnon's harsh reply stilled the chatter – all conversation ceased at this breach of etiquette. Arsites picked another grape and popped it into his mouth.

"I have news for you." Arsites' eyes were hostile. "The Macedonian is in Troy. He crossed from Elaeum!"

"What?" Memnon swung his feet off the couch and glared at his host. "How many men did he bring?"

"Sixty triremes; a small force of three thousand."

Memnon clutched his goblet on the table. "If we had known that we could have sent ships, had a force waiting for him. I thought he'd cross with the rest to Abydos and then make his way south. What's the use of a spy in their camp? Shouldn't he have told us?"

"Apparently he never knew in time. A late decision by Alexander."

"What an opportunity! I thought he'd cross with the rest." Memnon was speaking to himself, staring at the tapestry behind

Arsites. "We could have trapped him, we could have killed him."

"He will be trapped and he will be killed," Arsites replied languidly. "But, General Memnon, who gave the orders to land assassins and send them into Alexander's camp?"

Memnon glanced at Cleon. The physician kept his face in his goblet.

"Yes, our good physician brought us news. Alexander killed the assassins and piled their armour as a trophy before his pavilion."

Memnon murmured a quick prayer, a farewell to Droxenius and the rest. "They were good men. They died honourably in battle. What more could a soldier want?" He glared round the room, not liking the atmosphere – his hosts were polite but guarded and reserved. They don't trust me, Memnon thought. His unease deepened and memories of Lysias squatting in that iron cage floated back. In the courtyard below were ten hoplites. Memnon now regretted not bringing more of his force of fifteen thousand mercenaries camped only a few miles to the east.

"Alexander will be trapped and killed," Arsites repeated, watching him intently.

Memnon heard a noise and looked over his shoulder. The door opened. Six of Arsites' bodyguard slipped in, armed with shields, swords drawn. Cleon stopped munching and also peered up, his blue eyes watery, mouth slack. He caught Memnon's gaze and winked.

"May I remind you, Arsites," Memnon kept his voice level, "that I enjoy the personal favour of the King of Kings."

"So you do. So you do."

"This Naihpat?" Memnon continued. "Who is he?"

"We don't know, do we, Cleon?" Arsites lifted his goblet and toasted the half-drunk physician.

"I searched and I searched," Cleon slurred. "And searched again. But who is it?" He moved his head backwards and forwards as if playing some childish game. "I don't know."

"Then you are not very good, are you?" Memnon snapped.

Arsites stared across the rim of the goblet. "He has his uses."

Memnon's disquiet grew. Since he had left Persepolis he had

215

kept in regular communication with Arsites and the rest. He'd suspected Droxenius and his companions had failed: if they had succeeded, the news would have spread as fast as a breeze across the sea.

"What uses?" Memnon asked.

"Whoever Naihpat is – and not even I know the truth; the spy corresponds in a cipher only the Lord Mithra understands – he has done good work. We have reports that Alexander is not so confident. The guides he hired," Arsites smiled, "have suffered casualties."

"What do you mean?"

"Some of them have been murdered as has the map-maker Critias. Alexander can advance south but he will blunder straight into our trap. This man who killed his own father . . ."

"You have no proof of that."

"We don't need proof," Arsites snapped. "He's a parasite, a stench in the nostrils of the Ahura–Mazda who will deliver him into our hands!"

Memnon shook his head. "No, you must not oppose him."

"And what do you recommend?" Niphrates, the young general beside Arsites, asked. He was lighter skinned than the satrap, and delicate faced, but his gaze was fierce, unrelenting. "What do you recommend, General Memnon?"

"That we retreat, burn every house, field and barn! Slay livestock or drive them away! Torch the earth!"

"Never!"

Arsites' sharp retort was applauded by his colleagues.

Memnon stared beseechingly at them. A peacock screeched. Further down the room the songbirds in their golden cages began to sing. Arsites moved his head and smiled slightly.

"The divine one," Memnon declared, "has given me a command . . ."

"He gave you command of fifteen thousand mercenaries," Arsites said. "And the right to sit at this war council. But, you are not King of Kings, Memnon. You must not give . . ."

"I will give whatever advice is needed," Memnon retorted, his face flushed with anger. "I have fought the Macedonian. Surprise, speed, savagery: you have never met the like before." Memnon tried to reason. "Listen. Alexander will march down the coastline. His fleet is pathetic, no more than a hundred and sixty ships and some of them are transports. A good part of this fleet is Athenian, or from other cities who itch to revolt against Macedon's control. It could soon be defeated, driven from the seas."

"I agree with that," Arsites declared. "The Macedonian has come but he will not go home."

"Then retreat," Memnon declared. "Scorch the earth, poison the wells! His men will grow tired and hungry, his famous cavalry will be devoid of honour. Let him stumble about, let mutiny and dissatisfaction be fostered. Let his allies desert, sue for terms." Memnon stretched out his hands, his fingers curled. "And then destroy him."

"So, you would have us burn our barns?" Arsites replied. "Poison our wells, kill our fish, our oxen, turn everything into a desert stinking under the sun. Yes?"

Memnon nodded. "Grass will regrow. New trees can be planted, extra oxen bought."

"And our people?" Arsites said.

"Let them flee further east. Promise them compensation, the joy of seeing Alexander in chains and any survivors of his army loaded with fetters and sent to work in your mines. Or, if you want, have them crucified on either side of the king's highway, a warning to the rest of Greece."

"Do you hate him that much?"

"I hate him that much."

"But you are a Greek."

"Aye, and Alexander is a Macedonian. A barbarian."

"And does he hate you?"

"He has vowed," Memnon replied, drinking quickly from his goblet, "that any Greek found in arms against him will be shown no mercy, given no quarter. My lord Arsites, I will stand, fight and, if necessary, die with you."

"But we have other news."

With one swift movement Arsites cleared his table, sending the bowls and precious goblets clattering to the floor. Cleon jumped.

Diocles was agitated. Memnon's hand dropped to where his dagger should have been but, of course, all weapons had been left outside.

"You are angry, my lord Arsites?"

"I am very angry."

The Persian leaned beneath the couch and brought out a small coffer which he placed on the table in front of him. With one quick gesture he undid the clasp and threw back the lid.

"These are reports from Abydos, from our spies in the harbour and the land around."

Memnon went cold. He suspected what was going to happen. He glanced quickly round the chamber: the swarthy, dark-haired Persians stared implacably back.

"You have estates there?" Arsites demanded.

"The King of Kings has been most generous!"

"I also have estates there!" one of the Persian commanders called out.

"And so have I!" declared another.

"Many of us," Arsites said softly, "used to have estates there. They are now burnt, ravaged and pillaged. Nothing but black ash and guttering flames. But your estates, General Memnon, are not touched."

"You know the reason why," Memnon declared. "The King of Kings has the utmost confidence in me. Alexander, advised by that sly fox Aristander, has probably given orders for my estates not to be touched so as to spread disunity and disharmony between us."

"Your loyalty, my lord," Arsites replied, "is not in question. Is it, Cleon?"

The physician stared quickly at the Persian, then back at Memnon, and shook his head sorrowfully.

"I really do believe," Arsites continued, "that Alexander holds the same high opinion of you as you have of him. He, like us, works hard to create division and sow suspicion." Arsites waved his hand airily. "But we do have proof of other matters. General Memnon, please read this."

He tossed across a small scroll, tied with a piece of ribbon. Memnon took a deep breath, undid the knot and unrolled the letter.

"Read it aloud, my lord."

Memnon found he couldn't. He sat, hands shaking. He recognized the personal script of Alexander and, at the bottom of the letter, the king's own seal. The room fell quiet. Outside, the peacock had stopped its screeching. The songbirds moved restlessly in their gilded cages, as if the oppressive atmosphere had silenced any desire to sing or trill.

"I agree with you, General Memnon," Arsites' voice rose just above a whisper. "If we had known Alexander was going to sail directly to Troy with such a small escort we would have been waiting for him, either at sea or on land. I tell the truth when I say this: if I thought your strategy of burning the earth and poisoning the wells would work, then my colleagues and I would agree. We trust you, General Memnon, but we do not trust those around you. Lysias was a traitor. He wished to meet Alexander in Troy. The divine one certainly spoke the truth when he claimed others were involved in his treachery!"

Memnon stared down at the letter, tears in his eyes.

"But, General Memnon, how can we fully trust you?" Arsites whispered. "When even your manservant Diocles is a traitor?"

Diocles sprang from his couch, knocking over the table. He stood, hands out, mouth trying to form words, eyes begging his master.

"That is a letter, is it not, from Alexander of Macedon?" Arsites continued. "It is in his hand, it bears his seal! It's no forgery. How does it read, General Memnon? I know the words backwards: 'Alexander, king of Macedon, Captain-General of all Greece, to Diocles, friend, servant of the traitor, greetings. The information you have sent us will be of great help in our march to the east as it was in the capture of the Persian spy, Leontes. The gods are with us. I will cross to Troy to make sacrifice to the gods and to my ancestors. Then we shall come searching for your master. Let him run.'" Arsites paused. "Yes, that's what it says, doesn't it?"

He ignored Diocles who had now fallen to his knees, arms across his stomach. "Yes," Arsites repeated. "And how does it continue? 'Let your master run. Let him do our task and burn all behind him. We shall still come on. As we march, we shall grow in strength.

219

The cities of Asia will open their gates and rally to the saviour who will save them from fire and sword. We shall be with you soon. Farewell.' "

"Where did you get this?" Memnon found it hard to speak, his heart beating faster. "Where did you get this?"

"I brought it," Cleon lisped.

"So, you just walked in to the king's tent, rifled through his correspondence and took whatever you wanted?"

"I didn't say that." Cleon was now smiling across at Arsites. "On the day, general, that your mercenaries tried to kill Alexander of Macedon, the camp was in confusion. I returned to my tent and lay down on my bed. Only then did I notice the scrolls resting there in a small leather pouch. I opened and read them. The letter my lord Arsites has just given you was one of them. There are others. In all the confusion at the Macedonian camp, they may not even be missed yet."

"How many?" Memnon asked. "Are there other Greeks in my company?"

Arsites shook his head. "No. Traitors in different cities. Don't worry, they will be dealt with. The letters provide an insight, my friend, into the Macedonian's soul." Aristander waved a finger. "Nowhere does Alexander express an eagerness to bring us to battle immediately. He hopes we will retreat. He counts on traitors in our cities opening the gates." Arsites paused. The sound coming from Diocles was heart-rending. Arsites sprang to his feet. "I will not continue talking until that traitor is removed and dealt with!"

Diocles would have crawled on the floor but Arsites clapped his hands. The bodyguards standing near the door came forward. They pushed by Cleon's couch and lifted the struggling Diocles to his feet. Memnon could only stare in disbelief. Diocles had been with him for at least ten years, his man in peace and war, but the letter in his hand? Memnon shook his head.

"It's not a forgery," he conceded. He glared at Cleon. "Could it have been deliberately left?"

Cleon shook his head. "The spy Naihpat left it in my tent." He sighed. "Which means, my lord, that he also knew I was the recipient of Persian gold. Perhaps he was warning me? After all, one of my colleagues had already been executed, probably betrayed by your servant. Aristander was watching me and the rest. If these letters were found on my person, I would find it very difficult to explain it away. So I decided to leave as quickly as possible."

"And no one tried to prevent you?"

"As I said, the camp was in uproar due to the attack on Alexander. I found it easy enough. I took my horse, said I had errands to do in Sestos. Instead, I went along the coast and hired a fishing boat." Cleon spread his hands. "And here I am."

Diocles tried to lunge forward.

"Take him out!" Arsites ordered.

Diocles struggled, sending a table flying. One of the guards drew his sword and with one blow knocked the manservant unconscious, blood spattering the marble floor. The songbirds screeched. Arsites screamed an order and Diocles was dragged from the chamber. Memnon still couldn't accept it as true.

"It's too easy," he protested. "Letters left in a tent? And you, Cleon, deciding to leave?"

Arsites sat down on the edge of his couch. "My lord, you forget. Our good physician Cleon has been a visitor to our court for many a month. He's in our pay, and worked at great risk, as did Leontes who was betrayed. If Cleon had been captured he might have been crucified. Anyway, why should he lie to us?"

"Perhaps Alexander himself left the letters there?"

"Why should the Macedonian mention he was sailing to Troy directly? And why *did* he do so? He must have known this letter was missing."

"Because Alexander is Alexander," Cleon slurred. "He set his mind and heart on it. And even if you knew, General Memnon, with all your talk of retreating, would you have really gone out to meet him?"

Arsites tapped the coffer. "You forget the other letters. We know how many men Alexander has brought. What supplies he needs. What route he will follow. Above all, his strategy. He's been received in Troy. He cannot afford for other cities to close their gates. Look, my lord, Diocles is now dead, his execution was immediate."

Memnon closed his eyes.

"A swift death," Arsites assured Memnon. "His head has already left his body. He took our gold, he broke bread and ate our salt. Our confidence in you, however, is unshaken. These same letters talk of you in the most unflattering terms. Alexander of Macedon fears Memnon of Rhodes. So, let us prove that fear correct." Arsites spread his hands. "We have sent out our writs. Our armies are assembling. We shall meet the Macedonian in battle."

Memnon was only half listening.

"General Memnon, you had best withdraw for a while," Arsites declared. "Compose yourself. Overcome your grief. Then return and we shall plot a revenge all of Greece shall witness!"

The blood-chilling scream alarmed the shepherds in the early hours of the morning. A long, drawn-out cry of terror which pierced the night and sent them huddling round their fire and their dogs howling at the starlit sky. The shepherds' leader wished to investigate but the others were more cautious. The windswept heathlands around Troy were haunted and the arrival of the Macedonian stirred ancient memories. The shepherds kept their dogs close and watched the sky for the first light of dawn. They wondered what the source of such horror could be. The Macedonian army had now been camped for five days around Troy, and others had joined them. To the shepherds' eyes it was a sea of men, herds of horses, a long, snaking baggage train with the weapons and engines of war; huge catapults, mangonels and battering rams. The Macedonian king had been glimpsed from afar. They had heard rumours, the occasional chatter of a pedlar or tinker, of how an even greater army, a veritable sea of horsemen, were moving west to trap the Macedonian, bring him to battle and utterly destroy him.

In their local patois the shepherds discussed who the victim could be. After all, the Macedonian camp was circled by a ring of steel, the countryside scoured by horsemen. Was it some Persian spy or scout? Or had one of those light horsemen come across some lonely country girl or a wandering journeyman with, perhaps, more coins in his wallet than was wise at such a time. Or was it something more sinister? A sacrifice to the gods? The Macedonian king was keen on sacrifices, setting up altars here and there, dressed in the sacred armour he had taken from the temple. The ancient ones talked of how, when the great Persian King Xerxes had crossed the Hellespont, he had sacrificed a thousand bulls. Would the Macedonian do the same? Or did he believe human blood was more effective in placating the gods?

"The Macedonian is not successful," the shepherd leader declared. "He has sent envoys to the cities but they refused to open their gates. The leaders of Lampascus," he referred to the nearby city, "closed their gates and sent his messengers packing."

"Will he march?" another asked. "Or will he stay in Troy?"

"They say he is about to march," the leader asserted confidently. "And when he does we'll move our flocks. They'll be short of meat: our springtime lambs would disappear like snow under the sun."

"Are they starving?" the shepherd boy piped up. Usually he'd play his reedy pipe, but that scream had silenced everything.

"They are short of food," the shepherd leader confirmed. "They've bought up all the supplies, the market is empty."

"Why haven't they taken our lambs already?" another asked, stretching his hands out to the flames.

"The Macedonian has issued strict orders – his troops are not to pillage. According to him," the shepherd leader laughed, "we are his subjects and our property is sacred. But, don't you worry," he added confidently, "once they are hungry, it will be a clout on the side of the head and our lambs into the cooking pot."

"So what will we do?" the boy asked.

"Into the woods," the shepherd leader declared. "Flocks, children, the lot. Bury everything you can't carry and wait till the buggers have gone!"

A shepherd looked over his shoulder at the trackway, white under the moonlight, snaking away to the south. The shepherds always camped here every night. It was safer. Wolves and other wild animals never came down where the scent of humans was strong.

"Does he know where he's going? Didn't the priestess take guides with her? I heard rumours that some of them were killed."

"But he doesn't need guides." The shepherd leader spread his hands. "You've seen those horsemen?"

The shepherds pulled their fur wraps closer about them and agreed. Macedonian scouts were constantly up and down the roads on their swift, lean horses. Sometimes they'd stop and question the shepherds, talking in their own patois. The questions were always the same: Had they heard rumours? Had they seen Persians? They had even travelled east to the River Granicus and taken two shepherds to show them the easiest ford, asking questions about how high the river could be. They had crossed the Granicus and scouted the wooded hillsides beyond.

"I still think we should see who it is."

The bravest shepherd took a brand from the blaze. He walked from the camp fire but then his imaginings took over: the dark trees moving in the night breeze, the shriek of an animal, the call of some night bird, and his courage faltered.

"We'd best wait until morning," he muttered.

The light in the sky spread, the sun began to rise. The shepherds doused their fire and, grasping cudgels and clubs, made their way up the trackway. The hillside to their right was honeycombed with caves and paths. They ignored these: the scream had come from the road. At first they could detect nothing until their sharp-eyed leader caught a blur of colour on the dusty gravel. They hastened over. The corpse lay rolled off the trackway; the victim's brown tunic, black hair and beard were covered in a fine white dust. One look at the terror-stricken face told them that the man had died a hideous death. They peered curiously at the hideous wound in his side, the strange winged dagger thrust between his ribs, the piece of parchment pushed into his curling fingers. They removed this and opened it up. None of them could read. They peered up the hillside. Had the man come from there? Had he been sheltering in one of the caves? He couldn't have come from the camp, surely? He wore no armour, the tunic was holed and darned, his sandals of poor quality.

"I know him!" the shepherd leader declared. He snapped his fingers. "He's from a village a few miles to the south. He's one of those guides hired by the priestess for the Macedonian army."

224

"What does the parchment say?" a shepherd asked. "Is it a curse?"

The leader took it, squinting carefully. He could make out a few letters but nothing else. One of the dogs howled. They froze at the thunder of hooves, then sprang to their feet but they couldn't flee. The horsemen who came round the corner, bursting out of the fringe of trees, were a squadron of Macedonian light horse, shields winking in the early morning sunlight, cruel barbed lances down, ready to strike. The shepherds huddled together. The squadron broke up and circled them. A shepherd tried to flee but one of the scouts, using his lance, expertly knocked him back. The shepherds sat huddled round the corpse. The ring of horsemen closed in, lances down at the ready. Young men, the shepherd leader thought, staring up at the hard faces. Eager for an excuse to kill, to draw blood.

"What's this?"

The squadron leader swung himself from his black horse, a pantherskin shabraque draping his mount from neck to withers. He took off his bronze helmet and wiped the sweat from his face with the back of his arm.

"A little bit of plunder, eh, lads?" He crouched by the corpse. "Do you know what the sentence is for murder?"

The shepherd leader realized the man was taunting him.

"We don't know who he is," one of the shepherds declared defiantly. "We heard a scream in the night. We came to investigate once it became light. That's what we found."

"You don't know him?"

"Yes, we do," the shepherd leader retorted, his courage returning. "We think it's one of the guides from your army."

The squadron leader was no longer interested in their words. He pulled the winged dagger out and, ignoring the pool of turgid blood which seeped out, examined it. The shepherd leader offered him the scroll. The officer studied it, lips moving. His eyes had lost the taunting look and he swallowed hard and sprang to his feet.

"He is from the camp," he declared. "You shepherds, bring in the corpse!"

He grasped his horse's rein and vaulted into the saddle. Some of his party were left to accompany the shepherds while the rest returned to the camp in a thunderous cloud of dust.

Telamon was with the king when the messenger arrived. Alexander was in good humour, teasing the barber trying to shave him, grinning at Telamon who had asked for this audience. When Ptolemy brought the squadron leader in and showed Alexander the blood-encrusted dagger and the piece of parchment, the king grabbed a cloth, wiped his face and dismissed the barber. He threw the dagger to the ground and passed the parchment to Telamon.

"Do you recognize it?"

"Well, of course I do," said Telamon. "The same old message, like a demonic chant: '*The bull is ready for sacrifice, the slayer is at hand, all is ready.*'"

"And the other quotations? You recognize them?"

"Same source as before," Telamon replied. "Euripides' *Bacchae*."

"Read them out!"

Telamon glanced up quickly. Just for a few seconds he caught that look of cynical amusement in the king's eyes. Are you pretending? Telamon thought. Do you know more about this than you've ever told anyone? He stared down at the verses. He'd spent the last few days in Troy sifting all the evidence he could gather; the more he reflected, the less certain he'd become.

"Read the verses, Telamon!"

"'When you realize the horror you have done, you shall suffer terribly.'" Telamon glanced up. "That's the first. The second is, 'Against the unassailable you run with a rage obsessed.'"

"And the third?"

"'We have you in our net. You may be quick but you cannot escape us now.'"

"And do you know what my response is, Telamon?" Alexander dabbed at his face with the rag he still clutched. "If I had to send messages back, I would take it from Book Seven of the *Iliad*: 'We shall fight again, until the gods choose between us and give victory to one or the other.'"

"Who is the other?" Telamon asked. "Alexander, who is the other? Who is Naihpat?"

The king indicated with his head for Aristander, lurking in the far corner, to leave the tent. "And close the flap behind you!"

The soothsayer, a smirk on his face, left.

"Another guide has been killed," Telamon said.

"Yes, out on the trackway," Alexander mused. "And no one knows how he got there. I could make enquiries, but I am sure that the story will be the same. He was seen in some beer shop or drinking booth just before he disappeared. Somehow or other he was taken through our ring of steel and brutally butchered out in the wilds at the dead of night with a dagger similar to the one which killed my father. And these haunting verses of Euripides . . ." Alexander sat down on a stool and rubbed his hands together.

"You should be worried," Telamon said.

"I am." The king grinned. "And if this news gets out among the men . . ." Alexander lifted a finger. "That's the real danger of all this! But Aristander won't tell anybody! The squadron leader will keep his mouth shut and, of course, Telamon talks to no one, apart from his red-haired, barbarian woman."

"I don't own her," Telamon retorted. "And she's not a barbarian, she's a Theban."

"Do you know something," Alexander continued, ignoring Telamon's outburst, "in a few hours we break camp. Parmenio has now joined us. We will march east to the Granicus. The gods will decide."

"East! I thought we'd go south along the coast!"

"So did everybody else." Alexander was smiling to himself, relishing this most secret of jokes.

"You decided this long ago, didn't you?" Telamon exclaimed. "It's all been a fable! You're aiming like an arrow for Darius' heart: the opening game is to be decided on one throw of the dice!"

"You lack confidence, Telamon."

"Naihpat, my lord?"

"I don't know."

"But you suspect?"

Alexander cupped his face in his hands, beating his fingers against his cheeks.

"I suspect. I suspect a number of people, Telamon."

"Nothing is what it seems."

"You're a physician! You know that."

"So was Cleon."

The king threw his head back and laughed.

Telamon flushed with anger. "Cleon isn't a traitor, is he?" he demanded. "I can't imagine our fat little physician saddling a horse and riding out. Is he Naihpat?"

"No, no, he isn't." Alexander became serious. "I'll tell you the truth about him. Cleon is one of Aristander's creatures. Cleon was born to spy, with his dull eyes, bovine looks and fussy little manner. No one thinks Cleon's dangerous, but he is. He's wandered the courts of Persia and, apparently, sold his soul to them. What they don't know is that Cleon loves me like a young girl would her suitor. He would no more betray me than fly to the sun!" Alexander laughed shortly at the surprise on Telamon's face.

"He's my spy, misleading the Persians, and Memnon in particular, creating confusion in the enemy's ranks with letters I've given him. So, before the battle is joined, let me assure you, we have no other spy in Memnon's camp. One of his cavalry commanders, Lysias, wanted to meet me secretly at Troy. Cleon suspected that it wasn't because he wished to betray Memnon but to kill me. Lysias was a Theban. He had the blood feud. He would no more kneel and kiss my painted toes than I would his arse! He thought Cleon was in his pay and asked the good physician to arrange a meeting.

Cleon, however, suspected the truth and, instead of selling me to the Persians . . ."

"Sold Lysias instead?"

"Very good, Telamon. Memnon has a number of weaknesses and that's one of them. He hires mercenaries whose first loyalty is to themselves. Lysias never told him anything about the projected visit; he only confided in Cleon."

"And Droxenius?" Telamon asked. "The leader of the assassins who nearly killed us?"

Alexander shook his head. "My life is in the hands of the gods. I am immortal, mortal no longer. Droxenius could no more have slain me than become king of Athens!"

"Did you know he was coming?"

"No, I didn't, but Cleon told me to be careful."

"And you had your revenge?"

"Yes." Alexander patted his thigh. "The Persians didn't send Droxenius and his killers, they want me to come on. The Thebans were Memnon's men so I thought I'd teach Memnon a lesson. Never to go hunting the lion, or try and sell its skin, as long as it rules as king of beasts. I'd struck hard and fast. Several letters were written in my own hand, attested by my own seal, to so-called traitors in certain Persian cities. I also addressed one to Diocles, Memnon's mute servant and lieutenant. I arranged Cleon's departure and made sure he safely arrived at the satrap of Phrygia's castle where, I am sure, Cleon is now doing what he does best, stirring up trouble."

"Ah, so he's the one who told Aristander about Leontes?"

"Of course. And Aristander went hunting." Alexander leaned forward and grasped Telamon's hand. "I also know about Ptolemy's little tricks. One of these days I'll teach him a lesson. The trouble with Ptolemy is he believes Philip was his father, that he's a better general than I, and a better soldier! Ptolemy may be good, but he'll soon learn his proper place in the scheme of things."

Telamon held Alexander's gaze and watched the shifting light in his eyes. You are more than one person, he reflected. You are an actor. You can take on roles, put on masks, with all the ease of a skilled professional: Alexander the bluff soldier; Alexander the general; Alexander the romantic; Alexander the daydreamer; Alexander the schemer and the plotter.

"I was well schooled," the king whispered. "With a mother like Olympias, and a father like Philip, can you blame me, Telamon?"

"Cleon could be in danger."

"Telamon, we are all in danger. Cleon takes his chances."

"But he won't be believed."

"Oh, I think he will be. I ordered old Parmenio not to touch Memnon's estates near Abydos. I have already sent Lysias packing. Now I'll drive the wedge between Memnon and his Persian masters even deeper. Never forget, Telamon – Persians don't like Greeks, Greeks don't like Persians. Persians don't trust Greeks,

Greeks don't trust Persians. Shall I tell you my real enemy? Not Darius or Arsites, but Memnon! Memnon is a good soldier. He has fought Macedonians. He has studied my father's methods, and mine. One thing I dread is the Persians following Memnon's advice. Imagine it. The countryside burnt and devastated. The Persians retreating before us. The cities keeping their gates locked. They won't open them unless I achieve a great victory. I must win one soon. We have only twenty days of supplies left. My fleet is small and I wouldn't trust some of its captains as far as I could spit. We need food. We need plunder. We need victory or the army will revolt."

"You're looking for a battle?"

"Telamon, I am praying every day for one."

"And Naihpat?"

"Victory will take care of Naihpat, as will you, Telamon. I just want to be certain."

"These guides," Telamon asked, "you don't really need them. You've already got maps. Your father must have had them made."

"It's all part of the web." Alexander rubbed his hands together. "Cleon will be stirring the pot. The Persians think I am frightened, demoralized. They will come out and fight. One way or the other, with a simple throw, I'll prove what I've always wanted to."

Alexander rose and patted the physician on the shoulder. "The rest I leave to you, Telamon, and to the gods!"

Chapter 12

"To the Persian, it seemed as if the opportunity for single combat was god-given. He hoped that by his personal courage, Asia might be relieved of its terrible threat and the renowned daring of Alexander halted."

Diodorus Siculus, *Library of History*,
Book 17, Chapter 20

A long the valley of the Granicus the farmers and shepherds talked for years about the great carnage, the bloody battle fought as the dust haze lay thick over the fields of sunflower and corn and the river breeze brought the first coolness of the dying day. For decades afterwards their children searched for weapons: daggers, swords, shields and spears. Occasionally the most fortunate found a jewel, a golden-encrusted dagger, a ring, or some other precious gem which decorated the cloths of glory the Persian chieftains and satraps wore. For days afterwards, beautiful horses roamed the valleys searching for their masters, while the kites and the buzzards and the scavengers from the forests filled their bellies on the flesh of corpses. The valley people would nod wisely. They had seen the beginning of it all: thousands upon thousands of Persian horsemen streaming down the hills through the clumps of ash, oak, fir and cypress. The troops of the King of Kings going out to confront Alexander, a glorious sight in their gold-embroidered cloaks with fish-scale armour, pantaloons of red-purple and green pushed into knee-high boots of soft goatskin, plumed steel helmets on their heads. The pretty boys, the sons of the Medes, with their faces painted and rouged, wearing horn-felt caps with lappets for their ears and a mouthpiece to protect their lips and nostrils from the clouds of dust and the hordes of black flies. Around their waists were silver-encrusted war belts carrying daggers and scimitars. In one hand they carried their rounded shields emblazoned with all the colours of the rainbow, in the other the light wood javelins with their cruel barbed points, sharpened to sink deep into the flesh of the barbarians from Macedon.

The cavalry slouched, reins in their hands, on horses of every colour and variety, embroidered with ornate harnesses and gorgeous saddle-cloths. They hailed from every province of the empire: light-skinned Persians from the west rode next to swarthy, turban-bearing light horsemen from the fabulous lands of the Hindu Kush. Behind the horsemen came their Greek mercenaries, heads shaven, moustaches and beards clipped, faces darkened by the sun. They marched lightly in tunics, boots on their feet, armour and harness, spears and shields piled on the carts which trundled alongside them. Their leader Memnon rode with the Persian princes but the brigade commander, the thin-faced, deeply scarred Omerta, swaggered at their front. The mercenaries were in a good mood. Well paid and provisioned, each man carried his own pack. The Persian lords had also filled the provision carts with the finest bread and meats, the best wines and beers of their own country. The prospect of pay was good: pure Persian darics with the promise of more when the battle was over. The mercenaries marched in unison – broad phalanxes of men, eight wide, sixteen deep, with a gap between each battalion. Trumpeters walked along the flanks, scouts searched ahead, ready to raise the alarm at the prospect of a surprise attack. The mercenaries' officers had informed them that the Macedonians were lost, confused and ill-provisioned. Memnon, Omerta and the rest of the senior commanders did not reveal their deepening unease – how they were deeply distrusted by the Persian commanders, the fierce debate on what would be their place, position and function in the Persian battle line.

Memnon rode with Arsites. The satrap and his commanders were arrayed in gorgeous gold and silver armour with purple-dyed cloaks. Their ears, throats and wrists shimmering with precious jewels. Memnon, however, was dressed simply in a plain tunic and a leather boiled cuirass, while a page carried his helmet and shield.

Time and again Memnon would ask Arsites to send out more scouts to discover where Alexander was. He had even tried to reopen the argument and beg the Persian commanders to retreat, to fall back, but Arsites was adamant. Their last council meeting had been held at the town of Zeluceia, the final decisions made. They would march to the gate of Asia, the river valley through which the Granicus flowed, and take up position on its eastern bank. Memnon had asked why and received shattering news: Alexander was not marching south along the coastline as expected but advancing east to confront them.

"I told you," Memnon confided to Arsites. "Alexander will change his mind at the drop of a coin. What he says and what he does are two different things."

"And what he plans and what will happen," the Persian retorted, "is also another matter again."

Memnon sighed and stared into the far distance. Somewhere along the plain of Adresteia his mortal enemy was marching to meet him.

In fact, Alexander was moving more swiftly than Memnon ever imagined. Some detachments had joined the king at Troy. He had then left that fabled city, joined Parmenio at the small town of Arasbio and struck east. Alexander dropped all pretence: the guides were dispensed with. Scouts were despatched in scores to scour the countryside. Time and again Telamon had seen them galloping back along the line. Alexander wanted to be seen: a great cloud of dust shrouded the army, the hills echoed with the pounding of marching men, the rumble of carts and the neigh and clatter of horses. The light caught the glint of weapons, the colours of the different regiments, and trumpets brayed constantly. The Macedonian army was in full battle array: two great columns, 750 men across the front, 16 deep, a gap between each eighth and ninth man so that the rear brigades, if necessary, could turn quickly to challenge any threat. Cavalry protected the wings and baggage trains trailed behind, shielded by a curtain of lances. Here and there soldiers sang ribald songs about their comrades in rival units. Alexander galloped up and down the ranks, giving his orders which were repeated so that every man knew.

"Remember the Macedonian way! The right wing is the hammer, the centre phalanx is the anvil, the left is the fire. Every man must know his place, watch your squadron commanders! Listen to the trumpets, memorize their calls!"

Telamon and Aristander accompanied the king in these morale-rousing gallops. Alexander was in fine fettle, exchanging good-natured insults and jokes with officers and men. Now and again he would rein in, call a man out from the ranks, tell him he knew his father or kinspeople, toss a coin and ride on. Debate was rife about where the Persians would make their stand. Parmenio, brigade commander of the left flank, urged caution. Alexander just laughed.

"If you were a Persian," Ptolemy called out, "where would you stand?"

"If I were Persian," Alexander retorted to hoots of laughter from his companions, "there would be no Macedon!"

The hot day drew on. Scouts came streaming back. They brought precise news: the Persians were on the far side of the Granicus deploying their forces. Alexander ordered his columns to halt. The baggage carts were immediately brought up and weapons distributed. The phalanx men grasped the long sarissas, pulling their causias firmly down on their heads. Shield-bearers put on corselets and armed with shields, swords and spears, donning their Phrygian helmets adorned with the colours of their units. Alexander dressed for battle, insisting on wearing the gorgeous helmet, cuirass, kilt, greaves and shield he had taken from the temple of Athena at Troy. The helmet was now decorated with white plumes. Cleitus, bear-like, remonstrated.

"The Persians will see you. They'll mark you out. My lord, must you strut like a peacock when the fox is absent?"

"Some peacock, some fox," Alexander retorted, winking at Telamon who stared curiously at the armour.

Over the last few days Telamon's suspicions about what was being plotted had only deepened. Time and again he had discussed it with Cassandra, and a hypothesis was forming. Sometimes he'd catch Alexander watching him out of the corner of his eye. Telamon suspected Alexander himself realized the truth, but the king was as impetuous, audacious and imperious as ever – even more so now. In his gold and silver armour, purple cloak and gorgeous helmet, Alexander would be a clear target for the Persians. The king leaned over and grasped Telamon's arm.

"You will ride with me, Telamon? As you did at Mieza?"

"Is that why you brought me here?"

"I missed you, Telamon, I always did. You were always truthful, not sly like Seleucus or sneering like Ptolemy."

The king ignored the agitation and bustle around him: men arming themselves, muttering prayers, making farewells to companions, giving messages to each other to pass on if they didn't survive.

"And my father?" Telamon asked. "I've always wanted to know. Why did he change?"

"You ask me that now!" Alexander joked. "Well, Telamon, the answer is what's happening now. Your father tired of hot blood being spilt, of carnage and the shock of battle."

"But not you, eh, my lord?"

Alexander shook his head, gathering the reins in one hand, the other smoothing down the fur of the leopardskin shabraque over his horse's withers. The legs of the pelt hung down, the claws unsheathed, specially polished.

"Not me, Telamon," Alexander whispered. "For me, the glory and the fire!"

The king dug his heels in. Aristander had disappeared. With Cleitus on his right, and Telamon just behind on his left, Alexander rode down the column urging a speedy double march. The army was now transformed. Squadron after squadron of horsemen: the Companions, the Thessalians, the Thracians, the different brigades and regiments of foot soldiers, Cretan archers, slingers and Agrainian footmen. At the core of the Macedon army, the regiments of shield-bearers and phalanx men, huge sarissas held high, all marched at double pace. Trumpets blared, the battle line deployed, moving from the road through the fields down towards the Granicus. Telamon glanced back. Cassandra was with the baggage train. He had left strict instructions as to what she should do if things went wrong. The die was cast: he was with Alexander and with Alexander he would stay, be it for life or death.

The Macedonians reached the reed-fringed river bank and deployed rapidly. Parmenio, with cavalry and a mixed brigade of shield-bearers and phalanx men, commanded the far left. Ptolemy, Amyntas and Socrates commanded the centre corps of phalanx men and shield-bearers. Alexander, with the royal squadron of Companions cavalry, supported by two battalions of shield-bearers and the same number of phalanx men commanded the right.

Alexander surveyed all from a small hillock, trumpeters and messengers around him.

"Remember how it is!" He pointed down the line. "On the left Parmenio! In the centre, Ptolemy, Amyntas and Socrates. Myself on the right! We are the hammer, the centre is the anvil, the left is the fire! So, gentlemen, let's survey the river!"

Alexander, accompanied by his staff officers and household, Telamon among them, left the hillock and rode down through a fringe of willow trees, wild gorse and bushes to the river's edge. The Granicus flowed sluggishly over its white and grey pebbled bed.

"Good! Good!" Alexander murmured. "Not too deep!"

"It's thirty yards wide!" a staff officer muttered.

Telamon looked across the river and his heart sank. On the far side rose high, clay banks, while a little further back were trees and bushes which would impede any assault.

"We will wait! We will wait!" Alexander ordered. "Let's see what mistakes Arsites will make!"

The Persian high command were in confusion. Their scouts had brought news of Alexander's rapid march and deployment. They lacked such speed: Arsites was still issuing his orders, which were impeded by poor communication between different units. The cavalry stretched eight deep in a long line, led by their commanders and tribal chieftains. The line extended for about a mile and a half – a human rainbow of steel, coloured cloths, banners and neighing horses. The air dinned with shouted orders and trumpet blasts.

Now and again similar faint sounds from their enemies drifted across the river.

Memnon sat on his horse staring in stunned disbelief at Arsites. The satrap's face was hidden by his helmet with its broad chain mail protection for ears and cheeks.

"My lord, this is madness!" Memnon exclaimed. "Alexander is moving too fast." He gestured at the sun, now beginning to dip in the west. "You expected him to camp for the night and he hasn't. We're now fully . . ."

"I have overall command!" Arsites snapped. "The Persian cavalry will advance through the trees to command the eastern bank of the Granicus. Alexander must cross, and he will fail."

"But my Greeks!" Memnon exclaimed, stretching out to grasp the bridle of Arsites' horse.

The Persian tugged angrily at his reins, his horse skittering back. The satrap's lieutenants glared at Memnon, hands falling to their scimitars.

"It is unheard of," Memnon pleaded. "My Greeks should be in the centre, a bristling phalanx of spearmen. They will hold back the Macedonians."

"You have my orders," Arsites replied coolly. "We will go through the trees. You will position your brigade on the high ground behind the Persian line. They will not occupy the place of honour!"

"It's not a question of honour!" Memnon screamed. "When the Macedonians come climbing up those banks . . ."

"They will be met by a shower of javelins," Arsites interrupted. "Debate is now ended!"

The satrap turned his horse away. Orders were shouted. Trumpets blared, standards dipped and the Persian line moved through the trees towards the river bank.

A Persian staff officer rode back to where Memnon still sat, staring in disbelief at the phalanx of Greek mercenaries dressed in order of battle – a dark square of spears, shields and helmets.

"My Lord Arsites sends his compliments," the staff officer said. "He asks you to be with him in the place of honour in the centre."

237

"I shall be there."

The staff officer galloped away. Memnon tugged at the reins of his horse and rode gently to where Omerta and his lieutenants stood in front of the phalanx.

"You have your orders!"

Memnon stared at Omerta and his second-in-command gazed back, eyes gleaming through the slits of his plumed Corinthian helmet.

"This is madness!" Omerta whispered.

"It's because they don't trust us," Memnon replied. "Omerta, be careful, stand your ground. If the Persian line breaks, only retreat on their orders. Do *not* move without Arsites' approval, otherwise they may suspect treachery."

Omerta lifted his spear in salute. Memnon stretched out his hand in reply and gazed across the serried phalanx of mercenaries.

"You have your position!" he shouted. "We have met Macedonians before and beaten them!"

A loud cheer greeted his words as they were repeated from file to file.

"Take up your place and await further orders!" Memnon shouted. "Do not move to the front or the rear!"

Tears stung his eyes. He tried to make his voice sound firm but his words of encouragement rang hollow. He was aware of the sun beating down, the call of a bird swooping over the grasslands, the distant buzz of a bee. His men were watching him intently. They truly believed that today they would see victory. Memnon found it difficult to deceive them. The beating of his heart and the lump in his throat prevented any further speech. He lifted his hand in salute and turned his horse away. He rode, surrounded by his officers, up to the Persian line.

"I didn't know they distrusted us so much," he whispered to himself. "If only I had known!" He reined in and looked over his shoulder at the phalanx, which was now moving slowly forward. He felt like riding back, giving the order to turn about and march as far away as possible, but Arsites would like that: proof that the Greeks couldn't be trusted and Memnon should not be the object of the King of King's favour. Memnon would be finished, his mercenaries attacked on every side by Macedonian and Persian alike. The die was cast. Memnon snatched his helmet from an aide-de-camp.

"My lord," the officer asked, "what can we do?"

"Fight and pray!" Memnon snapped, putting his helmet on. Digging his heels in, he urged his horse into a gallop.

The Macedonian battle line now stood above the dark clay river bank overlooking the Granicus. The men looked at the cool water, licked dry lips and stared fearfully across. All they could see was the clay bank and the copse of trees and bushes beyond. Alexander, surrounded by his officers, watched and waited. Somewhere along the line a man began to chant a hymn. Alexander despatched a messenger ordering silence. The last of the wine was drunk. Alexander poured a libation and watched it seep into the mud. He glanced at Telamon, who had now also donned a helmet and cuirass, and had a sword belt looped over his neck and shoulder.

"Nothing more magnificent than an army in battle array!"

Telamon could only agree. Alexander, with commanders of the Royal Brigade, stood on a small rise – to their left stretched the entire army in battle array: ten thousand infantry, five thousand cavalry.

"The Persians have about the same number," Alexander declared as if he could read Telamon's thoughts. "About twelve thousand cavalry, five thousand Greek mercenaries." The king raised his fist in excitement. "I want to see how they manoeuvre!"

A low murmur broke from the ranks. Telamon looked across the river. His heart skipped a beat. The Persian line was debouching from the trees, row upon row of brilliantly garbed horsemen, armour glinting in the late afternoon sun. More and more came, the line now stretching out to match the Macedonians. Alexander could hardly keep still in his excitement.

"See, see what they are doing!" he exclaimed. "They'll try to outflank us!" He turned to one of the pages. "Go down and tell Amyntas, Ptolemy and Parmenio our line is to be lengthened. Tell Parmenio in particular to watch his opponents."

A huge roar rose from the enemy ranks as a group of gaudily dressed officers made their appearance. They pushed through the

Persian ranks and galloped along the river bank. They paused and stared across at Alexander and his party.

"Arsites!" Alexander whispered. "They say he dresses like a woman but fights like a wildcat." His keen eyes searched the enemy command. "Memnon's there . . . oh, the gods be thanked!" Alexander's eyes were bright with excitement. "I don't believe this!"

"What is it?" Telamon asked.

"Oh, Cleon, I could kiss you!" Alexander whispered. "Can't you see, Telamon? The Greek mercenaries are nowhere to be seen. The Persians must be keeping them in the rear." Alexander held his hand up as if lecturing a group of recruits. "Never have infantry behind cavalry. They must be in front, supported by cavalry, never behind them!"

The Persian line now fully debouched to take up its position: row upon row of men, a wall of colour, shining shields, helmets glittering, horses neighing, moving backwards and forwards with the excitement of their riders. Faint shouts drifted across along with the sound of trumpets, jingling harnesses and the chilling rasp of weapons being drawn.

Telamon looked down their own lines and took in the coloured helmets of the shield-bearers, the phalanx men, the Thessalians and Thracians. He glanced over his shoulder. Aristander had arrived, on foot, surrounded by the chorus, all of whom were armed with great oval shields; some carried swords, others two-headed axes.

"How quiet it is!" one of Alexander's officers murmured.

The Persians, arrayed in a long line of mounted men, stared silently across at the Macedonians. The only movement on the Macedonian line were the mules on the far left, bringing up the hideous engines of war: mangonels, catapults and giant slings.

The river breeze wafted away the dust. It was a serene spring afternoon, lit by the dipping sun, the Granicus meandering slowly over its gravel bed. Above, birds swooped and called. Sunflowers and blossoms, shaken down and crushed under the hooves of the horses and the hard sandals of the fighting men, bathed the river banks with their fragrance.

There was no excitement or tension now – only an awesome stillness, as if the armies confronting each other wondered whether this bloody business should begin or not. Abruptly a catcall echoed through the air, a stream of abuse from some of Alexander's phalanx men in the centre. A Persian urged his horse forward, riding almost languidly down the bank to the river's edge.

"What are you doing?" he called out. "Where are you going in the territory of the King of Kings? Have you his permission? Have you brought tribute? What are you? Men in women's skirts! I bring you a message. If you lay down your weapons, we'll smack your bottoms and let you go!"

The Persian turned his head slightly as if eager for a reply. A Macedonian phalanx man ran forward. He turned his back to the enemy, lifted his kilt and broke wind, to the glee of his comrades, some of whom picked up stones and flung them aimlessly across the river.

"It is time!" Alexander ordered. "You will all follow me!"

He put his helmet on, drew his sword and thundered down the bank and along the Macedonian front. Telamon and the rest had no choice but to follow. The physician felt relieved to be moving, to catch the breeze from the river. Alexander thundered in front, sword held high, his armour-encased head and body dazzling as if he were a god. He did not ride Bucephalus, his precious pet, but a sure-footed warhorse. Each unit he passed raised their lances, rattled sword against shield and greeted him with the Macedonian battle cry, beseeching their ancient god of war: "Eynalius! Eynalius! Eynalius!"

The cry thrilled through the river valley. Telamon was aware of staring eyes, helmeted faces, the smell of leather, the pungent stench of sweat; the fear and the courage in so many faces and eyes. They passed the shield-bearers, weapons clattering to greet their king. They reached the centre and Ptolemy, his face relaxed and cynical beneath his bronze helmet. Socrates was fighting to control his horse. Amyntas, leader of the elite brigade of shield-bearers, roared the war cry, eager to release the tension and excitement within him. Finally, they reached the left wing of the Macedonian army under Parmenio, a veteran of many campaigns. He, too, was incredulous at the Persian's mistake and claimed he couldn't believe his eyes.

"The mercenaries should be there, my lord." He pointed across to the Persian centre. "Who knows? Perhaps they've left them at home?"

Alexander, however, was no longer interested in anything but his battle plan. He clasped Parmenio's wrist.

"You have my orders. Hold your line." He pointed down towards the line of catapults and mangonels. "When the attack begins, keep them silent. Don't force the Persian right to move."

"Is this wise?"

Alexander, already turning his horse, made a cutting movement with his hand. He galloped back down the line and stopped in the centre.

"Socrates, go first! Two squadrons of cavalry. Tell them to kick up as much spray as they like. Take a troop of lancers and auxiliaries. Aymntas, follow after with a brigade of shield-bearers – they will establish the bridgehead. Let the phalanx men come up behind – Ptolemy, that's your concern!"

"My lord," Amyntas protested. "We have to cross a river. True, it's shallow, the current is weak, but then we must climb a bank. The Persians will hurl down javelins."

"Let them hurl!" Alexander's voice was cold with repressed fury. "But if you think you are unable to do this . . ."

"No, no." Amyntas shook his head and put his helmet back on.

Alexander leaned across and chucked him under the chin. "Move obliquely to the right," he whispered. "Don't despair, don't give way. You have it now. Socrates first, move straight across. Amyntas behind, moving slightly to the right. Amyntas, stop being so excited. The Persians have no foot soldiers, they have few archers, they each carry two javelins. Once they have thrown them, they must draw their swords and come down to meet you."

Beneath his helmet Amyntas' face creased into a smile.

"They can't charge," Alexander added. "Their horses will slither, push and jostle. Riders will slip. Wait for my signal. Let them feel the full fury of Hades."

Alexander rode back to the small hillock. He made the sign to his

242

trumpeter – one long shrill blast, the sign for the advance. Socrates'
trumpeter answered this. A wild roar broke out from the Macedonian ranks as Socrates led his squadrons into the water. Alexander
watched horse and rider battle against the river. Some Persians,
unable to control their excitement, rode down to the water's edge
eager to engage the enemy. Socrates' men fanned out. The
movement of such a large force sent up a thick spray. Another
trumpet call. Amyntas led his brigade of foot soldiers into the water.
They didn't follow Socrates directly but formed a wedge and
moved obliquely to the right. The Persian commander noticed this
and began to move troops to check them.

Socrates' line reached the far bank to be greeted by a hail of
javelins. Horses and riders went down, the animals screaming and
kicking, riders clambering off. Telamon saw one kicked by a hoof.
The man fell back into the river, his body turned and twisted, and
floated face downwards past his companions, still struggling to find
a foothold.

Here and there Socrates' men managed to scale the bank only to
be attacked by the Persians thronging down, a sea of gleaming
scimitars eager to push them back. The air echoed with the clash of
steel, the neigh of horses, the shouts and screams of men. One
horse, its rider headless but somehow trapped by his reins, thundered along the river before missing its footing and collapsing,
throwing off its grisly burden. The pure water of the Granicus
turned a dull red. Bodies floated in mid-stream. Men screamed for
help, their faces drenched in blood.

Alexander watched, motionless. Amyntas' men reached the far
bank, shields locked together in close order. They were met by
Persian cavalry. First came a rain of javelins and Amyntas' ranks
dissolved, men falling or turning away in bloody agony, forgetting
all discipline and fleeing from the terror which confronted them.

Alexander sat stony-faced. One of Socrates' riders came galloping up, hands and arms covered in bloody cuts.

"My lord!" he gasped. "We cannot gain a foothold!"

"Tell Socrates to stay where he is," Alexander said quietly.

The brigade of shield-bearers was now fighting on the water's
edge, finding it difficult to find a secure foothold. Some men

slipped, to be trampled by their companions. Others moved away. The more zealous clambered up the bank. One small group of shield-bearers was surrounded. Scimitars rose and fell in flashing arcs and bloody corpses slid back down the bank. Once again Alexander looked along the still silent line of Macedonians.

"Now for the hammer!" he murmured.

He secured his helmet and snapped his fingers for his shield. A white-faced pageboy handed this up. Alexander thanked him, told him not to worry and led his own squadrons down to the water's edge.

Telamon followed in a dream. The horse he rode had been chosen by the king, a sturdy, sure-footed animal. Telamon felt uncomfortable in the leather cuirass, a heavy shield on his left arm. He wore a sword but carried no spear – he was a poor horseman and would need both his hands to stay mounted. All around him thronged Alexander's attacking force: the Royal Brigade of Companion cavalry, supported by shield-bearers and lancers.

Once he was in the river, Alexander moved quickly. He moved obliquely to the right, well away from the Persian line. The air echoed with the thunder of hooves, the splash of water, the neigh of horses, the gasps and shouts of men. Alexander rode like a man possessed. They were across the river, climbing the bank. A group of Persian cavalry appeared at the top. Alexander rode straight for them. Lances jabbed at face and chest. Telamon followed behind. Hephaestion suddenly appeared on Alexander's left. On his right was Black Cleitus, a giant, awesome figure in his black cloak bearing his Medusa shield and his broad stabbing sword.

The rest of the attacking force fanned out. They secured the top of the bank. To their right Telamon glimpsed the Greek mercenaries standing on a small rise, spears in the upright position. Directly in front was the Persian line, its flank now exposed to Alexander's attack. The Macedonians screamed their war cry and thundered towards them. The Persians were already alerted to the danger. A wave of cavalry charged to confront the Macedonian menace.

Telamon was soon in the thick of the fighting. He pressed his thighs tighter against his horse in order to stay mounted. Being so close behind the king, he faced very little opposition but saw the evidence of Alexander's bloody handiwork – Persian cavalry men knocked off their horses, crushed under the charge, bodies crushed or slashed by lashing hooves. Those who met Alexander and his companions in hand-to-hand combat were brutally overcome and thrust aside. The sheer savagery and energy of Alexander and his fellow killers brooked no opposition. They jabbed at horse or rider. With one stroke of his sword, Cleitus took a Persian's head clean off his shoulders, while another sat on his mount and stared in disbelief at the bloody cut in his stomach, his entrails slopping out into his lap. Another came in. Cleitus' horse seemed to brush him. The man swept by. Telamon turned to face the threat but the Persian's sword hand had gone leaving only a blood-spouting stump.

Eventually the sheer press of Persian cavalry slowed the Macedonian assault. Alexander and the others in front of Telamon became locked in hand-to-hand combat: horse and rider against horse and rider, pushing and shoving, jabbing and slashing. Occasionally a Persian would break through. Telamon met one, shield to shield, lashing out with his sword and catching the man more by luck than skill in the exposed flesh between neck and shoulder.

At last they were through. Alexander was not concerned about what was happening on the river bank below – his only aim was to reach the Persian centre. Despite the crash of battle, Alexander's tactics were working. More and more Persian cavalry flowed from the centre to meet this new threat and more Macedonian foot soldiers crossed the river, hastily following in Alexander's footsteps. A tremendous roar came from the river bank followed by the Macedonian battle cry: the phalanx men were across, pushing back the Persian horse.

Telamon became confused, caught up in a nightmare of whirling steel, curses and shouts, falling bodies and trampled corpses. He heard shouts of "Lances down!" and "Forward!", accompanied by a bray of trumpets. Cleitus was screaming something. Telamon looked up, wiped the sweat from his face and knocked his helmet off. They had beaten off the first assault by the Persian cavalry but a second wave, led by gorgeously caparisoned officers, were heading directly for Alexander. The king screamed his war cry and charged to meet them, his companions thundering behind. Alexander reached the Persian leader: with one thrust of a javelin he'd snatched from somewhere, the king took the Persian directly in the chest bone, lifted him out of the saddle and sent him sprawling into the dust. Telamon was behind, lashing out with his sword. Cleitus, the battle rage on him, fought to protect Alexander's back. He gazed wild-eyed at Telamon.

"The armour!" he screamed. "It's the armour!"

Telamon was aware of dark faces: Persian officers in beautiful helmets and armour. He understood Cleitus' panic. They were now being attacked by the Persian high command. The leading officers and chieftains had recognized Alexander and, supported by their bodyguard, were intent on trapping and killing the Macedonian upstart. The fight became a vicious hand-to-hand struggle, shield against sword, sword against shield. Telamon simply lashed out at any danger. The smell of blood and mud, sweat and human waste, the hideous odour of battle, was all about him. Persians grabbed at his arms. One, dismounted, tried to unhorse him. Telamon kicked him away. Alexander was locked in combat with a Persian officer. He killed him with one slice across his chest bone. Another circled behind, one hand raised, scimitar gleaming in the sun for the killing blow. Telamon screamed. He tried to move forward. Cleitus appeared. He had gone round, in front of Alexander, and now came back, riding between his king and the Persian: with one blow he sheared off the attacker's arm, clean at the shoulder. Blood gushed out in a hot spray, splattering Alexander and his horse. The animal, now in a fighting frenzy, whinnied and bucked. Alexander fought to stay mounted but slipped off. He pushed the horse away even as a Persian cavalry man thrust his way through and aimed a killing blow at the king's helmeted head. Alexander saw the danger and moved. The sword gave a glancing blow as Cleitus and the rest of the bodyguard thronged round the king and he fell to his knees. The Persian attacker was trapped and dragged from his horse. Cleitus yanked his head back and cut the Persian's throat as he would a chicken's, before kicking the corpse away. The Macedonian bodyguard ringed their fallen king. Telamon slipped off his horse, throwing shield and sword away. He removed the helmet from Alexander's head. The king's eyes were staring, his skin, white as snow, was splattered by blood. Telamon feverishly searched the red–gold hair and felt a bump and the sticky wetness of blood. Cleitus was beside him. The ring around Alexander had now grown and deepened as units of Foot Companions took up their positions. Alexander, dazed, stared around.

"How goes it?" he whispered.

"Don't you realize?" Cleitus' grim face broke into a smile. "My lord, can't you hear?"

Telamon felt Alexander's pulse, searching for any wound. He, too, sensed the change. The pressing danger had passed. Macedonians were moving quickly forward.

"They've broken!" Cleitus roared. "Ptolemy's phalanx is across the river. The Persians are in full retreat!"

"Is it possible?" Telamon whispered. "Is it over?"

"How is the king?" Cleitus snapped.

"Bruised and battered," Telamon replied. "But he'll live."

A little colour had returned to Alexander's cheeks. He smiled and, using Cleitus, scrambled to his feet.

"Let's kill them all!" he said thickly. "And quickly, before night falls!"

Chapter 13

"After sacrificing in Athena's temple, Alexander deposited his own armour: taking in exchange arms which had hung there since the Trojan War . . . He is represented to have worn them at the battle of the Granicus."

Quintus Curtius Rufus, History, Book 2, Chapter 4

Memnon was screaming with rage. Helmetless, a deep gash in his sword arm, he glared at Arsites. He had no compassion for this arrogant Persian commander, now a shadow of his former self. Arsites' exquisite dress armour was dented and splattered. A sword thrust had cut open his left cheek and his face was caked in blood.

"What shall I do?" the Persian wailed. "Darius' own kinsmen have been killed!"

"Hang yourself!" Memnon swore. He savagely tugged at his horse and looked back from where he had retreated. The sky was darkening. A breeze stung his face. All around was the hideous din of battle. The last elite units of the Persians were breaking free, fleeing through the dusk. Riderless horses galloped everywhere or careered around hysterically, their blood-battered owners slumped over their necks. One galloped in a mindless circle until its gore-spattered rider slipped off and the horse cantered away. Memnon turned back. Arsites had gone. A roar rose from the river bank as if the very sky was cracking.

"Eynalius! Eynalius for Macedon!"

Memnon rode up the ridge and stared down in speechless horror. The entire Macedonian army, led by Ptolemy's brigade, had crossed the river. The phalanx men had secured a footing, their soaring, death-bearing sarissas lowered – a veritable wall of moving, pointed steel shoved at both horse and rider. The Persians were exhausted, their javelins flung. They could only hack at this advancing hedge of corneal wood and jagged steel with their useless curved scimitars.

The Granicus glowed red in the setting sun. Corpses bobbed mid-stream, floating backwards and forwards. The bank was littered with dead men and the wounded were trying to crawl away. The first Macedonian casualties were already covered by fresh dead, many of them wearing the caparisoned cloaks of the Persians. Even as he watched, Memnon heard another roar further down the bank. The trap was being closed. Parmenio and his force . . . The Persians on the river bank broke and fled back up the slope. Horses slipped and slithered, crashing down, their riders rolling back to be cruelly stabbed and trampled on. The phalanx gained speed, moving effortlessly up the slope. All Persian discipline collapsed; riders thundered past Memnon.

Memnon's surviving staff officer grasped his commander's rein. "It's finished!"

Memnon couldn't reply. His throat was dry, his tongue was swollen. He could not understand it. The savage speed. How the Persians had neatly fallen into Alexander's trap. So simple, so deadly in its lucidity. Alexander's feint from the centre, the brutal blow from the right, Arsites' forces turning to face that threat. Still the Persians hadn't realized what was happening. Memnon recalled Arsites and the rest still confident, quietly discussing how Alexander was distinguished by his exquisite armour and how they would deal with him personally! The Persian chieftains had charged. All of them were killed but a few. Mithridates,' arm had been severed clean from his body; the rest were cut down and trampled like rotting sheaves of corn.

"My lord."

His staff officer leaned over and shook Memnon's shoulder. Memnon stared into the man's wild eyes. Already the Persians who'd held off Macedon's charge were thundering by them. The air was now sickly-sweet with blood. Heart-rending cries for help and assistance cut through the gathering dusk. Memnon allowed his horse to be led away. He knew what would happen. The Macedonian pincer movement would trap them in a circle of steel: this would tighten and then the real slaughter would begin.

"I must see Omerta!" Memnon shouted.

They galloped across the battlefield. The mercenary phalanx still stood helmeted, shields up to form a wall of steel on all four sides, lances down, oblivious to the Persian horses streaming by them. Memnon felt sick; his men were trapped. If they ran they would be pursued by Macedonian cavalry and slaughtered.

"Their only chance," the officer shouted, "is to stand their ground and sue for terms!" He pushed his horse up against his commander's. "My lord, if you are taken you'll be crucified!"

Memnon stared across the battlefield, ignoring the fleeing Persians. The Greek mercenaries were now one long rectangle of waiting steel. His officer was right. They were mercenaries, they fought for pay. They would sue for terms. Alexander would take them into his army, allowing those who refused to give up their arms, take an oath they would never fight against him again and go where they wished.

Memnon and his officers joined the flight. As they rode, the Rhodian's mind cleared, frustration and anger being replaced by a desire for revenge. Arsites had been trapped. Memnon suspected that the fat physician Cleon had played a role in this. The Macedonian had fed Arsites and his commanders false information. Alexander had done the exact opposite of what they had expected: marching east instead of south, seeking a battle as quickly as possible while giving the impression that his army was confused and demoralized.

They reached the Persian baggage train. Memnon, like a man possessed, rode around the baggage carts, sword drawn, searching for Cleon – but all the camp followers had fled. He glimpsed Arsites and his minions near a cart. A great roar rolled in from the battlefield. Mamnon stared back through the dusk. He knew what had happened. The Macedonian battle line had breasted the ridge. The Persians were utterly defeated. Memnon's rage boiled over. He galloped across to where Arsites stood hurriedly divesting his armour and summoning servants to find fresh horses. Memnon dismounted. Others thronged about him, Greek survivors from the battlefield. Some were unrecognizable, covered in blood from head to toe. Arsites stood like a frightened deer.

Memnon strode up to him. "You stupid bastard! You were not only defeated, you were tricked! Where is Cleon?" He grasped the Persian's shoulder. Arsites struggled to break free but Memnon held fast.

"I am the King of Kings' . . . !"

"You are *nothing!*" Memnon snarled, and drove his sword deep into the Persian's stomach, turning it savagely.

Arsites' entourage fell back. No one raised a hand or voice in protest. Memnon kept digging the sword in. The life faded from the Persian's eyes and Memnon withdrew his blade and shoved the corpse away. He remounted his horse and gathered the reins.

"This day is finished!" he yelled. "Pray to the gods there will be another!"

Darkness was shrouding the battlefield. The Persian army had fled. Alexander found another horse. Slightly pale and shaken, he had remounted and, surrounded by his officers and commanders, received their congratulations and cheers. Telamon, distracted, stared across at the ominous phalanx of Greek mercenaries still standing to arms. They were completely surrounded: Macedonian phalanx men to their front, shield-bearers on their flanks, cavalry to their rear. Through the dark rang the shrieks and cries of the dying and wounded. Already some of the auxiliary light horse were slipping away to plunder the dead for rich pickings.

Alexander urged his horse forward. He seemed to be oblivious to the cheers of congratulation and sat slumped in his saddle, staring hollow-eyed at the serried ranks of his enemies.

"Alexander of Macedon!" a voice shouted, clear and carrying from the mercenary ranks. "Alexander of Macedon! We ask for terms!"

Alexander raised his hand and beckoned to a trumpeter. He whispered to him. The man lifted the salphinx to his lips and blew a chilling blast.

"Listen now!" the herald cried. "Who commands?"

"Omerta!"

"Omerta of Thebes," Alexander whispered.

The herald repeated the question.

"Omerta of Thebes, Macedonian!"

"Where is Memnon?" the herald bellowed.

"Dead or fled. What terms do you give us?"

"None," the herald replied, "but unconditional surrender!"

A deep moan of protest rose from the mercenary ranks.

Ptolemy pushed his way forward. "My lord, they have asked for terms!"

"Give them my reply!" Alexander snapped, turning his head to catch the cool breeze.

"You are Greeks who fought against Greeks, in defiance of the decree of the Greeks!" the herald shouted through the hushed darkness. "Lay down your arms!"

"Molen labe!" a voice retorted, echoing the ancient call of Sparta to the Persian king's demand for submission: "Come and get it!"

Alexander lifted his hand and a trumpet blast rang out, quickly taken up by others. Telamon watched, dry mouthed, as the Macedonian phalanx advanced, sarissas lowered. Alexander himself led the cavalry charge into the enemy ranks. The Macedonians closed in and the massacre began.

Telamon, cold with fear, sat as the night air was shattered by the fresh clatter of arms, the hideous yells of dying men. The ranks of Greek mercenaries disappeared in a welter of bloody fighting.

"I have seen enough," Telamon whispered and, turning his horse, made his way over the ridge and down to the river. The effects of the battle lay everywhere. In some places corpses were piled two, three high. The ground was slippery with blood. Dismembered limbs sprawled grotesquely. A severed head, eyes staring, tongue clenched between the teeth, lay like a ball, caught in the branches of a bush. Wounded, frenzied horses writhed on the ground, desperately trying to rise. The walking wounded were staggering away, faces and bodies gruesome and bloody. A Persian sat with his back against a tree: he had been sliced from neck to crotch; his innards had spilled out yet his eyes still blinked and his lips moved, a strange clicking sound coming from the back of this throat. A passing Cretan archer crept up, slit the man's throat and began to pillage his body, oblivious to Telamon's presence. Here and there were pinpricks of torchlight as soldiers prowled the battlefield for plunder or looking for lost companions. Alexander's mercenaries were doing bloody business. The Greek wounded were being moved, tended by some of the leeches and camp followers – all the Persians received was the mercy cut, their throats slit from ear to ear.

Telamon heard a scream from a group of bushes at the top of the bank. He dismounted and led his horse over. A group of Thessalian cavalry men had caught a young Persian, stripped him and had him sprawled on his stomach, legs apart, ready to sodomize and inflict other obscenities upon him. The Persian struggled as a Thessalian knelt down in front of his face, kilt up, penis exposed.

"Stop it!" Telamon shouted.

The Thessalians clambered to their feet, drawing their swords.

"I am Telamon! Physician to Alexander!" He searched for the seal and brought it out.

The Thessalians drifted away. The Persian clambered to his feet. Telamon reckoned he must be a youth of no more than seventeen summers. The physician picked up a cloak and threw it at him.

"Dress!" He pointed to the horse. "Take it! Ride as fast as you can, as far as you can from this place of abomination!"

He didn't wait for the Persian's reaction but turned and slithered down the river bank. He came across a group of shield-bearers. They asked for help. Telamon paused to bind wounds but was so exhausted he couldn't even remember how to tie a knot. One of the shield-bearers took him by the arm and led him across the ford. He reached the other side. He saw torchlight; voices shouted. People clustered around asking questions. Cassandra, her face pale and anxious-eyed, held out a cup of wine. She grasped Telamon by the arm and made him drink. He was aware of stumbling through the dark and, crawling under a cart, fell asleep with Cassandra beside him.

He was awoken early in the morning, a guardsman kicking his foot. Cassandra was screeching objections – the man responded with obscene gestures.

254

"All right! All right!" Telamon crawled out from beneath the cart. He stared up at the sky and reckoned it must be late in the morning. The baggage park was busy. Prisoners were being led away under guard. Booty and plunder from the Persians was being ferried across the ford. Stretcher-bearers hurried by, their makeshift pallets carrying the Macedonian wounded to a small copse of trees where the hospital tents had been set up.

"Do you want any help?" Telamon muttered.

The guardsman, drunk and unshaven, his hands and wrists still caked with blood, shook his head.

"Please, sir, tell your red-haired bitch to shut up! The king wants to see you."

He paused as loud jeering broke out. A long line of men, naked except for their loincloths, chained together at wrist and ankle, were being led up from the river. On either side of them were two files of shield-bearers, pushing and shoving the prisoners. They trudged past the carts: a long line of miserable men, caked in mud and blood.

"Poor bastards!" the guardsman muttered. "All that's left of Memnon's mercenaries!"

"How many were killed?" Telamon asked.

"About three thousand, the rest surrendered. They're for the silver mines of Macedon."

News of the arrival of mercenary prisoners swept through the camp. Soldiers thronged about; mud and stones were thrown amidst catcalls and jeers.

"There are Thebans among them," Cassandra declared. She glanced at Telamon. "I stayed here all day and night guarding our possessions. There are more thieves round here than leaves on a tree. Most of them are Macedonians."

The guardsman stepped forward, an ugly look on his face.

"I'll see the king now," Telamon said quickly.

Alexander's pavilion was already erected, close to where Parmenio had held the left wing the previous day. The king sat on a camp stool in front of the tent. He hadn't slept and his face was pale and unshaven. He was dressed in the tunic he had worn underneath his armour during the battle. Splashes of dried blood stained his

255

arms and legs and, a makeshift bandage covered the bruise on the back of his head. Around him in a semicircle sat the scribes of the secretariat. Alexander was engrossed, watching squads of soldiers piling up the costly coats of Persian armour taken from the battlefield.

"I want nine of those sent to Athens!" Alexander shouted. "With this message: '*Alexander, son of Philip and the Greeks, to Athens and all the Cities of Greece except Sparta . . .*" The rest of the message was short and curt, describing a great victory. Behind Alexander Telamon glimpsed other commanders seated round a table inside the tent, scribes between them, poring over maps. More letters were dictated. Alexander talked quickly, giving instructions, receiving reports. Then he turned, shielding his eyes.

"A great victory, eh, Telamon? The gods have made their will known." The smile faded from his lips. "Have you seen Cleon?"

Telamon shook his head.

"He probably fled as far as he could," Alexander remarked drily, "and is making his way back slowly. But we have unfinished business, haven't we? The truth to be known!" Alexander waved a hand. "Make it quick! Do it secretly. Let me know. Oh," Alexander summoned Telamon forward, "you're not taking the red-haired one. A group of lancers will see you safely into Troy."

He stared in mock innocence at the consternation in Telamon's face.

"What's the matter, physician?"

"Troy!" Telamon exclaimed angrily. "I'm going back to Troy now?"

"As our good teacher Aristotle would preach," Alexander whispered. "In all things be logical. You do know who Naihpat is, don't you, Telamon? The true identity of the murderer and how the killings were carried out, the treachery?"

Telamon felt weak; uninvited, he sat down on a stool.

"You suspected all the time!" Telamon whispered. "We've been through a charade, a shadow play. Now we have Alexander the victorious general, the wily politician. What role were you playing in the camp outside Sestos?"

256

The King screwed his eyes up. "Er . . . the rather confused, inexperienced soldier."

"More than that!" Telamon retorted. "Sacrificing to this God, sacrificing to that! Worried about what route you would take; the maps, the guides, the festivities at Troy. It was all nonsense, you had already planned what to do, where to go and how to accomplish your dream. You were playing a game! You misled me, you misled everyone. During the last few days I reached my conclusion by logic, reflection and evidence. You knew all the time!"

"Well, of course I did." Alexander laughed sharply. "No, I am lying but I did suspect, I did wonder. I had to mislead everyone. Do you remember when we fought Droxenius? I defeated him, not because we were stronger or better swordsmen but through trickery. The same is true here. I misled Arsites and his commanders. Now the game is over. It's time to sweep everything up, clear the rubbish away, confront the traitor."

"How do you know I'm ready to do that?"

"Oh, Telamon, you might study me, I certainly study you. I watched your face on our march to the Granicus, how quiet and withdrawn you'd become. Now is the time . . ."

"To enforce the King's justice?"

"Precisely." Alexander waved him away.

"I shall see you this evening, yes? Or perhaps tomorrow? Tell me everything that happens."

By the time Telamon reached Troy, night had fallen. The garrison Alexander had left to guard the ruins and the town it housed were eager for news. They clustered about with a litany of excited questions. Telamon ignored them. He felt weary and agitated. He wished he could have brought Cassandra with him, or at least said goodbye, but the officer in charge of the lancers was under strict orders.

"I am to take you straight to Troy, sir. Guard you and bring you back."

The crowd of questioners dispersed. The officer led Telamon up the winding streets and into the forecourt of the Temple of Athena. The porter sleeping on the steps sprang to his feet. A short while later Telamon was ushered into the small chamber at the back of the temple where Antigone was working. She sat at a table on which four oil lamps glowed; others had been placed in niches in the walls. She was busy peering at a roll of parchment, a stylus in one hand, a small inkpot close by. She hardly looked up as Telamon entered but sat tapping the stylus against her cheek.

"Are you alone, physician?"

"I have an escort outside."

Antigone leaned her back against the wall. Her hair was undressed, hanging down in tresses around her beautiful face.

"Close the door, Telamon! Draw the bolts!"

"Have you been expecting me?"

"For years," she retorted. "I've been expecting you, or someone like you, for longer than I care to remember."

Antigone got up, went to a shelf and brought down a goblet. She filled this with wine and took it to where Telamon, the door now secured, sat on a narrow ledge which ran round the wall. She offered the cup. Telamon didn't take it. Antigone grinned. She took a long sip and thrust it into his hands.

"You've travelled far. You bring news of Alexander's great victory. I have already heard about it. Arsites was such a fool. The Macedonian has got what he wanted. He's come to bring fire from heaven down upon the Persians! What a raging inferno it will be!" She retook her seat and pushed away the parchment. "Only temple accounts. You've got more pressing news, eh, Telamon?"

"Naihpat."

Antigone smiled.

"I forgot my education," Telamon confessed. "But you are the priestess of Athena. You know all about it. In one fable Athena took human form, that of a king called Taphian. If you reverse Taiphan, a popular child's game, you get Naihpat."

"You thought of that?"

"No, Aristander's creature, Hercules, did. He loved turning people's names around. He did the same with Naihpat and spelt out Taphian. What happened, did he come and see you? And what did you do, Antigone, Naihpat, Taphian? Did you entice him out to one of those lonely glades on the plains of Sestos? A swift blow to the head and burial in a marsh?"

"If I had, his body would have surfaced."

"Not if it was tied down with stones. I am sure it lies at the bottom of one of those quagmires, weighted with small boulders. It will lie and rot for years! The dwarf's questioning, his furtive brain are silenced for good. Who killed him? You or Selena? Or was it Aspasia? He was wandering around the camp that day – you must have followed him, or had him followed."

"Has Alexander sent you?"

"He suspects."

Antigone turned on the stool to face him squarely, sipping elegantly from the wine cup. "It's a very rare story. Very few people know of the name Taphian, or the legend attached to it. You are right, Hercules was a chattering little monkey. He came to ask me if I knew who Taphian was. I dismissed him, told him I'd never heard the name."

"Of course, if Hercules ever found out about the legend, he would wonder why a priestess of Athena didn't recognize the name."

"Very good!"

"In the beginning?" Telamon asked.

"In the beginning I was a distant kinswoman of the royal house of Macedon, though I was Athenian born and raised. My father worked in the theatre."

"Where you read the works of Euripides?"

"Ah yes." Antigone smiled. "The quotations! I entered the service of Athena outside Corinth. That's where I met Philip, one-eyed, one-armed Philip! He looked like an old goat. He smelt like one!" She laughed. "And was as lecherous as one, yet I fell deeply in love with him. He lied to me, of course, said he was wary of Olympias. He wanted me to come to Troy to be the priestess of the temple here, far enough away from Pella to enjoy his pleasures. He said he had work for me, that he could visit me: when he planned his conquest of Persia, Troy would be his new home. I would be his wife. He was a liar, of course." Her eyes brimmed with tears. "I truly did love him. I came to Troy. Outwardly the virginal priestess of Athena, in fact Philip of Macedon's lover, or one of the many. Once here, I realized what Philip really wanted. Troy's only a few miles from the Hellespont, the crossroads between Greece and Asia."

"You became his spy?"

"I became his spy. Philip's ardour began to wane. Mine only deepened but the harsh reality became obvious: the rare visits, the lack of letters, though he always insisted that I send him news. Then one fine morning a wild-eyed, half-insane young man came to the temple."

"Pausanias, Philip's assassin?"

"Yes. I should have removed his name from the visitors' roll but that would have been suspicious." Antigone looked round the cavernous room. "I would have stayed imprisoned here, in a place like this, for a million years as long as Philip loved me. Pausanias was as mad as a hare. He told me everything – not only about Philip's lechery." She laughed sharply. "Everybody knew about that. But, you see, Pausanias had also visited Alexander's mother." She paused. "Olympias gave full rein to her bile. She listed Philip's conquests: my name figured prominently and, being the most recent, Olympias poured on the scorn. She informed Pausanias how Philip had boasted about his adventures with me. She also poisoned Pausanias' mind against Philip and let slip a secret: Philip was going to divorce her and marry someone else."

Antigone clutched the cup close to her chest: her beautiful eyes were staring into the darkness. Telamon suspected she had described this story many times to herself, reciting it until she'd learnt it by rote.

"Only then did I realize how I had been not only seduced but tricked."

"Did you encourage Pausanias to kill Philip?"

"No, no. Olympias started the fire." Antigone shifted her gaze. "But, may the gods forgive me, I certainly fanned the flames: a moment of hate I later regretted. I also decided to turn the game against Philip. Everyone visits Troy. The King of Kings, Darius, has a man close to his right hand."

"Who?" Telamon asked curiously.

Darius calls him Mithra and keeps him well hidden, I wrote to Darius offering to share secrets. I gave my name as Naihpat and said

I could be found in the town of Troy. I sat and waited. Eventually, well, you can imagine what happened. Mithra appeared. He was disguised as a merchant. He'd made enquiries in the market-place. The traders, of course, had directed him to the temple. Did I know who Naihpat was? He promised me protection, talents of gold and, when I wished, a place of honour at the Persian court. But, in the meantime," Antigone pushed a wisp of hair from her face, "I would serve him and his master. Only the two of them would know of my existence. In return I promised that I would provide as much information as I could about Philip, the Macedonian court and, above all, their projected invasion of Asia. Once Philip had sent Parmenio to establish a bridgehead, my usefulness increased. The Macedonians often visited here. I, in turn, visited their camp. They honoured me as a kinswoman of Philip, a priestess of Athena, a Greek. I learnt confidences, secrets."

"And you passed these to Mithra?"

"Of course!"

"How was it done? By letter?"

"Sometimes. Sometimes he visited here."

"But how?" Telamon asked. "Parmenio has his spies. This temple was surely watched."

"Troy is an ancient city. An underground passageway runs from the temple out into caves well beyond the city walls."

Telamon narrowed his eyes.

"I showed Mithra the entrances. The passageway is very ancient, built of rock, secure. He would come and go whenever he wished. He was always pleased with what I gave him. Philip's intentions, the intrigue at the Macedonian court, the number and quality of troops, supplies, movements." She shrugged. "And, above all, Olympias' plots against her husband: Philip's murder and what I thought of Alexander."

"And the Thessalian maidens?" Telamon asked. "The offerings to the spirit of Cassandra?"

"One of Philip's more bizarre, wild ideas. He wanted me to establish a college of priestesses and use them as spies, listeners."

"But, of course, you didn't want that, did you?"

"I was fortunate. Selena and Aspasia were the first to arrive. I was at a loss what to do. They loved each other. They were what you would elegantly term 'followers of Sappho of Lesbos'." She laughed. "Both fell in love with me. They were infatuated. I took them into my confidence – they were only too willing. They would do anything for me, and pointed out the danger of others joining us. The second year none came but, the following year, two did . . ."

"And this year?"

"We were waiting for them. Out in the caves, on that lonely trackway into Troy. The legend says that they have to make their way by themselves."

"You had no compunction?"

"At first, yes. But, after the first murder, none whatsoever. They had to be killed or we would be betrayed. They were invited up to the cave. Selena and Aspasia's looks belied them – they were killers born and bred. The maidens were murdered. You can still find their corpses in the tunnel. There's a pit just before the entrance."

"But this year, one escaped?"

"Yes. Alexander continued the practice. Once again the hundred families of Locri chose two maidens to send to our temple. Naturally, we were alerted. Once again we met them, only this time, by mere chance, one escaped. The rest you know. She was found and brought to the temple. If anything had happened to her, suspicions would have been aroused. As it was, she was confused, disorientated."

"And, of course, with the use of drugged wine that mood would be deepened?"

Antigone nodded. "Aspasia and Selena wanted to kill her immediately but, as I've said, suspicion had to be avoided. At the same time, Alexander was making his presence felt. He'd slaughtered Thebans, made himself Captain-General of Greece and was in regular communication with both Parmenio and myself. He blamed Parmenio's lack of success on poor knowledge of the terrain. He told me that he was mustering his army at Sestos. He instructed me to hire guides who knew the western seaboard of Asia. How he needed a map-maker: he ordered me to assemble these and bring them to his camp at Sestos." Antigone swirled the wine in the cup and smiled grimly. "I misjudged Alexander, didn't I? But, I suppose, everyone does. He has more sides than a dice. A man of masks. He often wrote to me, playing the role of the young, inexperienced king. Eager to launch his invasion of Persia but full of fear about the practical problems as well as securing the favour of the gods."

"So you went to Sestos. You took that maiden with you, along with Critias and the rest."

"Yes. I had talked to Mithra. He told me to do as much as possible to confuse Alexander, spread unease, make things difficult. One thing I hadn't counted on," her face turned ugly, "was that stupid Thessalian girl. Alexander ordered me to bring her with me otherwise I would have left her in Troy. Selena and Aspasia were very anxious." She filled the wine cup and smiled from under her eyebrows at Telamon. "I didn't agree with them until I met you. I thought, here is a physician who will put this woman into a deep sleep, soothe her humours, calm her mind, placate her soul and provoke memories." Antigone paused. "Even in her muddled state she was wary of me. You suspected I killed her?"

"Not till afterwards when I gathered more evidence. I recalled that night in your tent." Telamon gestured at his own wine goblet which he hadn't touched. "There were cups and beakers on a small chest. However, you went deeper into the tent and brought a goblet back. You filled it with wine."

Antigone's smile widened. "But you drank from it. I drank from it."

"That's right. And others may have touched it. It was a poisoned cup. I have seen and heard of such vessels: they possess a false base, a small disc which can be opened and shut by a hidden device, allowing whatever powder lies beneath to seep up into the wine. You did that before the maiden drank. And why shouldn't you? After all, the king's own physician was advising her."

Antigone sipped at her goblet. "But I could have been discovered when you came back."

"I don't think so. You would have protected yourself. We were looking for a poison and trying to remember who touched the cup. I never thought the answer could lie in the cup itself." Telamon grasped his goblet and spilt the wine onto the hard, black floor.

"You have, in fact, two cups, haven't you? Both identical. The poisoned one you hid or threw away. The second one, quite ordinary, you offered for examination."

"Very sharp!"

"No." Telamon pulled a face. He fought back the wave of tiredness. "More a matter of logic and common sense: it didn't occur to me till long afterwards."

Telamon leaned his head back against the wall. The young woman sitting so elegantly before him had been provoked by love which had turned to hate. He quietly marvelled at the chaos and destruction caused by Philip, Olympias and Alexander.

"The murder of the guides," he continued, "was easy. The first was killed on the cliff tops. He probably felt homesick. He met Selena or Aspasia. One of them struck quickly, viciously like a viper. His corpse was supposed to be found on the cliff top but, in his death-throes, he slipped over onto the rocks below. Who would suspect one of your moon-faced girls?"

"And the second guide?"

"Oh, the same. He and the rest were filling their bellies and drinking themselves sottish around the camp fire. You were busy with me in Alexander's tent. It would be easy for Selena or Aspasia to slip out. One of them did."

"How?" Antigone taunted.

"Are you genuinely curious?" Telamon asked.

"The guards said both of them slept!"

"Ah! Now we come to the tent." Telamon paused. "After I arrived in Alexander's camp I learnt my pavilion had been burnt down. Tents are costly with their leather awnings, peg ropes and frames. You, or one of your helpers, started that fire. In the confusion you stole seven or eight pieces of twine used to lash the leather awnings to their poles. You had to get them from there because, as in any army, the quartermasters jealously guard their stores. You needed an identical twine in colour and texture to that used in all the other tents throughout the camp. Erecting a tent is a special skill. When the leather awnings are stretched across the pole and secured, they are tied in a certain way to prevent them being unpicked or, indeed, coming loose."

264

Antigone was chewing the corner of her lip, gazing sardonically at him.

"You, Selena or Aspasia stole the pieces of twine, burnt down my tent to hide your theft and began your campaign. I don't fully know what happened the night the first guide was killed, but it would have been easy. No one was watching. After his murder you had to be more vigilant. You went to Alexander's pavilion while Selena and Aspasia pretended to be asleep. The flap of their tent was pulled down and the guard was reluctant to be caught spying on temple handmaidens. One of your helpers rose, put on her sandals, cloak and hood. The twine lashing the leather awning to its pole was cut and one of your handmaidens crept into the night. The other stayed behind. She used the twine you had stolen to refasten the awning. The guides were mournfully drinking round the camp fire. One of them got up to relieve himself. Your accomplice followed. The man was drunk: standing there in the dark, half-witted and half-asleep, swaying on his feet. Selena – or Aspasia – struck, swift and sure-footed, a mere shadow in the night. The man was stabbed. He died quickly. His assassin left the message and slipped back past the guards into the camp. The avenues between the tents are dark, full of shadows. Who would notice? Who would care? She returned to her tent, slit the cord and crept back through the gap: she retied it with an identical knot, using the twine taken from my pavilion. I suspect it was Aspasia, she seemed the stronger of the two." Telamon paused at a sound from the temple.

Antigone smiled. "It's only the porter. You're not frightened, are you, Telamon? I have no weapon. Your wine was untainted and Macedon's men are not far away. Why did you suspect Aspasia?"

"I visited you in her tent after her death. She had her belongings packed. I noticed how the same knot had been used as that on the tents. I thought it a strange coincidence: it was a fairly unique pattern, twisted with two knots pulled tight, very hard to undo, except with a knife. All three of you must have studied the tent-maker's knots carefully."

"And Critias?"

"Once again your assassin slipped into the night. She cut the twine of Critias' tent and crept in. The map-maker was tired, drunk; at such an hour he probably always was." Telamon spread his hands. "After all, you hired him. You'd know his habits. It was easy to slit his throat, plunge the dagger into his side and leave the tent. Outside, Aspasia, if it was she, knelt down. She probably only had to cut two or three pieces of twine to enter: these she replaced, and then crept away. Critias' death, apparently, was caused by some malevolent force or the anger of the gods."

"And the maps?"

Telamon smiled. "Cunning. Aspasia took with her a small identical coffer filled with ash. She simply replaced one with the other."

"How do you know it was identical?"

"Because I have seen them on sale in the market outside. You bought two and gave one to Critias for his maps."

Antigone sat tapping her fingers against her lips, staring at a point above Telamon's head. "Does Alexander know all this?"

"He will. Things went wrong, didn't they? Aspasia was the real killer. Swift of foot, deadly with a knife. She followed Hercules out of the camp, killed him. A swift blow to the head. She weighted his body with stones and drowned him in the marsh. She returned there early one morning . . ."

"Why?"

"She had to get rid of Critias' small coffer. She had hidden it in a basket, pretending to go out and collect flowers or herbs. The Furies weren't far behind. Aspasia would be agitated, excited, eager to rid herself of the incriminating evidence. She made a mistake. She put the basket down, took out the small coffer and either slipped in or, perhaps, the leather handle on the side of the coffer got entwined in her fingers. She stumbled and fell into the marsh. The casket explains the scuffing on her fingers, while the bump to her head was probably caused when she hit the coffer she was trying to hide. She lost consciousness. The coffer slipped from her hands and sank to the bottom. Aspasia struggled and, the more she did so the worse it got. Mud caked her nose and mouth. In a short while she died, and her corpse was left floating on top of the marsh."

"She was a silly girl," Antigone agreed. "A stupid, simple mistake: she endangered us all."

"You were very worried. Aspasia had got rid of the coffer but Selena was distraught: she was the weakest of the three of you. Only the gods know what she may have done in her hysteria. You are a cold-hearted bitch, Antigone. You decided to use your own handmaiden to cause further bloodshed and deepen unease. You gave Selena a cup of wine heavily laced with a sleeping potion. She lay on the cot bed, at the far end of your tent just near the awnings, her back to the entrance. Before you left for Alexander's feast, you leant over her to kiss her goodnight and, as you did so, drove one of those winged daggers, bought from an itinerant pedlar, into her side. Deeply asleep, her mouth smothered by your traitorous lips, Selena would have struggled for a while, then lain still. You left the message, got up and walked away. To all intents and purposes Selena, the temple maiden, is fast asleep on her cot bed, her back to the guard."

"But she was found sprawled on the floor."

"You are a priestess. You carry a shepherd's crook as a walking stick, a symbol of your office. Before you left, I suspect you put the hook of your crook around the leg of Selena's bed, the other end just within hand reach of the tent awning. I walked you back that night: you were only too pleased to use me as a witness. You bade me farewell and slipped round the tent to the precise spot. You placed your hand under the awning, grasped the stick and simply tipped the bed. Selena's corpse rolled onto the ground. You then walked round to the front and the drama began."

Antigone clapped her hands softly. "You have very little evidence, Telamon: as the sophists would say, 'It's all surmise and empty hypothesis.'"

"Alexander's engineers could drain that swamp. Aristander's men could question the market vendor. We could conduct a thorough search." Telamon leaned forward. "But I don't think it will come to that. Alexander left Sestos. You had done what damage you could and you returned to Troy. The murder of the third guide was very easy. He and his companions must have been terrified. They wanted to go home, leave Alexander's army. Did you arrange to meet him in the temple? Or, half-drunk and maudlin, did he come to seek your advice, ask for your help?" Telamon didn't wait for an answer. "He must have done. You offered to show him a way through your secret passageway out under the town into the lonely countryside. You led him down those rocks. He stood there bemused and you stabbed him. You left the message and returned the way you came."

Telamon got to his feet. His whole body ached. He walked to the door, opened it and stared down the narrow temple. His escort squatted in the antechamber talking to the porter. Telamon closed the door and came back. Antigone had refilled the cups.

"Why didn't you just kill Alexander?"

"Oh you know that, Telamon." Antigone had decided on the truth. "The Persians were insistent. If Alexander was assassinated in Greece he would be seen as a martyr. The Persians were worried at his hold over the Greek states. Alexander had to be enticed away from there. Once he was gone, Greeks would return to what they're good at – squabbling among each other."

"And Alexander?"

"He would be left to blunder around with his puny force, brought to battle, defeated and either killed or captured. By which time the Persian fleet would have returned to the Middle Sea. No Macedonian would go home. Greece would be disunited again. Macedon would be gone and Persia would have taught the world a lesson. The Persians were insistent: Alexander was to be either killed or captured in battle."

"That's why you gave him the armour?"

Antigone threw her head back and laughed. "I studied Alexander's mind. His superstition, fear, and guilt about his father. Above all, his passion to be a second Achilles. The armour he took from here was specially fashioned, bright and blazing: that's how the Persians wanted him in battle, so they could seek him out and destroy him. Alexander snatched them up as a child would sweetmeats. Like a boy playing a game, he had to ride into battle as the great hero."

"It nearly succeeded," Telamon agreed. "The Persians were

within inches of killing him at the Granicus. Every kinsman of Darius sought him out and tried to bring him down."

"Everything is as you've described it, but we made one mistake," Antigone mused. "We forgot about the gods: their luck is with Alexander. Memnon was right, Darius was wrong and I, Telamon, am for the dark." She lifted the cup in a toast. "Spotted hemlock, the same drink as Socrates."

Antigone drained the cup and leaned back, singing softly under her breath. Telamon recognized the love song. Antigone moved slightly as she began to lose the feeling in her legs. The cup slipped from her fingers and crashed to the floor. She glanced up, dazed, like a person falling asleep. She smiled, put her arms on the table and bowed her head. For a while she shuddered, fighting for breath, then one arm slipped off the table and the room fell quiet.

"You left immediately?" Alexander picked up the bowl of cooked meat to serve Telamon himself. They were seated alone in the antechamber of the royal pavilion. Alexander was washed and shaved, wearing a cloth-of-gold tunic taken from the Persian camp, silver sandals on his feet and a green and gold braid round his head, keeping the bandage in place. Apart from cuts, a bruise high on his cheek and a slight stiffness when he walked, he had recovered quickly from the effects of the battle.

"She was dead," Telamon said. "I checked her corpse and left the porter to carry out the ritual."

Telamon had left Troy and ridden straight back to Alexander's camp. The entire army was celebrating their great victory at the Granicus. Captives were still being brought in, together with cartloads of plunder and booty from both the Persian baggage carts and the battlefield itself. The sky above the Granicus was black with plumes of smoke from the funeral pyres.

Cassandra had been welcoming and sardonic. She had helped herself to some of the plunder as well as the foodstuffs, claiming that "When you are with Macedonians you become Macedonian." She'd also managed to secure better quarters and had everything tidy and ready.

On his return Telamon had acted as if in a dream. Faces came and went: Aristander glaring malevolently at him; Ptolemy full of his own valour; even Cleon, flustered, red-faced and a little bruised. He'd managed to reach the Macedonian camp, his task completed.

Telamon had slept for a while and been roused in the early evening by two of the bodyguards and brought to the king. Alexander had been cold but courteous. He was no longer the impetuous general, but the astute politician eager to gain every profit from his great victory. Letters had been sent out to neighbouring provinces, demanding their allegiance. Proclamations had been issued to every city in Greece. Telamon felt his hand touched and started.

"You are tired, physician?" Alexander's voice was mocking. "Are you sad Antigone died? I could have crucified her. She was allowed to take the gentle way."

Telamon thought of the dead piled high on the battlefield.

"Are you like your father, physician? Does the smell of blood upset you?" Alexander leaned his head slightly to the left as if seeing Telamon for the first time. "A gulf exists between us," he murmured. "I wish it didn't. I am just fulfilling my destiny."

"Does that include massacring those mercenaries?"

Alexander slapped himself playfully on the wrist. "That was wrong – the bloodlust of battle, and I cannot revoke a decree. But Antigone?" Alexander stared into the wine crater. He picked it up, swirled the wine about, sipped and passed it to Telamon.

"Did you suspect?" Telamon asked.

"I would like to say . . ." Alexander hesitated. He pulled himself up on the quilted chair pillaged from the Persian camp. "I would like to say I knew everything, but I didn't."

"Did you know about Philip and Antigone?" Telamon asked.

"Of course! Father told Mother about all his conquests: that's why she's half mad. Olympias told me. I wondered about Antigone: She was well placed to pass information on. Aristander had the temple watched but we never discovered anything." Alexander spread his hands. "A spy was busy betraying us but, to a certain extent, that was irrelevant. I wanted to mislead the Persians. Cleon did a marvellous job but that was nothing . . ."

270

"Compared to deceiving the Persians?"

"Naturally." Alexander laughed. "Darius called me a callow youth. I wanted to give the impression that I was confused, not as confident as my father, guilty about his death."

"Are you?"

"No, I am not." Alexander's eyes became hard. "I never was. I never shall be!"

"Did Antigone have a hand in his death?"

"Possibly, but there again, so did Mother. I half-suspected Antigone but couldn't prove it – that's why I needed you. Telamon with his sharp wits and keen eyes. The surveyor of cause and effect! Treason is a disease, Telamon. It, too, has its symptoms." Alexander took a deep breath and plucked at the tunic he was wearing. "This belonged to Arsites. I've sent a message to Darius. By the time I am finished, I will have the entire imperial wardrobe. I used Cleon. I used Aristander. Above all, I used Antigone. I told her that I needed guides, maps. She passed this on to the Persians. I sent those handmaidens from Thessaly, hoping one of them would discover something but, of course, Antigone took care of them. So I asked our beloved priestess to join me in Sestos with her guides and the map-maker." Alexander made a circular movement with his hand. "I'd stir the pot to see what came out. Antigone knew what she was doing: the death of those guides, the mysterious murders, the sombre warnings, the references to my father. She was much suspected but nothing was proved. I had to be very careful. I did not wish to give offence, incur the wrath of the gods by executing a priestess of Athena. I needed proof: I needed you. All the time the Persians thought they were dealing with someone confused and burdened with guilt. Well," Alexander smiled brilliantly, "I've shown them they were wrong. The real danger was Memnon. If his strategy had been followed, I would still be marching through a countryside where the cities had closed their gates on me, bereft of battle, of victory, of glory and divine favour. Now I have them all." Alexander picked up his wine goblet. "So, Telamon, let us toast, to my glory and to the ends of the earth!"

Author's Note

The events of 334 BC are as described in this novel. Darius, Arsites and Memnon were divided over the tactics they should employ to check and destroy Alexander of Macedon. The primary sources – Arrian, Diodorus Siculus, Plutarch, Quintus Curtius Rufus and Justin – all describe the detailed plotting in the Persian camp. In the end, Arsites had his way and as a result Alexander won his great victory. According to Arrian, Arsites fled the battlefield and disappeared: he may have committed suicide. In view of Memnon's later promotion by Darius, I have given another interpretation – namely that Arsites, as was customary for a Persian satrap who lost so disastrously, was executed for his failure.

The battle of the Granicus has often been debated by historians. Some claim Alexander actually waited until the following morning to launch his attack, but I have followed the primary sources who talk of Alexander's speed, savagery and surprise. The best evidence for my interpretation is the fate of the Greek mercenaries who were literally caught wrong-footed and, being unable to retreat, had to stand and fight. Alexander ordered their massacre, a deed he later regretted. Those who survived were loaded with chains and sent to work in the mines of Macedon. Archaeologists recently found their skeletons, manacles still in place.

Alexander's tactics at the Granicus are as described in the novel. The sudden lunge across the river, the distraction of the Persian commanders and their intense personal desire to claim the honour of killing Alexander led to a breakdown in command, the weakening of the centre and eventually the utter defeat of the Persian army.

Alexander's troops and tactics are also faithfully recorded: the use of the phalanx men, protected by shield-bearers, as well as the ingenious way Alexander used fast-moving cavalry to deliver hammer blows against the enemy flanks. True, the evidence regarding Alexander's tactics is sometimes confused. We have a range of primary sources, mentioned above, but we also know that the king kept a journal, while General Ptolemy, who later became pharaoh of Egypt, also published his own version of events. Alexander's other commanders, as today, were also keen to proclaim their greatness while serving with Alexander: the fragmented remains of these self-glorifying biographies and military treatises make interesting reading.

I have faithfully reflected the mood of Alexander's companions: Ptolemy and Seleucus, Amyntas and Parmenio. Aristander the soothsayer is a true historical figure – Olympias' creature, but for some strange reason very close to Alexander's council. Ptolemy was perhaps the most brilliant of Alexander's generals. He entertained ideas of greatness and viewed himself as Alexander's half-brother. At times the rivalry between them became intense.

The physician Telamon is based on a true historical figure, Philip the doctor, whom Arrian and other sources mention.

The story of the Thessalian virgins being sent to Troy is mentioned in two ancient sources: Aeneas "the tactician" work and in Lycrophon's poem "Alexandra". Robin Lane Fox, in his brilliant biography (*Alexander the Great*, Penguin Books, 1986) claims that the king, on his arrival at Troy, decreed the practice should end. Both Aeneas and Lycrophon refer to a secret passageway which ran under the ancient ruins of Troy.

My plot is based on a study of Alexander's movements at Sestos, Troy and the Granicus. In the previous months he had acted with great speed, crushing the northern tribes and bringing all Greece under his sway but, at Sestos, Alexander suddenly became rather nervous and superstitious. He did make sacrifices both there and at Elaeus. He also sacrificed halfway across the Hellespont in order to placate the gods. My description of his landing at Troy is based on ancient sources. When he reached the ruins, Alexander acted as if he were wonder-struck. He sacrificed in different parts of the city and expressed his great love and admiration for Achilles by

274

organizing the race to his hero's burial mound where he, Hephaestion and the rest laid flowers and made libations.

The story of the Achilles' armour is also true. According to Diodorus Siculus, "Alexander . . . made a splendid sacrifice to Athena, dedicating his own armour to the goddess. Then, taking the finest of the armour deposited in the temple, he put it on and used it in his first battle [i.e. the Granicus]." (*Library of History*, Book 17, Chapter 17, Verse 18). Arrian says that "the armour was simply carried before him in battle" (*The Campaigns of Alexander*, Book 1, Chapter 11). There is no doubt that Alexander's armour singled him out for the Persian high command. Both Arrian and Diodorus Siculus, as well as other sources, describe how Darius' commanders left their posts and engaged Alexander and his companions in fierce hand-to-hand combat.

The medical theories mentioned in the novel are also based on fact, particularly the use of heavy wine, honey and salt. Greek physicians may not have understood the full complexity of the human body but they were keen observers. Physicians did travel the known world acquiring knowledge, as Telamon did. A good account of ancient medicine can be found in the splendid book *A History of Military Medicines* by Richard A. Gabriel and Karen Metz (The Greenwood Press, New York, 1992). We tend to think of medicine as one long advance: this is not so. For example, some authorities argue that a Roman soldier in Britain in AD 90 had a better chance of survival from a spear thrust than a British soldier serving in Africa in the late nineteenth century. The practice of fastening bandages tightly over battle wounds persisted in hospitals until the First World War.

Alexander is a chameleon-like figure, one of Hegel's great figures of history, a "shooting star" whose life and exploits still fascinate us thousands of years after his death. He was deeply influenced by his parents: his filial relationship can be succinctly described as one of love and hate. He adored both Philip and Olympias and their constant feuding wreaked its psychological effects on him.

Alexander was a Greek who wanted to be a Persian. A man who believed in democracy but could be as autocratic as any emperor.

He could be generous to a fault, forgiving and compassionate but, when his mood changed, strike with a savage ruthlessness. The fate of Thebes and that of the mercenaries after the Granicus illustrate Alexander's darker side. Sometimes he could be child-like, as when he visited Troy. Trusting and innocent, he would regard life as one great adventure, then change to be as cunning as Philip or as spiteful as Olympias.

He was a loyal friend and companion. Once he gave his word, he kept it. He had a passion for poetry, particularly Homer's *Iliad* and, due to his tutor Aristotle, a deep interest in the natural world. He could be superstitious to the point of being neurotic but, as at the Granicus, display a personal bravery and courage which was breathtaking. His genius as a general and leader have, perhaps, not been surpassed, yet he also had a streak of self-mockery, even humility.

His drinking has been the subject of much debate. Some authorities, such as Quintus Curtius Rufus, claim he was a drunkard, given to homicidal rages. Aristobulus, his close friend, quoted by Arrian, claims that Alexander's long drinking sessions arose, not so much because of his love of wine, but out of comradeship for his friends. Whatever, Alexander had his faults and failings and wine brought these out! Perhaps this explains Alexander's continued fascination for us – not just his great victories and exploits, but his personality which, at times, could sum up the best and worst in humanity.

Paul C. Doherty, 2001